"Dark and atmospheric. . . Erica Monroe delivers a different kind of Regency Romance. Weaving suspense and romance, *A Dangerous Invitation* takes you on a ride through London's rookeries and into a unique new series." - Deb Marlowe, Award Winning Author

"*A Dangerous Invitation* is gritty, engaging, and emotionally compelling, with a hero and heroine who will break your heart and have you rooting for them!" –Vanessa Kelly, Bestselling Author

"I lived this read. It touched me on a very personal level...be ready to enter the world Monroe paints with an impressive prose, dialogue, and reality-soaked brush." –Bookworm2Bookworm, 2013 Favorite Debuts Pick

"Deliciously gritty romance." - Emma Locke, Author of *The Problem with Seduction*

"Fabulously researched with a fantastic love story and page-turning adventure. This promises to be a great series!" -Darcy Burke, Bestselling Author

"Walk on the Regency's wild side with this gritty tale of rookeries, wrongdoing, and redemption." -Ashlyn Macnamara, author of *A Most Devilish Rogue*

"The book is outstanding, presenting a realistic picture of life in London in conjunction with a beautiful love story." –The Kindle Book Review

Tokella –

A Dangerous

Invitation

THE ROOKERY ROGUES
BOOK 1

ERICA
MONROE

So nice to meet you! Enjoy. Erica Monroe

A DANGEROUS INVITATION
Copyright © 2013 by Erica McFarland
Excerpt from *Secrets in Scarlet* copyright 2013 by Erica McFarland
Cover design by Amber Shah/Book Beautiful
Cover photo copyright © by Jenn LeBlanc/Studio Smexy

Quillfire Publishing

ISBN: 978-0-9900229-1-6

For information, address Erica Monroe at ericamonroe.com.

For my husband, Kevin,
who still tells me I'm beautiful in yoga pants and glasses.
Thanks for putting up with me always. I love you.

ACKNOWLEDGEMENTS

I am sure you have heard the old adage "it takes a village to raise a child." For many writers, our books become like children to us. In the course of writing A Dangerous Invitation, I have found that while the actual act of writing may be solitary, by the end a published book reaches its intended audience it has been touched by many hands.

To my mother, who bought me my first Jane Austen novel and didn't blink when I said I wanted to go to school for writing. Thanks for supporting me even in my literary purist days when I claimed I'd only read dead writers.

To my father, who unfortunately left this world before he could read this novel, but I know he'd like it because for some reason, he was always certain I could take on the world.

To my grandmother, my brother, Aunt Arlene, and the rest of my family for being ridiculously proud that I write novels. Thanks for believing I could do this.

To my wonderful critique partners and dear friends Jennelle Holland and Amy Nichols Pfaff, thanks for always answering my hare-brained questions from what to do when your flintlock won't fire to how to slit a man's throat in twelve seconds or less. I love you guys.

To the wonderful people who either beta read or critiqued this book in some state. Emma Locke, who gave me some of the best line edits I've ever gotten in my life. Darcy Burke, who is excellent at pointing out consistency errors that completely stump me. Evangeline Holland, who taught me about deep POV and helped me read maps (I hate maps). Lisa Lin, Jessica Grey, and Patricia Marquez, who always made me feel better about my work. Olivia Kelly and Andris Bear, for telling me that dark and angsty was definitely the way to go with my writing. Rachel Grant, who helped me with suspense elements.

To Deb Marlowe, who gave me the best cover quote I could ever ask for. I'm still stunned you think I'm something special.

To Isobel Carr, who answered my endless questions, helped me pick out new research materials, configured a print template for this book, and for a thousand other amazing things. I'm delighted to be your Muppet.

To the Secret Curtsy Society of Valerie Bowman, Erin Knightley, Anne Barton, Ashlyn Macnamara, and Sara Ramsey, who read the first fifty pages of this book when it was in draft stages and still enjoyed it.

To Jenny DeWoody, who introduced me to regency romance novels and who forced me to realize I could write a book and that I was being a ridiculous ninny for not trying.

To the girls from the old Silvrwings RPG, and to Samantha Maurice, who have all known me since I was a bossy middle schooler convinced I knew everything about writing. I didn't—and I still don't—but thanks for making me feel like I did.

To the ladies at Heart of Carolina and the Beau Monde, who have taught me so much in the last year. I am forever grateful to be part of your groups, and so proud to be a member of the Romance Writers of America.

To my Teatime Romance sisters, thanks for giving me a blog to call home. You're fabulous.

To my research goddesses, Máire Claremont and Delilah Marvelle, thank you for sharing your endless wisdom with me. I am forever in awe of your brilliance as writers and historians.

To my editor Meghan Hogue, thanks for never minding that I plan obsessively in advance. You are invaluable.

To the greats of nineteenth century British literature: Wilkie Collins, Charles Dickens, Jane Austen, Charlotte Brontë, George Eliot. From you I'm inspired.

And lastly, to everyone who said they were ready for a dark romance with nary a duke, earl, or viscount in sight. You're my people and I love you.

CHAPTER 1

London, 1832

KATE MORGAN'S NECK prickled with awareness. Someone was following her.

It was not an unusual occurrence. As a fence for stolen goods living east of the City in tenement housing with more thieves than honest men, Kate had grown accustomed to being followed. They approached slowly, until she crossed the alley that divided Upper Shadwell from Broad Street, where the light from the lamps grew dim.

There they met her, thinking the darkness would give them sufficient cover to filch her valuables. That was their grave mistake.

She had nothing of value left.

Her pace was steady as she neared the alley, but her hand clenched around the worn wood handle of a Forsyth flintlock pistol. She breathed in deep, instantly regretting it when the sick smells of excrement and bodily fluids assaulted her senses.

She glanced over her shoulder discreetly and saw the tall,

muscular frame of a man with a hat pulled down low on his brow. Without a lantern, she could not distinguish his exact features. She moved her finger to the trigger. The pistol was fully cocked and loaded.

His footsteps echoed in the alley. He made no pains to keep his presence unknown. When he was several yards away, Kate spun on her heel, lifting the gun upwards. She took a step back to lead him into the lamp glow that shone bright in a nearby window. If he would attack her, he must do it face to face, so that she could describe him to the Metropolitan Police. The Peelers had at least one use: there were more of them around than there had been of the old Watch.

No man would make a victim of her again.

She leveled the gun at the stranger's chest. "I don't want to shoot you." Her voice was calm, even confident. In the past two and a half years, she'd learned to lie, to steal, and to brazen through the worst of situations. She'd had no other choice.

One more step forward, and she could see him clearly in the light.

The man stood his ground. Fear tightened her throat and she forced it down, until it was only a burning sensation in her stomach. Like every other useless emotion, fear was meant to be mastered.

He stood in front of the window, his damnably handsome features on display for her. Doffing his hat, he carded a hand through his short ginger hair, a gesture as familiar to her as the soothing weight of her pistol. His wide forehead was creased with worry, strong jaw set with determination. His straight nose led down to lips reddened from the cold.

"Kate." His voice sent a shiver up her spine. A hint of a brogue, mottled with thicker country English, like he'd been raised by Irish immigrants.

It could not be Daniel.

He had fled London three years ago. Surely, he'd not be foolish enough to return. One hint of his whereabouts and the Peelers would be out for his blood.

"I won't hold you accountable if you shot me." His gaze never left her gun, green eyes wide.

Her heart pounded in her ears, every part of her body awakened by his presence. She didn't meet his eyes, instead letting her gaze travel down from his face to his broad shoulders and narrow waist. He was lanky and well-built like a bar brawler, with powerful hands that had once brought forth the most salacious of moans from her lips.

Powerful hands that an eyewitness claimed had been used to slit a man's throat with such force that it ripped out his esophagus and severed his windpipe. Those hands were currently raised, unarmed, in supplication. But Kate knew better: a man could secret away many weapons on his body.

With Daniel, his greatest weapon had always been the destruction he wreaked upon her carefully ordered existence.

"Put down your barking iron, love. I'm not going to hurt you. I only want to talk." He placed his hat back on his head.

She narrowed her eyes. "There is nothing you could do to me that you haven't already done." Her hold on the gun shook and she quickly steadied it.

"While shooting me might be justifiable, it'd make a hellish mess..." A small smile creased his lips, an attempt at a joke she didn't appreciate.

Kate lowered the gun but left it cocked. Stubbornly, she held on to that last defense. She tried to make herself believe she would fire on him—if the need arose.

She should be furious. Enough to *want* to shoot him, for if anyone in England deserved shooting it was Daniel O'Reilly. She should want to do anything but fling herself in his arms, crush up against his chest, and press her lips to his to see if they still fit so wondrously against hers.

This, like everything else, was a situation that could be met with order and rationality.

Kate tapped the butt of the pistol against her leg. "What are you doing here?"

"I'm proving to you that I didn't kill Tommy Dalton."

So simple, so direct, she almost believed him. As if the years were nothing and losing him hadn't torn her carefully arranged world apart. But things had changed, and she couldn't stand across him from as the besotted girl she'd been, desperate for his love and willing to do anything for him.

"Three years I've waited for you to bloody come back," she hissed. "I thought you'd *died*, Daniel. For so many nights, I imagined you lying in a ditch off Brighton Road, with nobody to identify your body. I can't come back from that."

"I'm sorry. I thought if I left—" He stopped. Bit his lip, like he'd done whenever he wasn't certain of something.

He damn well better not be sure of what they were to each other. She'd gone through too much to get him out of her head, too much to let him back in only to hurt her again.

Her eyes narrowed. "You should have stayed if you were innocent."

"I know."

Was that guilt in his tone? He tugged on his hat brim, pulling it lower over his eyes until it was a mourning shroud. Did he grieve the time lost, the life he could have had with her if he hadn't been so foxed? Maybe he would have remembered more about the murder and proven to the police he wasn't guilty.

No, he couldn't regret the past. Because a repentant man—a caring man—would have reached out to her again.

She sunk back into anger, her voice rising with each question. "If you knew you were wrong to leave, why didn't you come back? How am I supposed to believe in your innocence when you escape transport to Newgate? When you don't write?"

He held a hand up to stop her. "Please, quiet your voice."

"Why should I? Because this isn't good and proper for you?" She spat the words out, refusing to lessen her volume. "Because someone might find you? God forbid, you finally face the Met's officers."

"Do you truly believe I could have slit that man's throat?"

His voice broke.

No. The local constable had an eyewitness to the murder. But here she stood across from Daniel, and part of her wanted to fall back against him and never be alone again. Even if being with him meant she'd lose everything she'd worked for—a life where she answered to no one.

His eyes never left her face, as if memorizing the contours. She fought the urge to cover her face with her hand. In the lamplight, every imperfection was on display. Time had not been kind to her. When he fled, she'd been on the cusp of the lowest levels of the *ton,* almost accepted but not quite. She had worn tailored silk, not a secondhand dress from the rag shops in Field Lane, originally made for a woman on a better diet than scraps.

Kate didn't know who she hated most: the spoiled woman she had been then, the harridan she currently was, or Daniel.

She stepped back from him. "It doesn't matter what I believe."

"It matters to me," he pleaded.

"You know, the Peelers interviewed me after you fled." She ran her finger along the handle of her gun, tracing the inlaid roses. The pattern was familiar, but a comfortable familiar, one that did not fling her headfirst into a strange abyss like his presence. "They dredged up every bit of our past, told me all about finding you with that warehouse laborer's corpse, and all I could think about was how we were supposed to be married. We were supposed to be *happy.*"

Happiness was illusive. It didn't come to ruined women like her.

"I never lied to you. I've done many wretched things, but I never once lied to you." His voice dipped lower, gentle and intimate, a caress to the tired parts of her soul that had ached to hear such confessions.

"What do you call telling me that you'd protect me? That we'd always be together? All you did was *lie.*" She flung each accusation at him with the same accuracy she shot her gun, knowing what weaknesses would hurt him most.

She hated every damn thing about him because he made her believe things that weren't true. There was no haven in loving him. Devil take it, when laws defined women as property, there was no safe man.

She stepped back. On the edge of Upper Shadwell, a carriage clopped by, for at this late hour London didn't sleep. Prostitutes lingered at the street corners, powder and rogue over skin stretched tight.

Daniel followed her out onto the street. He lingered too close. She wondered vaguely if he'd smell like bergamot and cloves, the scent that haunted her dreams. He'd obliterate the odor of rotting refuse of the rookeries, and make her believe she could go back into the past.

That woman didn't exist any longer.

Kate retreated quickly, so fast that she didn't notice the drunken sailor leaning against the doorway until she'd already backed into him. A hand brushed against her bottom, thankfully protected by her thick skirts. She tore away and turned to face the offender. His eyes were red-rimmed and a knife hung limply between his fingers, forgotten over the pursuit of her rump.

"'Ello, Merry bird, ye got somethin' for me? Look at 'er, Jay, 'ave ye ever seen a better dimber mort?" The sailor gestured to a man hidden in the shadows of the doorway, his face clouded and barely visible in the darkness. "I tell ye, Jay, when we get 'em Things down by the Fortune—" The sailor's knife twitched between his fingers.

Kate took another step back. The Fortune of War public house was a known haunt for grave robbers. Her fingers clenched around the handle of her fully cocked pistol. She could defend herself if it came to that.

The man in the shadows snapped something under his breath, and the sailor's expression changed. Paleness swept over his yellow skin, his lower lip quivering. She felt the tension rise between them, thick and choking. A fight brewed.

She wanted to leave, but she wouldn't turn her back on Daniel. Before she could form a plan of attack, Daniel grabbed hold of her arm and tugged. He kept moving until they had rounded one corner and then another, reluctantly releasing her when they entered a more populated area. In the distance, a low-pitched scream echoed from where they had been. It died off in the distance.

Another one killed, and no one to mourn him.

She doubted the sailor's death would make the papers. He'd slip through the cracks like so many others. The warehouse laborer Tommy Dalton had only warranted a few broadsheets because of the gruesomeness of his murder and the connection to her father's old company, Emporia Shipping.

Daniel had pulled her onto another part of Upper Shadwell. The road buzzed with activity, from the influx of patrons who wandered in and out of the dram houses to the dockworkers on the prowl for a cheap whore. Their noise filled her ears, snippets of various conversations clouding her thoughts.

"It kills me to see you here," Daniel murmured.

A lover's tone, softer and warmer than she wanted. "If it hurts you so bad, leave again. This is where I live now."

He shifted his weight from one foot to the other. "I couldn't have known Emporia would go bankrupt. I thought your father's company was insoluble, as did the rest of the shipping industry. You've got to believe me, Katiebelle."

"Don't call me that. You've got no right to call me that." Her throat clenched at her father's nickname for her, a sting of grief that had lessened but not dissipated in two and a half years.

"Once you liked it when I did."

"Once I liked a lot of things you did." She stepped out into the street, under the beam of the street lamp.

But now I don't. If she told herself that enough times, she might start to believe it.

Daniel remained in the shadows, unwilling to risk the exposure offered by the lamp. He would always be in the dark: an accused murderer too scared to atone for past mistakes. He'd drag her down with him. She couldn't risk tying herself to him, and the Peelers investigating her criminal activities.

She took one last look at him. He smiled at her, accepting her perusal as a sign of good will and not the goodbye it truly was.

When patrons came out of the nearby Three Boars public house, Kate took advantage of their exit, slipping in unnoticed by Daniel. From her vantage point at the door, she saw him turn slowly, first to the left and then the right. Eventually, he might follow her, but by the time he did she would be tucked away at a table far in the back.

This was her world. The rookeries were her life.

He could not change that with a simple reappearance.

DANIEL'S STOMACH LURCHED. He should have known he'd have to enter a public house again. The single-floor dram joint was jammed between several other shops on Chapman Street. Set up above were tenements, reached by an entrance unseen from the road. Flaked green paint on the walls revealed bare, rotted wood in areas. A circular sign hung above the street, bearing the image of a three-headed boar on a rampage.

The Three Boars was in short, a public house like any other in the borough of Stepney. His breath came in short, irregular pants.

Devil take him, he wanted—he needed—to see Kate again. She had gone inside, leaving him no choice but to go in as well. He lingered too long at the door, blocking the entrance. People gathered behind him, shouting their inquiries on the wait. That was attention he didn't need: should the police find out about his reappearance, he would surely be taken back to Newgate to face trial, not only for his escape, but for the murder.

But he had to be something better. He hated the man he was when he drank. His sister, Poppy, claimed he was ready. She supported him, and damn it all, he would not fail her again.

He stepped inside the door.

Almost all of the battered circular tables were occupied by a squalid collection of rogues, men with bleary red eyes and hard grips around mugs of gin. The whole place reeked of blue ruin, assaulting his senses and triggering memories of times after he'd left London, waking up on the floor of another brothel. He remembered fights he'd started because the gin made him wild and reckless.

He leaned on the end of the bar, searching the room for Kate.

"Care for a penny's worth?" The barmaid ceased wiping the counter-top.

He blinked. Her accent was distinctly East London, yet her speech was polished. The lady had airs that didn't fit with Ratcliffe. Her head barely rose above the tall counter; if she leaned down, only the simple white cap that confined her raven locks would be visible.

"I'm looking for a woman," he said.

"And you think this is a brothel?" Her face hardened, brows knit in distaste. "This is Chapman territory. If you leave now, I won't call them to escort your vile rear out."

"No, no, you misunderstand me." He quickly held up his hand. "I'm looking for Miss Kate Morgan. I saw her come in here."

Recognition dawned in the girl's green eyes, but she clamped her lips shut, taking a moment to survey him. "What do you want with Kate?"

"She is an old friend from when I lived in London. Please, I just want to speak to her. I don't mean her any harm." He scanned the room again. He couldn't see Kate in the hordes of people. The bar was deceptively large, extending far beyond his view.

The barmaid stared at him a moment longer. Her button nose wrinkled as she thought. "She is at a table in the back."

"Thank you." He turned away, the tightness in his chest from the putrefaction of gin weighing heavily on him each breath was a struggle.

The barmaid called after him. "And sir? If you hurt her, not only will you have Chapman Street gang at your back, but I'll personally draw your claret."

"I've no intent to hurt her, Miss—?"

Her guarded expression was back. "Putnam. Jane Putnam."

He nodded. "Miss Putnam."

He made his way through the crowds. Finally, he pulled out a chair at her table. Kate had removed her greatcoat and bunched it underneath her to ward off thieves. Her gaze never wavered as she searched his face. He thought he knew what she saw: a marred image barely resembling who he had once been. His breath sucked inward, a futile attempt to draw in courage with the air.

Kate glowered. "Must we do this again? Whatever you want, Daniel, I'm not interested."

"I don't want anything except your company." He wanted many things: to win her heart back, to prove his innocence, to regain some sense of control over his existence. But for now he'd settle for a civil conversation with her.

She folded her hands over each other. Her gloves were threadbare, the seams about to burst. "Tell me what is so important that you felt it necessary to linger in the exact alley I'd take to get home from the market. I don't want to think of how long you may have been spying on me, biding your time."

"I've been in London for five days." Five long days in which he'd holed up at Madame Tousat's Boarding House and pored over information from his friend, Atlas.

Finally, he had the names of people who might know something about the night of the murder. If he could avoid being captured by the Peelers long enough to figure out who had really killed Tommy Dalton, he might have another chance to prove to Kate he could be the man she deserved.

He glanced at the tables surrounding them. To their left, a group of sailors sat huddled around what was likely a pornographic pamphlet, from their jeers at the contents. One man in shirtsleeves with an anchor tattooed on his neck looked directly at him. Daniel pulled the brim of his hat down lower to shade more of his face, a lump high in his throat.

He couldn't recognize me, not in this light.

The barmaid came by, setting Kate's plate of mutton and a glass of ale in front of her. Jane turned to him. "Would you like something?"

"He won't be staying," Kate interjected.

Jane simply shrugged, unconcerned.

"I don't need anything to drink." Daniel managed to keep the right amount of calm in his voice, like he'd practiced with Poppy. He didn't *need* a drink, but he wanted one with every fiber in his being.

As soon as Jane left, Kate turned back to him. "I never thought I'd see the day when Daniel O'Reilly wasn't thirsty. You used to be a crank man."

"I used to be a lot of things." Stalwart, honorable, respectable: those were the terms which had once been applied to him. The taste of crank lingered on his tongue, though he had not drank the blessed gin and water in months.

Pulling the plate closer, Kate cut into the mutton with gusto, as if it was an epicurean treat served by her father's old cook.

Daniel lowered his voice, deciding to play it safe. "Do you know a man named Atlas Greer? They call him the Gentlemen Thief."

Kate drew back from him. "Do you really think I'd be foolish enough to confess my associations, so that you have something to hold over me if I don't comply with what you want?"

"Christ, Kate, why do you think I'd do that?"

She gave him a look that told him exactly how little she thought of him.

"I asked because he's a friend of mine. I wrote to him a few months ago to ask him to look into my case." Daniel had penned that letter a month into sobriety, but he held that information back. "Atlas is a savant when it comes to puzzles. He sees conspiracies in a simple trip to the market. I thought maybe he'd find something the constable missed."

"When we were together, you never once mentioned your *friend* Atlas." Kate's eyes held a hard glint.

"I'd been appointed your father's assistant. Somehow I didn't think it in my best interest to confess my affiliation with a known thief, brilliant lad that he is or not. That doesn't matter much now, does it?" He'd always wanted Kate to meet Atlas, but not like this.

"No, I suppose not. All those hours Papa spent grooming you to take over the company, and you threw it away as if it was nothing. I don't understand you, Daniel." She spoke around bites of mutton.

"Your father was never going to let me lead the company." He had known Morgan had plans for him, but he couldn't see himself as the head of a large shipping company. Her father had never specified that Daniel was his successor.

"Why do you think he introduced you to all his damned suppliers, his business partners? Because he believed in *you*." She hissed the last word as though it was the gravest insult.

Once you believed in me, too.

"When you got arrested, Papa's good name was dragged through the ditches. Everything he'd done for you, and instead you brought shame to our door."

"I'm sorry." He'd been a fool to not imagine what wide-reaching effects his departure would have.

"Apologies won't bring back the company or my life." She wouldn't look at him, gaze intent on the mutton.

He was so unimportant to her he didn't deserve her

attention.

They lapsed into silence. She patted at her hair, parted in the middle with short curls on her temples. When he had last seen her, she had worn her chocolate curls in ringlets with silk flowers. He liked this new, simpler style better. It felt more genuine.

He let his gaze run down her frame. She had always been tall, but she was gaunter now—her thinness was emphasized by the swell of her wide skirts, the puffed sleeves of her azure dress.

Yet she remained the most beautiful woman he'd ever seen.

Kate finished her mutton and took a swig of ale. He watched the line of her throat as she swallowed, imagined the taste of the frothy brown liquid on his tongue. Her fingers curled around the clay mug. An angry scratch ran across her wrist, in the space between her glove and sleeve. Dark circles lined her eyes.

I doomed her to a life of hard labor and injustice.

"After I left..." He didn't know how to finish that sentence without hurting her, and so the words spilled out like the rapid clip-clop of horse hooves on cobblestone. "What happened to you? Why did no one help you when the company collapsed?"

He didn't add what he truly wanted to know: *why didn't you marry? Could you still love me?*

She sat up straighter, spine stiffened. "That is none of your business."

When Atlas had told him she lived in the rookeries, he was aghast. She was the daughter of an upper middle class merchant; someone in her social class should have helped her. Even without her father's money, she should've been able to marry well based on her beauty alone.

"You should have better than this, Katiebelle." He leaned forward, pretending the smell of her soap pierced through the haze of gin.

"And who shall give that happy future to me? You?" She gave a harsh, guttural laugh.

"I could." He hated the pleading tone of his voice. "If I can prove my innocence, then I'll be able to find work in London again."

She snorted.

"I deserve your scorn." He deserved far more than that, yet he kept silent, lest he give her ideas on the best ways to throttle him from across the table.

"Damn right you do," she muttered.

"But if you give me a chance, I'll show you I've changed." He searched her face, deluding himself into believing he saw a ghost of compassion in her brown eyes, in the slight quiver of her bottom lip.

Slowly, her posture rigid, she rearranged her thick skirts. She patted the greatcoat underneath her, where she had slipped the pistol. "You have five minutes to tell me what the Gentleman Thief has discovered."

CHAPTER 2

WHEN HER FATHER died, Kate had not cried. Her body had ached with a sadness she could not begin to fathom, but she kept those emotions hidden, to be released only when she was finally alone in their Bloomsbury townhouse.

But that privacy had been short-lived, for after Richard Morgan's death, representatives from Lloyd's Bank descended upon the townhouse, seizing everything as payment for the unpaid loans. The company her father had built from the ground up—the very company he'd always claimed would secure her future—was bankrupt. Emporia Shipping had already been under scrutiny since Daniel had escaped arrest, and the papers ate up this new scandal. Broadsheets caricaturized the failing of a company once rivaling the East India Trading Company in strength.

She'd absconded with four gowns worn on top of each other, her father's greatcoat, and the flintlock pistol. The bank notes she'd managed to stuff in the pocket of the coat had run out all too soon.

Faced with starvation or selling her flesh, Kate had chosen a third, seldom-considered alternative. She'd formed a plan: use her knowledge gleaned from years of cataloguing Emporia's export and import inventory and set up as a fence for stolen property. It had been a good plan, and damn it, it continued to be one. Though she had few funds, she decided her own fate.

Yet as she sat across from Daniel O'Reilly in the boisterous Three Boars, she was eminently aware she'd fallen through a vortex that would consume her if she was not careful. She'd been foolish before, and her naiveté had led to far worse hurt than him leaving. Daniel saw the woman she had once been, pure and untainted, not the new scars upon her soul.

"Atlas has gone over every record he could get of the murder. Several names have come up repeatedly." Daniel's eyes never left her face, tracking her reaction. "But he can't find any other commonality between Tommy Dalton and me besides the fact that we both worked for Emporia."

"As far as I am concerned, you are partially responsible for Emporia's failing, so don't you dare continue with that line of thought." She clenched her fists, eyes narrowing until she saw him only through thin slits. "When you were arrested, the investigation started into Papa's company. They discovered the deficit, and from there Lloyd's made certain Emporia would never rise again. Leave it be, Daniel. Much like our relationship, the company is in ashes."

And in ashes their life together needed to stay.

"Emporia was a very large company," Daniel said. "Morgan can't be held responsible for the actions of all of his employees. If someone knew Dalton and had an involvement in his murder, don't we owe it to Dalton to bring his murderer to justice?"

"*We* don't owe him anything," she corrected. "*You* should have talked to the constable when you were arrested."

"I didn't know who had set me up to be bummed. I still don't—even if I had, the constable wouldn't have listened. He was delighted he'd found his man without any real work." His voice was tense, yet so quiet she almost couldn't hear him over the disharmony of the public house. "But if we keep digging into the past, we can find proof that I was innocent. Atlas has been combing through Dalton's personal life, and he's discovered connections to a gang of resurrection men. Maybe even to the London Burkers."

She shook her head. "Then you don't need to dig about in the past. Bishop and Williams have already been hanged. The entire City is abuzz since the trial of the Italian Boy's killers. If they were responsible, then they've already paid the price."

"Maybe it isn't related. Maybe it means nothing, but I have to find out."

"Find out without me. If the Peelers come looking for you, I can't risk that they'll dig into my fencing." She pushed back her chair, but his words stopped her.

"Someone paid an affidavit woman to say she saw me with the knife in my hand. Dalton was dead when I entered that alley, you have to believe me, love."

Kate squeezed her fist tighter. He sounded so desperate and raw. There was that word again: love. His brand of love ripped her to pieces, left her with only the bite of gin to remember him by. If she let him back in, he'd take her for all she had once more. She'd barely managed to create this new life for herself. Free of him, and free of other men who wanted to use her as a punching bag.

Learn from your past mistakes, Papa had always said.

"The next time you think of contacting me, change your mind." She stood and as she did, a man from the next table rose too. He bore an anchor tattoo that she recognized. She snatched her greatcoat up off the chair and threw it on. A quick escape would be necessary.

Al McNair was a caper-witted porter, but he was at least a full head taller than her and twice her weight. He lumbered toward them, worn top boots pounding into the planked flooring. Dust sprang up as he walked and his ham-fisted hands swung to and fro with every stride. His linen shirt was stained with grease and his loosely tied neckerchief bore the same.

"Someone you know?" Daniel asked, following her gaze. He stood up from the table.

"If by know, you mean despise, then yes," Kate said. "He is a member of the Chapman Street gang and as bacon-brained as they come."

People parted at the sight of him, moving quickly out of his way. Soon he was across from them.

"Must we do this now, McNair?" Her patience was thin. She didn't even bother to disguise the irritation in her voice.

"Ye owe me fer cuttin' me outta th' dock job." McNair's bushy black brows knitted together as he stared her down. "An' I wan' my share."

Kate let out a long, melodramatic sigh. "We all want things, McNair. For instance, I wanted to never see your daft hide again, but here you are. You know I was only on the end part of that job. I didn't have anything to do with payment. See Jason Baines if you've got complaints."

Daniel's shoulders were back, his legs spread wide. That stance, full of righteous indignation, had been enough to make her quiver for him at one point.

She didn't need him to save her.

McNair snorted. He turned, his bleary gaze appraising Daniel and taking in his worn clothes and the red locks peeping out from the brim of his hat. "Ye got my money, Irish? Or were ye too busy sayin' th' Holy Mary?"

Daniel searched his pockets but came up empty. McNair stepped forward, looking like he was ready to punch them both. Daniel lifted his chin, determination etched in his face.

Kate pushed Daniel back and crossed to stand in front of him. Her hand closed around the pistol stowed in her greatcoat. In such close quarters, the shot would attract far too much attention. Better to use the butt of the gun to bludgeon McNair, and escape when he was down.

McNair stepped forward, his hand going to the sheath at his side. He drew out a knife, the long blade serrated. The remains of the last victim were dried on it in stomach-turning brown dots. "I oughta show ye what I do to pope worshippin' bastards like ye."

The knife gleamed in McNair's hand, catching the light from the candles. Kate's eyes darted toward the door. The exit was clear.

The thief stood stock-still, holding the knife away from him. With his gaze trained on Daniel, he paid little attention to Kate. Surging forward, Kate grabbed his arm, twisting it behind his back. She exerted pressure on him, turning the knife in the direction his grip was weakest and then pulling it from his fist. When the knife was out of his grip, she let it drop on the ground, kicking it away.

Realizing what she had done, McNair smashed his fist into her cheek. Sharp pain ripped through her skull, blurring her eyesight for a second.

Bollocks. She'd show him what happened to cowards who struck women.

Kate wheeled back, fisting her hand and smashing it into McNair's nose. He fell back against the chair of another patron as his blood oozed down his face. The man McNair hit was on his feet in an instant, bellowing out insults and grabbing his empty tankard. He slammed it into the side of McNair's head. A second passed before McNair rammed his fist deep into the other man's gullet.

Barely in time, Kate jumped back as one of McNair's friends threw a punch. One by one, cohorts of either miscreant added to the mix, until the bar had descended into a swirling fray of pointed limbs striking sensitive contours. The guttural groans and shouts of the vagrants made up a vulgar cacophony, spliced with the ping of broken pottery as empty tankards were smashed on the table and used as weapons.

Out of the corner of her eye, Kate saw Daniel jump back as the sharp edge of a shattered tankard slit his arm. The fabric of his shirt was ripped but there was no sign of blood. He bobbed to the right, clearing the fray. Taking advantage of his distraction, Kate ducked behind a pillar, out of sight.

Daniel had spent most of his nights in public houses like this one. He had tried to hide his drinking, but she had seen through him. He had never been a capable liar, and so she found herself believing in his innocence.

If she didn't leave now, she'd stay to help him with not only this fight, but his crusade for justice. Stay until he ravaged her soul again, leaving only pieces where a whole person had once been.

She could not risk being around him. Dodging right hooks and onslaughts of sharp glass, Kate wove her way through the fighting and into the night. If only she could make the memory of Daniel O'Reilly disappear as easily.

MADAME TOUSAT'S BOARDING House rose up high above the crumbling buildings on this long-forgotten stretch of the Ratcliffe Highway. Built in a strangely haphazard fashion of additions onto the existing foundations, Daniel had thought upon first seeing it that it was bottle-shaped because the top levels tapered inward. If the rent wasn't so cheap, he'd have gone elsewhere. He was not entirely sure the building was held up by anything more than dumb luck.

Each time he approached the flat, he took a different route, moving through the back alleys and streets. Perhaps he was being overly suspicious—but he couldn't take the chance that someone would find him.

At three in the morning, two stragglers loitered on the stoop. Daniel didn't recognize either of them from his earlier days. Nonetheless, he thrust his hands deep into the pockets of his greatcoat to both keep out the cold and ward off possible thievery.

He pulled open the door and headed down the hall toward his room. For the first time since he'd arrived the groan of a well-pleasured man didn't meet his ears, nor the bang of the bed against the wall. Perhaps he might get some sleep tonight—yet with the thought of Kate out in the cold, her thin body huddled in that ridiculously large coat, he doubted it.

He slid his key into the lock and opened the door. Darkness met him, the tiny room a cavern without a lit candle.

"Did you find her?" A man's voice called from inside.

No one should have known where he was staying, not even Kate. Daniel stepped back from the door and grabbed the knife tucked into the lining of his boot. Holding the knife out, he advanced.

The last time he'd been caught off-guard, he'd lost everything he loved.

A match struck and a flame appeared. Held between two fingers, it cast a small circle of light on the jovial features of a man he'd known since he first came to London four years ago.

"If the Watch could see you now, Danny-boy, they'd need no further convincing of your guilt." Atlas Greer's voice held only a trace of slurred East End, beaten out by the nuns of St. Helene's orphanage who prayed equally to God and proper English. The thief leaned forward and dropped the lit match into the oil lamp.

"What the devil are you doing here?" Daniel closed the door and tucked the knife back into his boot. "Quite eerie to find you sitting in the dark, you old cove."

"Guilty as charged." Atlas's lips twitched mischievously, as though he knew a secret. No doubt, he did. Given the time he put into intelligence gathering, Daniel wouldn't have been surprised if he knew every major heist planned for a fortnight.

Atlas perched precariously on the lone chair in the room, tilting it back against the wall. The thief still kept his blond hair shaggy with side whiskers. His blue eyes observed more in an hour than most people in a day, and his nose was slightly off-center from the only fight he'd ever lost.

His fashion sense was impeccable. Dabbling in dandy dress, his white pantaloons were spotless, and his shoes shined. A neckcloth tied into a large bow adorned his neck, while his coat was elegant, tailored wool.

"You smell of gin." Atlas let the chair clatter to the ground as he stood. He was shorter than Daniel, lean and spry.

"If I wanted to talk to Kate, I had to enter a public house. But I didn't drink."

"Then I congratulate you for making it through the evening." Atlas clapped Daniel's arm warmly. "Did anyone see you?"

"At first I thought I was being followed, but it was simply a blackbird looking for an alley to set up in." The freed black beggar had trailed him down three alleyways, before sitting down in the doorway of a pawn shop.

"Good then. The less people who know of your return to town, the better—no telling what the new Met will do. Bloody nuisance, the lot of them, in their ridiculous blue uniforms." The thief wrinkled his nose.

"You don't have to tell me twice. I have no desire to end up with a noose around my throat." Daniel undid the three buttons down his greatcoat, but didn't shrug out of the heavy material. The flat was frigid. He missed the warmth of gin sinking into his bones.

"How's Poppy?" Atlas asked.

"She is well." Daniel sunk down onto the battered straw mattress, weariness weighing on his limbs. "She's got a seamstress job in Dorking. It's not much, but it keeps food on the table."

"And the babe?"

"As smiling and mischievous as ever," Daniel managed a small smile. Poppy's daughter Moira was growing up quick.

"If the babe's good, and your sister's well, then why do you look like death?"

"I saw her." He rubbed his neck, sore from hunching over the information Atlas had gleaned for him. His legs were stiff from spending the past five days constrained to a desk.

"I knew you would." Atlas smirked. "What do you have to say to me, then?"

"Pardon me for doubting you." Daniel rolled his eyes, too

fatigued to pander to Atlas's egotism.

"I'm sorry the gel's in the rookeries, but it could be worse. A rich lady like her shouldn't have survived the first month, let alone the first year."

"If you are trying to comfort me, you are doing a wretched job."

Atlas's expression sobered. He sunk down into the chair by the door. "I want you to be realistic, Danny. What you've set yourself up to do is herculean and adding in the unpredictable Kate Morgan might be what pushes you to the edge. The people you're going up against won't hesitate to slit your throat the way they did Dalton."

"Kate's here in Ratcliffe because *I* didn't stay. Because I took your advice not to contact her." Daniel rubbed at his arm. He had been bruised when escaping the Three Boars.

Kate had left him there to fight his way out, without a single glance back to see if he survived.

He wouldn't do the same to her, not again.

"I gave you sound advice, Danny. The gel would have been tied to you, an escaped murder suspect. This life's not for everyone." Atlas shrugged. "But since your chit has decided to associate with the criminal lot, circumstances have changed. You don't know who she's acquainted with or what trouble she's started."

"It doesn't matter. Whatever she's done, I'll accept it." He couldn't imagine anything that would make him love Kate less. "It doesn't change what I'm here to do."

"You'd best be prepared to fight this battle, then." The warning tone to Atlas's voice didn't sit well with Daniel, for it was so different from the thief's customary jubilance. "There's a man named Jasper Finn you need to know about. He started out as a cart-boy moving the Things—that's what the bastards call the bodies they sell—but has worked his way up to having his own crew."

"Kate mentioned the Italian Boy's murder. Do you think there's a connection to Dalton's death? The circumstances sound too different." Daniel knew from the papers that the new Superintendent of the Metropolitan Police, Joseph Sadler Thomas, had arrested the grave robbers for the murder of an Italian pauper child. The crime had been discovered when the exhumators sold the boy's corpse to a surgeon for anatomization, who noticed marks of foul play.

Atlas tapped his chin in thought. "Thievery is an art and stealing bodies should be no different. May, Bishop, and Williams were idiots. The police made fine work of them. If Finn is trafficking in bodies, then he'd want to cover his movements. It's enough to make any resurrection man worried for his neck."

"But what's the connection between Finn and Dalton?" Daniel asked. "And what does he have to do with the other names you've given me?"

"According to rumor, Finn and Dalton were going in on some sort of job. Finn met with Dalton several times in the weeks before his death." Atlas's lips pressed together in a thin line. "I can't make heads or tails of it, Danny. None of my associates can say exactly what Finn looks like. He's careful to do business where he won't be seen, and when he absolutely has to go out in public, he's disguised in some way."

Daniel thought of Kate alone in her flat, unprotected from rogues. He didn't know this new bloodthirsty version of her, who was apparently comfortable shooting a pistol. But somewhere—somewhere beneath her hardened exterior—was the woman he loved and he had to keep her safe.

"I need to find Kate again." He scrubbed a hand across his chin. "She's alone, Atlas, and she faults me for escaping. I don't blame her—if I'd only stayed, maybe I could have convinced the constable I was innocent." Even as he said the words, he doubted the veracity.

"If I hadn't arranged for your transport to Newgate to be stopped, you'd have been topped after the trial," Atlas stated, with his usual certainty. "Perhaps she'd have rather attended your funeral? The Lady Fence is a fool if she thinks you would have survived gaol, gone off on drink like you were."

"You're right," Daniel frowned.

He hadn't been prepared to be Morgan's assistant. Before, he'd been a simple warehouse laborer, and no one had wanted to hire him for a higher position because he was Irish. Others pointed to his Catholicism and decreed him worse than the freed black slaves. After a year of racial insults, he'd been ready to head back to Sussex, where at least in his small home town of Dorking he knew familiar faces. But Richard Morgan had seen something in him.

It was that desire to prove his worth that had undone him. Long nights working had worn him down until he took to the gin to get through.

Kate had been the only thing in his life that had made sense, and he'd destroyed that.

"I merely urge you to use caution," Atlas said gently.

"I could advise you of the same with your various thieving jobs." Daniel didn't expect Atlas to understand. His friend had been named the Gentleman Thief for a number of reasons, but one was his loyalty. When Atlas Greer made a promise, he kept it. He wouldn't know what it was like to live with the guilt of the lives ruined by his failures.

First Morgan, then Kate, then Poppy. Everyone Daniel cared about got hurt by him in the end.

"I can't change the past." He said that more to himself than Atlas, a note of new conviction in his voice. "But I can make sure Kate doesn't get hurt again."

"I had a feeling you'd be bloody determined." Atlas sat up straight and fished again into his pocket. He pulled out a scrap of parchment, dirty and creased into a triangle. Leaning forward, he handed the paper to Daniel. "Kate Morgan's address. You don't want to know how many thieves I had to meet with to get this. Your Lady Fence is a mysterious woman."

Daniel unfolded the paper. Scrawled across the left margin was the street Kate lived on, deep in the heart of

Ratcliffe. A slow smile crossed his lips—today wasn't the last day he'd ever see her again.

He had another chance.

CHAPTER 3

THE NEXT MORNING was bright, the city free of the perpetual London fog. Kate glared at the blue sky, visible above the rotting tenement roofs. Daniel's return to her life should have been cast in dark clouds warning of a storm to come. Even the sun was a traitor.

She ran her hand down the door frame of the lodging house. Flecks of white paint from the rotten wood came off on the fingers of her glove, little reminders of where she lived. From across the alleyway, Mrs. O'Malley, the tired mother of seven Irish children, waved a brawny hand at her. "Might 'ave a bit of bread for ye, lass, if ye've got some coal to spare."

"Been trading with the mudlarks. I'll take a cold night for your bread any day." Kate smiled back at her. Though it was hard as a rock on the outside, the inner core of the soda bread was moist and smelled of caraway seeds.

She wouldn't dignify the thought that the smell of the Irish bread always reminded her of Daniel, or that every time she ate it she imagined what his childhood had been like before his family had moved to England.

Down the street bustled Bridget Malone, her arms laden with herbs and flowers to take to the market. Bridget had managed to formulate a soap that closely mimicked Kate's old black pepper and jasmine blend. She got the soap from Bridget at a discount, since she fenced goods for Bridget's husband.

Kate knew these people, characters deemed sordid by her father's ilk. They took what they needed to survive, and she couldn't judge them for it. Gone were her delusions about right and wrong. Sometimes the goods she received had been stolen from people as poor as she was. Sometimes the items were heirlooms. There was no way around it, not now.

She'd learned the hard way that if she didn't fence, she'd end up on the streets.

She'd die before that happened again.

At first, Kate had been only an apprentice to another fence – one of Jane's friends through the thieving Chapman Street gang. But she had been a quick learner, and with her knowledge of antiquities from Emporia, she'd graduated to her own clients within a year.

Now she was dependent only on her own take. She had a gold watch to find a buyer for and then if she could get a few more pick-ups from the boys in Chapman Street, she would be set for this month's rent.

If she couldn't—she wouldn't think of that now. Her landlord's tolerance would not extend much further.

"Kate!"

She looked down the street, eyes narrowing at the sound of a male voice. Owen Neal approached, a charmer and a housebreaker of the best sort, if such existed. He was smart about his jobs, and he always filched the best jewels.

Kate started down the alley to meet him, not bothering to hide the smile on her lips.

"Good morning." Owen sketched a quick bow to her.

She curtsied in return, though she felt slightly ridiculous. So far from the woman who had waltzed at balls held by her father's associates, she barely recognized these movements.

But Owen was sweet, so she'd humor him. He didn't treat her as a common whore, expecting a bit of fun in exchange for a good turn on receivable goods. Nor did he judge her for her readiness with the Forsyth, declaring that he liked a woman with a bit of fire in her.

He had brown eyes that seemed to light up whenever they saw her. That gave her hope that maybe someday when she was ready, she'd be able to attract a man whose past did not include "fleeing from a murder charge."

A man who wouldn't care that she'd been broken apart and used up.

But when he reached forward to touch her arm, she felt nothing more than a tiny tingling. The mere proximity of Daniel in the damned flash house had nearly undone her, sparks of warmth flooding her skin.

Bastard.

"Do you have something for me?" Work would distract her. A new bauble to sell was what she needed.

"Wish I did." Owen frowned, looking apologetic. He scuffed his feet against the sidewalk. "Last few jobs, luck's not been with me. Almost got bummed on the Rearden townhouse."

"Didn't you say they were supposed to be in the country until the Season started?" Kate pursed her lips.

"Thought so. Don't know why they're back." Owen shrugged.

"Why'd you stop me then?" She leaned against the doorframe, two steps away if he decided to increase contact. Old habits were hard to break, despite the fact that Owen had given her every reason to trust him.

In the end, he would hurt her like every other man.

Owen smiled, his eyes twinkling. His face was all angles, from his chiseled cheekbones to his clean-shaven chin. She reached a hand up to her hair to check that no curls had fallen loose from her bun, doubly secured by a gray ribbon headband and a cottage bonnet.

"I wanted to see you." Owen took a step closer to her, his scent of musk and leather invading her nose.

He would never smell of bergamot and cloves, but he was a good man.

"I like seeing you too." She had said too much, given a commitment she was not entirely sure she wanted, and so she slid back into a casual teasing. "Especially when you bring me things I can turn around."

Owen pressed a hand to his heart, pretending to be stricken. "You wound me, my fair Miss Morgan."

"I thought you stronger than that." She grinned.

The smile on her lips froze as a familiar flash of black and ginger met her sight—the black of Daniel's hat and the red of his hair under the brim. With his hands stuffed deep in the pockets of his greatcoat and his wide shoulders back, he looked like a god walking down the street, an arrogant, infuriating, selfish god. Perhaps the god of war, Ares—that would fit perfectly.

Her stomach tightened at the sight, unwanted heat spreading into the core of her. So much for her body listening to the voice inside her that said she shouldn't want him.

Damnation.

"Something troubling you, Kate?" Owen asked, concern flitting across his face and darkening his eyes. He followed her gaze.

"It is nothing. Would you excuse me?" She didn't wait for his response. She was off running back into the building, the door slamming behind her.

Owen didn't attempt to follow her, leaning back against the wall and watching as Daniel approached. Daniel was dastardly quick—he came inside and called up to her. She reached the first landing of the staircase.

"What part of 'I shall make you bleed' did you not understand?" Kate kept her hands hidden behind the solid wood of the banister, preferring him to think she might be armed.

He rounded the last step, coming to a stop in front of her.

Kate retreated against the banister, which came up to her

hips. "Why are you here, Daniel? I already told you I wouldn't help you."

"I need to know." Daniel took another step forward, effectively boxing her up against the banister.

She leaned back further, unbalanced. What did he need to know? Who had killed Dalton? If she believed him? Or worse, if she still loved him?

Cold air swept in through a broken window on the first floor, ruffled the knotted ribbon of her straw hat underneath her chin. Her fingers clenched around the worn wood of the railing, gripped so tightly her knuckles became white.

She might never feel sure of her footing again.

"You let it pass for three years," she charged. His urgency made no sense.

"I shouldn't have. I won't this time. Dalton deserves justice, and so do I. I'm going to investigate Dalton's murder whether or not you help me." Daniel brought his hand to rest on her arm, heat penetrating through her greatcoat. "But truly, I came back for you."

He leaned his head down, so that their eyes met. His gaze pulled at her. Her body longed for his touch, craved it, as if he was the answer to every question she'd had in the past three years. He could not love a woman so wrecked.

She retreated back again. With her body bent against the banister, the wood sagged against her weight and a threatening groan echoed. She didn't move, knowing that if she did she'd be back in his arms within seconds.

He took one look at the banister, then at her, and tugged her closer to him. His hold was strong, but not unrelenting. She was flush against him, so close she could feel the beating of his heart. Warmth replaced brisk wind, and his presence blotted out loneliness until she was part of something greater, something powerful beyond herself.

She feared that heady sensation. Passion didn't stick to predetermined routes and checklists.

When he spoke, his breath tickled her skin. His voice

rumbled in her ear. "I don't want to lose you again."

A tremble tore through her. In those few months after he left, she'd woken with those words on her lips, whispers from dreams wherein he'd fulfilled his promise to return for her. He was here, and she forgot the reasons why she should loathe him.

Everything but the smell of bergamot and cloves disappeared. An altogether familiar aroma, one intrinsically locked in her mind as his, yet different this time without the overlay of pine needles. It enveloped her, clouded her senses. She lifted her head from his chest.

She looked him in the eye. But that was a mistake, for his eyes shone with the same desire she kept trapped.

"If I didn't know better, I might believe you." She forced herself to step away from him. "I can't be with you again."

"Kiss me."

Her eyes widened. Could he read her thoughts?

"I will do no such thing."

"Just once. If you feel nothing, I'll go and you won't ever hear from me again. You have my word." He brought his hand up to cup her cheek.

She found herself nodding. One kiss. That's all it would be—one kiss and he'd understand he didn't know her anymore.

He grinned, a lazy, slow grin that made her insides pool with warmth. Quickly, he undid the knot that tied her bonnet on and swept it off her head. Her breath stopped in her throat, died because she knew damn well that there was no stopping this. She would be his. She would submit. Submit as she always had, begging for euphoric release.

His mouth covered hers, perfectly fitted, pieces of a whole that had always made far more sense when they were lying together. He'd loved her when she was a bluestocking with little life outside of her father's company. Could he love her as a fence? It shouldn't matter.

This was all taste and desire, of mint on his lips, of

sensations she had long banished from her mind entirely. She gasped, but that was in error, because the slightest move of her mouth gave him more access. His hand came up to grasp her chin, thumb and forefinger tracing delicate circles that made her shiver. He pulled her closer, angling to take the kiss deeper, to drive away from her any semblance of normalcy with his wicked, wicked mouth.

She fell hard against his shoulders, hands fisted in his greatcoat, not trusting her knees would keep her steady. His other hand trailed the small of her back, the bonnet he held crushed against her dress. His lips rediscovered the curvature of her mouth and planted hot, impatient kisses along the corners. She leaned into that hand and the bonnet slipped from his grasp. His devious fingers descended on a downward course to cup her rear, clenching the plaid cotton of her skirt in his strong grip.

His tongue probed at the seams of her lips and she opened for him, allowing him to sink into her wet heat before she thought of what it meant. He thrust into her mouth again and she forgot all those objections in favor of the pulsating need building in her core. A fire burning bright within her, coaxed by sense and touch, stoked only by him, for no one else's attempts had this effect.

Her nipples pebbled, neglected for too long and straining against her short corset. He sensed her need, as he'd known without fail when they were together exactly what she desired, and his hand left her chin to brush against the inopportune confines of her dress. She wanted more—devil take it all, she'd fall into an inferno because this was all she remembered and it was all she'd dreamed of these past three years.

His groan penetrated the air, breaking Kate from the haze.

She tore from his hold. Cold crept up her back, the absence of him paramount. Kate rubbed at her lip frantically. It would be no use; hours later she was certain she would still feel him, taste him on her skin.

Daniel smiled smugly. "You don't kiss like a woman who feels nothing."

THERE WERE MANY things that Daniel O'Reilly was not skilled at, but he could read the kiss of a woman like a journal in which she would transcribe all her secrets. He knew the difference between a kiss with passion and one where the lady was simply completing a professional act, for he certainly had locked lips with enough harlots these last three years back home in Sussex.

He would trade all those gin-fueled, desperate lays for this one kiss with Kate. He'd never wanted anything more than to be back with her, and no amount of drink or clumsy tups made him forget her. She was too deep in his soul, sunk into every part of him.

But now he had a chance with her. *Because she wanted him as much as he wanted her.*

He knew it as she pulled from him, swiping at her lips furiously. He knew it as she slid across the landing to lean against the solid wall, like her knees shook too much to hold her up. And most importantly, he knew it as her lightning-flash eyes and rosy cheeks wished him to hell.

"You surprised me," she said, as if that could explain away everything.

"Were you caught unaware by your feelings for me, or by the memory of how much better I am than your current paramour?" He gestured toward the door, where she'd been in deep conversation with the other man before.

She scowled at him.

Damn it all, he couldn't stop smirking. He picked her bonnet off the ground and handed it to her.

"Owen Neal is not my paramour, as you put it." Kate addressed the second part of his question first. She set the bonnet back on her head, leaving the strings untied around her chin. "But even if he were, it would be none of your business."

Owen Neal. Daniel stored that name in his mind to ask Atlas later for a full report. Not that it mattered in the end; he felt assured he would completely obliterate Owen from her memory soon.

Reaching for her, his hand brushed up against knotty wood instead of tender flesh as she scooted away from him.

"This changes nothing." Her tone was flat. Gone was the ardent woman who had been in his arms mere minutes ago.

"It changes everything," he argued. "You want me, Kate."

"Even if I did, it doesn't make a difference." She stuffed her hands into the deep pockets of her greatcoat. "You can't erase the last three years with one kiss, Daniel. I'm always going to know you as the man who broke my heart. So you can follow me, and you can knock on my door until two in the morning, but I'm not going to answer."

"Wait, Kate, please don't go." He was too quick this time for her, catching hold of her blue plaid sleeve. She kept moving and he was towed along with her, unwilling to let her go again.

"I need you." His chest shook with the effort of those three words. How could he make her believe him?

"And I needed you three years ago." She came to a stop in the hall, refusing to turn her head back toward him. "But I learned that was weakness. You'd do better to realize it too."

He wracked his brain, trying to think of some way to get through to her. He looked around at the rooms surrounding them—mere closets compared to her old townhouse.

"I know what you do, Katiebelle." He lowered his voice, so that only she could hear him. "I know you fence goods and that you must be stiver-cramped."

She stiffened. "Did you have the Gentleman look into my dealings too? Have I no privacy?"

"I didn't need to, once he told me where you lived," he said. "If you could afford to, I know you'd move from the East End, find a little townhouse on the edge of Bloomsbury so you could be closer to where you grew up. I know you don't want this life."

"You know *nothing*." She spat the accusation at him.

"I know that when you were twelve, your father bought you a pony so you could learn to ride, but you preferred the roll and fall of a ship to a horse's canter." He edged closer to her. "I know that you wrote a paper to *The London Magazine* under an assumed name about cryptography when you were sixteen. But most of all, I know that you're the only woman I've ever loved."

For a second, her expression softened, as if drawn into the memories. Yet the past could only hold her for so long.

"Even if I wanted to help you, I can't risk it." She cast a furtive glance down the hall, making sure that no one was listening. "The people I work with won't like you being back. Your case was too publicized. If the Peelers find you, you bring down all my hard work. No one will do business with me if I've been bummed."

"What if I could promise you an honest wage, better than you'd make at fencing?" He pulled out a shilling from his pocket.

She stared at the coin, a mixture of fear and want flashing over her face. Her hand crept out to snatch it from him but as her fingers were about to brush against the metal she pulled back.

Lifting her jaw, she faced him imperiously. "If you think I would whore myself out for a shilling, you are sadly mistaken."

He cringed. Her censure was warranted, for he had taken her virginity and not married her. "Kate, if this is because of what we did in the past, I'm sorry. But I will be the most proper of gentlemen, if you want me to be."

Her eyes narrowed. "What do you want me to do, Daniel?"

I want you to let me into your life long enough for you to see that I've changed.

Daniel held onto the plan he'd developed on the mail

coach ride from Sussex to here. He might have been a drunk, but he was a damn good gambler. The boys who played in Dorking's main public house didn't hold their liquor as well as him—and he'd made good use of their propensity to drink and empty their pockets. He had enough saved up now that he could pay for this trip to London and have blunt left over to offer to Kate.

"My knowledge of London begins and ends with the docks. That was my home, and while I could ask Atlas for help, he isn't as familiar with Stepney or the East End."

"You want me for my knowledge of the rookeries then." She didn't sound like she believed him.

He couldn't blame her, not when he could think of seventeen other distinct reasons he desired—no, *needed*—her and not one of them had anything to do with the ruffians she cavorted with.

"I do require your help." He softened his tone. "There's a man named Jasper Finn who sells cadavers out of Bethnal Green. If I find out more about him, maybe I will be closer to discovering who set me up. Tommy Dalton was a warehouse laborer, Kate, a warehouse laborer like I was before your father took a chance on me. He died in the most brutal, sickening way and I can't get him out of my head."

He wouldn't tell her of the dreams that haunted him every night, of seeing Dalton's body convulsing one last time.

"You've got the most logical mind of any chit I've ever known, and I'm sorely in need of your expertise. I've seen you catalogue all of Morgan's shipments in the time it would take three able-bodied men to do so." Pride seeped into his voice, for she was the smartest damn woman he knew and he'd missed that. "And I know from Atlas that you keep company with some nefarious people."

She nodded, her eyes having never left the shilling poised between his two fingers. "This is true. I do know a lot of rogues. But I won't help you investigate my father's company."

He shrugged. "Maybe that link means nothing. Maybe I

was someone picked out of a hat because I was an easy mark. Wouldn't you rather know?"

She pursed her lips in thought. "Perhaps."

"So will you accept my invitation? I can't say that it is going to be easy, but Dalton deserves justice." He fought back the urge to reach for her arm again to feel her soft skin against his.

Every time they touched, things began to make sense again. She was his anchor. She'd keep him steady when he needed it most.

She nibbled her bottom lip uncertainly. "I don't know."

"Then take the shilling, as fee for dealing with me these past two days." He pressed it into her hand, closing her gloved fingers over it. "And if you decide to assist me, I'm at the Madame Tousat's on the first floor."

He lingered too long with her hand in his before reluctantly parting. "I promise you won't regret it this time."

BEFORE KATE MET Daniel, she had been a proper debutante, drinking only sherry or Madeira with dinner, or champagne at social functions. She'd learned how to drink from him.

Four years ago, when he had been first hired as her father's assistant, she went to his office to deliver a shipping report to him. It was late, and most of the staff had already gone home; she thought he'd already left. But instead, she found him leaning back in his chair, feet up on his desk and a flask in his hand.

"That gin?" She'd asked him. At nineteen she was certain she knew it all.

He nodded, hand poised on the flask. He didn't lift it to his lips, didn't put it back down on the desk, unsure of whether or not she'd run to her father. His cheeks were as flushed as his ginger hair, his hand trembling.

She remembered thinking that he was the only man to be

unnerved by her boldness. The rest of Papa's employees found her brashness irritating, unbecoming to a lady. They were quick to correct and shun her.

"I've always wanted to learn to drink gin," she'd said, flopping down in the chair across from his desk.

He'd relaxed. Passed her the flask like it was completely natural for a debutante to make such declarations. In that moment, she decided that Daniel O'Reilly was worth her notice.

"It'll burn," he had cautioned. "Normally, I'd tell you to get some ice to water it down."

"I can handle it," she'd declared. "I can handle anything."

"I've no doubt of that." He smiled, a slow, mischievous smile that made her stomach flip. Passing her a shot glass, he poured out a sixth of gin into it. "My uncle taught me a little rhyme that I used to say before drinking, until I got used to the sting. 'Over the teeth, past the tongue, down the hatch it goes.' Say that, and then drink it as fast as you can."

She repeated his words, gulping down the gin. It stung like hell, but it pierced through her inhibitions. Daniel had laughed at her reaction, and took a shot himself. He could handle the spirits without showing any effect. She felt like she'd learned something that no other girl in her class could claim.

She'd felt alive for the first time.

Tonight, Kate sat with her feet propped up on the top rung of the wood chair, nursing a six and tips. She needed something stronger than her—something that could hold her up when she was in danger of falling down. The whisky cut with water had a bite to it that made her lips pucker and her throat burn every time she took a sip.

The Three Boars had become Kate's second home. It was not by any means an exceptional public house, but it was an easy walk from her flat and she knew the clientele. On the best days, she got wind of pick-ups that would soon happen so she could properly align herself to receive the stolen goods before anyone else heard of the deal. On the worst of days, she witnessed a bar fight; even that had its appeal, as long as she was not the one being pummeled.

Then there was Jane Putnam, who had worked as a barmaid since Kate had moved to Ratcliffe. The Three Boars was owned by a member of the Chapman Street Gang, and with Jane's brother Penn being a member, Jane was the logical choice for a barmaid. She was practical and diligent, but most importantly, she was discreet.

And she was the best friend Kate had, and perhaps the only one she trusted.

"Whisky is not your normal drink," Jane noted, leaning on the clean bar counter. On nights when Jane worked, the public house was tidier than most upscale gentleman's clubs.

"Sometimes I wish you had the memory of a normal human being." Kate swirled the whisky in the glass, watching the amber liquid as murky as her current situation.

"Yes, but then you'd actually have to place your order like a normal human being, and what would be the fun in that?" Jane propped her elbows up and rested her chin in between her hands.

Kate sighed. "Lord pity me if I should have to make a decision for myself."

Jane's brows furrowed in concern, her voice softening. "I was only quizzing you."

"I know," Kate smiled ruefully. "I'm out of sorts tonight. Nothing is in its proper place and not a single thing makes a bit of sense." She knocked back the last sip of the six and tips.

"Your Irishman is back in town, isn't he?" Jane inquired. "Hearing you talk about him before and with his bit of a brogue, I put the pieces together when he came in last night asking for you."

Kate sputtered, whisky burning her throat. Shock turned into a coughing fit that at least allowed her enough time to process. If Jane knew Daniel had returned, then how many other people did? He would be forced to flee before he had a chance to prove his innocence.

Wasn't that what she wanted, for him to leave without a trace and never come back? That would be the logical thing to crave. But if the Peelers got to him first...

An icy hand twisted in her stomach, dousing the fire of the liquor. The tightness was almost unbearable. All she could think of was Daniel on collar day at Newgate, hanging by the loop of a noose.

Jane passed her another six and tips. "I've told no one. It's been ages, and you didn't frequent this part of town before. I highly doubt anyone else is going to figure it out."

"They will if he pokes into Tommy Dalton's murder," Kate said.

"Faith," Jane murmured.

Kate drained half out of the shot before continuing. "He wants me to help him, and has offered to pay me. He gave me a shilling."

Jane pursed her lips. For a second, she simply looked at Kate, her green eyes wide.

"Oh, don't stifle yourself so. Out with it," Kate demanded.

"I have been thinking..." Jane paused, her nose scrunching as she tried to find the proper wording. "Maybe there's less danger to be had in reuniting with him. You might convince him to leave town with you, protect you."

"I don't need Daniel's *protection*." Kate set the whisky back down on the tabletop, unfinished. "Nor do I want to put my fate in his, or anyone else's, hands. People are fallible and cannot be trusted."

"You can depend on me," Jane insisted.

"Of course." Slowly, Kate smiled. Growing up, she had two friends she had thought she could tell everything to—they'd left like the rest.

Jane arched a brow at her. "You'd better believe that. You're family now, and neither I nor Chapman Street takes that lightly."

Family. Her mother had left when she was a child, and she hadn't any relations that lived near London. She had thought she'd build a new family with Daniel. Some days, when the ache of Papa's death did not consume her, she almost managed to forget what family had felt like.

She was safest that way, for without those connections she could not be hurt.

Yet Jane was made of sterner stuff. Kate had once witnessed her lie to four Metropolitan Police officers about a theft to protect her brother from harm. Perhaps Jane was the one person left in the whole lot of London who could be trusted.

"I do believe you," Kate said, even though she knew she shouldn't.

"My point was that if you are bummed for fencing, you might be imprisoned or transported. If Penn had simply been more careful, sought out honest work—"

"I won't end up like Penn," Kate assured her. Jane's older brother Penn had been arrested for assault and thievery. He was being held at Newgate Prison.

Worry creased Jane's brows. "That is what everyone thinks. Then it is off to the gaol with you."

Kate reached forward, patting Jane's hand. "I'll be careful. I always am."

"I know you've been hurt before," Jane started, her tone hesitant. "Not only by Daniel. But you didn't know how to handle yourself and the whoremongers preyed on that. You're not that naïve girl anymore. Don't let the past affect how you conduct yourself now."

Raising the whisky to her lips, Kate gulped down the remaining contents. The burn settled in her stomach, warmth to replace the cold chill of memory. No matter how far she came from two and a half years ago, she felt like that same girl in a brothel, clutching the remains of her ripped chemise and fleeing for her life.

"I know," she lied. It was what Jane would want to hear:

that she was fine and she'd moved on. That she thought of herself as something other than shattered.

"What about Owen?" Jane asked.

"I haven't the foggiest notion," Kate frowned. "He is charming and we get along well. I suppose that we'd suit nicely."

"Which is all one can ask. Passion and intrigue are best left to those tawdry novels read by the lazy *bon ton*," Jane said.

Kate nodded, not from agreement but because it was the safe thing to do. Owen Neal made her feel at home. That was a sensation she should not take lightly. He didn't have a history of drinking or abandoning her, and he was too damn clever to get caught.

But he didn't look at her as though she was the only woman he'd ever love.

Only one man had ever done that. She would not think of the kiss with Daniel.

"Daniel wants to see if Emporia was involved, because that's the only link between Dalton and him that he can find," Kate explained. "I don't want to dig further into Papa's company. If Daniel finds out someone in the company set him up, then it's Emporia in the papers once more. Papa's good name will be dragged through the ink again."

"So control the information," Jane said shrewdly. "If you know what he's uncovering, you can make sure no one sees it. Find another angle to investigate."

It's us against the world, Katiebelle. So Papa had always claimed. She could take Daniel's money, and leave him without a shred of evidence against her father's company. Without evidence, Daniel would leave again.

She would always be better off alone, where no one could hurt her.

"It's an idea," Kate mused. "It's an idea indeed."

CHAPTER 4

THE KNOCK RESONATED through Daniel's small quarters at Madame Tousat's Boarding House, one solid pound and then another. He crossed the room in three strides, dilapidated Hessians smacking the scratched wooden floor. Once the boots had been new, but now they were as cracked as him.

Nervous energy flittered through his body. What would she say when he saw her? This unsteadiness was absurd—hell, when they'd been together, he'd buried himself so deep within her he forgot where he ended and she began in the most intimate of couplings.

He could do this. She couldn't hate him forever. Daniel breathed in and pulled the door open.

Kate's fist was outstretched to pound the door once more. She wore a worn gray walking dress with puffed sleeves and frayed ebony piping on the hem. He wasn't entirely sure, but he could guess from Poppy's work as a seamstress that the dress was not on the cusp of fashion. Underneath her arm was a leather portfolio, ragged and stained.

"Daniel." She said his name with little pleasure. "Do you intend to let me in?"

"Of course." He backed away from the door and into the

cramped room, stumbling over a footstool jammed in front of a sagging armchair. Sharp pain pierced his calf, where bone connected with the wood frame of the footstool. He bit back an oath, pressing his lips together tightly.

"Stools do have an odious habit of jumping out at you, don't they?" Deadpan, she peered up at him from beneath her wide-brimmed bonnet.

"I am devilishly clumsy." He ran a hand through his hair, offering her a small, tentative smile.

Kate shut the door behind them. Memories assailed him as his eyes trailed down her frame. She sashayed away from him, and he followed the lean line of her neck where his lips had burned against her soft skin to her shoulder blades, which he'd gripped to steady himself as he thrust, to that shapely rear men should've written sonnets about.

His breath quickened as she turned around, shrugging off the giant greatcoat. Her bodice crisscrossed in the front, giving the slight hint of her pert breasts. God's balls, she was stunning. He couldn't remember a time in the last four years when he hadn't wanted her.

This was the woman he'd lost, too fucking foxed to know where he'd been that damned night.

He cleared his throat. "I have the funds for you. When we clear my name, I'll pay you an additional sum."

Daniel pointed toward the two-legged desk in the right corner of the room. He felt a kinship to that rickety desk, precariously balanced with one leg in the past, one leg in the present, and neither in complete agreement.

"I haven't agreed to help you," she said tightly. Her gaze locked onto the small purse, a calculating gleam in her eyes.

He had been clever with the promise of an additional sum after completion. She couldn't take his money and run if she wanted the full payment.

He shrugged, feigning nonchalance. "The funds are there for you when you want it."

The single shilling from before wasn't enough to ensure

she was safe, and he doubted she'd allow him to pay for her lodgings. Devil take the modern set to her now. It'd been easier to deal with her when she'd been willing to accept his protection.

"I came to give you these." Tugging the portfolio out from underneath her arm, Kate dropped it on the desktop unceremoniously. The folder landed with a thud and the coins clinked at the movement. The frayed ribbon around the portfolio split, unable to contain the aged parchment of varying sizes.

Daniel reached for the papers. Quickly, he leafed through the stack. Three broadsheets in total, more than he would have thought the murder of a warehouse laborer like Dalton would have warranted. But Daniel's position as assistant to Richard Morgan had made the murder more interesting to the papers.

"It is a bit odd, looking at one's name in the paper." He stared at the clip from *The Daily Advertiser*, yellowed from age and indented from the folds of the portfolio. His grip tightened on the parchment, creating a crease at the right corner from where his thumb pressed. "I didn't even know the *Caledonian Mercury* reported on trials."

"I thought it best to add variety. If you only consult one source, you risk biased information."

With her ordered mind, he wasn't surprised she had found success as a fence. She plucked up the article from *The Morning Herald* and handed it to him. He skimmed the contents. The papers had interviewed Richard Morgan.

Daniel O'Reilly was a highly competent and skilled assistant. I was privileged to know him, and the charges against him are the basest of falsehoods.

"Christ." He rubbed his hand against his neck, squeezing at a knot. "Morgan didn't have to do that."

Her face darkened. "No matter what I said, he believed in you. He was sure you'd come back and fight for me. His loyalty to you made him appear weak to his business partners. They wanted him to disavow you." She looked toward the purse again, as if weighing her options. She gave a toss of her head, her black velvet bonnet flapping with the motion.

"I'm sorry, Katiebelle," he said gently, reaching for her hand.

"I don't need your apology." She pulled back, his fingertips barely brushing the shabby leather of her glove. "But when Papa got sick, he needed you at his bedside. Instead, you were off gallivanting somewhere. Maybe you would have been able to bring Emporia through—maybe if you'd been there, the accountants wouldn't have stolen money from us. Maybe...I don't even know. I can imagine a million scenarios, but they all end in you leaving."

He hadn't been there to hold her hand when Morgan died. He hadn't been there when the bank took everything, and he hadn't been there to keep her from having to live on the streets.

"I wanted—" He stopped. It didn't matter what he had wanted.

"You wanted to run, from the accusations, from the constable...from me." Her unflinching gaze fell on him, not the purse of coins.

"I never *wanted* to leave you. It was the hardest thing I ever did. I can't even begin to describe how unbearable it was." He ached to hold her in his arms, but he wouldn't reach for her again.

For a second, her expression softened, and he thought he'd infiltrated her stony defenses. Then her spine stiffened as she drew herself up to her full height. She peered down the bridge of her nose at him.

"I don't despise you for running," she said flatly.

He sensed there was an addendum to her statement, something that would tear his heart out from his chest and stomp upon it with her half boots. "Then why do you?"

"Because you got yourself entangled in this hellish situation. If you'd been sober, maybe you wouldn't have ended up in that damn alley." She frowned. "You taught me to drink gin, Daniel. Did you really think I wouldn't know the depth of your problem?"

He shifted under the weight of her gaze. Boring into him, reminding him of everything he'd ever done wrong. "I hoped you thought I drank socially."

"Casual drinkers are not found with flasks in their offices."

"I didn't want you to worry about me."

She flinched, wounded by his words. "I *loved* you, Daniel, with everything I had. Of course I worried about you. When you love someone—when you care so deeply about them that the very loss of them breaks you in two—that's what you do."

"I never meant to hurt you, Katiebelle." He stepped closer to her.

"Don't." She held up a hand to stop him. "Don't think that we can magically repair things because you want to. I would have stuck by you through anything, if you'd let me. But you didn't."

"I thought it would be better if I gave you a clean break. I thought you'd move on to someone better. Get married. Live in the sort of big house I couldn't buy for you."

"You thought wrong." She scowled. "But that is the past, and we can't change it. We were meant to live separate lives."

Separate lives. He could not think of a worse fate than to live without her. He had nearly imbibed himself to death because he could not have her.

She looked toward the dingy window in his flat. He wondered what she was thinking, if she'd rather be anywhere but here, with him. His confidence was waning—he'd been so sure he could convince her to take him back. But this Kate, this hardened woman who spoke like there was nothing between them at all, baffled him.

He moved his thumb on the broadsheet to cover up the word "murder," as if he could hide the horrendous details if he didn't allow Kate to see it. From the soft texture of the paper, she'd read the contents many times, the oils from her fingertips smoothing the print.

"Why did you keep these, Kate?"

She flushed, fists balled up at her side. "I kept them to remind myself of the truth."

"Whose truth, Kate? The constable's? Mine? Yours?"

She flinched, eyes narrowing warily. He'd struck a nerve. Woodenly, she sat down on the chair by the door and arranged her thick smoke-gray skirts. She looked down at her hands, examining her gloves. When she finally met his gaze again, the sadness in her eyes caught him off-guard.

"I don't even know anymore."

"Then help me find Tommy Dalton's murderer. We'll find the truth together." He sounded too earnest.

"Truth is a particular notion, Daniel. I have found it can be bent and twisted to fit the speaker's best interests." She laid her head back against the chair, arm draped across the side, appearing to all others like she could not be bothered to care.

But he knew better. Life might fatigue her, but she'd fight and crawl her way to the top.

He held up the purse, giving it a shake. The coins tinkled. "So twist the truth for our benefit. I've got a list of names from Atlas to go over. Have a look and tell me if you recognize any of them." He went for the foolscap on his bedside table.

"Very well then," she nodded. "We'll start with why you were too foxed to remember a damn thing. What in your life was so bad you had to drink it all away? Was it me?"

"God, no." The words came out quickly. "You were the only thing in my life that made sense."

How could he explain to her the pressure from the long hours at Emporia, the newness of their love, constantly feeling like he had to prove himself? She'd think him mad, or worse, weak. He would be a better man if it killed him. With Kate facing him, disbelief struck upon her pale, thin face, it just might.

Instead of picking up the list, he crossed to the teapot, perched atop his trunk. He had boiled water in the tea kettle downstairs in the fireplace before Kate arrived. Adding tea leaves into the pot, he poured the water in on top to let it steep.

"Tell me what you know about that night," she said.

Daniel ran a hand through his hair. He'd practiced what to say—what details to reveal and what details to leave out because they weren't suitable for a lady—but it didn't make it easier.

"All I know is somehow I ended up in the North Quay, my head pounding and the taste of stale gin on my tongue. I stumbled into the alleyway and there was Dalton."

"Was he dead when you arrived?"

It would have been easier if he had been. "No."

"How are you sure you didn't kill him? You said yourself you were in your cups."

His jaw clenched. Had he been foolish to assume she believed in his innocence? He'd thought she knew him. "Because no matter how foxed I was, I would not have murdered a man."

"I am merely asking you what the Peelers will, Daniel." She gave him the smallest of smiles, a tiny hint that she did trust his word.

He relaxed. "Dalton's throat had already been slit when I turned the corner."

She nodded, apparently satisfied. "Did you see anyone else?"

He shook his head. In his dreams, he saw a cloaked man, tall and lean, flee the site. A faceless man, more phantom than corporeal, whom he didn't trust was not an invention of his nocturnal mind.

The tea was steeped. He picked up the pot, strained out the leaves, and poured tea into the two cups provided by Madame Tousat. He kept the chipped one for himself and handed Kate the other.

"Thank you." She held the mug close to her with two hands, relishing the warmth. "I can't remember the last time I had tea."

"If you take the blunt, you could buy yourself a case," he suggested, regretting it when she frowned at him.

He chose a safer course and returned to her earlier question. "No, there was no one else present at the docks. It was simply Dalton and I, until that wretched scavenger of a woman showed up. I swear to you, I never saw her before she began to scream."

But her voice haunted his nights. "You killed him! I saw you do it."

"Evidence is like any other item. It can be bought and sold to the highest bidder," Kate mused. "There are people who make their living selling affidavits."

"I had Atlas look into the woman, but he could not find any evidence of Anne Turner. She simply does not exist." Daniel sighed.

"I am not surprised. Names are tried on and dispensed with at random here, like hats or dresses."

"Yet you never took up a false identity." He had wanted to believe she'd kept her name as a signal to him. That maybe she wanted him to search her out and save her.

"Why should I?" Her tone didn't allow him room to respond. "I won't be ashamed of who I am, or who I come from. Lloyd's may have tried to sully the Morgan name, but I know my father was a good man."

He was distinctly aware that she had challenged him. His heart wrenched as he looked toward the broadsheet with Morgan's declaration of his innocence. Emporia was the only link between his life and Dalton's.

"It was a large company, Kate," he stated delicately. "No man can be fully aware of the activities of that many employees. I am not suggesting your father was involved with the death of one of his warehouse workers, but you must recognize the connection between his *company* and the crime."

She scowled at him but kept silent, and he considered that progress.

"How did you get away from the constable?" She asked.

"Atlas bribed the guards for my time of transport to Newgate. Once he knew the route and when they'd be at each stop, he was able to intersect the carriage with bruisers he'd hired and get me to safety. Then I left for Dorking."

Where he had spent the next few years trying to erase her from his mind. But nothing could make it hurt less. He needed Kate far more than she needed him. Without her, he was nothing but a shell of a man.

He was damn tired of being broken.

IT ALL SOUNDED so simple.

Kate hated him for that, how easy he made his escape from London sound. Because it had been arranged by the Gentleman Thief, she knew the plan had accounted for every single thing that could have gone wrong in the transport. She wondered if Atlas Greer had developed a contingency for her involvement, or if she had been deemed so insignificant he didn't need concern himself with the lover Daniel left behind.

She kept her hands on the teacup, the warmth against her gloves a reminder of what was real and tangible. Sitting in this small room across from the only man she'd ever loved was the present, and the whispers of old memories could not be relied upon for veracity.

Only one thing could be relied upon: lour. She needed money to pay her rent. Owen had nothing new for her, and the Chapman Street Gang split their deals between multiple fences.

She set her teacup down on the table beside her, and stood up from the chair. In a few paces, she was at the desk again, overturning the purse. Three one-pound notes flew out. Six shillings clanked onto the table. Provided she was economical, that sum could set her up nicely.

All she had to do was spend a week or so in Daniel's company to get it.

A week, and then would he leave again?

She grabbed onto the thumb of her right glove and pulled until the fabric slid from her fingers. The cold air stung her bare flesh as she grabbed a shilling, rubbing it between her forefinger and thumb. If she knew exactly what Daniel uncovered about Emporia's involvement, she could keep her father's name from the press.

Control the information. She dropped the coin onto the desk.

Kate pulled her glove back on and turned around to face him. "I think that it would be best if we went to the docks tomorrow. Perhaps seeing that particular spot will stir something suppressed in your mind."

"So you'll help me?"

She scooped the coins back into the bag and tucked them into her pocket. "I will help you find Dalton's killer, but that is all. Do you understand? There is nothing more between us."

Daniel's brows arched, but he didn't argue. He set down his mug on the arm of the chair and rose to collect the foolscap rolls from the bedside table. As he handed the papers to her, their hands brushed in subtle, aching familiarity.

The longer she spent with him, the more she wanted to lean into his touch. Kate snatched the papers away, spreading them out in front of her.

"I've spent the past few days trying to think of anyone who might have known Dalton," Daniel said. "Atlas gleaned a few names from some of the logs from Emporia."

"He was able to find old logs?" She shouldn't have been surprised. The Gentleman Thief could filch or locate anything. "Do you still have them?"

"No, I left them with him for further examination."

She stifled a sigh, longing to run her fingers over the aged parchment and trace the familiar invoice wording. For a second, it would be like she was back in the office, sifting through paperwork. She'd served as her father's secretary since was sixteen, filing the company secrets he didn't trust with his other employees.

That Kate didn't exist anymore.

The first list identified eight individuals. Four of the names she didn't immediately recognize, another she knew of through Jane, one was dead, and the last had moved away to become a sheep farmer shortly after Emporia's collapse.

"I don't recognize Jeremiah Farner or Ezekiel Barnes. As for Patrick Corrigan, unless you fancy making bah noises at sheep in Northumbria, we should look elsewhere first." She handed the list back to him.

"If I wanted to see sheep, I could have stayed in Sussex."

"I've never seen sheep," Kate shrugged.

"You are not missing much."

She had never been outside of London. Growing up on a farm like Daniel did seemed strange. What did one do without stucco townhouses, high-class phaetons, and tall ship masts? She preferred her countryside clearly marked, like Rotten Row in Hyde Park where the Upper Ten Thousand rode.

"Why is this name starred?" She pointed at the last name, Jasper Finn, which was written in all capitals.

Daniel hesitated.

"I haven't heard of him, if that is what concerns you. Who is he?"

Hesitantly, he rubbed his forefinger against his ginger side whiskers. That gesture was as familiar to her as the alleys in the East End that would keep her from the Bobbies' notice.

"It is a tad unseemly."

"I run with Chapman. Whatever you have to say, I assure you I've heard worse. Is this related to the resurrection men you spoke about at the Three Boars? They sell the corpse to the surgeons for anatomization, and the clothes of the dead to the pawn shops in Field Lane."

To the very shops she bought her dresses from. She laid her hand against her stomach, willing the impending nausea down.

"According to Atlas, he is one of the most ruthless," Daniel grimaced. "Perhaps Finn saw me before? Knew what I faced and figured I'd be a convenient foil. If you know what to look for, it's not hard to spot someone in the thrall of gin."

She pictured her father's round face, his fine clothes and his need to control his surroundings. He'd been a man of principles, ruthless in company politics but devoted to her. "Then my father couldn't be involved, if you think the culprit is a resurrection man."

He reached for the list. "Outside of Finn, that leaves Charles Hester and Cyrus Mason. I liked Hester for it—it's not much of a stretch to imagine him digging in the ground with a spade. Though I suppose I'm unduly biased, given that he never addressed me as anything other than 'Bloody Irish.'"

"At least he never looked at you like dinner to be devoured. I asked Papa to teach me how to shoot after meeting him." She cringed.

"Did he hurt you?" Daniel's voice was sharp, protective.

"No."

He hadn't, but others had.

"Hester is dead, regardless. He fell from one of the ship decks into the water and drowned. I suppose no one told him it'd be wise to learn to swim."

"Devilish bad luck, for him and us," Daniel frowned.

Us. She hated that word, a temptingly succulent promise that they'd be something more than strangers passing in the night. Better to solve Dalton's case as quickly as possible, so that when he moved on she would have fewer memories to torment her.

"What about Cyrus Mason?" Daniel pointed to his name. "He's not connected to Emporia, so that's one in his favor, don't you think? Atlas told me he was Dalton's closest friend at the docks. Used to work as a porter."

"I am acquainted with him. He's had ties with Chapman Street in the past. His brother runs a gaming hell. We won't get anything from him there. Joaquin Mason has too many guards." Kate pursed her lips. The King of Spades was notorious, not only for the games of chance that drew select members of the nobility into the darkest parts of the rookeries, but for the vice parties given by the proprietor.

"It would be easier to talk to Cyrus at the Red Fist," she continued. "The boxing fancy turn out to drink there after the bouts. When East India figured out he was stiffing from their shipments, he fled. I believe he suckered some rattlepated aristocrat into sponsoring his mills. He's a brute of a man."

"How comforting." Daniel's tone was strained, his humor falling flat. Concern sprung into his eyes before he snuffed it, expression again neutral. He'd looked the same outside of the Three Boars, she recalled.

"You needn't go." Kate shrugged. "I've been to the Red Fist more times than I can count. I'm perfectly capable of extracting information from Cyrus without your help."

"No way in hell."

"This protective streak is misplaced and irritating, Daniel."

"You'd best get used to it." His jaw set, his green eyes focused solely on her. Fist at his side, shoulders back, determination was writ across his features.

The only person I need protection from is you. Her heart pitter-pattered against her chest, desperate to fly to him and his perfect words. What little sense she had left, she'd kept locked away, even to charming men like Owen Neal.

"We will meet Wednesday afternoon at the Red Fist."

He nodded. "I'll see you then."

She felt the weight of his words, heavy on her gut. Another promise, another day together reliving what they had once been. "The docks tomorrow at sundown. Don't be late."

He blinked, likely surprised by her commanding tone. He opened and shut his mouth, then simply nodded again.

With no goodbye, Kate left him standing there, watching her retreating form disappear.

CHAPTER 5

As DUSK DESCENDED upon the foggy sky, Daniel stood at the principal entrance of the London Docks. Strewn to both sides of the gates were empty carts and wagons, deposited by porters who had finished unloading the ships. Beyond him rose a seemingly never-ending confluence of masts and brightly colored flags flapping in the wind. Sailors streamed from all sides of the docks, dozens of nationalities represented in this relatively small part of the city.

Every gust of wind brought a new prick of attentiveness down his spine. These docks were the stuff of his nightmares. He dreamed of black masts, of ghost ships crewed by a thousand dead Tommy Daltons.

He looked to the right and then to the left, his eyes wide and his mind ever-vigilant. In one hand he grasped a truncheon. The vendors had mostly cleared up for the day, but the smell of roasting meat lingered and reminded him of barbecued flesh. Suddenly the savory fish pie purchased for Kate from one of the donkey-carts didn't seem so appealing.

Once he had moved through these crowds with ease, certain of his place as a shipping assistant to one of the most powerful companies. He'd let his guard down because he'd believed he belonged.

He would never be so careless again.

"Daniel."

He turned to meet Kate, almost slamming into her. She'd sneaked up behind him, her gait soundless. That was a new skill, perhaps taught to her by the man he'd found her with. His chest tightened with jealousy.

"For you." He thrust the hot pie into her hands awkwardly. Everything he did around her these days seemed awkward. "I thought you'd want it."

"Thank you." She looked at it suspiciously for a second. "What do I owe you?"

"What? Nothing." He shook his head. "I was hungry before and I thought you'd like dinner too. Consider it part of your working wage."

She bit her bottom lip. Her desire for the pastry won out of over her pride. Biting into the pastry, her expression changed to clear relish of the food. "Mmm. Did you buy this from James the Penny Pieman at the lower loading docks?"

He nodded. "Of course I did. You always loved them."

"It's lovely." She devoured the pastry; eel, parsley, and sauce oozed out of the doughy bread. "I haven't eaten one of these in…bless it, I don't know how long."

"I'm glad you like it." He was rewarded by her smile as she took another large bite. This was how it should be between them, him taking care of her. *If only she'd let him.*

She ran a hand across her mouth when finished with the puffed pastry, getting the crumbs that dotted the lines of her lips. Flawless lips that he ached to kiss, reading their language with his own.

"Shall we go?" Kate turned back to him, her hands stuffed in the pockets of that absurdly large greatcoat.

If he looked closely, he thought he recognized the buttons on the coat: rounded with an anchor etched into the gold enamel. *Morgan's coat, like Morgan's pistol.*

He didn't want to set foot on these docks, and he certainly didn't want to go further toward the North Quay. It defied logic to think Dalton would somehow appear again, but he could not shake the notion.

Kate was here, and he had to be strong for her. He steeled himself up, took her arm in his, and started down the way. The bully stick remained in his other hand, poised and waiting. He cut a sharp left through the Crescent, past a two-story warehouse with barred windows. Empty barrels scattered the courtyard, to be removed by the next shift of workers.

He was ready for anything—or anyone—that might jump out from behind the many barrels containing used wine corks, sulfur, and ore. He rested his hand on her arm as they walked, ignoring how she became rigid under his hold. They were in the bowels of hell, and he would keep her safe if it was the last thing he did.

"I can't help but be on edge here," she muttered.

He nodded. This had been her second home too, before it had been ripped away from her by Emporia's debts.

A loud crash echoed in the quay. Daniel pivoted to place himself in front of Kate, breaking contact with her arm. He missed the solidness of her flesh, even as his eyes darted across the path.

"Sounds as if a barrel has been knocked over," he muttered. "But not close enough to here."

Kate thrust her hand into her pocket and pulled out her pistol, a cloth-wrapped load pouch, and a rod. Quickly, she loaded the pistol and switched it to half-cocked with a self-satisfied grin. "Better to be prepared, Papa always said."

His grip tightened against his bully stick. He preferred the truncheon to a gun, for it could be used at a moment's notice. "Let it never be said that Kate Morgan was not a wise woman." He winked at her.

They walked on, past more wine facilities that housed great vaults underneath the streets for the storage of the tested spirits. At last their path converged where the North Quay met the West. To their right were the warehouse complexes, numbered one through five, while to their left and a few paces over was the Superintendent's Office. A lone lamp shone from the nearby warehouse and the light spilled out into the alleyway in dim rays.

When the wind changed direction, he swore he heard the hollers of foxed sailors. What had happened to the men he used to drink with? Had they met their demise too soon, succumbing to the effects of gin? Or had they finally sailed back to Ireland, fighting a war against the very nation they'd found work in?

He stopped, running his hand down the clapboard side of the warehouse. The wood was cool against his palm, smooth from a fresh coat of paint. No matter how many times workers tried to cover up the stains, the wood would always smell sickly sweet with spilled blood to him. He could still remember each splatter. He slapped the bully stick against the wall, the sound bringing him back to reality.

Kate came to a stop next to him. She slipped the flintlock back into her pocket. "If you were on your way home, you could have cut through here to get out."

He glanced around. Nightingale Lane separated the London Docks from the newer St. Katherine's Docks. He could have taken the same entrance they'd used, and from there gone to either East Smithfield or Upper East Smithfield.

"That would make sense. I've done that before."

"What time did you leave Emporia?" Kate's gaze was rapt, like she could read all the secrets his mind had repressed. Often, he had thought she could. "You were supposed to meet me at home at ten, after Papa had gone to sleep."

He didn't recall that conversation, but how he wished he had gone straight to her townhouse that night and lost himself in her embrace instead. "I don't remember leaving at all. But that day Morgan had asked for us to catalogue some inventory before the next shipment arrived. I've often thought that maybe I stayed to finish those." It was the only theory he had.

"It would fit the usual schedule." Kate tapped at her chin with one finger. "The shipments always came in on a Tuesday, and it was Monday when Dalton was found. But it was two in the morning when the Watch got the tip about you. What were you doing between when you left Emporia and then? That is a large window of time to be unaccounted. Did you go to the public house?"

"Most likely." He could not hide past failures if he wanted to learn the truth.

"I suspected as much. I think it would help if you closed your eyes," Kate suggested. She reached for him, taking his hand in hers.

His fingers closed over her soft glove. In the darkness, the wounds of his past would be made fresh. He met her reassuring gaze and nodded.

"I'll be here with you," she murmured gently.

Daniel closed his eyes and let the blackness take over. He heard the gurgle of blood bubbling out of Dalton's mouth. He saw the slick red liquid coat his chin. Dalton's bruised, splitting nails were pressed to his neck in a desperate attempt to keep the blood in.

One stab wound would have been enough, if placed strategically, for Dalton to die instantly. The man's death had been drawn so that he felt every cut of the knife to his tender chest. Four slices, each not deep enough to kill him on their own, yet combined were enough to end his life. Dalton's hands were raw from fighting against his attackers, bits of the murderer's flesh probably stuck under his fingernails.

Footsteps had echoed. A woman had screamed. Daniel remembered lifting his head to look as the patrolman scurried into the alley between the first warehouse and the second, flanked by a hysterical doxie. He was glad at first for her screams—for her agony meant that someone at least cared that a man had been murdered—but his face soon drained of what little color left as she extended her pointer finger toward him.

"That man," she gasped. "I saw him do it."

The portly officer had moved with greater speed than Daniel thought possible. In an instant, the patrolman had pulled Daniel up from the ground, hands locked behind his back and bound. The patrolman dragged him from the alley, leaving Dalton to rot in the coming sun of the morning. Cornered, brutalized, and drained of life.

Daniel's breath now came in pants, jagged like the dagger that had severed Dalton's larynx.

Kate squeezed his hand. He opened his eyes. Dusky grayness framed her face, giving her pale skin a ghoulish cast. Yet to him, she was everything he needed. He clung to her hand, pulling it up to his lips and placing a kiss on her knuckles.

She blinked back at him, a faint blush across her high cheekbones. All too quickly she wrenched her hand from his.

"Did you remember anything?" Her features schooled into flatness.

He wanted to tell her he'd remembered something that would solve the entire case. Something that would bring them back together, with no future impediments.

But he refused to lie to her again. "I have never forgotten."

"Did you see anything *new*? Perhaps someone leaving as you knelt by Dalton?" She stepped closer to him, her mere presence buoying him.

"I entered the alley from the left, which does suggest that I was coming from the Prospect of Whitby." He tried to separate himself from the vision, to look at it logically. "Sometimes, when I dream about it, I see a man in a black cloak leaving the alley. But that is all a blur. I remember nothing so clearly as Dalton's body. I've no idea what brought me to that particular alley at that particular moment, when there are a dozen other ways I could have chosen to get home."

Kate's face grew thoughtful. "I once heard the Chapman Street Gang discussing a drug that could make you forget where you'd been. Mixed with alcohol, I expect the effect would be semi-permanent."

His chest tightened. Drugging indicated a pre-meditation, with him being the intended target instead of a convenient drunkard. *You'd best be prepared for this fight,* Atlas had said.

He gulped, sucking in air that smelled of cooked meat and dank wood. "If that is true, then we must look further into the connections between Dalton and me. Not only do we ask who wanted Dalton dead, but who wanted me to take the blame for it?"

His gut tightened. She didn't want to hear it, but it had to be something with Emporia. Perhaps something going on in the warehouses that Dalton worked in—Daniel had been responsible for overseeing all deliveries. Had Dalton seen something he shouldn't have, and been hushed for it?

Kate tapped her chin. "Who hated you enough to want to send you to the hangman's noose? Even I didn't want that after you left."

For a moment they both stood there, staring back at the alley that had changed everything between them.

SHE SHOULD NOT have held his hand. It was a sign of feebleness and it would give him hope that things could go back to the way they were before.

His kiss burned her knuckles. Surreptitiously, she looked down at her hand. The tan leather of her glove had not been obliterated by the gentle brush of his lips, but it might as well have been, for all that her body was enflamed.

She slipped the offending hand into her pocket, her fingers wrapping around the two shillings. She had stowed away the rest of Daniel's money in the secret recess in the wall of her flat with the rest of her received goods, but these two shillings she kept as a reminder she was doing this for the blunt and for the blunt alone.

As Daniel leaned back against the warehouse, strong arms crossed over his muscular chest, she had a distinct notion she'd already failed. Intensity flared in his green eyes, his ginger brows furrowed, and worry lines were etched into his wide forehead. She missed the scratch across her skin from the hint of stubble on his sharp chin, longed to run her hands through his short red hair until portions of it stuck out at awkward slants.

She couldn't think clearly when he looked so much like the man she'd loved before.

Three years without a single note.

She started to walk, forcing herself to move away from him. Closeness was hazardous—she needed to remember that. She moved toward the entrance to the docks, toward the road that would take her back to her flat and her normal life and everything that wasn't him. She advanced about five paces before he jogged after her, closing the distance in a minute with his long strides.

"Kate, wait." He grabbed for her arm.

She spun to the left just in time, for if he touched her again, she didn't know what she would do. His hand fell uselessly to his side. A frown darkened his face.

He could have taken another route, one that would leave him closer to Madame Tousat's. Instead, he followed her. She would not interpret that as a sign he would not leave this time. One hour made no difference, when he had the rest of his life to change his mind.

They continued on in silence until they broached the far side of the West Quay. Tall warehouses bordered the basin, housing everything from wine to wool. From a distance, she heard footsteps.

She thought nothing of it at first. Dockworkers skittered by, finishing up last-minute jobs before heading off to the Prospect of Whitby public house. When she stopped to let a porter with a full cart of goods pass in front of her, so did the footsteps.

Something was definitely wrong.

Her hand slipped to the flintlock in her pocket. She

darted a glance over her shoulder. From the shadows of another warehouse a man watched them intently. He was average-sized, yet he was built like a bruiser. In the dimming light of dusk she could not clearly make out his features.

She frowned. Earlier when Daniel had heard something, she should have trusted her instincts.

She quickened her pace. "Daniel," she said through gritted teeth. "I think we are being followed."

"Damnation," he cursed.

They continued on for a few more paces at a brisk walk. Neither looked behind them. The footsteps echoed still. She was almost at a jog, but the man continued to come after them. At this rate, he would catch them out in the street, where the crowds were fiercer and the lay of the land had changed somewhat since she'd been here last.

"He has not stopped," Daniel murmured.

"I think that I can lose him," she whispered.

He reached for her hand, wrapping his strong fingers around her own. This time, she didn't fight his hold. He doubled the odds of their survival—that was the only reason she wanted him near to help her fight.

It could not be that she felt safer with him around.

Some girls grew up watching the fireworks in Vauxhall Gardens and taking trips to Hatchard's Booksellers. Kate's upbringing had been confined largely to these docks, playing in the various quays and touring the warehouses while her father worked. She knew every passage like others would know the flavors of ices at Gunther's.

She set off at a full-fledged run, cutting in front of another porter. Down this alley, across this street, past the wine warehouses until they reached Warehouse No. 5 and the wine quay. Emporia's warehouses had been located close to here.

A glance over her shoulder confirmed that the man had kept pace with them. At his side was an angular object, vaguely resembling a cocked pistol.

She had to be quicker, smarter.

With one final squeeze to Daniel's hand, she stole to the left, rounding the side of the wine quay. To the south was the gigantic tobacco warehouse, but to the north-east were the wool warehouses. Emporia's old warehouses weren't close enough—she'd have to take a chance with the wool weavers.

If the patrol was the same, then she knew the north entrance of this warehouse would be unlocked. The Thames River Police's officer chatted up a pretty doxy on Pennington Street at this time of night. She ran toward the warehouse, Daniel two steps behind her.

Please God, let the door be open.

The door was propped open by a chunk of old barrel. She let out a breath she hadn't realized she'd been holding as Daniel thrust the door open. They skidded inside, slamming it behind them.

"We must find somewhere to hide." Daniel struck a match, illuminating a small circle of the warehouse.

For as far as she could see, bales of wool lined the floor. She wrinkled her nose. The warehouse stank of shorn wool, four stories high and spanning a courtyard. The walls and roof of the upper floors were made of glass to allow for better visibility of the many bales. They stood knee-deep in discarded wool, which had been drawn for inspection and then discarded. A public sale must have occurred recently, and in the morning the workers would return to clean up for the next showing.

The door slammed.

"Quickly!" Kate pointed to a nearby bale.

Daniel extinguished his match and crawled in after her. Without her legs tucked up against her chest, there would have been no room for him. As it was, sandwiched nearly on top of each other, there was little room in between the back of the bale and the wall.

Darkness surrounded them, all light from the glass ceiling blocked out behind the bale. So close together, she breathed in the scent of bergamot and cloves. She leaned her head against his shoulder, convinced she was conserving space and not giving in to temptation. The warmth of his body against hers felt so good, so safe.

It was not folly if he offered decent protection against an attacker.

Never mind that their current position blocked access to her gun. Out of the hundred or so bales on this floor, she doubted that the man following them would choose *this* exact bale to search behind. They simply had to remain here long enough for him to think they'd left the warehouse completely and go about his way. In the grand scheme of her adult life, this would be the least difficult of all nefarious activities.

She clutched Daniel's hand as the man walked through the warehouse, making a circle of the floor. His lamp swung back and forth. Finding nothing, he stopped in the middle of the warehouse and listened.

She could not breathe.

The man frowned. He strode toward the entrance. The door slammed shut.

She dropped Daniel's hand. Her breathing was ragged, overwhelmed with relief. Until Daniel's hand brushed against her leg. Lower at first, content to move along her ankle before scooting upwards. His thumb nudged at her thigh, traced the fold of her kneecap before moving upward to land on her hip.

Oh, but it felt so devilishly good to be stroked by him. It took off the edge of all this, but it was a new danger in itself.

Kate pulled back from him suddenly, upsetting her balance. She toppled over into a pile of castoff wool.

"What's wrong?" Daniel asked, as he crawled out from behind the bale. Concern clouded his face and he struck another match. "Why are you blushing?"

"You—" She blinked. "Your hand—"

"Was on your waist." He nodded, not in the least bit ashamed. "You seemed frightened."

Her jaw fell slack. "And so your normal response is to

stroke fear from people?"

"Not people. Just you." He blinked.

She looked away from him, for his confused expression made her stomach flip-flop dangerously. She'd always thought him adorable when perplexed, for his nose scrunched up just so and he'd blink rapidly. He had hated the idea of problems he couldn't solve, but together, they'd been able to change Emporia's shipment intake procedures to greatly increase productivity.

He did not speak. That perhaps was worse, for in the silence she heard his earlier words. *But most of all, I know that you're the only woman I've ever loved.* Her body craved his touch, the coiled-up tension within her begging to be released. It'd be deliriously perfect, until she crashed back down to reality.

She glowered. Stepping back, Kate turned toward the door. "I have to go."

"I'll walk you back." He closed the distance between them.

She started. "No. Absolutely not."

"But I'll see you at the Red Fist?" He was puzzled by her reaction.

She could only nod before she fled. If she never saw another bale of wool in her life, it would be too soon.

CHAPTER 6

THE RED FIST was located in the midst of a small but crowded area known to residents as Mid-Shadwell. To Daniel, it was simply another circle of hell in Dante's *Inferno*, meant to torment and remind him of his flaws.

He could smell gin as soon as he turned from Shadwell Highway onto Fox Lane, where the pugilist's public house loomed high above the crumbling houses. Juniper and coriander, a fragrant bouquet marginally fascinating to the casual drinker, but to him it was the most wonderful scent in the world. His feet moved forward without his consent, advancing toward the front of the public house to seek his ruination in the form of a stubby glass.

The once-white brick Red Fist filled the first story of the towering building, the top floor being used for tenement housing. The fancy crowd was out in full force tonight, though he'd heard no rumors of a mill. They came to discuss the latest bouts, to exchange strategy and bets, and they came to drink. In his darker days, he'd been like them. Two men bleeding each other had appealed to him on a basic level, the part of him that wanted vengeance for the mess of his life.

He didn't go through the front doors. *Too much exposure.*

An easy excuse, a lie he could tell himself when he was well aware of the real reason he didn't want to enter. Crossing into the back alley, he stood outside the kitchen. Even here wasn't far enough for him.

Off to the side was a rubbish bin. A burly beggar hunted for scraps, bent so far over the bin that only his backside, legs, and split-soled shoes were visible. Daniel leaned against the wall, watching as the man gave up rooting, righted himself, and turned around.

"What're ye lookin' at, cub?" The beggar's nose wrinkled, as if Daniel was the one gripping a burnt shank of mutton and a crusty, half-eaten roll in his grime-soaked hands.

"Kill the Bogger! Down with Popery!" The shouts echoed from inside the public house, followed by rousing agreement.

The beggar squinted, looked at Daniel's red hair peeking out from underneath his low-brow hat, and snickered.

Daniel swallowed. The winter air was stifling, full of spiced mutton and gin. He tapped his truncheon against his leg, fingers clenched harder around the handle. He half-expected the back doors of the public house to swing open, unleashing a torrent of men upon him. Fueled by vitriol from the debates over the Catholic Question, they'd hate him for nothing more than his nationality and religion. It didn't matter that he'd lived in England for most of his damned life, or that his memories of Ireland faded with each passing day.

He should stand on the side of Ireland, waving a flag of patriotism because the British had invaded the land of his ancestors, but he couldn't bring himself to care. He had enough bloody problems.

He was mad to think the crowd meant him, when he knew full well there was a pugilist fighting under the name Bogger, a strapping Irishman who used the slur to suck dry English pockets.

Daniel was mad to be here in the first place.

Where was Kate? Furtively, he glanced up the alley and back again. Did she expect him at the front entrance? Perhaps he should move toward there, let himself indulge in a single pint to add to the image that he was just another fancy…

No.

He knew better. He had a family to think of, of his sister Poppy and her daughter and his uncle. And Kate, gorgeous Kate, depending on him to prove he could be a better man.

Kate, whose hips swayed so devilishly when she walked, who emerged from the shadows of a snowy London night with the tails of her men's greatcoat floating out behind her, pistol in her hand. He grew hard at the sight of her, supple and imperial. For a second, he was not sure if he'd imagined her appearance, as he'd done so many times before.

"What are you doing all the way back here?" She asked. "Cyrus's sponsor is holding court by the bar, so Cyrus can't be too far off."

He gulped, unwilling to admit his weakness. "I thought I'd attract less scrutiny if I sneaked in through the back."

Her eyes narrowed like the beggar's, who candidly observed them from his place atop the rubbish bin. She leaned down and scooped up some ash from the sidewalk.

"If you were worried about being seen, you should've done something about your appearance. We shouldn't take chances, not after last night. Here, take your hat off." Not waiting for him to do so, she reached up and grabbed his hat. Scattering the ash atop his hair, she spread it out with her fingers and patted it down. "There. A brunette if I ever saw one."

He set the hat back down on his head. They walked around front, the crunch of their boots against the snow like a thousand explosions to his ears. Kate opened the door and he slid in after her.

"There's Cyrus." Kate pointed toward the bar where a man sat off to the side, nursing a pint.

Cyrus looked up from his ale as they approached. A candle flickered on the bar-top next to him, illuminating his glowering features. His hair was black as coal, his forehead wide, jaw square, and he had a bulbous, off-center nose that had been broken badly and not properly set. His left lid was blackened, the skin puffy from a recent hit, while his right eye regarded them with discernment. A mammoth of a man, he hunkered over the bar-top, bruised hands wrapped around a dwarfed mug.

Daniel gripped Kate's arm, ready to pull her away from the pugilist. He'd humor her need to be in control only as long as it didn't endanger her safety.

"Morgan. Who's the cull?" Cyrus asked.

"I'm Patrick Sweany." Daniel inclined his head, his natural half-Brogue thicker, like his uncle's.

"You always did have a thing for the Irish, Morgan." Cyrus shrugged, turning his attention back to Daniel. "Betting on the Bogger then?"

"'Course. Heard he was gonna fight Izzy Lazarus next," he fibbed, unflinching at the fighter's uneven gaze. "He'll win for sure."

"You kiss your mother with that lying mouth, Clanker?" Cyrus crossed his arms, his bulging forearms straining against the cut of his linen shirtsleeves. He wore no coat.

"Care to make a wager?" Daniel asked. "I'm damned certain the Bogger will take your man tonight, just as he'll defeat the Jew, Izzy."

"I've got a pony on Jim Friar," Kate interjected, appeasing the fighter.

"Not a good place for a lady tonight." Cyrus tilted his head toward the masses around them, bent on heavy drinking and exodus. "Why are you here, Morgan? Finally coming to your senses about my offer?"

"Don't make me retch." Kate rolled her eyes.

Unbidden, an image of Kate with Cyrus came to mind, the fighter's muscular chest pressed against her bare breasts, his riven lips on her neck.

Bastard. It didn't matter whether it had happened or not, the man had opportunities to get to know Kate when he'd left and thus Daniel hated him.

"You're not the fighting sort." Cyrus sat back on the stool, surveying her. "You only come when you want something. I haven't sent you any goods. Something wrong with Jane?"

Kate's expression became guarded. "Jane is fine, or as fine as she can be with her brother in gaol. I saw her the other night when she was working. You know she doesn't want you asking about her."

Cyrus sneered, fresh blood speckling his split lip. "She don't know what she wants, that lass."

"You weren't good together. You've got to let her go."

Was that how Kate saw their relationship too? Like poison disguised as wine, warm on her lips but fetid in her stomach.

We are meant for another chance. Daniel held on to that faith, clutched it tight as his gaze flitted from her back to the scowling Cyrus.

The tapster inquired what they wished to drink. Kate ordered an ale. Daniel's mouth watered, his throat tightening.

"Coffee," he said.

"A man who won't drink's not a man." To demonstrate, Cyrus knocked back the rest of his ale and slammed down the tankard.

Daniel bit back a retort, for Kate had stiffened next to him. She glared at Cyrus, hackles raised in his defense, and he wanted to see what she'd do.

"A man who needs to hide behind drink isn't a man," she snapped. "I don't remember you being so devilishly judgmental."

Daniel squeezed her arm in gratitude. So he had not descended so far in her esteem after all. Cyrus's features relaxed, as if he were pleased by Kate's retort and she'd passed some sort of test. Daniel folded his hands in his lap and did what he hadn't done when he was drinking—he listened.

"YOU REMEMBER MY betrothed," Kate said.

That simple statement left her raw. Somehow calling Daniel by that title, with him present, seemed far too intimate for their current state. It was a word of promises, households to manage and children to raise.

Cyrus took the new pint offered to him by the bar-wench, winking at her with his one good eye. "Irish's lucky he got away when he did. I'd like to rip *his* throat out for butchering Tommy."

Daniel stiffened. His hand rested on the bar-top, mere centimeters away from her fingers. Close enough that if she moved a hair's breadth to get her drink, she would brush his supple gloves.

"Been a long time since Tommy died, and you never quizzed me about it before." The boxer turned his attention to Daniel. "Sweany, you said? I've not heard of any Sweanys in these parts."

Panic clogged Kate's throat, but she shoved it far down. He couldn't know of Daniel's identity, not with the hat pulled low, the darkening of his hair and his deep accent. She could only remember Daniel sounding like that when aroused, when he was too far gone to care about modulating his speech.

Those were the realest times she'd had with him.

"I moved a few months ago. From Cork," Daniel supplied.

Cyrus gave a short nod, but his eye still held a hard gleam. He was suspicious, and he'd keep on digging until he eventually found out that Sweany was no more than the quick thinking of the man he wanted to maim for killing his best friend.

Unless she did something.

When Cyrus's attention was on her, she intertwined her fingers in Daniel's. Glove to glove, she could not feel the callouses on his palm, but she knew they were there and that was almost as poignant.

"I've found someone new." She turned her head toward Daniel, letting the silence serve as emphasis as she looked into his eyes. Eyes she could get lost in, swimming in jade. "How can I possibly move on until I know that I didn't have something to do with Daniel O'Reilly's descent into madness? I never suspected a thing. I would've married him, Cyrus, married a man capable of brutal murder."

Cyrus seethed. "Tommy was a good man, you hear me? Damned besotted with some doxy. It's always the woman. You tempt and tease us but you never give it up. You'd string us along until we're only fit for Bedlam, and then you leave us because we make one mistake. Jane don't know—"

"*Cyrus*," Kate snapped. "Do you want me to tell Jane that I found you belly up in a bottle, bemoaning your fate like a melodramatic chit? Because I will."

Cyrus bared his teeth, but she refused to be intimidated. For all her days, she would never understand what Jane had seen in the pugilist.

Daniel raised himself up to his full height, ready to attack Cyrus if he came after her. That was insanity, Kate knew, for the man was far larger than Daniel and made a living pounding the shit out of others.

Regardless, the show of support sent a little flutter through her. Stomach flipping, Kate looked back at Cyrus.

"What's a bit of reminiscing between two old friends?" Cyrus relaxed back into the chair. "Not that I've got much for you, Morgan. Tommy might have known some bad blokes, but your lad was Emporia, and Tommy did warehouse work. One can obviously see the connection, though you don't like it."

She made a fist, nails digging into her palm. *There had to be more than that.*

"What happened before Daniel killed Dalton? Surely you must know something?"

"Do you think me dim because I'm a bruiser, lass? I'm not going to risk my hide for nothing. Show me a little something for my troubles." His eyes roved down her frame, gaze settling at her chest. Her greatcoat was open, revealing the lower neckline of her gold walking gown.

Damnable, damnable fashion. In the Red Fist, where most of the women were lightskirts, the less she wore the better she fit into the crowd.

"Say that again, Mason." Daniel's voice was low, lethal as he pushed himself up and off the stool.

Fury radiated from the firm set of his jaw to the soles of his worn top boots. She saw the man the constable claimed he was—the potential for violence hidden underneath his calm exterior. So why then did she feel a tingle through her body, comfortably stealing away the bitter taste Cyrus's proposition had left in her mouth?

He would not let her honor be tarnished. She'd forgotten she could even have such a notion as honor.

Cyrus leaned on the counter-top lazily, unperturbed. He held all the cards and he damn well knew it.

"Are you deaf as well as dumb?" Daniel's hand slammed on the bar-top, fisted and ready to punch Cyrus in the jaw. The noise drew attention to them, in the form of several turned heads toward their little congregation at the end of the bar.

That would never do. She hopped off the stool, pushing herself between the two men.

Cyrus stood, towering over Daniel. He took a step toward them, his movements surprisingly agile considering his size.

"Get out of the way," Cyrus barked at her.

The situation was getting out of control quickly. How could she not have accounted for this?

Another error in judgment to add to her already long list.

When she didn't move out of Cyrus's way fast enough, he grabbed for her shoulders, lifting her up and off of her feet. By the time she'd managed to form a protest, she was back on the ground away from Daniel, giving Cyrus a clear shot at him.

"Bollocks!" Her shriek got their attention. In tandem, they looked at her, confusion flickering.

Daniel took another step forward, edging on Cyrus. Kate stifled a groan, reaching into one of the pockets of her greatcoat. She pulled out a gold watch and set it down on the counter.

"It's clean," she said grudgingly. "I checked it myself." The watch was supposed to be a good payday for her. She had bought it from a drug-addled pickpocket, who was easily convinced the market was saturated with watches and thus it was worth far less.

Daniel needed the information, but more importantly, *she* needed to know Emporia wasn't connected to this. Papa had been vigilant in knowing the affairs of his employees. If Papa had known about a plot and not stopped it...she couldn't countenance that.

"Kate—" Daniel started. He shut his mouth when she glared at him.

"It'll do." Cyrus snaked it up from the counter, depositing it in the inner pocket of his coat. "Would've preferred a lay with you, clever doxy, but it'll do."

Daniel's face became stormy. Kate grabbed for his hand, warning him not to challenge Cyrus again. He threw his arm over her shoulder and pulled her closer to him. She stayed put, not because it was so comforting to lean her head back against his sculpted chest, but because it would not perpetuate their deception if she pulled away. She breathed in bergamot and cloves until her senses were caught in the fragrant haze.

"Tell us who the beaters that Dalton knew are," Daniel demanded. "You said he had connections, or was that you spinning tales?"

"I ain't no liar." Cyrus took the stool next to her, leaning in so that his words were only audible to her and Daniel. "I don't know any names."

"Sweany here is a grand thief. Do you really want him to lift that watch from you?" Kate had no patience left.

"Listen now, that doesn't mean I know nothing. Tommy and I, we grew up together. I was in better circles, due to the

Mason name, but I never cared much for the *bon ton* and we were on the fringes regardless. Tommy wasn't a bad man, but he sure as hell wasn't lucky. That much ought to be obvious." Cyrus swiped a palm across his brow, a misplaced attempt at hiding his sadness over his friend's demise. "We ran in the same gang. Small stuff, mostly, anything more and Joaquin'd have my head. I did it for the thrill, but Tommy—he thought he'd make a life for himself and the whore who'd caught his eye. Never listened when I told him he was being duped. No bit of baggage cares enough about our lot to run off into the country and start over."

I cared about you, Daniel. I would have run away with you. Those thoughts rose up, gossamer threads to be snipped by rusted scissors when she remembered their place.

"So what kept him from leaving?" Daniel asked.

"Well, Morgan's bloke sliced his neck clear through, I'd say that stopped him, wouldn't you?" Cyrus lifted his glass. "Bunch of bastards brought him on what he thought was going to be the greatest deal. Stealing bodies from the graveyards and selling them to doctors who didn't give a rat's tail about where they came from. I told Tommy not to do it, told him it'd end badly. He never listened to me, never—"

Cyrus stopped. He blinked rapidly, then the emotion was gone from his face, snuffed out.

"Do you recognize the name Jasper Finn?" Daniel leaned forward on the bar, overeager.

Cyrus shook his head. "He some kind of exhumator?"

"The best, apparently, but I haven't found anyone who's seen him." Kate drew her bottom lip between her two front teeth, biting down on the tender skin. "If he truly exists, *someone* must know him."

She would turn over every rock in London if she had to, if it meant finding another tie besides Emporia.

"I can't help you there, lass, even if I wanted to." Cyrus shrugged. "I don't make a business of sorting with the resurrectionists. Bunch of skin-flints, the lot."

"Yes, because bareknuckle boxing is such a noble pursuit." Kate rolled her eyes.

Daniel patted her shoulder in a gesture most likely meant to quiet her. She stiffened against his hold, shooting a glare at him.

He was undeterred. "The woman you mentioned earlier—do you remember her name?"

"That bitch couldn't be bothered to come to his funeral. Of course I remember her." His voice rose, increasing in volume. Another ale appeared in front of him without his asking. The barmaid would keep him drinking, in hopes he'd draw in more business with one of his legendary brawls.

"I can understand how that would upset you. Women, they can be ruthless. Hell, I've got a friend in the same situation, enamored with a woman who probably wouldn't mourn his death." In contrast to Cyrus's escalated anger, Daniel was calm, verging on sympathetic.

For a second, her eyes met Daniel's and her next question died in her throat. She said nothing, but in that silence the weight of their wrongs crashed down on her shoulders. They could never be the same people again, not now.

I've mourned you for the last three bloody years.

Cyrus snorted, oblivious to their exchange. Caught in his own grief over his friend's death and his irritation toward the woman who had failed Dalton. "Her name is Sally Fletcher. Attached to a brothel on Jacob's Island. Devilishly dimber, but don't let her angel's face fool you."

"I'll try not to be taken in." A mischievous smile tugged at Daniel's lips, that telltale sign he thought he was being witty. Kate pushed back her bar stool, ready to be gone. That smile was not for her any longer. Some other woman would be the recipient of it.

They had information now that lead away from Emporia, and that in itself was worth the price of three gold watches. She nodded to Cyrus, waiting as Daniel fished out coin from his pocket for the ale and coffee.

"Give my best to Jane. Pleasure doing business with you, gel." Cyrus winked.

She wouldn't dignify that with a response.

CHAPTER 7

THEY WALKED DOWN Shadwell High Street, the street alive with a vibrancy that failed to lift Daniel's mood. Snow crunched under his feet. The smell of gin had left his nostrils, allowing him to breathe easier again, but the heaviness in his stomach came from the knowledge of Kate's sacrifice. She'd given up part of her livelihood, all to answer questions from a man she shouldn't have had to speak to, let alone develop an acquaintanceship with.

"You didn't have to do that," he said.

"Cyrus would never have told us anything otherwise." Kate cocked her head toward him, her voice flat.

She walked with her hands shoved into her pockets, her shorter strides two to his longer ones. He slowed to match her pace. This city, with all its grit and crime, didn't deserve the brilliance of Kate Morgan.

Devil take it, he didn't either.

"That doesn't make it right." He halted her progress down the street, gripping her thin arm. "I'll pay you back for what that watch costs, on top of what I've given you for your help already."

"That's not necessary." She stiffened against his touch.

He didn't release her arm. They stood in the middle of the

street, the traffic diverting around them. If he got through to her—well, he didn't know what he'd do then.

"I don't want you to have to pay for my mistakes." Reaching out with his other hand, Daniel brushed his thumb against her cheek.

Her eyes closed for a half-second, transfixed by the moment. His breath caught in his throat.

Her eyes fluttered back open, chocolate abysses deadened to his attempts. Steeled against what she must believe were lies. Maybe he'd never change. Maybe he was a drunk for life, doomed to repeat the same patterns.

He let out the breath he'd been holding, let it out like he wished he could free himself of doubt. Time flowed once more, rapid and bitter.

"I've paid for your mistakes and I'll pay for mine." Her voice was full of resignation.

He sighed. Poppy had been seduced by a rogue because he hadn't been there to protect her, and Kate had been tossed into the rookeries as though she were fresh mutton.

"It shouldn't have to be that way. Last night, in the wool warehouse—I couldn't think of anything else other than the fact that you were in danger because of me." His hand tightened on her arm, holding her close to him.

She shook her head. The feather stuck into the trim of her gray straw bonnet bobbed too. "Nothing is perfect. For all we know, that man was after me for my own activities. You talk as though things will change because you wish them to. I don't remember you being that naïve."

"It's not naïve to dream. You used to know that." He shrugged.

"Look around you," she commanded, stepping back from him to motion to the rest of the street. "Does this look like a place of dreams? The man loitering in that doorway there, covered in rags, do you think he cares about your high ideals? No. He wants to take whatever money he can glean from begging to buy enough gin to forget his very existence."

Daniel followed her glance to the same beggar he'd seen in the street before. As Kate turned her head to look further down the street, the beggar sneered sinisterly. Warning bells rang in his head as soundly as the old Charley's time and weather announcement. He couldn't explain it, this feeling that the vagrant knew something about him, that he had been watching him. Daniel tugged his hat lower on his brow.

Kate stepped out into the street. As she did, a vendor moving the last of his merchandise out of the square bumped into her, jolting her forward.

She fell into Daniel, face pressed against the metal buttons of his greatcoat. The bonnet perched on her head flopped askew. Her scent filled his nostrils, crisp and spicy. He breathed in deep, for she was the air surrounding him and all he needed to survive.

He had to keep her close to him.

That knowledge burned through his mind, even as all around them Shadwell High Street ebbed and flowed with nighttime activity. In their current stance, they could easily be trampled as the remaining vendors finished boxing up their stands from the day's market.

"We should go." He took her hand in his once more, fully expecting her to protest.

"Right." She blinked twice, looking dazed.

He tugged on her hand, leading her to a less crowded side-street near Surin. They crossed underneath the front awning of a three-story tenement house, with balconies spanning the second and third levels. A sheet hung from the rafters, once clean but now coated in soot drifting from the chimney. The decaying roof was patched in sections with swollen boards. Two young children played in the courtyard, their bare feet sinking in the sludge of snow and muck. Next to them, a goat chewed on a scrap of fabric.

Pulling Kate into a darkened doorway off to the side of the house, Daniel released her hand with chagrin. The dying winter light barely penetrated the cavern of brick and grime, casting her features in a gloomy gray. She looked tired, gaunt.

"I told you that you were wrong." She crossed her arms over her chest. "Papa was a good Christian man. Good Christian men don't go digging up dead bodies in graveyards to sell for dissection."

Good Christian men do a lot of things you wouldn't expect.

"It is too soon to make assumptions," he said vaguely. "We don't have all the facts."

Kate pushed off from the wall she leaned against, coming to stand directly in front of him. "I've had enough of people harboring grudges for my father's company. He didn't do anything wrong. Investments sour all the time. It is the nature of the business."

"I am not endeavoring to—" He stopped, realized what she'd said. "Other people with grudges? Who are you talking about?"

"Did you think I came to Ratcliffe because I wanted to?" She let out a laugh, harsh to his ears. "Had I other options, I would have taken them in an instant. So many people lost their jobs when Emporia collapsed. No one wanted to help the daughter of the man who had ruined them."

"What about your old friends? Diana, Justine—what happened to them?" He treaded dangerous territory by inquiring into her past, but he couldn't stop himself from asking.

He remembered the two girls being Kate's constant companions, the daughters of Emporia's department heads. One a blonde, one a redhead—the warehouse laborers had called them the Terrible Three.

Her jaw clenched. "Mr. Balfour was furious over the loss of his job. He forbade Justine from associating with me because of Papa—as if it were Papa's fault he'd gotten sick and the investments didn't pan out."

"So she simply stopped speaking to you?" Outrage crept into his voice, when he had no right to be judgmental of Justine. Hadn't he done the same by not communicating with

Kate?

"Yes." She leaned her head back against the wall, closing her eyes. The admission seemed to pain her, and he wanted to drag her closer to him, to tell her that he'd never leave her again.

She wouldn't have to be alone.

But he didn't. He simply waited for her to open her eyes again, for her breath to return to normal rhythms before he made his final inquiry. "And Diana?"

"Diana married and moved to Yorkshire. I couldn't afford the mail coach ticket." Her gaze drifted toward her feet and stayed, unwilling to meet his questioning eyes.

He vaguely recalled how she and Diana had been delighted to become engaged around the same time.

He'd ruined everything.

"You should have had the big wedding, from the announcing of the banns to the celebratory breakfast to everything in between."

She gave a half-hearted shrug. "It doesn't matter now."

"Did you ever write to Diana?" He hated the thought of her cut away from her past, whether or not she had this new set of thieving acquaintances.

Kate shook her head. "I didn't want her to see me like this. I didn't want *you* to see me like this." She mumbled the last part, so he was not certain he'd heard her right. She didn't look up at him.

His voice softened. He leaned in closer to her, arm outstretched against the wall for balance. "You haven't anything to be ashamed of with me."

A gentle flush spread across her cheeks but she remained silent. She shifted her weight from one foot to the other, the smallest hint of a smile appearing. He seized onto that smile and the hope it presented.

"Please, Katiebelle, if you take nothing else from this time spent with me, know that you needn't feel shame," he pleaded. He was emboldened enough to slide his hand forward, his fingers curled under her chin, bringing her eyes up to meet his own. "You are bold and beautiful and I would not change a single thing about you."

The flush deepened, spreading from her cheeks to her pert nose. "Such pretty words," she mused, tucking a loose russet curl behind her ear.

He didn't release her chin, wanting to hold on to her forever, keep her in this moment where she was not fighting him. They were simply a man and a woman together, as they should have been all along.

"Pretty words for a pretty girl." The line sounded trite even to him, but her smile grew so he would not doubt the prowess of the tried and true. He grinned back at her. "Though I'll admit I'm not entirely fond of your flintlock. It is far too often pointed in my direction."

His joke seemed to jar her. She ducked underneath his arm. She stood in the alley, as if torn—not wanting to leave, yet not willing to stay in such close confines with him.

"I held you at gunpoint *once*," she said. "In the alley, when you first confronted me. It was justified."

He couldn't help himself. He threw his head back and laughed. That startled her.

Her brows furrowed quizzically. "I can't see what is so amusing about my gun. I have been told I am quite intimidating."

"Oh no, you most certainly are." He supposed his agreement was less convincing when he grinned like a buffoon. "But you must admit it's absurd. Once you and I were lovers, and now you greet with me a gun up my nose. We are a pair, you and I."

"A match made in hell, I'd venture." She tried to play off the comment with a smirk, but he saw through her.

Once we were perfect together.

She returned to the task at hand. "I assume now we try and find the lightskirt Cyrus mentioned."

"Yes, but I thought we'd visit Atlas to see if he knows of

Sally Fletcher. There must be hundreds of prostitutes on Jacob's Island alone. I don't fancy checking each brothel." Daniel frowned.

Kate arched a brow. "A man who does not want to go to a brothel. I never thought it possible." She turned away from him, about to head down the alley.

His hand snaked out, grabbing hold of her wrist and spinning her back to him. Her eyes widened, alarmed by the sudden change in his demeanor. He closed the distance between them, backing her up against the wall.

His taller frame loomed over hers, leveraging his weight to keep her trapped, hands placed on either side of her head. His hips pressed into hers, his legs spread so that she fit in between his thighs.

God's balls, this was how they should always be.

She shivered. Her eyes were locked on his lips.

"Listen to me," he said, his breath hot upon her cheek. "You are the only woman I need. Every woman I've ever been with—they were substitutes for you. Nobody's ever read me like you could. I've made every mistake a man can make, I know that."

She leaned her head back against the wall, exposing the long, kissable line of her neck. "I can't be that woman I was with you anymore. I know you want me to, and maybe a part of me wants to go back, but this can't work."

"Why not?" He kissed her neck, right underneath her left ear, continued to nuzzle her down the column of her throat.

"I can't—" Her protest broke off, turning into a little moan of pleasure.

"Maybe you don't want to forgive me right now. Maybe I have to work for it, earn your trust back." He nipped at her ear and she shuddered, pliant against him. "I promise you, love, I'll convince you I'm worth the trouble if it's the last thing I do."

He laid a kiss upon her cheek, his whiskered chin scratching against her soft skin for a second before he pulled away. "Come, let's get you a carriage home."

THAT NIGHT, WHEN the clock struck three in the morning, Kate perched on a barstool at the Three Boars. She should be sleeping, but her mind was far too alert for rest. She would not think of Daniel, would not ponder the delicious way his lips glided against her skin, and she definitely would not remember the thrill of being between his thighs once more.

Except in not thinking about it, she somehow managed to recreate every single bloody moment in vivid detail. She needed a drink. Or four.

"He's here." Jane came to her side of the bar, a glass of crank already in hand for her. She slid the glass across the bar-top.

"Who's here?" Kate croaked. She checked her hair to make sure her headband held back her coiffure nicely.

Jane cracked a smile. "Owen."

Kate's breath released in one loud exhale. What was that niggling feeling in her gut? It could not be disappointment at Owen arriving instead of Daniel. No, Daniel was nothing but trouble. She should be overjoyed to have a break from him.

Too slowly, she composed her face, plastering on a smile.

"Somehow I don't think that is who you expected," Jane remarked. "But whether or not you want him, he is heading this way."

Kate hazarded a glance over her shoulder. Owen strode toward them, shoulders back, tight beige pantaloons stretched across lean, Corinthian legs. He wore a black and silver striped neckcloth, a silver waistcoat with a starched white shirt, and a black jacket wide and oval in cut. In this room of unwashed drunks and scoundrels, Owen was ripped from the pages of *The Gentleman's Magazine of Fashion*.

She thought of Daniel's worn coat, his scuffed low-boots and cheap trousers. When had such tattered apparel begun to appeal to her? She ran a hand down her patched gold skirt, smoothing out the wrinkles.

Owen slid into the stool next to her without asking if it was occupied; he assumed she'd saved it for him all along. He winked at Jane, who simply stared back at him, humorless. Owen wasn't Chapman Street and Jane had little patience for thieves outside of the gang. She stood with one hand on her hip.

He angled his stool closer to Kate. "Three threads and a refill for Miss Morgan."

"Miss Morgan drinks gin," Jane said testily, moving to pour a glass of half-double ale, to mix with stale and double beer.

"Bloody wretched stuff," Owen pronounced. "But if she prefers it, then sky blue it is."

Jane harrumphed. She pushed Owen's tankard to him, along with another glass of gin for Kate. A customer called for her attention.

When Jane's back was turned, Owen leaned closer, his knee brushing against Kate's. Leather and musk filled her nose. His hand came to rest on the back of her stool. In the dim light of the public house, she doubted anyone else could see his fingers.

Why shouldn't she let him touch her? Hitherto, he had been a gentleman. They had a sort of understanding, given their mutual interests. She was no untouched virgin, and it had been a long time. Too long.

"I have something for you." His voice rumbled in her ear, smooth without the hint of a brogue or East London sloppiness. She had heard a prostitute compare his voice to melted caramel.

"It's something shiny." He pulled back from her, hunting in the pocket of his coat until he found the small bit of gold. Triumphantly, he dropped it on the counter, the ring twinkling.

She picked it up and stood, holding the ring up to the lamp that hung from the bar. In her palm, it felt right. The oil light tinged the gold with a fiery glow, highlighting the two outstretched hands braced around a heart. A crown perched on top of the heart.

Her stomach plummeted. There could be a thousand rings like this in England, it didn't mean—she ran her thumb across the inner ridge of the ring.

Devil take it.

There was a deep scratch in the gold, confirming what she already knew. The ring was hers.

Or rather, it had been hers, once. Three years ago.

"Where did you get this?" Her voice came out strangled, her breath in tiny pants. She held the ring so tight that blotches of red appeared between her thumb and forefinger.

Owen watched her, confusion flickering in his deep brown eyes. His chiseled cheekbones appeared even more statuesque when cast with concern. "My man cloyed it off some toff on King's Street. Standard bungnipping, a dumb bob cull who couldn't watch his pockets and so my man got lucky." He stood, coming up behind her. He was shorter than Daniel, almost her exact height, and so his chin fitted over her shoulder. "Do you like it? If it isn't up to snuff, I can get you something else."

"No, it's fine." She closed her hand over the ring.

"Are you quite certain?" Owen reached forward, his hand covering hers.

"*Quite.*" Her nails bit into her palm, so tightly latched was her hand over the ring. She knew a thief like Owen could lift it from her otherwise, and damn it all, she wasn't going to part with this ring again. "It's lovely. I don't have the funds on hand for it now, but I think I could get you a good price—"

Owen held up a hand, cutting her off. "Kate," he said quietly, his breath a whisper on her cheek. "I meant it as a gift, not something for you to fence."

"Oh." She wasn't quite sure what to say to that. Could she accept a gift from Owen in good conscience?

And then there was Daniel, who had given her this bloody ring as a token of his love for her. The ring had been passed down through generations of his family. It was an embodiment of what it meant to be an O'Reilly, and the life she *should* have had. A life that she now knew she couldn't have.

Bollocks.

She must have appeared startled, for Owen sat back down. "As a thank you for all the work you've done for me," he clarified. "The crown made me think of you. You're very regal, Kate. A man could fall in love with you and you'd hold his heart right there in your pretty hands."

His gaze softened as he reached for her hand again. His larger palm covered hers, yet no flurry of emotion filled her. "I think we would make sense together, but I won't push you. Keep the ring. I wanted you to have something that would remind you of me." He leaned in closer, locking eyes with her and ignoring Jane's glare from across the bar.

He released her hand. "If in time that ring puts thoughts in your head, you know where to find me."

CHAPTER 8

ST. GILES TEEMED with activity even in the early morning. Men spilled out of the dram shops, bottles of Old Tom's in their hands to take home. Pilferers lingered, watching for culls. Kate forced herself to look away from their cold, empty eyes.

Sympathy to others was a rich man's prerogative, along with clever notions like charity and honest work. Most thieves had lived out their lives on the streets, learning to steal as children from the family that should have kept them innocent. She couldn't judge them. When faced with starvation, she did the same. If she wasn't the one fencing, someone else would. That was the evolution of the rookeries.

Outside of her Forsyth pistol and her father's greatcoat, she didn't own anything she wouldn't pawn for a quicker profit. She wore the O'Reilly ring on a string around her neck, underneath her dress. It would bring a nice bit of funds, better now that she knew what she was fencing. There was a shop in St. Giles that would do nicely. The gold was good quality and the sale wouldn't trace back to Owen.

That damn ring shouldn't mean a thing to her. It was a product of a life long gone.

What about Owen, who had given it to her not knowing

its significance? He had expectations for them, hopes that she hadn't jarred. "I don't like him," Jane had said once he left. But even Jane couldn't place what struck her as odd about Owen. e was charming, if a bit arrogant, and he seemed to care for Kate. It would be easy to lie with him and pretend that she was a different woman, one without jagged pieces that needed to be pasted back together.

She shook her head and focused on the street in front of her. Daniel had wanted to share a ride, but she refused. Better the cost to her pocket than to spend another moment cloistered with him. He would take the omnibus, though the fare was higher than the hackney, while she would count the few pence in her purse and ponder how far the money he'd given her would get her from London.

Seven Dials, on the borders of the Irish slum St. Giles, was familiar to her as a fence, but knowledge didn't breed ease. Shoving her hand deep in her pocket, fingers curled around the handle of her pistol, she moved at a brisk pace.

She turned down Newton Street, known for its various thieving dens. The snow lining the alleyway was tinged brown. From further down the street, voices pitched in rage drifted, carrying insults about whoresons and their disease-ridden daughters.

"Kate!"

She stiffened at the sound of her name. Whirling around, her outstretched hands landed flat on the muscular expanse of Daniel's chest, clad snuggly in a double-breasted navy wool coat. He reached up, his grip tightening around her elbows to tug her closer to him.

She pushed him off of her. "How was the omnibus?"

"A bit too fast for my taste. And loud. And large." He grimaced. "Frankly, it rather reminded me of herding my uncle's sheep, except I was the sheep."

They turned down another street, then another, and still a third after that. He navigated without thought, each turn automatic to him, and she wondered how long he had been friends with Atlas Greer.

She wondered how much of their past relationship had been based in fact.

Daniel finally came to a stop in front of a split-level building patched in random places with mud. Kate reached for the doorknob, turning it to no avail.

"How utterly uncivil of him to lock the door." She hunted in her pocket for her set of lock picks. Each tool had been fashioned by hand from metal scrap she had found in the streets of Ratcliffe, crafted in her first few months as a fence. She flipped open the case and surveyed the lock. "Thankfully, I come prepared for occasions just like this one."

"Do you practice the black art now too? This is my friend's house. We needn't pick the lock." Daniel made a grab for the case, but Kate was too quick for him, skirting back.

"This is quicker." She slid the slender tension wrench into the bottom of the lock and applied torque. "Besides, with a lock that simple your friend is begging to be dub laid. I'm surprised that the Gentleman Thief wouldn't have more security against lock pickers." Turning the knob, Kate opened the door and walked inside.

"You haven't seen the inside of the house," Daniel said.

Only the barest of furniture resided in the room, yet it felt cluttered. A table sat by the fireplace, accompanied by one grandiose chair twice the height of the table. Kate's glance flicked from one end of the foyer to the other. She could have sworn the house was bigger from the outside.

"Where is he?"

"Upstairs." He crossed to the end of the room and put his hand out onto one of the bricks in the wall, pressing it hard. Creaking echoed through the room as the wall moved to the right, disappearing into a crevice. In its place appeared a stairwell, painted moss green and carpeted.

At the top of the landing, Daniel opened the door to a room far beyond anything Kate could have imagined. In the farthest corner from the door stood a coat of armor, next to a marble table with iron-claw feet that boasted a huge tray of jewelry. There were books everywhere, on the various tables, piled in chairs, and atop the fireplace mantel. Somehow, Atlas had managed to maneuver the stuffed carcass of a bear poised to attack into the loft.

She had entered the world's strangest treasure trove.

"St. Nicholas be praised." She traced the lines of latitude across a map of France, following a route Emporia's ships used to take.

"Do you like it?"

Kate started at the sound of the thief's voice. Atlas came toward them, ink-smeared fingers placing a well-worn copy of *Titus Andronicus* spine-up on a chair in the corner of the room. She was face to face with the man who had most likely saved Daniel from the noose.

All she could think was that he had taken Daniel away. It didn't make rational sense and she knew that, as she knew that shan was counterfeit money and a darkman's budge slipped into houses in the dead of night to let in other thieves. She harbored no illusions about the legal system. They would've hanged Daniel. She could not imagine it without feeling tightness in her chest and sickness in her stomach. So why did she loathe the sight of this man?

Because he had known a side of Daniel that she didn't. Because Daniel had turned to him in his hour of need, instead of her. Because he had succeeded in this strange world of the rookeries, and made something of himself.

Blackguard.

She focused on his physical features. What struck her most was the transmutability of his features: nothing stood out. If one took away his black tailored clothes, he could slip through a crowd without any notice. He had a cherubic smile, round cheeks, and kind green eyes. His blond hair was kept short, to minimize the natural wave. He was a head shorter than her, lean and spry.

"Danny-boy." He clapped Daniel on the back. "Help

yourself to some tea, bitter cold out there." He spoke with no trace of East London, his sentence structure as polished as any of the *bon ton*. Little was known about his upbringing. Some claimed he'd been born to a wealthy family, while others purported he'd been raised on a pirate ship.

His gaze settled on her, green eyes gleaming roguishly. "So this is the illustrious Kate Morgan, ship magnate's daughter turned fence."

Kate stood up straighter, forcing him to look up at her. "So this is the illustrious Gentleman Thief. I thought you would be taller."

Atlas smirked. "Good things come in small packages."

She highly doubted that. The notice of bankruptcy had been folded to not more than the size of her fist.

"I have never found that to be true," she sniffed.

"Perhaps you've not met the right ones." His grin was unstoppable.

She should be nice to him. At his say, factions of St. Giles committed grave larcenies. She patted her pocket. With the blunt from Daniel and what she might earn from fencing the ring again, she could set herself up for a few months. The approval of the Gentleman Thief meant she'd earn a round sum, much more than she had now.

If she didn't ram the butt of her pistol into Atlas Greer's overly cheery face.

Daniel offered her a mug of steaming tea. She accepted it, taking a seat in the armchair Atlas had vacated, for it was the only clear spot in the whole bloody flat.

"Mind the pages, luv," Atlas chirped, gesturing to the book on the arm of the chair, spread flat. "Don't want to lose my place."

She flipped the book closed, grimacing at the damage done to the spine by hours of misuse.

Atlas bristled. "You didn't mention your pet was so detestably rude, Danny."

Plaintively, Daniel looked from Kate to his friend before

his gaze landed back on her. Without words, she knew he begged her to get along with Atlas. *Fine.* She would comply, for him.

And she refused to think of why Daniel's preferences mattered.

"We met with Cyrus," Daniel said, taking a seat on a clear edge of the table littered with jewels. "He mentioned Dalton was indeed involved with a gang of resurrectionists."

"Did you doubt me?" Atlas sounded insulted.

"One of these days, you will turn up wrong, old chap." Daniel grinned. "I'm glad it's not today. Actually, I'm more concerned about the bounder who followed Kate and me when we were at the docks."

"Someone followed you?" Atlas's brows shot up. "Bloody bad luck if you've been spotted, Danny. Told you to be careful—these men aren't ones you want after you."

"We can handle it." Kate tapped her pocket, secure with the flintlock.

We. She'd best be careful, before she began to think of them as a unit once more. That way led only to madness.

"So you can shoot and pick a lock passably," Atlas scoffed. "How are your skills at hand-to-hand combat? Have you dealt with murderers? I'm not willing to risk Danny's neck because you think you can 'handle' it."

"He asked me to help him. Not the other way around. If you want to lecture someone about safety—"

Daniel broke in. "Atlas, it was my decision to come back to London, and I stand by it. Have you been able to locate the fen that Dalton associated with?"

Atlas flicked a glance of disapproval over to Kate before he plucked a sheet of paper out from his pocket. "First, let's note that there are at least forty well-known brothels, flash houses, or ill-reputed places on Jacob's Island alone. That doesn't include the ones that aren't recorded and exist in the back of some bloke's house." Atlas paused for them to emit the proper sound of shock. "It took me all night, but I sorted through every altamel I've got on file and I sent out carriers to do the rest. 'Course, reading through bawdy house ledgers isn't so bad, all things considered."

"Normally, I expect you to see the pattern in something inconsequential, but this goes beyond." Daniel took the scrap of paper Atlas handed him with the address of the bordello.

Atlas stood, dropping a mock bow. "I am at your service, Lord O'Reilly. May you use me as any good serf should be used."

"All right, all right." Daniel rolled his eyes.

"The blowen's go-between is Benjamin Wilkes. He used to keep half the constables on his payroll, and a good chunk of the Night Watchmen used his girls. Beyond me what the Peelers think of him now. No one can tell what those bloody blue uniforms think." Atlas said.

Kate's stomach churned. She knew of Benjamin Wilkes, and had gone out of her way to avoid the brute. Gossip claimed he had taken a knife to a girl when she refused to let three men lay with her at once. The girl was found in the alley outside of the Three Boars, but by then she had lost too much blood to be saved. Sally Fletcher had likely sold her soul long ago to survive in a brothel where Wilkes was the bullyback, hired to keep the customers—and the girls—in line.

"We have to get her out of there," Kate murmured.

"Absolutely not. She's a case vrow. Any attempt to break her from the bawdy house that owns her is only going to bring attention to Danny," Atlas said. He spoke as though he was discussing the weather, not the life of a girl. He didn't know the fear of being raped, or what it felt like to have beefy hands paw at him.

"Better to keep to the schedule I got of Wilkes's whereabouts," Atlas continued. "I know a doxy by the name of Mary who helps me with some jobs. She says Wilkes will be out for part of Monday."

Kate balled up her fists at her side, nails digging into her palms. "We will be lucky if Sally Fletcher will say a word to us.

Men like Wilkes rule by terror, stealing a basic part of your soul. No one deserves that."

"We will see what we can do." Daniel came up behind her, his hand on her shoulder.

She leaned her head back against his chest, gazed into his concern-clouded eyes. She would have expected him to take Atlas's side, for the girl was another prostitute among thousands.

"Find out what ties the girl has to Jasper Finn and then worry about her fate. I've got trackers out there looking, but I haven't managed to turn up any clues as to Finn's appearance." Atlas frowned. "The exhumators are being particularly cagey since the trial."

"Understandable. The London Burkers's executions must have been a wake-up call for them all." Daniel nodded.

"No one is particularly eager to be a-swinging by the hangman's noose." Atlas's expression became thoughtful. "When I think about how that could have been you, Danny…"

Kate cut him off. "Yes. We all recognize what might have happened."

Visions of Daniel's body—high up, hands bound, neck broken—danced before her eyes. Her stomach lurched. She fingered the string around her neck, the scratchy yarn stiff on her skin. The ring fell between her breasts, but when she moved it swung right near her heart.

She had to get rid of it and soon, for if she didn't, it would always hold her down. Remind her of the life she'd once had, a dream now departed and broken. "If we are done here, I have an errand I have to run."

"I'll go with you then." Daniel looked up from the table of jewels he'd been examining, starting to come toward her.

Kate shook her head quickly. "That won't be necessary."

Atlas folded his arms over his chest. "This is Little Ireland, lass. Not the place for you to be wandering about by your lonesome."

Her eyes narrowed. "I have my pistol and I don't hesitate

to shoot."

Daniel was insistent. "I would feel better if you allowed me to accompany you."

"And *I* would feel better if you didn't treat me as a child." Her voice dripped with ire. "I have survived quite well without you thus far and I will do so again."

It's just you and me against the world, Katiebelle.

So Papa had said on her eighth birthday when her mother left. So she had reminded herself when Justine would no longer to speak to her, and the rest of Emporia turned against her family name.

She was better off alone.

DANIEL WATCHED KATE go with a deadened heart. He wouldn't give up. After he finally convinced her to share a cab with him back to Ratcliffe when she was done with her errand, she had fled from the room with no more detail about her mysterious task. Something having to do with receiving, he guessed, for she had given him no opportunity to ask further questions.

He watched Kate stop at the edge of the alley and look over her shoulder. No one followed her. She took the corner and then she was gone, onto the cross street and out of his view. Daniel wasn't entirely sure she'd show up at the hack stand in an hour like she had promised.

"Are you certain this is worth it?" Atlas stood at the window with him.

He plowed a hand through his hair. "I'm not certain of anything anymore."

"It's not a bad life being a criminal, Danny." Atlas gestured at the scene before them. From their vantage point high atop the road, Seven Dials stretched out in all its unholy glory, narrow streets with filth-overflowing gutters, pavement spattered with rotting cabbage and meat, houses with moldy foundations and peeling white-washed walls.

"Might not be much to look at, but it is home." Atlas pointed across the landscape to a place east of Bloomsbury, in the stretch of St. Giles to the north of Ivy Street where the old leper hospital had once been located. "Do you see that over there? That's the Rat's Castle, and a bigger den of iniquity you'll never find. No Bobbies for miles and even the bloody Runners won't touch it. They treat me like a king there, and you'd be family."

Daniel turned away from the window. "I've told you before, it's honest work I want."

"And it's honest work that almost got you collared." Atlas shook his head. "You'd make a great cunning man with your straight face."

"I made a promise to Poppy I'd live life right. That's what I intend to do," Daniel said. "This thieving, it might be fine for you, but I need something different."

"Maybe you take the Lady Fence and you set up deep in the heart of Little Ireland where I can protect you." Atlas held his gaze, his countenance serious—out of place on the normally jovial thief.

Suspicion crept up Daniel's spine, cold and icy as the hand of death. "There's something else beyond your usual antipathy toward legal vocations, isn't there? Something you're not telling me. Have out with it, old chap. I don't need more secrets in my life."

"I looked into Kate's friend Owen Neal." Atlas shifted his weight from one foot to the other, arms locked across his chest.

"And?"

"And he doesn't exist."

"That's impossible. I saw him outside her lodging." In the past, he had nights when he couldn't vouch for his memory, but he'd been sober for seven months and he damn well knew he'd seen the bastard with Kate.

"You might have seen a man who goes by Owen Neal,

but as to whom he is the other twenty-three hours of the day, not a soul knows." From the table beside the window, Atlas selected a small bit of parchment and handed it to Daniel.

Daniel stared at the paper, flipped it over, and then peered at the original side. "It's blank."

"Because that is all I know about Owen Neal," Atlas retorted. "The man is a phantom. Three years ago, he appears as a housebreaker. He does a few jobs here and there, nothing too difficult and nothing that will put the Runners on his tail. He may pop up in a flash house one night and then not turn up for six months at a time. I can't find a single source who knows where he actually resides."

"You checked with everyone?"

Atlas's annoyed glare was answer enough.

He hurried to soothe his friend's nerves. "Of course you did. You found our blowen on Jacob's Island. I'm sorry I asked."

The thief moved back to the window, drumming his fingers on the sill. "I am as bloody stupefied as you are, Danny. Somewhere out there is a man who has clearly gone to great lengths to hide his identity, and I don't know if I should admire him for his talent or send a bounder to waylay him."

"While you ponder that, Kate has been working with him and God knows what he has planned for her." Daniel gritted his teeth. "Hell, she could be meeting with him now."

A combination of fear and jealousy burned through him and roiled in his gut. The look in Neal's eyes had been enough to fire him up, but then the bastard had touched Kate's arm with such familiarity and ownership. Kate had not shied away from him, despite her claims that they were merely business associates.

"Steady, lad," Atlas cautioned. "That chit's got escape artist written all over her. If you push too hard, she'll flee faster than Mary Cut-Purse from the Peelers."

"So what should I do? I can't leave her alone in the rookeries, prey to the devices of someone calling himself

Neal." He couldn't bear that.

"Have patience," Atlas said. "If you continue on with this hunt, you're going to need all the allies you can find."

KATE PUSHED OPEN the door to Osborne's Pawn, a small shop not more than two rooms in total. The front consisted of a lobby where Osborne packed inventory into every corner with no discernible manner of sorting. Vaguely, Kate wondered if Osborne knew Atlas Greer, for their scattered assortment was similar.

Paul Osborne was one of the many freed black subset living in St. Giles. He operated a shop off of Oxford Street and was not as well-known as the fence Mrs. Jennings on White Cross Street, but that was his charm. While Mrs. Jennings deeply resented encroachment into her territory, Osborne cared about one thing and one thing alone: blunt. If profit could be made, he cared not the source.

Osborne looked up from the glass counter in the back, his long fingers nimbly picking through a tray of buttons. He was tall and lean, with the physique of a pugilist yet no love for the ring. His angular face was marred by a scar up his left cheek, which gave him an air of devilishness. With far too much charm for his own good and a flair for fashion, he was never short a whore for long.

His body stiffened as she came into the light of the lamp hanging over the counter, and his hand slid below the glass.

In a flash, Kate had her flintlock drawn. The pistol was already cocked, ready in preparation for touring St. Giles's streets. "Must we do this every time, Osborne?"

"'Ello, luv, always nice to see a chit who can prime and pump." The fence's dark eyes twinkled as he placed both hands on the counter.

Kate smiled, indulging him. There were certain routines that became dear because they were familiar, no matter the initial idiocy. "Your games will one day get you shot."

Unabashed, Osborne grinned cheekily. "I'd consider it an honor to be shot by the likes of ye."

"Do cease, Paul, you know I'm not one of your girls. That smile won't work on me." She rolled her eyes.

"Ye fancy the Irish. No accountin' for taste." Osborne smirked. "What brings ye to darken my door, luv?"

She plucked the twine from underneath her bodice, lifting the necklace up and over her head. She placed the ring on the counter.

"Ye plannin' on releasin' it?"

She peeled her fingers back from the ring. Osborne snatched up the piece, catching it in the lamp's light like she had done when Daniel had first given it to her.

He squinted. "Detail's good. Ten shillings."

"For that price, you don't get to touch it." Kate pried the ring from his grip. "It's worth at least double that, as you should damn well be aware."

"Be takin' it elsewhere then." Osborne shrugged, his keen eyes never leaving her face as the necklace dangled from her fingers.

"I will." She started to pull the necklace back on over her, but Osborne's hand darted out to catch hers.

"Sixteen and not a penny more."

Sixteen shillings was a solid price, a good deal which would cover three weeks rent with still a bit left over. For a moment, she simply peered down at his hand covering hers, skin the color of rich coffee. His fingers curled around the gold and he attempted to yank the ring from her fingers. She slapped his hand away. Osborne shook his head. "Ye won't get any better, luv. Not for this Irish piece. No wantin' for it with the outcry over the new laws for Catholics."

"Perhaps I won't." But she didn't release the ring.

Through three generations of O'Reilly women, the ring had been passed down to the wife of the first-born son.

I want you to have this, Katiebelle. So you know I'll always be with you, no matter what happens. You're my heart, my ruler, my best friend.

She might get twenty shillings for the ring, if she went with a shop down in Bethnal Green that dealt in high-end jewelry. Unlike Osborne, she could not vouch that the owner wouldn't sell her name to the Peelers, but it might be worth the risk.

"That ring—where'd ye get it?" Osborne gripped his sharp jaw between thumb and forefinger with a thoughtful mien.

Kate arched a brow at him. "I should think you'd know not to ask those questions."

Osborne frowned. "Usually, yes, but when I get a bounder comin' in lookin' for somethin' like this…"

"You said no one wants an Irish ring, and now you've got a market for them?"

Osborne's gaze darted to the door. In the street outside, two men argued, or so she guessed from the adamant hand gestures. As the more portly of the two men swung the pawn shop door open, Osborne leaned forward on the counter.

"One toff does not make a market." He lowered his voice. "Ye be careful, Kate. A pretty chit like yerself…I don't want to see ye endin' up in the gutters. Somebody's out lookin' for a ring like that, and I don't got a good feelin'."

"I can take care of myself." Two and a half years without a damn bit of concern, and suddenly everyone worried over her welfare.

Not everyone. Daniel.

She stifled a sigh. "What did the man look like?"

"Black locks, solid build, cheekbones that sent my girl Fanny into fits." Osborne sneered. "If that weren't enough, bastard came with muscle, like I was goin' to cheat him."

Could that be Owen? He had said one of his boys had gotten the ring from a usual pilfer. To search through pawn shops in the rookeries indicated intent—as if he knew about the importance of the ring to her.

She swallowed, throat suddenly dry. As a new customer

approached the desk, she slipped the ring into the pocket worn under her skirt. To have it on her skin felt too much like old times.

"Don't be a stranger, luv," Osborne called before she exited.

She began to suspect everyone she knew was a stranger of some sort.

CHAPTER 9

DANIEL BREATHED A sigh of relief when Kate emerged from the shadows of a crumbling building on King Street. He slipped his pocketwatch back into the folds of his coat. She was fifteen minutes late, but he didn't care, for she was here.

They caught the next available hackney from the stand. The slightest touch of Kate's gloved hand against his own as he handed her into the hackney surged desire through him. He wanted to be close to her again, hands intertwined, being a team as they'd been at her father's company. Whenever he'd had a question on company policy, he could always come to her. Soon, he'd created reasons to seek her out in private so he could see her smile. She never had any reserve with him, and he loved her fiery spirit.

He had to believe that working together now was a step toward reconciliation.

He ducked inside the cab and closed the door behind him. There was only one bench, lined in gray velvet with a twisted gash down through the center.

The carriage rocked once as the horses found their footing, and then they were off. If he moved a bit he'd touch her, feel the heat from her thigh. Her skirt was black as a mourning shroud. He resisted the urge to grab the hem in his hands and tear it in two, as if by destroying the dark fabric he could break them free of the tragedies of the past.

He laid his head back against the seat cushion and breathed in deep. The carriage had a faint odor of perfume from the last passenger. The team's hooves hit the road in a steady rhythm.

Seek absolution for your sins by recognizing the wrongs you committed. The priest in his uncle's parish had told him he could only repair the damage of his actions by proving he wouldn't return to drink. He couldn't ignore his failures.

"Kate?" He shifted on the seat toward her, the movement bringing her closer to him.

"Yes?" She looked at him expectantly.

"Do you remember me telling you of my sister, Poppy?" He rifled through the pocket of his greatcoat, pulling out a miniature not bigger than his thumb. Poppy when she was fourteen, her hair as blisteringly red as his, swept up into maiden braids.

She nodded, glancing at the picture. "What about her?"

"She has a theory that if we remain accountable for our actions, then we will never be sucked in by remorse." Daniel slipped the picture back into his pocket.

Kate shrugged. "Regret is a useless emotion. I've learned from living here that I'll do anything to survive. If that makes me wicked, then so be it."

"I don't think that about you," he said. "I think you're incredibly strong. You've been dealt a bad faro hand and you've made the best of it."

Warily, she turned toward him. "Thank you. I'm proud of my independence."

"You should be." He'd half-expected her to chafe at his praise. "As your experiences have taught you, so have mine. I know I'm responsible for some of your pain. When we were together before, I wasn't the man you deserve. You may have noticed some things have changed about me."

She thought for a moment. "You didn't order crank at the Three Boars."

"No, I didn't." Pride edged his tone. Every day was a struggle and he'd take his victories when he could. "I haven't had a drink for seven months and three days. I'd tell you the exact hour, but I made the decision when I was on the cut."

She fell silent. The need for her to understand welled deep in him, a driving force since he'd quit drinking. Outside their window, Covent Garden flashed by in a flurry of activity: theater employees readying for tonight's performance, women of pleasure already at their stations to ply their wares. This was the London he remembered, but none of it felt the same.

Become a better man, or die trying as a proper Irishman.

"I know, it sounds absurd," he continued. "A Teague-lander without his spirits is no Irishman at all, as Mason made particularly clear." He scrubbed his hand through his hair, tugging at the scarlet roots.

"Don't listen to him. He's too cowardly to be a real man, so he must poke fun at those who are." Indignation lit up her face, anger on his behalf.

He grinned. "You think I'm a real man, love?"

She nodded, so slightly he might have missed the incline if he hadn't been watching her. Her words gave him strength.

"I've done a lot of bad things. Spent too much time in hells and other places so dark no sane person would ever venture." Hands clasped in his lap, he stared at an old stain on the sleeve of his navy greatcoat. A blot of whisky, held down by a droplet of ale and left to sit so long on his passed-out form that Poppy could not blot the stain away.

"Why are you telling me this?" Kate's glance flickered from him to the window uneasily. "Everyone knew you drank, Daniel."

"I'm telling you because I'm not that man anymore." He didn't cower under her distrust, or move closer to her. "That man was a bastard who hurt everyone he loved. My sister paid the price, and so did you."

Kate sat up straighter. "What happened to your sister?"

"I didn't think I was meant for farming when I came to London, and I didn't want a damn thing to do with it once I went back to Dorking. I left Poppy alone, Kate. Alone when I should've protected her." He ducked his head down, but that couldn't hide his shame from her.

"Poppy had your uncle, didn't she?" Kate asked.

He frowned. "Most of Uncle Liam's time is spent managing the farm. Aunt Molly used to take care of us when we were young."

"I remember when you went home for her funeral." Kate reached over, squeezing his shoulder. Her touch lasted only a second, but it was enough. Kate had sat with him when he received the news about Aunt Molly, her arms wrapped tight around him.

With her at his side, he used to feel he could conquer anything.

"I guess I thought things would be the same as they'd always been. Poppy was apprenticed to a seamstress in town, so I didn't think much of her being gone." He swallowed down rising guilt. He should have known better.

"When I was off on my tour of Sussex's touting kens, a wealthy merchant visited Dorking's main inn for a fortnight, out on some sort of shooting expedition or whatever it is jackanapes do with their time. He met Poppy around town." His fists clenched against the cushion, knuckles white. "Blackguard thought he'd have a bit of fun while he was away from London. He plied Poppy with lies."

"I'm not surprised," Kate said. "She was what, seventeen? Too young to know any better. It happens all the time here."

She looked straight ahead in the carriage, her expression blank. Stripped of any emotion. Had other men preyed upon her because he hadn't been there to protect her? Or worse, did she classify him in the same category as Mr. Clarendon? He hoped not. Yet he'd taken Kate's virginity and hadn't married her.

Damnation, he was almost as bad as Clarendon.

"Clarendon seduced Poppy. By the time she realized she was with child, it was too late. He'd already left town." Daniel brought his fist down on the cushion, pounding into it. It wasn't Clarendon's face, but it'd do for the moment.

Kate shook her head. "He wouldn't have done anything to help. Perhaps suggested a way she could get rid of the child."

The carriage banged along, churning gravel and bouncing with each wheel turn. His stomach sloshed at the idea of little Moira not being in this world.

"Who is Poppy staying with now?" Kate asked.

"There's an older woman in the village whose daughter moved away recently. Poppy needed help with the baby and Mrs. Daubenmire missed having children around. She was happy to come live at Uncle Liam's." Daniel relaxed against the bench, comforted by the knowledge that Poppy was well taken care of back home.

Kate nodded. "That sounds like the perfect solution for both of them."

"It is. Watching Poppy, I figured if my sister could take the news of her increasing in stride, I'd best puzzle out a way to deal with my own issues. So I stopped drinking, went back to my uncle's farm and there I've been until this trip."

"And you haven't taken a drink." She smiled. It was a slow, small smile that didn't compare to the eclipsing grins she used to give him, but it was something.

He didn't tell her of the short relapse he'd had after Moira was born. It didn't matter. "Every time I want gin, I drink a cup of tea. I am down to four cups from twelve."

"That's growth, I think." She nodded.

The carriage came to a stop and she leaned back to peer out the window. He followed her glance. A merchant wheeled his cart across the road, cutting into traffic.

He dared to readjust, sitting closer to her. Her long ebony skirt brushed against his tan breeches, dark to his newly gained light. "My niece Moira is the most comely of babies, and Poppy the best of mothers." He let his fist open up, splaying his fingers across the edge of the seat.

"Strange how a newborn babe can make the most depraved of situations seem sweet," she noted wistfully.

His heart squeezed. Her knee brushed against his, hip next to hip. He angled his body so that he could face her, knee still touching.

"Do you ever think of it?" His voice broke, too vulnerable to stop when he knew damn well he should. "Of the life we might have had together. I do all the time, Katiebelle. I picture a little girl with your high cheekbones, hair as red as mine to mark for the entire world that she's an O'Reilly. Or a lad with your stunning eyes and my nose. When I thought I'd never see you again, I mourned the loss of them as I mourned you."

She gulped for air, gaze locked on the window. "I did—I do."

He looked over her shoulder. The granite towers of Newgate Prison rose in the distance as the carriage turned the corner of Newgate Street and the Old Bailey courthouse.

"I was scared." He hated the rawness of his words. How could she respect him, when he was a broken man?

He wasn't even sure he respected himself.

SEEING THAT MONSTROSITY of a prison now with Daniel not even an arm's length from her, it struck Kate harder than she'd imagined. Four wards arranged in a square around a central courtyard, though they could only see one wall of the horrific structure.

"I couldn't face gaol." Daniel's voice barely rose above the din of cab wheels striking gravel. "They would've kept me in a cell not fit for a dog, the stench of waste so thick in the air I'd retch the second I entered. Mindlessly running the treadmill and listening to the screams at night, waiting for the turnkey to call my name for collar day. I know you think I should have taken my chances with the trial, but I couldn't. I won't hold it against you if you find me weak."

Her eyes stung with the tears she struggled to keep back. "I don't think that about you."

She hazarded a glance at him. A single look and then she'd return to perusing the City. Except her breath caught in her throat, ripped from her lungs by his wide green eyes. He penetrated her reserves, until she knew she wouldn't have any resistance left if he kept talking.

He held his breath, waiting for her to continue. Her hand darted out, connecting with his. She didn't know how to stop moving forward with him. His knee was against hers, warmth penetrating the wool of her skirt like it was nothing but a gauzy chemise.

"If I did before, I don't any longer." She pursed her lips, not allowing a smile to show. To give him that would be too much of a concession. "Weak men don't try to atone. If I'd known about your abstinence from spirits, I wouldn't have made you go to the Three Boars. Or let you come with me to the Red Fist. Lord knows I can handle Cyrus by myself."

"There's no way in St. Patrick's name I would have let you go to that hole by yourself." Daniel's eyes darkened protectively as he turned over her hand so that his was on top. He squeezed, his touch somehow managing to comfort her and set her body aflame all at once.

"I've told you before, I can fend for myself," she said. If she kept repeating it, she might believe that she didn't need him. That she could live without his touch again.

"I've got no question of your ability to defend yourself. You're quite handy with the cap gun, love. I think you almost blew my head off in that alley." His smile was wry, offset by the sadness in his eyes.

"I considered it. Violence comes easily to me, since you left. Perhaps too easily." Absently, her thumb stroked against the inside of his gloved palm.

"I hadn't noticed. You've been nothing but delightful." He winked. "Do try not to kill anyone, love, while I'm off on Monday interviewing Miss Fletcher. I think our relationship can only stand one arrest for murder."

Our relationship. So he already classified them as together again. Kate looked down, loathe to break apart their joined hands. The madness started here, with reluctance to leave his company.

There was no place for relationships in her life. Fence the goods, make the rent, and continue on living without answering to anyone. Those goals were logical. Those goals meant she wouldn't have her heart torn apart again.

"We are not in a—wait. What do you mean *you're* interviewing her? I'm coming with you."

Daniel's jaw clenched. "Absolutely not. If you think I would allow you within ten paces of a bordello, you'd best check yourself into Bedlam."

He said "bordello" as if it was the basest place in England, all because of the tainted women inside.

Women like her.

He'd never understand. Those women came from different backgrounds, some forced into prostitution and others seeking shelter from the gruesome outside world. They'd lay with men, trading their bodies for a bit of blunt until their souls were crushed and the pain lessened. She'd seen perdition in the face of a brothel, and she wouldn't be owned by anyone ever again.

"You don't have a right to *allow* me to do anything." She snatched her hand away from his.

"I care about you. What do I have to do to make you see that?" He threw his hands up in the air.

"I do see it," she admitted.

He'd been nothing but fucking conscientious since he got back. That made it worse, so much worse. If he'd simply been a scoundrel, she'd have refused him outright and moved on.

Once she had thought she knew everything about him. He liked roasted mutton with carrots but not turnips, he preferred *A Winter's Tale* over *King Lear,* and he felt embarrassed about never going to a school like Eton.

But all of those things didn't make a lasting relationship. Love was a temporary notion, seizing hold of her heart. It was beautiful and powerful in those moments, but when it ended she'd be nothing. He had family and a life in Sussex, and she had neither. Didn't she have to safeguard her own sanity? When he left, she'd only have herself to rely on again.

"Let me help you," he pleaded.

"No, let me help *you*." Kate held her hand up to stop him from speaking again. "If the constable talked to Sally Fletcher about Dalton, then she would know what you look like. She'll be on guard for a redheaded Irishman, especially one suddenly digging into the past."

"Blast it." He frowned. "I didn't think of that."

"So I will go with you. Maybe she'll talk to me."

He sighed. "I still don't like it. Stay close to me, then."

Like I could leave you. Not trusting herself to speak, she nodded.

"I can't help but believe this is all my fault." His eyes bored into her. "When I ran, I thought I was doing the right thing for you. You'd have a chance to set your cap at a better match, one who could give you financial security. Who wasn't a drunken Irishman. But instead you've had to learn how to survive independently."

When he looked at her like that, seeking her inner secrets, she knew she'd eventually tell him everything. "If you'd talked about how you were to blame at the beginning of this week, I would have agreed with you in an instant."

"And now?" He shifted on the seat, breaking the contact of their legs.

"Now—" She bit her lip. "Now I haven't the faintest idea what to think. You complicate things, Daniel."

"In a good way, I'd hope." He chuckled softly.

She knew that laugh, so rife with intimacy. Had heard it so many times before, a precursor to a kiss that curled her toes. God, she wanted him. Wanted him even though she knew it'd break down the walls she'd built up around her heart, and leave her standing in a pile of rubble.

"Before you came back, I knew exactly where I stood. There were lines, clearly demarcated and categorized. Things I promised myself I'd never do again if I wanted to survive, and I lived by that code. It's kept me alive."

"Some lines are meant to be crossed, Katiebelle." His voice dipped lower, a caress to her tired body. Their eyes locked. Heat sizzled between them, an almost palpable spark. Slowly, his face inched closer to hers. "Live dangerously."

No amount of fighting or sensible decisions would save her now. "Devil take it all," Kate whispered.

Before her mind had a chance to reason, she leaned forward, closing the distance between them. Her lips came down upon his savagely in a desperate attempt to consume him. She nipped at his lip, and he opened immediately for her with an eager, surprised moan. She relished the fact that she'd taken him by surprise, given him one-tenth of the displacement she felt from his presence.

Yet whatever power she'd gained in that one instant dissolved in the luxurious bliss of his lips. He kissed her with the almost heart-stopping intensity of a man who would worship at her altar if she gave him a chance. She drank him in, eager to be his precious gin, for in that moment it only made sense that she should be the one to save him.

Their lips came together, over and over again, each press of delicate skin more desperate. The friction was enough to tear her asunder, starting in her fingers and gradually moving downward to that secret juncture between her thighs. Her breaths became jagged, stolen between kisses. Her ricestraw bonnet banged against his forehead as they fumbled for closeness.

He will see the ring. She reached up, expecting to find the twine chain but remembered it was in her pocket. She wanted this moment—this one desperate grab at touching him and holding him close to her—without complications of the past. Without having to explain how she'd come upon the ring again and what it meant that she'd kept it.

Because she wouldn't, she couldn't, make that commitment to him now. Not when she knew nothing about what her heart felt and what she wanted. But she could tug him close to her and crawl into his lap because that was what she had done before and *that* was natural.

He broke away and she murmured in protest, desire clouding her rationale. "Not leaving, love." His voice was ragged, chest quaking with the effort of drawing breath.

Quickly, his fingers made deft work of the knotted strings under her chin. He grabbed at the bonnet, tossed it haphazardly to the other side of the carriage where it bounced off the wall and to the floor. She watched it for a second before he tugged her forward, lips meeting hers fervently. The constant sway of the carriage mimicked the thrust of his tongue, toying inside her mouth. Every spot of her body was familiar to him and he sought that ground with the practiced expertise of a rogue.

His lips left hers to venture down her neck, to the sensitive hollow at her throat. She whimpered and he bit her tender flesh, tongue then rushing to soothe the pain. Her head lolled back in rapture. He was fixated on her, a wicked glint in his jade eyes.

He began to slide the hem of her skirts up her legs. Her petticoats fluffed around her waist and she reached down to gather up them in her hand so that he would have better access. Arching against him, her sensitive breasts brushed once more against his greatcoat.

He lifted her up and onto his lap, so that her center came directly in contact with his erection. She should pull away. But desire lapped at her, so insistent that she felt quickly certain that if she didn't heed its call she would surely descend into madness.

She pushed against him, feeding her desire.

His breath sucked in. "Christ, love, you'll make me spill."

With a salacious grin, she braced her hands against his shoulders and rocked. Hard. He cursed, the sound dying out as he buried his mouth in hers. One hand threaded into her curls, while the other fell to her breast, squeezing her through her dress. She squirmed against him, wanting to get closer to him.

He slipped his finger in the slit between her drawers. The rough pad of his thumb rubbed against her bud. A shot of pleasure rushed through her, knocked out all other sensations until all that was left was bliss. He knew her rhythms, knew the exact places to touch. She fell against his chest, moving her hips in time to his strokes.

She drifted higher up, higher and higher, until suddenly the carriage was pulling to a stop. When the door slid open, his finger was buried deep within her core.

CHAPTER 10

DANIEL BARELY MANAGED to catch the door as the coachman pushed it half-open. The wooden handle was slick in his sweat-soaked hands.

"Give us a moment, lad," he barked out, his voice raspy.

The door slid back upon its hinges, shutting out the street. One catastrophe averted. He was bloody uncomfortable. His cock was thick, his body randy. His fingers ached to touch Kate again, to run against her silky skin and finish what they'd started. He shifted on the seat, doing up the fall of his trousers.

Daniel sunk back upon the bench, his gasps for air uneven. Breathe in, breathe out. He repeated that mantra to himself.

"Let me help you." He scooted forward.

"I get dressed every morning without your assistance." She slid her petticoats back down her legs and patted her dress back into place.

"I'm only trying to help you, love." He held up his hands.

She scooted farther away from him on the bench. "Don't call me that." Quickly, she did up the ties to her bonnet.

He shifted on the seat uneasily. To think that only a minute before he'd had his finger thrust into her, watched her squirm with desire. That was how things were supposed to be with them—they'd work together on a problem and head home to bed. They were better together, damn it, better than they could be apart.

"Has nothing changed between us at all?" He asked.

"No. We don't change." Her words were shaky, her breaths in jagged pants. "We shouldn't have done this. I said I'd help you find the resurrectionists who killed Dalton and that's all this can be. I can't give you more. Not now, not ever. Not when you're going to leave again."

"If you'd stop being cod-witted for two seconds, you'd see I'm making no attempt to go anywhere." Frustration seeped in, constricted his limbs and left him useless.

"Well, I am." She got up off the seat, grabbing for the door and tugging it open.

The driver jumped back, almost tripping over the curb. He'd likely listened to their whole conversation. Frantically, Daniel replayed their words. *Shit.* Kate had mentioned Dalton and the resurrection men.

She jumped out of the carriage onto the street in front of her tenement house. He reached too slowly to pull her back in, his fingertips grazing the leather of her ankle boots. "Kate, wait!"

She didn't turn around. Instead, she hiked a thumb over her shoulder, pointing at him. "He'll pay your fare." She nodded at the coachman, and then she was gone.

Damnation.

He stood, hunching down as he dismounted from the hackney. The coachman looked at him expectantly. Fishing in his coat pocket, he pulled out enough to cover nearly twice the amount of their drive. He slipped the coins into the man's waiting hand, pitching his voice low enough that only the coachman could hear him. "Tell anyone what you heard, and I'll find you. I'll make your life very, very bloody."

"Yes, sir," the man stuttered. He remained a second later. Daniel's eyes narrowed. The coachman scurried off, back to his seat on the hackney. He picked up the reins, giving them a flick and setting the horses off at a trot.

Daniel watched until the carriage turned the corner, the driver so spooked that he almost steered his team into a child playing in the street. He looked back at the tenement house. A light winking in the upstairs window went out.

She'd shut him out again, but he refused to give up.

TWO DAYS LATER, Kate was certain that time didn't heal wounds. It made a pretty dressing over top of past errors, dulling the mind in moments of stress. Until clarity was regained and the entire situation spilled out before her in all its wretched glory.

She'd kissed Daniel. More than that, she'd let him touch her—and if the carriage hadn't stopped, who knew what else she would have let him do.

She now waited on the docks with Daniel, her hands shoved into the pockets of her greatcoat as if that would stop the longing to reach out to him. His chest had felt so firm against her body, so strong. If she leaned into him again, she'd find temporary respite.

Damn it all, she was weak.

The ferry drifted toward the shore, a rickety wooden contraption built of boards strapped together to form an open platform that might hold about ten people at most. On two sides, rails were built up and fastened together by twine. The ferryman steered through a long pole dipped into the water. One could not expect more when seeking transportation to and from Jacob's Island.

Once they were onboard, Daniel broke the silence between them. "I wasn't sure if you'd show up."

"I said I'd come, didn't I?" She kept looking forward, at the backs of the other passengers. At mid-day, the small ferry was crowded with people making the trek back to the island.

"Yes," he agreed.

She arched a brow at him. "Then you should have known I'd be here."

His hand snaked out, landing on her arm. She glowered up at him. His forehead creased, brows furrowed. He kept his voice low so that the other passengers wouldn't hear him. "I don't understand. Are you embarrassed? What we did in the carriage is completely natural."

That was the problem: it had all been too natural. Kate stared down at his hand. She tried to will herself away from him, yet his touch was warm. Staid. Constant. All of those things she knew were only true for now.

"I let myself get carried away. It won't happen again."

"Would it be so bad if it did, Katiebelle?" He asked.

"It would be…difficult. Chaotic. Complicated." She shook her head. "I can't handle that right now. So much of my life is random, Daniel. I don't want to add to that."

"Do you remember when Bartleby called me an incompetent Paddy in front of the staff? I wanted to quit. But you held my hand and told me I couldn't let him win." He pressed her arm lightly, smiling at her. "You told me the best things in life are worth the challenge."

She relaxed slightly, her shoulders no longer ramrod straight. Laurence Bartleby had gone out of his way to make Daniel's life miserable at Emporia. "That accountant was an ass."

"Yes, he was." Daniel nodded.

"But that was a long time ago, and we were different then." She shook her head. "And what we did last night was a mistake."

"I disagree." He ran his hand up her arm, the light brush of his fingers setting her afire.

"Then you are a fool." She stepped back from him. "Look at what I do for funds, Daniel. You keep saying you want to be a better man. That once you prove your innocence we'll have some great life together. But did you ever stop to consider that maybe *you* deserve better than me?"

How could she be with him, when she knew he'd disapprove of the life she'd led?

"Katiebelle," he murmured.

She cut him off. Forced a harder note into her voice, one that would convince him she couldn't be swayed. "The worst part of it is, I *like* what I do. There's a certain joy in finding buyers for those objects that I can't explain to you. I make it happen. It's my knowledge that moves objects."

"And you like being in control of your fate." He nodded. "I understand."

"Do you really?" She tilted her head to the side. "When we got engaged, I was content to sit beside you and help you achieve your goals. But I don't think that's enough for me now."

"I don't want you to be anyone but who you are," he said. "Accept what we were in the past, and what we'll be again."

No man would be content with a fence for a wife. Daniel had been raised traditionally on a farm. Could he really still love her if she didn't give up her activities? If she didn't follow his lead in life? He'd always said he loved her intelligence before, but then she had been working with him to help him take over Emporia someday. Their roles had been clearly defined.

She didn't know how to be a fence and be the woman he'd loved at the same time.

The ferryman stopped the river barge in one of the man-made tidal ditches in front of the ugliest stretch of houses Kate had ever seen, each built on top of the other in a haphazard, jigsaw fashion with their ends jutting out over the Neckinger River. The windows were patched with scraps of broadsheets, a little space left from which onlookers could see out into the grime and muck of the drenched streets. Doorless privies opened out into the river. A house door opened and an occupant stepped out onto the makeshift porch, scooping up the scummy water into a battered clay pot. The woman raised the pot to her lips and took a deep sip.

Kate sucked in a hard-won breath, her stomach tumbling. In all of the rookeries, she'd never seen such filth.

Daniel dismounted from the river barge first, helping her onto street level. Jumping down off the barge and landing on the sludge, her boots sunk into the puddles of water the color of marbles. She wrenched her hand from his and shoved it deep within the pockets of her patched black coat.

He started forward, turning to look over his shoulder. "Come now. We've got a murderer to catch."

She scurried after him, skirt bunched in her fist to keep the fabric from dragging on the ground.

Daniel shaded his eyes. "Atlas said Sally lives east of St. Saviour's Dock."

Every building was in an equal state of squalor, and the chipped wooden signs announcing each business were strung so close together that it all formed an indecipherable maze.

"There should be two more bridges that we need to cross, then we will turn left at the next ditch." She nodded.

He took off for the closest bridge, a rickety wooden contraption stretched over thick water that ran red from the clothing maker's dyes.

Like a river of blood. The dead would be cold to touch when their bodies were dug up, clammy skin caked in grave dirt. She shook her head, picking up pace as they waded through the mud puddles. Cold air smacked her face and she pulled her coat tighter to block out the wind.

"This bridge?" Daniel stopped in front of the swollen planks that stretched across Mill Lane.

The first board creaked but didn't collapse, and so she took another step forward, growing braver with each advance. Crossing another bridge in similar state, they turned at London Street. In between roofless warehouses and crumbling squat houses sat the flash house where Benjamin Wilkes pimped his girls in conjunction with the abbess, one Mrs. Stuart. Though it was but nine in the morning, already the sounds of drunken revelry spilled out into the street where they stood.

Daniel reached for the doorknob, but Kate didn't move. She stood outside the brothel, transfixed.

How many times had Daniel ended up in places like this? Did he ever think of these girls as anything other than objects to bend to his will?

At her hesitance, he hung back. Catching his eye, Kate glared back at him and pulled open the door.

They were met by a man who easily towered over Daniel, his shoulders alone the width of Kate's outstretched arm. He leered through his one good eye. The skin was as swollen shut as melting cheese around the other eye.

"Flash panney's that way." His beefy hand extended to the left in the direction of the public house. He had a voice like the wheels of a curricle churning gravel.

"Actually, we wanted the fen, Sally Fletcher. I heard she docks here." The patter words for whoring came too easily to him.

"It'll be another bit of socket money if ye are both rough tradin' on 'er commodities." The man looked from Kate to Daniel and back again. "One shilling."

Her stomach lurched. Daniel's grip increased on her arm, but he said nothing. The less the broker knew of their business with Miss Fletcher, the better.

Daniel handed over a shilling. Snagging a tallow candle from the wall, the broker led them down the hallway. Daniel's hand didn't move from her arm, guiding her forward as they passed between throngs of intoxicated men. He kept her close to him, protected by his larger frame. Unexpectedly, she didn't want to prove her independence.

The walls were thin, the doors thinner. Bed confessions spilled out into the hall, clouding her thoughts.

"Tup me harder." *The pain will remind me I'm alive.*

"Ye're nothin' but a used-up cunt, ye bitch." *No one will love you once they know your past.*

"Ye'll do what I ask, whore, unless ye wanna die out on the street." *You'll be snatched up again, stripped of everything you love as they make you fuck for your dinner.*

They were shown into a room, bare of all trappings but a straw mattress strewn on the dirt. A soiled blanket stretched across it, not long enough to reach from corner to corner. A battered coat, rolled up into a ball, served as a pillow. Nothing to mark it as different from the brothel she'd been at before.

Her hand clenched tighter around the handle of the flintlock in her pocket. She wasn't that same girl anymore. No one could hurt her now.

She'd make damn sure of it.

Willing herself not to think about whatever might live in the godforsaken mattress, Kate took a seat on the edge and folded her long legs up underneath her. They might appear less intimidating to Sally if they were sitting.

She let her gaze flick over to Daniel. He had to duck to enter the room. His broad shoulders appeared wider in these confines; his hands were stronger, his stance more intimidating.

The vulgar cacophony of the couple next door embraced the air like choleric death, squeezing out the life in her. Her gaze fell to the dirt floor.

The mattress sagged as he dropped down next to her. He doffed his hat.

"Kate." He hesitated, as if he didn't believe she'd allow him to speak. "About before—"

He would never think her worthy of him. He'd say he did, but when he got the full picture—her life, the things she did to survive, he'd change his mind.

Anxiety clenched her stomach as she met his gaze. How could he still want her? Her lip quivered under the intensity of his stare. She shouldn't be ashamed. She'd endured the damn streets and become something more. She had a flat of her own and connections with the thieves of Chapman Street.

He ran a hand through his thick ginger locks. Her stomach tightened. God's balls, she loved him when he looked disheveled, roguish and ready for anything. Kate tugged her knees closer, wrapping her arms around her legs.

The door swung open, the creak of unoiled joints echoing. A small, ethereal -looking woman stepped into the room and shut the door behind her. If it had not been for the threadbare clothing she wore, Kate might have believed she was a fairy. She was beautiful, with golden hair that hung down her back unrestrained and round cheeks that would have been cherubic had she proper food. The threadbare gown that hung loosely from her shoulders had a neckline cut precariously low to reveal her small bosom. Her lips were heavily rouged. She stared at Daniel and Kate, her blue eyes widening with surprise that was almost childlike. Likely she'd been at this since she was just above adolescence.

"Shall we be gettin' started?" She shuffled toward the straw mat, her bare feet kicking up clouds of dust.

"Are you Miss Fletcher?" Daniel pushed himself up from the mattress. He turned to face her.

"That be my name." Only for a second did Sally look up. Her eyes narrowed in upon Daniel and her tiny body trembled. Had she recognized him?

"Ezekiel says ye paid double. I don't want trouble, sir. I'll do what ye want." Sally's unsteady fingers reached behind her and undid the back closure of her dress. The fabric gaped around her. On the top of her left breast a vicious w-shaped brand scarred her skin.

"Er, you see." Daniel swallowed, shifting his weight from one foot to the other. "What I mean to say is—"

"That won't be necessary." Kate's voice rang out firm and clear, that same commanding tone she had always used when dealing with the workers at Emporia. She had fought for their respect, winning it through her hard work and acumen. "You may do up your dress. We came for information, Miss Fletcher."

Her almond-shaped eyes blinked rapidly. She looked behind her shoulder at the door. "Who told ye I was a snitch? If Wilkes 'ears—"

Kate understood the girl's fear. Sally's pimp owned her body. In the eyes of the law, she had few real rights.

The men we trust with our lives will hurt us in the end.

"No one said you were," Kate murmured. "We found you on our own. I promise you, Wilkes need never know of our visit. I'd rather cut my own wrists than have you be hurt by that bastard again."

"Please, I beg ye." Sally's chin wobbled, her voice but a whisper. Her pale face was ashen, the streaks of dirt on her cheeks in stark contrast. "Ye're with the Peelers, aren't ye? I won't wag my lips. I can't."

"We don't work for anyone. My name is Daniel O'Reilly."

"I thought it be ye." Sally clasped her hands together to hide the shaking of her body but Kate recognized it. She didn't look at them as she mumbled. "'E was a good man, my Tommy."

"Miss Fletcher, I didn't kill Tommy Dalton," Daniel declared.

Kate shivered. His voice rumbled, thicker and rougher. She remembered that tone well: he'd used it to win every damn argument with her.

Sally began to shake harder. "Ye slit 'is throat. 'E didn't deserve to die, and ye slit 'is throat." Sally's words tumbled out quick. She clamped her hand over her mouth.

"He *didn't* deserve such a fate, and that's why we're here," Kate said.

"Don't tell me yer lies." Sally traced Daniel's every movement warily, her bruised knuckles whitening as she clutched her spindly arms to her chest. "Peelers 'ad a witness, and still ye got away with it. There be no justice 'ere— no one to 'elp Tommy when 'e needed it."

"I wanted to help him. Miss Fletcher, I see his face every night before I go to sleep." Daniel propped his elbows up on his knees, resting his chin in his hands. "But when I got to that alley, he was too far gone for me to save. Someone else killed him, and I want to find that person."

"I 'eard ye ran." Sally's voice quivered.

"I did. But I'm back now, and I won't leave again." He locked eyes with Kate, holding her gaze.

"Why should I believe ye? Ye took him away from me." Sally bit at her bottom lip.

Why should I believe you won't tire of me?

Daniel broke their gaze, angling his body toward Sally. "Because if I was guilty, why would I be here asking you to help me find his killer? I'd be as far away as possible, hoping that the case stays buried forever."

The prostitute stood up straighter, her expression thoughtful.

Kate patted the space on the mattress next to her. "Miss Fletcher, come sit down with me, would you? No one is going to hurt you. We merely want to talk."

Gingerly, Sally took a seat on the edge farthest from Kate. She suspected obedience had been trained into Sally at the penalty of death.

No one should have to live like that, sacrificing their free will to the caprices of another.

"Wilkes did that to you, didn't he?" She pointed toward the brand on Sally's breast. It was covered by the bodice of her dress, but nothing could erase the knife mark from Kate's memory. "He's a fucking bastard. What he's doing, it's not right, and it's not just. He wants you to think that he owns you, but I don't believe that. Maybe I'm still naïve. Devil take it, I refuse to think that you can't be something more than what Wilkes has made you."

"'E controls everything, 'im and the abbess," Sally whispered.

Kate leaned forward, lowering her voice so that only Sally could hear her. "Everything but your mind, Miss Fletcher. What you're going through…the fact that in spite of it all, you found Tommy, that's pretty amazing. Wilkes couldn't touch that part of you. It's yours and yours alone."

Sally's small fingers tightened against the rim of the straw mat. "I'm scared."

"Of course you are," Kate whispered. "Can I tell you a secret? I'm scared too. Bone-numbingly terrified that if I take a chance on the unknown, I'll get burned. I know what it's like to wish you'd die so you could stop hurting. People tried to break me before, but I survived. I think you're stronger than you realize. I think you'll survive too."

Sally sucked in a breath. Slowly, she let go of the straw. She nodded, her posture straight, shoulders back, and a glint of determination in her ocean eyes.

Daniel leaned forward. "Tell us about the days before Dalton was killed. Was he acting out of the ordinary? Did he say anything that might indicate he was in trouble?"

Sally smiled wistfully. "Tommy was always in the muck, runnin' on the edge of the law. 'E was small as a tot and could fit through the windows of 'ouses so thieves used 'im as a diver. As 'e grew, Tommy moved up in the ranks. Stole more, better stuff. When 'e found warehouse work, 'e might've been clean."

"It's hard to break away from of those kinds of connections." Kate thought of Osborne, Owen Neal, Mrs. O'Malley and her damn soda bread. All of them stuck in patterns of iniquity because the alternative—to starve and die out on the streets—was far worse than Newgate Prison.

"'E always said 'e'd buy my freedom." Sally's face had taken on a forlorn quality, her wispy frame huddled on the mattress. "When 'e got enough saved, we'd leave England and never look back. Two weeks before 'e died, Tommy came to me all cocksure, like 'e'd won a bleedin' fortune."

"What did he say?" Daniel asked.

"'E took my 'ands and said, 'Sal, I've got all we need. I found us a cull and that's goin' to give us our lives. Ye'll be able to paint those pretty pictures ye like and I'll be a farmer." Sally's eyes grew misty. "I should 'ave known it was all Bedlam."

"Did he talk about the job? Did it have anything to do

with a company called Emporia?" Daniel sounded far too eager.

Kate stiffened. Her cheeks flamed. Daniel hadn't been there when the papers had ripped apart the Morgan name, when Kate's dearest friend Justine had betrayed her. When she'd learned that the only person she could depend on was herself.

He wanted Papa's company to be guilty.

Sally shook her head, befuddlement crossing her ethereal face. "I don't know. 'E'd go meetin' with Wilkes and some other men after work. That's how 'e found me, you see, 'e knew Wilkes. A few days before Tommy—before they killed 'im like an animal—I saw them fightin' outside 'is door. I didn't get close enough to 'ear much. I ran like a coward, and then Tommy was dead." Tears fell down her face, mixed in with the grime on her cheeks. "I didn't save 'im. I didn't tell nobody 'bout Wilkes's involvement. The boys 'ere, they never liked Tommy."

"Do you know who the other men were?" Daniel asked. "Perhaps Jasper Finn?"

Sally nodded, biting her lip nervously. "Finn's the only one I know by name. 'E comes by to lay with Amelia. But if ye come to take 'im on, ye'd best think again. 'E's got men everywhere."

Daniel placed his hand on top of Kate's, squeezing. For a second, their eyes met and her chest fell with the breath she'd not known she'd been holding. She angled her body toward Sally, dropping his hand.

"We don't know what he looks like. Would you recognize him if you saw him again?" Kate asked.

"I can do more than that." Pride seeped into Sally's voice. "Like I said, I draw. Don't go thinkin' it's any good now, but it's better than nothin' I figure." From the depths of her dress, Sally pulled out a rumpled stack of foolscap, held together by three strings of twine tied in bows. She flipped through the sooty parchment, giving them quick flashes of faces and landscapes as the pages turned.

"When Tommy died, I asked around. Stopped when Wilkes got wind and gave me a beatin' for not mindin' my own matters." Sally stopped on a particular sheet and handed the book to Kate. "That there's Jasper Finn."

CHAPTER 11

KATE HAD BEEN lied to again.

Her hand clenched around the page. Owen Neal's chiseled features stared back at her, rendered with skill in charcoal. His high forehead, tapered cheekbones, straight nose. Even the few streaks of gray in his black hair were caught in perfect replication. Dalton had been right about Sally's talent at least—in another life, she could have been renowned.

"He can't be. How could I have missed this?" She hated the shake in her voice from the little pull on her heart.

Over two and a half years, she had gotten to know Owen. Danced around his overtures, never allowed herself to become serious with him, for she knew damn well the heartbreak that came from attachment. A few kisses here and there didn't constitute a relationship. With him, she felt safe.

Daniel looked over her shoulder. "Isn't that the man I saw you with?"

The movement brought him closer to her, his breath on her neck. Kate scooted away from him, turning back to glare at him. "You are not helping," she hissed.

Somebody's out lookin' for a ring like that, and I don't got a good feelin'.

Osborne's warning came back to her. The ring was safe in the secret box in the wall of her lodgings where she kept jewels too high profile to fence right away.

How well did she truly know Owen? She'd checked him out before doing business with him. People knew of him at Three Boars. They said he'd moved to town a few years ago from Surrey, established himself quickly as the ken cracker to beat.

She shoved her hands into her pockets. She must think, arrange the facts carefully. Kate inhaled, kept her breathing even. Owen had brought her numerous items from jobs he pulled. Enough that she believed in his identity, when names and faces shifted in the rookeries without warning.

If he was truly Jasper Finn, he had operated with planning and an attention to detail that would have befitted a man framing another for murder.

"Bloody by-blow, I'll kill him." She snatched the page from her lap and flung it forward.

Sally's brows knitted. She folded the scraps of paper carefully and tucked them back into her dress. Those drawings were probably the only things she had that were truly her own. She ran a hand across her threadbare dress, playing with the seams. "Miss, I don't mean no disrespect."

All evidence pointed to Owen—Jasper Finn—keeping watch over her. Kate sighed. "I don't mean you, Miss Fletcher. It's…I know that man. Or at least, I thought I did."

Sally nodded sagely. "'Tis oft the case."

Kate crossed her arms over her chest, hugging herself. If she had not been saved that day, she'd be like Sally…it was pointless to dwell on memories.

Sally broke the silence. "'E's not been by in a fortnight."

"If you hear word that he'll be by again, will you contact me?" Daniel asked. When Sally nodded, he gave her the address to Madame Tousat's. He looked at his pocketwatch and signaled to Kate. Their time was reaching a close.

From his purse, he withdrew four pence and slipped the

coins to Sally. "Don't let Wilkes know you have that. We're rightly appreciative of your time."

Sally's face lit up with a gentle smile. For the first time in probably months, she might eat a decent dinner tonight.

Kate reached out, taking Sally's hand in her and squeezing it. "Bless you," she said.

Sally pressed her hand before releasing it. "Find out who killed 'im, Miss."

"We won't stop until we do," Daniel vowed. His determination echoed in Kate's ears. After meeting with Sally, she didn't doubt that he would do anything to prove his innocence. He had made the prostitute a promise, like he made to his sister Poppy.

But he'd promised to stay with her forever too.

They slipped out the door and down the hallway. Daniel kept his head down, the collar of his coat pulled up to cover his neck and part of his ears. He tugged the brim of his hat low across his brow and she did the same with her bonnet, shading her eyes.

Down the hall, a door opened. Into the lamp-lit gallery stepped a curvaceous blonde woman, dressed a step above the other women in a purple bodice with a lace-trimmed black skirt. Her green eyes gleamed shrewdly as she caught sight of them.

The prostitute didn't advance. As they passed by her, Kate locked eyes with the woman. Her stomach roiled, for the woman's gaze was cold, deadened, as if her soul had been ripped from her years ago and she'd given up trying to retrieve it.

"Amelia!" A male voice called.

He comes to lay with Amelia. So Sally had said about Jasper Finn. Kate grabbed hold of Daniel's arm, tugging him down the hall and not stopping until they reached the alleyway outside the brothel. If Finn hadn't already known they were here, she suspected he would now from Amelia.

DANIEL PAID THE fare and stepped onto the platform. It swayed under his weight. The bright moon lit every uneven plank, leaving no room for doubt on the unsteadiness of the ferry.

"She's a safe one," the ferryman promised, with a cheeky smile that displayed his crooked, gnarled teeth.

Daniel sincerely doubted that. He helped Kate onto the ferry and breathed a sigh of relief. They were the only passengers for this night journey. The fewer people who saw him in England, the better.

Kate rubbed her hands up and down her arms, cracked leather against the wool of her greatcoat. The blistering wind sliced at them; it had only gotten worse as the night fell. Daniel unwound the red woolen scarf around his neck and handed it to her. She took it, a small grateful smile playing on her lips when she'd finished tying it about her neck.

Jacob's Island was falling to pieces around them, yet Kate was radiant. The brisk gale had given her cheeks a rosy glow. She held on to her straw bonnet against the wind with one hand, and she wore the blue plaid dress underneath her father's greatcoat. He envisioned stripping her of that large, battered coat in her rooms that night, so that she was once again the woman he'd fallen in love with, free of the trappings of the past.

He plucked at his Belcher, readjusting the fall of the cloth against his neck. He'd babbled on when they were dockside about everything but what he really wanted to discuss. Kate had stood stock still, her expression unreadable. He should know exactly what to say to prompt her to open up, but he didn't. Not anymore—maybe not ever.

"I'm sorry about Sally Fletcher."

"As am I." She looked out at the water, eyes narrowed like she was disappointed the mud-clogged Thames didn't magically reveal all its secrets to her. She leaned against the rickety rail, her palms gripping the wood.

"Once we get my name cleared, if there's anything I can do for her, I will. Maybe she'd like a new profession. I don't believe that's all there can be for her in this life."

Kate's head tilted toward his. "An odd belief for a man."

"Are you surprised because it's me saying this, or because you've grown to think that no one will ever understand the problems a woman alone has to face?" He covered her hand with his own. She didn't pull back, yet her mouth tilted downward. He didn't blame her. She had no reason to forgive him. "You're strong, and you made something of yourself despite these circumstances. Who's to say Miss Fletcher couldn't do the same? Everyone deserves a second chance, love."

"I'm different from Sally. And don't call me love."

He turned his head to look her in the eye, the haunting darkness of her face startling him. Devil take it, the visit to the brothel had stricken her. His stomach churned. The selfish part of him couldn't help but be grateful she'd gone with him, for he doubted Sally would have ever spoken so frankly about her past lover if Kate hadn't been there.

Kate swallowed. "Sally never had a choice. I'd venture she was a child thief before graduating to prostitution. She'd be in too deep to get out before then. But me—I've done things, kept things to myself, looked the other way." Her other hand extended to touch her lip, where he'd kissed her days before.

"Steady now, lass, we are all in some way victims of our circumstances. We all make mistakes. Don't trouble yourself with the past, unless you intend on making good on something. The rest, it's all stuff and nonsense." He moved to slide his fingers in between hers, clasping their hands together. With God as his witness, he'd never let her be hurt again.

"Kate, the life you've led here, it can't have been easy. If things happened, you can tell me. I'll listen." His voice shook. He sounded too Irish, too raw, but he couldn't be bothered to be anything but a broken Teague.

She wrenched her fingers from his, her eyes flashing twin warning signs. "I don't need you to fight my battles."

"I know. Hell, I watched you start a bar brawl." Daniel forced out a laugh in a fruitless attempt to cut the tension. He felt the absence of her closeness like the worst of hangovers, a pounding in his head and a seizing of his gut.

His throat was dry for the burn of gin. It'd make everything better, at least for a short while, and he'd be able to fathom what had happened to her.

A minute passed and then another, the whistling wind surrounding them. Illuminated by the moon, she looked fiercer than ever, her high cheekbones emphasized. Water lapped against the wooden planks as the ferryman steered them closer to a shoreline Daniel had once hoped would welcome him.

Daniel moved closer. When everyone else had shunned him, he'd found a home away from home in her arms before.

She didn't say anything as she leaned back, gloves wrapped around the wood of the railing. For a second her eyes closed and she breathed in deep. The wind roared, cold blasts that ate up his words.

"Your friend—Owen," he started, not knowing how to finish the thought.

She opened her eyes, lips pressed into a firm line. "He's no friend of mine now."

Daniel frowned. "I'm concerned he knows where you live. Maybe we should have Atlas find you a new place."

"Not exactly. He knows the building, but there are at least sixty flats in my lodgings. He has no idea which one."

Worry flickered in Daniel's eyes, unconvinced by her explanation. "Perhaps we should still look into moving you."

"I'm not leaving my flat." She shook her head. "All my stuff's there. It's my home, Daniel, and I refuse to part with it. Besides, Finn has apparently been watching me for all this time. He doesn't know that we're aware of his true identity. If I suddenly disappear, doesn't that bring more suspicion onto me?"

Daniel let out a sigh, but he nodded. "I suppose that makes sense. But I don't prefer it."

"You don't have to," she said. His preferences meant little, or so she kept trying to persuade herself.

"I have a confession to make." He leaned against the rail next to her, shoulder to shoulder. If he thought she'd allow it, he would take her in his arms, breath in the jasmine scent of her hair and know that everything would be fine. "I asked Atlas to look into Owen Neal."

"You did *what?*" Her body shifted to angle toward him stiffly.

"I didn't know about him being Jasper Finn. If I had, I would have told you immediately." He squeezed the rail in his hands, holding on to it for support. "If he hurt you, I'll kill him."

"The bastard didn't do anything but lie to me." The edge to her voice told him she classed him in the same category as Owen Neal.

"I don't regret the interference. This place eats at me—even the damned dead aren't safe from disturbance. The thought of the months you've spent here, in part because of my actions..." He looked out across the water, murky and dark. A lone top boot—perhaps taken from a corpse and lost in transit—floated in the gently lapping waves. It was coated in thick, black mud.

"And I confess I was jealous of the bounder, for getting to be near you, for seeing your smile when all you did was glare at me." His knuckles whitened as he gripped the rail harder. Gripped it as though it was her body, and in her arms he found safe harbor.

"He was nothing to me," she said.

He doubted that, after seeing them together. Her smile had been radiant. But if she wanted to believe Owen had no place in her life, he wouldn't stop her.

"After I stopped drinking, Poppy said the only way I'd find peace is if I accepted what had happened to me." He leaned back against the rail, surveying Kate. "I could move on then, start making sense of my life. At the time, that motivated me—I wanted to be something other than the miserable sod I'd become. But now, I think there are things in life we shouldn't have to accept. That we should fight against with every gram of our being. If someone hurt you, I'm not going to think that's acceptable."

"Don't talk like that, like I'm better than you. I'm no saint. You should know that by now." She didn't look his way as she shifted her weight from one foot to the other.

Bugger. After seeing how Sally Fletcher lived, how could he possibly think she'd done something wrong in fencing goods? She'd done what she had to survive.

God, he admired her.

"When I judged you for picking Atlas's lock, I shouldn't have. It's a damned treacherous slope to be on the wrong side of the law. Wondering if you're going to end up in the gallows, everyone you've ever known attending your hanging like the newest spot of entertainment at Covent Garden. But you didn't succumb to that terror. You've thrived in your new surroundings." Brazenly, he chucked her chin, holding on a moment too long.

"Thank you." For a second, her gaze fastened up on him with something akin to devotion.

Could it be? He blinked and she had already pulled back from him. Her fingers traced the cast-in anchor and Greek letter for E on the bronze buttons of her inherited greatcoat.

The outline of the London Docks appeared in the distance, the many colored flags on the ships like a kaleidoscope of nationalities. He breathed in, then out, searching the black sky for the familiar gold of the Emporia flag only to remember that flag would never again grace the shoreline.

Perhaps they'd never escape the memory of Morgan and his company.

Her hand brushed against his arm as she moved to

disembark, so casually that he almost forgot where he was. They stood on the Gauging Ground in the western docks, facing the complex labyrinth of warehouses and sheds. Kate turned toward the warehouses.

"Good night, Daniel." She looked over her shoulder and gave a nod clearly meant to dismiss him. She started to walk away.

He had become used to her running away and matched her stride easily. "Where do you think you are going?"

"Home." She shook off his hold yet didn't move forward. "I don't need an escort. I practically lived at the docks. I should think I know my way to Ratcliffe Highway by now."

"It is at least a half hour's walk. There is no way I am going to let you do that by yourself." He set his jaw and shoved his hands into the pockets of his coat. If he had to stand out here all night in the frigid air in an argument with her about her independence, he would.

Kate's hands formed fists held down at her sides, likely in debate if she should punch him or shoot him. She shook her head and then bit out a short, "Fine."

FROM THE DOCKS they hired a passing hack. Sitting in the bench seat across from Daniel, Kate couldn't focus on his attempts at light conversation. Eventually, he lapsed into silence, seemingly lost in his own thoughts. As the carriage pulled up in front of her lodgings, she sneaked a glance at him. His eyes were half-closed, only a slit of emerald visible in the dim light from the street lamps. She shouldn't care what he thought, shouldn't wonder if he'd meant what he said out on the ferry.

If someone hurt you, I'm not going to think that's acceptable.

She ached to believe him, for then it would mean that someone understood her pain. That in itself was frightening; enough that she started to doubt the veracity in his statements.

People said things they didn't mean—he'd think her changed, broken.

She would never be a victim again.

The carriage door opened. Daniel jumped down and reached in to hand her to the ground. Hesitating in the doorway, Kate held her breath as he stood in front of her, his intense gaze on her face. Dread filled her, this sensation that if she stepped from this hack all would change between them. Somehow, in some uncertain way, she'd lose her grip on reality as she knew it.

At her hesitation, he grasped her arm, tugging her out and onto the ground. He didn't release her until she stood upright, feet planted steadily on packed snow.

Damn him and his ability to know what she needed.

They stood outside her lodgings as the hack drove away. A gust of wind wafted the red wool scarf against her cheek. Daniel's scarf. Another indication of his kindness that she did not want. Had she learned nothing in two and a half years? Kindness from a man most often meant they wanted something from her. Quickly, Kate unwound the scarf and handed it back to him. His nose wrinkled as he took it from her, but he didn't comment. He still had some tact, while she felt stripped of all decorum.

"Shall I see you tomorrow?" He wrapped the scarf back around his neck, over top of the blue Belcher.

"No."

"What about the day after?"

"No."

He reached for her arm and she skidded away from his touch. That was the last thing she needed. She turned and started to walk toward the building, three steps from the door before he called to her.

"Kate, wait. Have I done something to upset you?" His boots crunched against the snow as he advanced.

"It's been a long night, and I am fatigued." If she were tougher, she'd not turn around to face him. She'd run into the boarding house and lose him in the warren layout.

"That is not what ails you, and you know it." Daniel's brows knit. He stepped to the right, positioning himself in front of the door.

"Get out of the bloody way," she demanded.

When he did not move, Kate threw her weight into his side, smacking into him with such force that he budged from the entrance. He spun her around so her front was against his back, his arm across her middle to keep her still. She pushed at his arm, slapped at his hands, as fear bubbled in her mind. Fear that she'd be trapped forever, subject to another man's demands.

Trapped like she'd been before on that cruel night.

"I'm not going to hurt you, love." His soft words were a balm to her tired soul; at once what she needed and what she hated needing.

Her bonnet tilted precariously. He reached up, setting her hat in place. She relaxed against his hard-muscled chest. The brush of his breath against her ear sent a shiver up her spine. Suddenly being so close to him was imminently dangerous, not for how her body might betray her but for the truth she might reveal.

In any decision, Katiebelle, weigh the odds. People rarely change.

What if Papa was wrong, as he'd been about the investments he made for Emporia? Hearts were breakable and fickle, but the memory of her father had always been steadfast until a week prior. He couldn't have been involved with Jasper Finn's resurrection men. It simply wasn't possible.

Yet if everything Papa owned hadn't been tied up in the company, she'd not have ended up in the rookeries in the first place.

"You don't have to tell me what's wrong, love, but you can't push me away." Daniel hugged her tighter to him.

She didn't want to feel safe in his arms. Kate slipped from his hold to stand away from him. She watched his expression change in the street lamp from one of determination to concern.

Her heart thumped against her chest. No matter how she tried to fight him, he'd keep prying until he learned her secret.

"Bloody hell. You can come inside." She took his hand in hers. It would be the last time they'd touch—she could let herself have this moment of contact.

They entered the tenement house, took the steps that led to her room. He followed in after her, sitting down next to her on the bed.

"I didn't bring you in here so we could have intercourse." She specifically chose a word that would sound clinical. Anything more maudlin would touch her too deep, nourishing that small part of her that begged to be treated like the rich merchant's daughter she'd once been.

"It didn't cross my mind."

That was a lie. Of course it had occurred to him; he was male and thus he thought about sex. Hell, as he sat so close to her, *she* couldn't stop the flow of memories. Daniel above her, plowing into her with powerful strokes in a perfect, blissful rhythm. The gleam of sweat upon his brow, head thrown back as he groaned his release. Kate gulped down much needed air, ignoring the building tension in her belly.

"Do you want to talk about what happened at the bordello?" Each word was slow, emphasized. That should've irritated her but somehow helped her to sort out her mind.

Shrugging off her coat, Kate hung it on one of the four posts of her bed. Without the voluminous material around her, hiding her frame for all to see, she was laid bare to him.

"It happened right after the bankers took control of our townhouse." She forced herself to meet his eye, determined to be strong enough to finally have a voice.

Daniel nodded, his attention rapt upon her.

Kate squeezed her hands into a fist, nails digging into the soft flesh of her palm until a quick prick of pain shot through her. "I had nowhere else to go. I ended up outside Emporia's old warehouses at three in the morning, damned cold and starving. A porter saw me and said he knew of a woman who'd let me stay in her boarding house in exchange for some light work. Mrs. Hartwick would be glad to have me and I'd fit in well. I'm certain you can surmise what happened from there. I should've known. I was foolish not to know."

Foolish, foolish, foolish. The litany repeated in her mind, over and over again as it had every day since that night. Put up in a room with twelve other girls, she shared a bed with a young Chinese woman named Mei, who had been sold by her parents to the abbess when she was twelve. Mei told her story with little aplomb, accepting her fate for it was better than she had back at home. Stuck in that room, the doors locked so the girls wouldn't try to escape, Kate suddenly understood that the last trappings of her prior existence were truly gone.

Her hand stroked the fabric of Papa's greatcoat absently. Daniel leaned in closer to her. Shoulder to shoulder, his mouth set in a grim line and his brows furrowed, the heat radiating from his body sung through her. She tilted her head toward him as he placed his hand over hers, a silent gesture that meant more to her than any words he could have said.

"When dawn came they placed me in a room with a man who smelled of piss and gin. An initiation for the new tail, they said, laughing when I yelled that they didn't know who I was and they'd have hell to pay." Instead she'd stayed, huddled against the wall, her dress stolen for the madam to sell to the used clothing stalls. Clothed in only her petticoat and chemise, the man's blood-red gaze on her bosom, she'd been powerless to do anything against him. No gun, no knife.

Daniel gave her hand a squeeze as the tears started to come. She rubbed at them furiously, hating the sign of weakness but unable to staunch the flow. "He didn't wait until they'd left to launch himself at me. I yelled, tried to shake him off but he kept coming." He'd undone his trousers, his cock hardened by her struggles. He maneuvered her against the wall, sliding his hand up her skirt, finding the slit in her drawers.

You like it when I stick my fingers in your cunny, don't you, you sick bitch?

"The things he said, what he was about to do…but I took care of him, didn't I, when I shot him in the shoulder later? The wound got infected and they had to amputate his whole bloody arm." A nasty grin slipped onto her lips. "He won't come after me again."

Daniel's expression was too blank. She knew she'd shocked him. In a second, he'd say what men always said: he didn't want her. He couldn't, now that he knew she'd been spoiled.

"How did you get away?" He asked flatly.

"My screams attracted attention." She wouldn't tell him that Mei had saved her, risking her own safety when she rushed into the room. With a force she hadn't known such a tiny woman could possess, Mei had smacked Kate's valise into the man's head. He slumped to the ground, knocked unconscious by the blow.

Go. You are not meant for this life. Mei had tossed her bag at her and opened the window. Once Kate touched the ground, she was gone, with a promise to never reveal Mei's identity.

Some promises were meant to be kept.

CHAPTER 12

BILE SEIZED DANIEL'S throat. He swallowed back the sickening taste, for this was not about him. He didn't get a chance to grieve for the loss of innocence in the woman he loved. He didn't know what to say. How could he? He couldn't take away this pain.

Her sniffles echoed in the silent room. A heavy weight on his chest made breathing difficult. The act of forming words seemed impossible. He must soldier on, for her and for her alone because he'd been a fool. He had acted like things could so quickly go back to the way they'd been between them, like nothing had changed. If it was the last blooming thing he'd do, he'd carve out a new life for her, one free of the stain and horror of these rookeries.

"Bloody hell." He thought of the brothels he'd visited when foxed out of his mind back home. Bollocks, how many women like her had he helped abuse? He'd never stopped to contemplate it.

Some bastard had hurt Kate, his Kate, and he'd finish the job she'd started on him. Maybe that'd be some sort of penance. Or maybe it'd make him what England already believed him—a murderer.

He didn't care, as long as it helped Kate find peace.

"Go on." Kate's command shattered his daze, her voice strong despite the tremor. "Tell me I'm a whore now. Tell me you couldn't possibly ever want me again, knowing what's been done to me."

"Christ, Katiebelle." He sat up straighter, like a bolt of lightning had shot down his spine and remained firmly wedged. "I'd never say that to you. This isn't your fault. You shouldn't have to expect that a blackguard would come at you because you agreed to do some housework. That's not how the world should work. I sure as hell would never judge you for it."

"You say that now." Her eyes glistened with tears.

He'd thought it obvious that he wanted her—that he needed her—but if she required proof he'd do whatever it took. Leaning forward, he held her chin gently and tilted it upwards. He kissed her softly, without the burning heat that always threatened to besiege him when he was with her.

Daniel waited until she responded before he pulled back. He let go of her chin, albeit reluctantly, and held her gaze. "You listen to me, and you listen to me now. You are still the girl I fell in love with."

She shook her head. "No, I'm not. I can't possibly be anymore."

"Then whoever you are now, I love you still. My feelings haven't changed because of this." He stroked his thumb across her palm slowly. "I am honored that you have trusted me with something so private. I'll prove that I didn't murder Dalton and I'll work to deserve you, Kate, for you are far braver and far stronger than I've been. That is what I want to work toward, without the aid of gin."

She exhaled, a long breath that he wondered if she'd been holding this entire time. Shifting to rest her head upon his shoulder, she snuggled in the folds of his coat and shirtsleeves.

"Thank you." Her voice was muffled, but he could distinguish what she'd said.

He blinked. "For what? I have done nothing."

"Just...for being here." She stifled a yawn, covering her mouth quickly.

"I am not going anywhere, love." He laid a kiss upon her head.

"For tonight, and tonight alone, I accept that." She tilted her head up to look at him, smiling slowly.

He'd do anything if she'd look at him like that for the rest of his life. He leaned back against the wall and she followed, eyes closing. He ran his hand through her hair, waiting until her breathing slowed into a quiet rhythm before he slept.

KATE AWOKE SUDDENLY. Underneath her head was certainly not a pillow, but instead a living, breathing man. She could hear his heartbeat, his slow, resting breathing echoing through her small flat. Hazarding a glance upwards, she saw Daniel's serene, sleeping face. His hand was on her hip.

Shit.

He wore no neckcloth, the top buttons of his shirt undone to reveal the strong line of his throat. She slid her hand down, touching his buckskin breeches. At least they were fully clothed. She wore the walking dress from the day before, the heavy fabric now set with wrinkles. It came back to her then, how she'd asked him to stay over. She had been too tired to change into her nightgown.

Her elbow collided with his side. He groaned, his eyes popping open.

Shit, and the sewers it collected in.

"Good morning." His hand came up to brush away a lock of hair that had fallen across her cheek. Tenderly, he stroked her hair.

She leaned into his touch, telling herself that this was acceptable because she was barely awake and no one expected coherence in the early morning.

"How did you sleep?" he asked, ceasing movement.

"The same as always," she lied. For the first time in three years, she'd slept soundly.

"That could either be a very good thing, or a very bad. Which is it?" There went his fingers again.

If this kept up, she'd lay in his arms all day. Kate pushed herself up fully, his finger snagging on a knot in her hair as she tugged back. Even her traitorous body was against her.

She vaulted from the bed, ignoring the crick in her limbs from sleeping so crammed into her tiny bed. She rubbed at her shoulder. Tender skin screamed back at her and she winced.

"Here, let me do that." He was up, feet on the ground and already over to her side of the bed. How did he move so damn fast in the morning? He should be groggy, like she was, so that she had an equal chance.

Daniel stood behind her, pushing her hand away from her shoulder. The back of his hand held her steady, while his fingers wrapped around her shoulder blade. His thumb found the sorest spot, rubbing back and forth in a circular motion until the stiffness started to ebb from her body.

"You're so tense." He brushed her hair back, kissing her bared neck.

Her stomach fluttered, a thousand butterflies begging to be released. Warmth coiled up in her, the same blasted fire lit whenever he was near. He worked at her shoulders again, his hands loosening the knots. He unbuttoned the top button of her gown, sliding his fingers in the opening created to continue massaging.

Kate jumped back.

"Daniel." Doing the button up hurriedly, she glared at him.

He was sheepish. "It's hard not get carried away around you."

"Contain yourself." She used the hard edge to her voice as a whip. If she cracked it hard enough, he might not remember she'd invited him to stay in the first place.

An awkward silence filled the room. It was worse than

their stilted conversation, yet she could not bring herself to break it. What could she even say? The night before, she'd felt close to him again. Perilously close.

He went to make tea, sorting through her smattering of cracked dishes. She frowned at his back. She could guess what he thought: this was a stark comparison to her suite in her father's old townhouse, with dainty antique furniture and bedding and curtains that cost more than his yearly salary. The lone chair she had was a hideous paisley and missing one arm. The only other furniture in her flat was a table, armoire, and her bed.

She went to the battered chest of drawers pushed up against the window, as far away as she could get from Daniel without leaving the room. From the top drawer she pulled out a fresh dress to change into when he left.

She kept her head up, eyes on the grainy wood of the door. Her stocking-clad foot stepped on a letter, slipped underneath the door by the landlord. Kate leaned down, scooping up the missive.

Daniel stared unabashedly, a crooked grin stretched across his lips. Spying upon her rear, as if they'd slipped back into their old courtship ways.

You let him think you'd take him back.

No, Kate reasoned, she'd done no such thing. At every point, she'd been completely clear—she was in this to show that her father's company had no connection to Dalton's murder and to collect funds from him. That was it, that was all, and the kiss in the carriage had meant not a damn thing.

If she told herself this often enough, she might start to believe it.

"Didn't think the Post would deliver this far back off the Highway." Daniel nodded to the letter clutched in her hands.

"They don't." Her nose wrinkled as she turned the sheet of foolscap over. "I try not to let it be known where I live. I don't receive goods here."

The stationary was flimsy and cheap, unlike the thick

paper her father had preferred. A brown stain dotted the right corner, the color of dirt or tea grounds. A dollop of cheap wax sealed the folds, with no signet pressed into the wax.

She flipped the letter again, scanning the back. No postage was applied. The back read "Kate Morgan - Ratcliffe, London" in a spidery scrawl. Someone had dropped it off specifically for her, likely employing a child to run an errand in exchange for a hunk of bread. Somehow that made it more personal, the intent behind it suddenly threatening.

Determinedly, she seized a butter knife from the table and slit the letter open.

M. Morgan, if you wish to know who truly killed Tommy Dalton, you will come to Friggard's Pawn in Bethnal Green at two in the afternoon tomorrow. Bring the Paddy.

A squiggle adorned the bottom of the letter. Kate squinted. She recognized the mark from countless accountings from Emporia's chief clerk, Laurence Bartleby. What could Bartleby possibly have to do with all this? A crotchety old man more apt to snap than compliment, he'd preferred numbers to people. Yet the use of the derogatory term aimed at Daniel's nationality did fit.

She handed the letter to Daniel wordlessly, address side up. He flipped the paper over, read the sparse contents, and set the foolscap down on the table.

"Cryptic, I'd say." He shot an expectant glance toward her.

Under the weight of his gaze, she was competent. Self-assured, ready to develop a plan that would leave them straight to Dalton's murderer. Her enemies would live to regret doubting her, starting with Jasper Finn.

"I think it was sent by Laurence Bartleby." Kate crossed to the bed, sitting primly on the edge of the thin coverlet.

"My old friend." Daniel ran a hand across the scruff of his chin, grimacing. "I'd ask you how he is, but I frankly can't be pressed to care."

"Understandable. I haven't spoken to him in years. Not

an estrangement I particularly regret." Absently, Kate plucked at a loose thread in the coverlet. The action spurred her mind onward until a plan started to form.

When Emporia fell, Bartleby lost not only a generous salary as head account, but his easy source for ready money. He had started to embezzle money from the company when her father became sick. Money the bank needed to pay off the loans; money she could have bloody used. Perhaps he'd been doing it for years—no one thought to look for the funds until the bank came to collect.

Bartleby had lost all chance at a good reference when his embezzlement was revealed. A bitter man with an agenda was a dangerous man. He'd make sure Daniel thought Papa was responsible for Dalton's death.

Spending time pursuing Bartleby's falsehoods would only slow them down. A killer was still on the loose.

"We must go." Daniel gestured at the letter. "As much as I don't want to see him, if he knows something, we've got to investigate."

Kate scoffed. "You and I both know Bartleby would as soon send his own mother onto a hulk if it'd save his skin. That bastard stole from the company. You've been back in town, making inquiries about Dalton's murder, and suddenly he comes forward? Where has he been these last three years? If he wanted to clear your name, he could have found me. He didn't."

"That is suspicious, I'll admit." Daniel held up a hand when she opened her mouth to interject. "I can't explain his motives without seeing him, and neither should you. Bartleby is a sniveling rascal, but he's hardly a threat. I'm rather sure if I drew his cork, he'd fall flat."

"As delightful as it would be to watch you punch him in the nose, I question what we'd gain." The coverlet thread had grown longer as she continued to pick at it, until it was the full length of her middle finger. "While I remember that being Bartleby's signature, how do we know that he sent it? Someone could have forged it."

"Or Bartleby sent it himself. We'll never know if we don't go." Earnestness lit up Daniel's face, giving him an almost boyish quality. "Come, Kate. You're always saying you can defend us."

Kate stiffened. "I can. But that doesn't mean I like this."

"We'll be careful. Leave at the first sign of danger," Daniel's posture was straight, his hands fisted at his side like he was ready to take on the world.

If she didn't agree to attend the docks meeting with him, he'd go without her and she'd lose any opportunity to stem the tide of Bartleby's lies.

"Fine. We'll do it your way." She pulled her jacket down from the bed post, digging into the pocket. "But I'm bringing my gun."

Daniel grinned. "I wouldn't expect anything else from you."

DANIEL TUGGED AT his neckcloth, pulling it up higher on his neck to block out the chill air. It had rained earlier, but an even bigger storm threatened to break, if the inky clouds were any indication. He'd take the weather as an omen that they were getting closer to the truth.

He held his handkerchief up to his nose. If nothing else, at least rain would lessen the stench of putrefaction that clung to all of Bethnal Green. In the afternoon, the streets were less crowded, the majority of denizens either at work or in the public houses. He tapped his truncheon baton against his leg to the beat of an Irish ditty he'd heard outside of his window the night before. Ratcliffe's heavy Irish population at least made him feel at home in that aspect.

"I could think of about seven hundred other places I'd rather be than here." Kate slipped her hand into the pocket of her skirt, pulling out her Forsyth pistol and keeping it at her side. She shot a disparaging look toward a rank pile of rags cluttering a doorway.

Only when the pile groaned did he realize there was a person underneath the debris, bone-thin and yellow in complexion.

"The letter was quite clear. Outside the pawn broker's on Anne Court." He kept his voice low, his mouth near her ear.

She pinked, stepping back from him. "What did Atlas find out about Bartleby's last known address?"

"He was able to locate a flat rented by one Laurence Bartleby in the heart of Westminster," Daniel said.

"That doesn't make any sense. Why would he want to meet in Bethnal Green? Quite a distance to travel, even in a hired hack." With her hand wrapped in the gray wool of her dress to hold her fraying hem up, Kate picked carefully around the cadaver of a feral cat.

They rounded the corner, dropping into a back alley. Here the street became busier, as patrons wandered in and out of a public house. Music drifted out from the doors.

"The pawnbroker's is another alley over." Kate stepped to the left to avoid a young mother, child in hand as she entered a flash house.

"Atlas said that Bartleby's neighborhood is moderately well-to-do. Trust the ass to find himself another Bloomsbury," he said.

Kate pursed her lips, a far-away look in her eyes for a second, most likely remembering her family's townhouse in Bloomsbury. Of all the neighborhoods he could have picked, why did he have to choose that one? He sighed.

"How can he afford that? He must have found another post."

"No record of it, at least that Atlas could find on the black market." Daniel refused to share Atlas's suspicions of what Bartleby was doing for money. Whether or not Kate believed it, she was a lady and there were things ladies didn't need to hear.

They stopped in front of the pawn shop, one of several businesses in the dilapidated building. The front section had been refaced with stucco, while the side was a mottled mix of brick and wood as if money for the renovation had dried out before construction was complete. In each shop's doorway, a crude wooden sign hung from the rafters. Painted on the dingy window of the shop in chipped ornamental lettering was "Friggard's Pawn." The glass was broken in the corner, most likely from a thief's hook. The usual display of wares to entice potential customers was empty.

Daniel pressed his nose to the glass, peering into the shop. Floor to ceiling shelves lined the walls, the thick coat of dust missing where articles had once sat. The case in the front of the shop held no paste jewels, an indentation in the grime the size of a cash box on the cabinet counter.

"Damnation," he muttered. "It's vacant."

The letter had been specific about this location. Daniel's grip on the truncheon tightened. He stood legs wide, posture taut. Whoever had summoned them, he'd be ready for them.

He wouldn't run any longer.

"No sign of Bartleby. Perhaps there's a back room. I wouldn't be surprised if the dolly shop was simply a cover for another operation." He tried the doorknob. It was stuck. "I'm assuming you have your picks."

Kate drummed her index finger against the walnut checkered grip of her pistol, her nose scrunched up in thought. Her gaze darted up the alley. Two men stood outside the clothing shop, deep in conversation.

"Of course I do." She came up to the shop window and peered inside. "But I'm not keen on discovery."

"Then we go around back by the chandler," he nodded. Stepping down from the platform, he started to walk toward the rear of the shop.

"The door isn't locked," Kate called. "It's merely stuck." She turned the knob and the door opened partway until she gave it a shove. As it swung open, she spun around, hand out to stop him. "Daniel, no! Don't come closer!"

She screamed. A brilliant white light flashed. One second, Kate stood at the doorway, and then a cloud of black smoke engulfed everything. He felt the percussive wave of sound as it rippled through the air, arm flying up to protect his face. Balance off-set, he stumbled, barely managing to right himself. Shards of wood, lead, and seemingly a thousand other razor-sharp things whipped toward him at an alarming speed. Windows burst, glass ricocheting into the street.

A second blast followed the first, stronger than before. This wave knocked him off his feet, tumbling him to the ground in a tangle of limbs and debris. He pushed himself up, hand hitting something pointed. Blood spilled from the wound, but he barely registered it. He couldn't see clearly from the black cloud, couldn't think. Instinct pushed his legs forward, away from the demolished building and toward the road.

No, he refused to leave. He forced himself to turn around. Kate was still in there. Where was she? "Kate!" He rasped out, coughing from the smoke.

She was gone.

CHAPTER 13

FLAMES LAPPED AT what had once been Friggard's Pawn. The blackness of the powder from the explosion was punctured with golden orange tendrils. The heat grew, sparks clinging to his coat and singeing the thick wool. A crash resonated, muted somewhat by his slightly deafened ears, as the walls caved in and a gaping hole was left in place of solid foundation.

Kate had been standing in front of the door a moment before. That door was no more, so Daniel could only assume the blast had blown her back, trapped her under the rubble.

The smoke weighed down on him, each breath a special labor. His eyes streamed with water, sensitive to the black powder. Ash flooded the air. He could not move without hacking and his head pounded. He unwound his neckcloth, holding it over his nose so that he could breathe easier.

Yelling her name, he kept on. He turned over piles of rubble, unsure of whether he should dread what he'd find underneath or be hopeful. He grabbed on to a large piece of wood, holding it up as a shield. Another explosion, another blast of fire sent his way. The flames rippled across the edge of the wood before dying out. He was near the front of the building, heat boring down on him, smoke almost unbearable.

In the darkness he could make out one silver flash of metal, a small tube. His gut tightened. Kate's pistol, flung from her hands when the bomb went off. Daniel ducked down and scooped it up, the heat of the barrel burning the tips of his already charred gloves. His pace increased, frenzied by the possibility of her being close. He moved without thought, relying solely on his instinct in the black cloud.

She might not be alive. But he wouldn't think of that—he would keep searching until he found her. He would not leave her now.

Throwing down his shield, he stopped in front of a heap of debris up to his shin. He shoved through the remains, pulling off pieces of wood from the pile. Flames licked close to the area, providing him with enough light to see a body covered by the debris.

"Kate!" he screamed, hurling pieces from the pile.

He uncovered a splash of gray fabric edged in black. Kate's skirt—it had to be. He kept digging, piece after piece until finally he saw her.

Crushed underneath a chunk of wood, face down with her limbs splayed at awkward angles, she didn't stir as he approached. He grabbed the door, pulling it off of her and setting it to the side of them so that it offered some shelter from the splintering building.

"Kate. Please, Katiebelle, please." Her name became an urgent plea for her to awaken. He couldn't possibly survive without her, couldn't become the better man she made him want to be.

He knelt down in front of her, leaning over her to press his ear to her chest. Faintly, her heartbeat reached him. He let out a sob of relief, rubbing at his eyes with the back of his hand.

She was alive.

But she wouldn't be for long if they didn't get to safety. Gingerly, he lifted her onto his lap. His fingers came back slick when he touched her face. Bile rose in his throat. Blood streamed from her forehead, matted in her hair and coated her left ear. Dirt, clay, and glass stuck to the wound. She must have hit the ground hard when the blast had thrown her down.

He hugged her to his chest, his heart pounding frantically. So much blood flowed from the gash, coating her face in sickly red. Gathering her up, he stood. With her in his arms, he hunched down, running as fast as he could. The flames smoldered, sending bits of building toward them. He deflected the missiles as best as he could.

His arms burned from the effort of carrying her down the street at such a pace. They were out in the open, and he dare not risk slowing down. He didn't loosen his grip on her until finally they were far away where a hack could be hired, and he'd lifted her into the carriage. Only then did he collapse on the cushion across from her, his body limp.

SHE'D TRIGGERED A tripwire.

When Kate awoke in the carriage that was the first thing she remembered. Her foot hitting a wire so thin it might as well have been a fishing lure spun from silk. It made a small plinking sound, and if the activity on the street had been louder, she might have missed it entirely.

She blinked open eyes prickly from exposure to flame and powder. Light filtered in through the hackney windows. Daniel's lips moved, yet she could not hear any sound coming out. Panic rose within her, clogging her sore throat until fatigue swept in. What if she could never hear again?

Her head throbbed. Too much smoke inhalation; too much pain drumming through her body to stay awake. She slipped back out of consciousness, letting the black take over.

Hours later, she awoke again. She was in Daniel's quarters, laid out on top of his bed with a pillow behind her head. Her dress was torn and dirtied. Her shoes and stockings had been removed.

"Daniel?" Her throat was raw, scratched like dirty laundry against a washing board.

"I'm here." Daniel sat in a chair across the room.

Tears formed at the sound of his voice, rich and with a hint of Irish brogue. She reached out for him and he was at her side in a flash, taking a seat on the bed next to her. Struggling to prop herself up, she ignored the answering ache within her. The pain didn't matter. It was immaterial when Daniel was near her.

Devil take it, she might have died without a final taste of his lips, the feel of his strong arms around her.

"I'm—" She started, her mind not clear enough to form the proper words. Instead, she grabbed for his hand, giving a weak tug.

He followed her guidance, maneuvering so that his arms wrapped around her shoulders. His touch was so tender she barely felt it. Leaning deeper into him, she rested her head on his chest, breathed in the sooty scent of him that reminded her further of what she could have lost.

Vaguely, she remembered being in his arms. He had fished her out of the wreckage, carried her to safety. She pulled back to look at his face, black-streaked and haggard. A fresh bandage adorned the hand slung across her right shoulder. He wore no neckcloth or waistcoat, his shirtsleeves ripped and ashen.

"I thought I'd lost you." His voice was raw, words stripped bare.

When he looked at her like this, shoulders hunched and dark circles around his eyes, she worried she would get lost in his unwavering gaze. His green eyes full of love, he stared at her as if she was the only woman he had ever needed, the only one he'd ever want—and she wanted so badly to believe him and fall into his arms.

You could not lose me because you've had me all along.

"It'll take more than a bomb to end me," she said.

She rubbed at her eyes. Her fingers scraped her brow.

"Bugger," she groaned, as pain shot through her temple and crusted blood flaked off on her fingers.

"Careful," Daniel cautioned. He stood, filling both a bowl and a teacup with boiling water from the tea kettle. Handing her a full teacup, he took a seat cautiously on the bed. He placed the bowl on the table, with a clean bit of fabric torn from the sheets hanging off the rim.

"Drink up," he said. "You needn't worry about the quality. I boiled it while you were asleep. It should be safer than tea, given what the coffeehouses here pass as tea."

"Bitter swill." She tried to smile as she lifted the cup and sipped. She tasted blood, coppery sweet, from where it had dripped down from the wound on her brow.

"How are you feeling?" He picked up the bowl, dipping the cloth into the soapy water and ringing it out.

"I'm not dead, so better than the alternative." Her body ached, she was certain she had a few bruises the size of fists, and her head thrummed, but she was alive.

All because of him.

"The door took most of the blast," he mused. "From what I can piece together of the initial explosion, the bomb must have been behind something. Maybe the counter; there were so many fragments of glass, more than should have been from the windows shattering."

"When I opened the door, it triggered something." She frowned. "I tried to warn you—"

"I think the bomb was wired to the door. So when it went off, the door blew off the hinges and knocked you backward. It gave you shelter from the rest of the shards, at least."

She nodded, as if it were an everyday occurrence to be trapped under a wooden plank, the smell of powder thick in her nose and the whirling of fragments around her. It had been so dark under that board.

Suffocating blackness that only ended because he'd risked his own life to save her.

He leaned forward, the cloth in his hand. "Let's try and

clean that mess on your brow, shall we? This may sting a bit and for that I am truly sorry." He ran the hot cloth across her chin, delicately cleaning the area.

The sting knocked her breath away. A thousand burning fires on her brow that didn't cease when he drew the fabric off. He dunked the cloth back in the water, wringing it out and returning to her face for more. She squirmed out of his grip, hissing sounds that didn't form full words.

He held her down, murmuring softly to her. Words she could not fathom, but they sounded sweet and comforting. Little by little she relaxed against his clutch, the pain ebbing into dullness.

Dipping the cloth in the now rust-tinged water, Daniel sat back on the bed. "There."

She drew in a shaky breath. Her shoulders ached from the movement but it made her calmer, for she had control over something at least if she could manage her breathing.

He stood and tossed the soiled water out the window. A shout echoed from the street below, where the water had apparently landed on a passerby. Daniel refilled the bowl with water from the kettle, grabbing another cloth. She squinted. He'd torn up a ragged bed sheet for this, sacrificing warmth for her health.

"Thank you." She dared not speak louder than a whisper, afraid of breaking the precious calm settling between them. Everything was as it should be, and if she didn't move, she might not believe she had been buried under a pile of wood and glass a few hours before.

"Say nothing of it." He soaked the second cloth in that water, his back to her.

Sturdy shoulders, solid chest, a perfectly sculpted rear she'd once slapped as he braced himself on her bed and drove into her—she knew every curve of his frame better than she knew the rookeries. That familiarity scared the hell out of her, but it was also oddly soothing. When her foot had hit the wire and she'd turned around to warn him away, the idea of him surviving even if she did not had soothed her.

"You saved me." She might have been crushed under the remains, forgotten about by the rest of society. Perhaps some would say she deserved it—a fitting end to the crooked daughter of a crooked man.

"What was I supposed to do? Leave you there?" He turned around, wet cloth in his hands, his brows furrowed. "What kind of man would I be if I did that?"

"The kind of man I've thought you were for three years." She frowned, whether from remorse or the constant ache of her battered limbs she knew not. This thing—whatever this was—between them was treacherous, something she could not easily define.

"You thought I'd leave at the first sign of danger." He sighed, coming to the side of the bed. He held the bowl of water and the cloth, setting both down on the table.

"I—" But she couldn't finish that thought. If she admitted she no longer thought of him that way, it would be akin to an admission of feeling for him. Of love, blossoming in her heart when she ought to crush it, for it wasn't safe and it wasn't infallible.

Beside her was Papa's greatcoat, now shredded. Closing her eyes, Kate ran her hand down the familiar wool. One more comfort of her old life in Bloomsbury stolen from her. There was nothing left, nothing but the flintlock—

"My father's Forsyth pistol," she said suddenly, her eyes popping back open. She grabbed Daniel's hand, pouring her hurt into a vice grip. "We must go back and retrieve it. Please, Daniel, it's all I have left of him."

He pulled his hand away from hers and patted it once before crossing to the other side of the room. Opening up the trunk off to the side of the room, Daniel emerged with the pistol held out to her in both hands.

"I found it when I was searching for you." He looked all too pleased with himself, his grin glowing and his eyes dancing with glee. Bringing the gun to her, he set it down in her lap affectionately.

"You..." She couldn't form words.

Her finger traced the roses carved into the wooden handle. The flintlock was heavy in her lap, a constant presence she'd grown to love. The gun had become her best friend these last three years, the only thing that still made sense. A crutch like gin had been for him once.

Daniel had brought this piece of her father back to her. Daniel, who had spent the first days of his return accusing Emporia of being involved in Dalton's murder.

Emotion bubbled in her throat until she could no longer contain it. Tears streamed down her cheeks. Too much had happened in the past two weeks to stay sane. Slowly, her walls were breaking down and she didn't know how to construct new ones.

"I knew it was important to you." He drew back, arm still around her shoulders as he kissed the top of her head. The gun stuck out awkwardly over her lap.

His gesture was so bloody intimate that she couldn't stand it, yet she ached for it to continue.

He sank down, the bed creaking under his added weight. The past hung in the air between them, tangible when he dared to link his hand in hers. She didn't pull back, letting the warmth of bare palm on bare palm surround her, smoothing away her concerns.

"Katiebelle," he started and stopped, seemingly as unsure as she was. "When I saw you hesitate after pushing the door open, I knew something was wrong. I should have been with you, sheltered you properly, taken the heat of the blast."

"Nonsense." She patted his hand. "Then who would have pulled me from the wreckage? I would say your timing was impeccable."

"You shouldn't have been there in the first place. You shouldn't be involved in any of this." His fingers tightened around hers, as if by the power of his grip, he could keep her away from harm. "But I bloody drew you into a fight that isn't yours because I was selfish and I couldn't bear the thought of not having you by my side again. I'm sorry, Kate. I jump from one foolish decision to the next, hurting those around me."

She sat up a little straighter, balanced her weight on her elbows so she could look him in the eye. "You listen to me," she commanded, echoing his earlier words to her. "You listen to me now. Maybe you shouldn't have come back to London—maybe it put me in danger. But I am *always* in danger, Daniel, and that's the life I've chosen."

Maybe it wasn't the life she wanted anymore. Maybe she wanted a life with him.

She squeezed his hand. Tried to remind herself that with the risk of fencing came her independence, but all she could think about was how she didn't want to be anywhere but with him. "If it wasn't Finn, it'd be someone else. You didn't arm the charges of that bomb. I've blamed you for a lot of things, but this attack I refuse to assign to you."

"I can't reasonably ask you to continue to look into Dalton's murder." Daniel squared his shoulders, determination wrought on his black powder-streaked face. "Whether or not you release me of culpability, it's too much. I won't do that to you."

She took her hand from his, grasped his chin and directed his glance to her. "It's too late for you to make that decision. Somebody tries to make me into a Guy Fawkes effigy, I have something to say about it and I'm not going to stop until that bastard hangs outside Newgate."

He grinned, a wide smile that sent a frisson of heat through her. "My bloodthirsty love."

She should correct him. She wasn't his, wasn't anyone's to own. This had been about Emporia originally, and maybe, a small part of it still was.

But as she sat shoulder to shoulder with him, she suspected that it had stopped being entirely about Emporia and become about them. She had known it would. Feared it deep down in those parts of her heart she kept locked up, for it meant for the moment she would not be alone.

She stole a glance at him, thinking she was being furtive, but his eyes locked on hers. He knew all her secrets and he didn't judge her for them. When he stared back at her, she got the distinct impression he could see into her soul. The most damaged parts of her were on display for him and he didn't run.

He stayed beside her. Removing the gun from her lap, he put it gently on the floor next to the bed. He angled his body so that he was closer to her, cross-legged on the bed, face to face. He inched forward, until his lips were so precariously near to her his breath tingled upon her raw skin.

"This can't continue," she murmured, fully aware she should back away, but caught up in him nonetheless.

"I disagree." His voice was richer, thick with the Brogue he could not suppress in moments of real emotion.

"We tried once before. It didn't work." Her chest rose and fell with staggered breaths, suddenly light-headed.

"Circumstances change." He traced her bottom lip with his calloused thumb.

"People don't." Little goose-bumps pricked her skin, far too alert to the feeling of his strokes.

"I've changed. I almost lost you today, Kate, and I won't have that." He pulled his thumb away and bridged the gap between them.

He kissed her with the laziness of a man intent on a long night of seduction, when before his kisses had been ones of claiming. He didn't need to do that now, when they both knew she'd always been his and she'd never be anything but his.

She broke away. "I can't promise you more than one night."

He brushed another kiss against her lips. "One night is all I need."

CHAPTER 14

NOTHING MADE SENSE anymore, only the glide of his mouth against hers. His kisses cascaded over her chin, until he found the hollow at her throat. His tortuous tongue flicked back and forth across her skin. Kate angled her head away, stretching out her neck to give him better access. The pressure of his lips made her insides clench with lust, until her mind was hazy. Only their clothes stood between them, fears cleared away by the devotion in their caresses.

He returned to her and she kissed him again recklessly, forgetting all her reasons why she'd resisted this until now. Forgetting the way he'd fled from London, the accusations that had been made against her father's company, the struggles she'd had, everything but the sheer weight of his body pressed up against her own and the deliciousness taste of him. Fervor erupted between them. His lips smashed against hers, bruising tender skin, the pain only making her feel more alive.

Daniel understood her past and did not condemn her. She needed him as he needed her, the wildness she'd held back bursting at the surface.

His fingers brushed against her breasts. She leaned into his touch, straining against the busk in the center of her corset, resenting the restriction. He dragged his thumb across her right breast, moving the tattered gray fabric back and forth with his movement against her sensitive skin. With each stroke, pleasure built up within her, devilish, wicked pleasure that she could not deny—would not want to, for it had been all she could think of since he'd come back.

She couldn't get close enough to him, couldn't lean far enough into his touch. He pulled back, caught her eye. His lips were red from her kisses. A whimper fell from her lips, a sign of weakness that gave her no shame.

He swung around the other side of her, undoing the many back buttons of her bodice. Some had popped off in the explosion, making his work simpler. She found it somehow fitting that this time with Daniel would be when she looked out-of-sorts. That's what they were to each other: chaotic, complicated, and utterly consuming.

He worked the long sleeves down her arms, his touch burning her. He unclasped the brass fixtures that joined her bodice to her skirt and then lifted her up. She kicked off her skirt with far more speed than she should have been able to muster—than was proper.

She wasn't a proper lady anymore, damn it.

He tackled next her petticoat with its heavy corded twine rings, throwing the offending garment off the bed and toward the County Cork trunk in the corner of his room.

She wore a simple corset, modified so she could lace it up without the help of a maid: spiral laced in the back, but with cords that came forward and weaved into tabs in the front. The two strings tied together in a bow underneath her breasts, a bow his heavy-lidded gaze fastened on. His tongue darted out to wet his lips before he made quick work of the laces, freeing her breasts to him. He tugged the shift out from underneath her skirt, up and over her shoulders.

"Kate." He said her name like a reverential prayer, his voice thick and husky. His gaze slipped down her frame, drinking in her breasts, pink nipples hardened into tight peaks for him.

She should want to grab the sheet back up, to hide herself from his scrutiny. Instead, she leaned her head back. She gave in to the lush pleasure of his open mouth against her skin, tongue flicking over her breast. Before she knew it, her fingers were locked in his hair, keeping his head down where she needed it most.

He pulled away only long enough to shrug off his own shirtsleeves. Then again he was on her, giving her a slight push so that she would land on the bed, the pillow behind her head. Her body shook as he trailed his thumb down her frame, a line of fire wherever he touched. He worked her drawers down her legs.

A rush of cold air hit her, but then his hot skin was against her, the warring sensations only sending her higher. He dragged his thumb across the juncture of curls at her thighs. She bucked into his hand, impatiently urging him on, but he wouldn't give in to her yet.

If this was insanity, then she'd go to it willingly. One night away from their problems, one night in which they didn't worry if they might die in the coming hours. One night to honor all they had been and all they might be if she just stopped thinking.

DANIEL HAD NEVER known a finer drug than Kate Morgan.

As he leaned above her, thumb lightly tracing her innermost folds, he was all too aware that nothing else would ever do. The gin paled in comparison, a makeshift attempt at replicating how he felt when he was laying with her. Her breathy moan echoed in his ears, until it he knew nothing but the fact that he'd brought her pleasure and he'd continue doing so until the day he died.

In his mind's eye he saw not her bare body writhing beneath him, coiled and ready for him, but the way she had looked underneath that broken dolly shop door. Still. Lifeless.

Her eyes were closed. Her chest rose and fell with precious, shaky breaths. "God, Daniel," she murmured, the raggedness of her deliriously rapturous voice sending a bolt of pleasure through him.

Unable to resist any longer, he plunged a finger deep inside her, stretching her. She arched against him, her head coming up from the pillow only to fall back again. He breathed it all in, the musky scent of her womanhood, mixed with the disturbingly real black powder. Black powder over everything, reminding him of what he'd almost lost.

He leaned down, pulling her legs high up around his neck, making her a veritable feast for him. Christ, he'd waited so long for this. He couldn't believe it was happening until his tongue slid against her core, drinking in the taste of her. She shuddered underneath his hold when he brought the tip of his tongue against her, taunting her with a sly touch. Her hands fisted around the sheet as she struggled in his hold, but he was firm, keeping her steady.

He would not stop.

He'd make it last as long as he could.

Finding a rhythm that had her panting, he alternated between a nip there, a kiss here, a slide down her folds with his tongue before he thrust deep inside her. His name became a staccato chorus in their room as he drove her higher, finally hitting the spot he knew would send her to completion. He remembered her body like the catechisms he'd been taught as a child, worshiped her as a savior. He sucked against that precise center, faster and faster as she shook, the tension building within her until she finally collapsed.

"That was amazing." She sighed contentedly. Tugging him to her, she gave his shaft a quick pump of appreciation.

He groaned, the touch of her hand upon him nearly enough to make him spill. Flipping open the clasp, he slid down his drawers and breeches, kicking them off. He had to be in her, joined at the hilt, until he could not tell where she began and he ended.

Through her he would come to grips with his failures, and rise again a new man.

Her gaze rested on him, heated and passion-soaked. She nodded, and that was all the approval he needed from her. With one knee on either side of her, he leaned forward, gripping the wooden headboard of the bed. He laid all his weight in his wrists to keep her injured body safe, though he couldn't be tasked to stop. He should give her time to recover, but he couldn't. Of all the fixes he'd had in the past three years, he couldn't shake her.

Nestled between her hips, he guided himself into her, and then drove in with one fell thrust. She fit him like she was made solely for him and him alone. Let no other man take their fill, trespass against her, or hurt her, for she was his again.

Thrust by thrust, he filled her, sinking deep into her cavern, pulling out until he was almost gone and then diving back in. He was urged on by her nails digging into his shoulders, the desperate crescendo to her cries. It was sheer unending glory to be between her thighs again. The place he'd longed for since the day he left, where he felt closest to her. Nothing could separate them.

Her hands clasped his buttocks, pushing him deeper within her. He thrust harder, the bed-frame shaking in time. His knuckles turned white from gripping the frame. He'd be done soon, coming without her if she didn't finish. He leaned down to kiss her, his tongue probing the inner corners of her mouth in sweet torture.

"I'm—I can't—" She shuddered underneath him one final time, lost to the bliss.

He could hold on for one more thrust. One more glorious moment inside her, body to body. Perhaps another, and then he'd be truly done for it. Even longer…but no, he couldn't. He tore from her, spilling on the sheets, not a moment too soon.

His arms gave out and he fell next to her. Idly, his hand ran up and down her arm, reticent to part from her. If he didn't have contact with her, the moment would fade into the famous London fog and he'd be left with nothing. A man more broken than he'd been before.

But he wouldn't think of that. He'd focus on the present, being with her.

Fatigue gnawed at him. He found himself too comfortable with lying beside her in the room that had so recently echoed with their lovemaking. When her breathing became slow and regular, he closed his eyes, finding respite in slumber.

DANIEL STRETCHED LEISURELY on the bed. His arm was slung across Kate's torso, her chestnut locks spilled out over his pillow in the most succulent display he'd ever seen. He was vividly aware what he'd been missing these past three years. Here, with her snug against his body, he could not have been happier.

Gingerly, his thumb traced where her breast met her side, relishing in the luscious slide of her smooth skin against his finger. Everything about her was perfect, from the slight curvature of her hips to the plump orbs of her bosom. He wanted to always wake up tangled up in the sheets with Kate, her leg draped over his thigh, the sound of her quiet breathing filling the room.

He dipped his head down to place a kiss on her injured brow. Even in sleep she was not peaceful. Her lips were drawn into a frown and her hands curled tight in his pillow, as if by clasping it she could keep her surroundings from escaping. He understood why she feared him leaving, and even why she expected it as an absolute.

But all that would change today.

Kate had said it would only be one night, but one night would never be enough between them. The smell of powder lingered on her milky skin, and little particles of ash dotted his sheets. He hugged her closer to him, needing that reminder that they were alive and together.

Already, she had decided that they could be no more. She didn't expect a commitment from him, but perhaps she needed him to make a gesture for her to see that they were meant to be. Perhaps then she could be certain of his affection, and give them a chance.

He hoped to God he was right.

She stirred, her eyes opening slowly. He looked down at her, smiling as she yawned.

"Good morning." He entangled his fingers in hers.

"Oh." She stared down at their joined hands, eyes widening as if the memories had flooded her mind.

He swallowed, throat dry. Would she flee now? He gave her hand a squeeze, wishing he could imbue that grip with all his feelings for her, so she could finally be certain he'd never leave.

She shifted on the bed, grimacing at the movement. Edging away from him, she pushed herself up into a sitting position. She hugged the sheet to her, covering her breasts, but she could not remove the memory of her bare skin from his mind. He missed the warmth of her thigh upon his, the gentle beat of her heart against his chest. His arm fell uselessly to the side of the bed, no longer wrapped around her torso.

"Did I hurt you last night?" He sat up too, not bothering to bring the sheet around him. He had no shame about his physique. "I should have given you more time to recover. But after what happened, can you blame me? The thought of you lost forever—I can't imagine not being with you. Having you near me is the only thing I've ever wanted."

He had to make her believe that.

She frowned. "You had the oddest way of showing it before."

"I'm not going to leave you again." He crept closer, taking her chin in his hands. He brushed his lips against hers in a kiss first tender, then heated, for now that he'd had another taste of her, he couldn't survive without her again.

She went pliant in his arms. He memorized the response of her lips against his, the sweetest of caresses. He could stay there forever with her, his tongue darting out to the taste the moist heat of her mouth, but nothing would get resolved.

He snaked a hand behind her neck, angling her head so that he could examine the wound better. "That cut worries me."

She winced when his fingers lightly stroked the tender skin above her brow. He patted the bed once and then pushed the sheet back. He felt her gaze on him, and he tilted his head back quickly to catch her looking at his bare bottom.

"I'll put the kettle on so that we can wash that cut again." He stepped into his breeches.

"It's nothing. You don't have to worry about it."

Out of the corner of his eye, he saw her lean over, fingertips grazing the wool of her gray gown. The gown was stained with blood and ash. He shook his head, lifting open the trunk and pulling out of one of his shirts.

He came around the edge of the bed, swapping the clean linen shirt for her soiled dress. "I like you better naked," he teased.

She rolled her eyes as he held the clothing up higher than she could reach without dropping the sheet. He grinned back, undaunted. Quickly, Kate released the sheet, snatching the fabric from his hands and throwing the shirt over her head.

"I would have gone and gotten breakfast, but I didn't want you to wake up alone." He poured water into the kettle and set it up.

"I won't be here long enough for that." She swung her legs over the side of the bed and winced at the sudden movement. Cautiously, she slid one foot onto the ground and then the other.

His shirt clung to her gorgeous frame, stopping at her knees and leaving her long, velvety smooth legs visible. She ran her tongue across her lips and swallowed. He was hard just seeing her again, recalling much better uses for her mouth.

"Where do you think you are going?" He leaned back against the tea stand, brows arched. "You haven't a clean dress. Surely you don't intend to slink through Ratcliffe with only my shirt."

Unabashed, he watched as she stooped down to pick up her boots. His shirt slid up further, letting him glimpse her rounded rear. God's balls, she'd kill him.

"It is not as if I have much of a choice." Boots in hand, she pursed her lips in thought. "I could borrow a pair of your breeches. Put my hair up under your hat and no one need know I am female."

"As Shakespearian as that sounds, I must refuse." He closed the distance between them, gathering her up in his arms.

Sweeping away her hair from her shoulder, he laid a kiss on the pulse point of her neck. With only the thin layer of his shirt around her nubile frame, her bottom against the hard ridge of his burgeoning erection was nearly enough to undo him. She leaned against his hold, giving him better access to her neck. His hand palmed the shape of her full breast until she whimpered.

He spun her around so that she faced him, nestled against his unclothed chest. "Stay awhile. Let me love you."

She wrenched from his hold. "You say you won't leave now. But you can't predict the future."

He tucked a stray curl behind her ear. His fingers lingered along the line of her jaw, tracing the familiar shape of her face. "No one can predict the future, Katiebelle."

Pain crossed her features as she closed her eyes. "Don't call me that."

"What else should I call you?" He kept his voice soft, as if she were an easily startled filly on his uncle's farm that he needed to calm. "Wife?"

Her eyes popped open, but she didn't look at him. She kept her gaze focused on the trunk across the room. He had never unpacked his belongings.

"Daniel, please." Her voice was achingly raw, but not in

the way he had wanted. Not with joy, not with passion, instead with the resignation of an already-decided mind.

"I mean it, Kate." He reached over, delicately turning her chin so that she faced him. "I want to marry you. I've always wanted to marry you. I'm nothing without you, love, and the thought of some other man with you rips me to bloody pieces. So say yes, Kate. Say yes to me and what we mean to each other because there's no one in this world better for me than you."

CHAPTER 15

KATE HAD MADE the worst of mistakes. One night had unleashed all the feelings she'd tried to keep hidden. Daniel's fingertips braced against her chin, that slight touch scorching red hot through her body. She couldn't think, couldn't breathe, as long as his gaze was locked on hers. He sat so precariously close she could fall into his arms.

His words tumbled like drops of honey upon her, sweet and rich, and she wanted nothing more than to believe in his promises. She could tell him she had his ring again. That she'd never stopped loving him, and she'd been lying before when she claimed she had no feelings for him.

She was wiser, stronger than she had been when they were together. She ought to know that love was a childhood fairytale.

"I can't." She found her voice, staring directly at the trunk across the room. Why had he never unpacked? Was he preparing for another quick escape?

He dropped his hold on her chin. Clarity triumphed over a hazy mind when he was not around.

"Tell me why not," he murmured, winding an arm around her waist and pulling her to him. He brushed her hair out of his way again, nibbled on the rim of her ear.

Those devious lips were her ruin. She could get lost in his arms, forgetting her place entirely. Forgetting who she had become without his help, and the life she had carved out for herself.

"Because last night was a mistake." She slipped from his arms and stood up quickly. The ground swayed beneath her, head spinning from the sudden rush. She grabbed for the solidness of the bed to steady her, brushing against his calf instead.

Damnation.

She flung her hand up in the air. But that wasn't clever either, for the movement brought the edge of his shirt up further on her thigh and he watched all too appreciatively.

Stubbornly, he tilted his chin up. "Last night was not in error."

"Think what you want." She shrugged. "I know what it was to me."

He shook his head. "I've never heard you say something more false. You're drawn to me, love. That hasn't changed— do you think you'd have slept with me last night if you didn't feel the same way?"

She stiffened. "For all you know, I fall into bed with men quite regularly."

He arched a brow at her. "I highly doubt that."

"We almost died, Daniel. I was caught up in the moment." She propped the lid open on his trunk and yanked out a pair of breeches. Stepping into the breeches, Kate tried the closure, but found that the fabric gaped wide. She was going to have to walk through Ratcliffe holding the damn breeches closed with one hand.

"Don't do this, Kate." He slid behind her, crowding her and pushing her up against the trunk. His scent filled her nostrils, thick with spice and soot.

"I'm not doing anything," she whispered. Yet the fight was dying in her. She knew it and he knew it, and soon she'd be no more.

"Yes, you are." His arms encircled her waist, drawing her flush against his hard pectoral muscles. "You've been doing the same thing since I came back to London. Running from me when you should be staying here, letting me love you. I made a mistake three years ago, but you're so stuck in your own head that you won't let me fix it."

"Some things are too split to slap a bandage upon." She leaned back into his hold, contradicting her own words.

"Some things, perhaps. But not this. You've got to allow me in first, and then you'll see."

"I've got goods to take in—"

"And I've got a murderer to catch. Those things will wait, at least for now. You have to talk to me. Tell me what you're thinking." He tweaked her ear.

"It's too soon." She said the first thing that popped into her mind.

"Oh." He paused for a moment, as though deep in thought. His fingers tapped out a slow beat against her waist. "Is that all? We don't have to decide this now, Katiebelle. But I need you to know that I came back for you because every day I was gone I thought of you. The way you laughed, that cute quirk of your lips when you smile, that sparkle in your eyes when you've figured out something that's been puzzling you." He sighed, his thumb tracing the bridge between her ring finger and pinkie. "I tried to drink you away and I couldn't. There's not enough liquor in the world to dull you out of my mind."

His words sunk deep in her, as if he'd taken a mallet and crushed at her defenses. She leaned back against the trunk, grateful for something to hold her up. Her knees were weak, heart thumping against her chest. Tears dotted the corners of her eyes. She wasn't prepared for this.

He made no move to wipe away the tears, as if sensing that his gentle touch would be enough to undo her completely. "So I stopped drinking, stopped trying to obliterate you from my memory. There's something Uncle Liam used to say to Poppy and me, after our parents died. '*Tá mo chroí istigh ionat.*' It means 'my heart is within you,' and Kate, I swear it is true. Without you, I'm nothing."

But with him, she was vulnerable.

"I—" She fell short, with no knowledge of what to say next. Happiness flooded her at his declaration, desperate, cloying bliss that clamored for her to give in and admit that she loved him too. "I can't do this, not now."

"So we don't run off to Gretna Green right away." He smiled, unconcerned with her refusal, like he'd expected it all along and it was only a matter of time before she gave in to him. "We stay here for the present, and we find Dalton's murderer and clear my name."

She nodded. "That is what I agreed to."

"And in the meantime, you allow me to go fetch us some breakfast and a change of clothes for you, as I highly doubt you want to wander about in those breeches." He moved his hand so that he clutched the waistband, tugging it out of her grasp so that the gap was visible. "Promise me you won't leave until I get back."

"Fine," she grumbled. "But that's the only promise you'll get out of me."

He hugged her to him once more before releasing her. "Shoot anyone who comes to the door that isn't me."

Target practice, she thought, was exactly what she needed to improve her mood.

DANIEL CHOSE TO cut through a back alley he hadn't gone down before. He was half-way up the street when a man darted out from a back alley, too close to him. Just in time, Daniel held up his hands. His palms collided with the other man's chest and stopped his momentum.

"Watch where yer goin'," the man spat, revealing a

mouthful of yellowed teeth.

There was something familiar about him. Knotted, dirty gray hair touched his shoulders in limp tendrils. His rheumatic eyes were brown. His clothes were ordinary: checkered neckcloth spoiled with dark spots, rumpled waistcloth, and double-breasted wool coat missing half the buttons hanging loosely from his stooped shoulders. Dirt streaked his shirt. As Daniel stepped closer to him, a dank odor drifted to his nostrils, foul like death. The man's shoes were coated with mud, grass, and stone dust, as if he had been rooting in graveyards.

"What're ye lookin' at?" The man sneered. Not waiting for a response, he turned away.

The beggar outside the Red Fist had said that phrase with the exact same accent and speech pattern. It could be a coincidence to meet him in two different places, but after the explosion Daniel no longer believed in chance. Caution was prudent, especially if it meant keeping Kate safe.

"I know you," Daniel called to the man.

The man tilted his head back over his shoulder to look Daniel square in the eye. "Yer testin' yer luck, cub."

"Why are you following me?"

"Yer an easy mark. Ye don't watch yerself."

Amidst the sounds of the street, sheets hung to dry from the rafters of the tenement houses whipped in the wind. The beggar's cloudy eyes focused in on him, and in that dull lifelessness Daniel suddenly felt he could see everything. "Who do you work for? Who sent you after me?"

"I'm a cartin' man. Movin' Things for the boys down at the Fortune of War public house."

"Who set Friggard's Pawn to blow?"

"Don't know nothin' 'bout no pawn shop, but if I did, I'd not be tellin' ye, cub. All I got is some bodies. Ye want a Subject, I got some smalls, some larges..." The ruffian's laugh descended into a hacking cough.

Daniel crowded him back against the wall, grasping the

man's collar and lifting him upward. The captured man flailed in the air, protesting loudly. One arm across his chest, Daniel held him solid against the wall. Daniel applied pressure to his throat, until he coughed and gasped for air. "I want you to take a message to Jasper Finn. Tell him Daniel O'Reilly is done running."

Releasing the beggar, Daniel stepped back from him.

The man slumped against the wall. "Yer a crazy codger. I'm Ezekiel. Don't know any Finn."

Daniel's eyes narrowed. He should have realized it when Sally Fletcher had mentioned an Ezekiel. A man of the same name had been on Atlas's list.

"You lie, Ezekiel Barnes."

"What ye gonna do? Ye can't touch me."

The bastard hurt Kate. Nothing else mattered. He deserved to be punished. With his free hand, Daniel pulled back and punched Ezekiel in the nose. Fist connected with cartilage and bone in a revolting smash. Ezekiel hollered. Blood squirted from his nose and onto Daniel's greatcoat. The same sticky, dark dots had collected on Dalton's body when Daniel had found him; that same crimson crusted Kate's eyebrow.

When would this bloodshed stop? When he'd lost everything he cared for, and Kate lay dead in the street?

Daniel shook his hand out, fist stinging from impact. "What Finn did to Dalton will seem like child's play when I'm through with your master. If he comes after Kate Morgan again, I'll cut every limb from his body and scatter the remains across the fucking Thames River."

Ezekiel ceased shuddering and stood up straight, his movements becoming quick. Thrusting out his arm, his fist connected hard with Daniel's forearm. Daniel grunted, teeth on edge as he took the blow.

Another bruise to add to his growing collection.

"Finn will make ye watch as he plows her, then kill ye where ye stand. I'll hold the bitch down." Ezekiel wheeled back for another attack.

But this time Daniel was ready for him. As Ezekiel's arm shot out, Daniel blocked with his forearm, wrist rolling over the man's arm so that he could not bend it. With his free hand, Ezekiel tried to ram his fist into Daniel's nose.

Anticipating Ezekiel's blow, Daniel ducked. He threw Ezekiel's aim off-guard and the brute stumbled, unable to compensate for the loss in motion.

Daniel needed a weapon. Foolishly, he had left his truncheon back in the room. Rough linen hung from the rafters of the tenement house, close to his position. In the second before Ezekiel righted himself, Daniel snatched the linen down from the rafters, wrapping it tight around his fist.

Darting forward, Daniel snapped his wrist, the sheet slapping against Ezekiel's leg so hard it echoed in the alley. Ezekiel backed off, howling in pain and favoring his right leg. Daniel pushed closer, shoulder connecting with the bully's chest and jostling him off-kilter.

Daniel shook the sheet out, throwing it over Ezekiel's head. The cloth deflected some of Ezekiel's flailed blows, softening the hit and creating distance. Hands gripped in the sheet, Daniel boxed his ears.

Ezekiel could not be trapped for long. Slimy and spry, he squirmed out of Daniel's hold. Ezekiel darted forward, landing a heavy blow to Daniel's ribcage.

Sharp pain seared through his body. The bugger had managed to find the exact spot where he'd been injured in the explosion. Daniel forced the pain down, using it to focus him. No matter what he felt now, Kate had endured much worse.

Have to keep Kate safe. That thought above all others kept him going. Send a sign out to Finn through his operative, save Kate, prove his innocence.

He deflected Ezekiel's next blow, grabbing his arm and twisting. A tight grimace stretched across Ezekiel's wan lips and he spat. His saliva landed on Daniel's cheek.

Still gripping his arm, Daniel pinned Ezekiel against the wall, using his weight and height to his advantage. The sheet slipped uselessly to the ground. His hands wrapped around the man's throat, squeezing tightly. The ruffian gasped for breath but could gather none. His eyes rolled back the harder Daniel pressed, cutting off his oxygen supply.

If Daniel kept hold of Ezekiel, if he didn't look at the whites of his eyes, the blue tint to his skin—

But he couldn't look away. He had to stop. With every bit of pressure he ended this man's life. If he did that, he'd be no better than the blackguard who stabbed Dalton and left him dying in that alley.

Daniel's grip lessened and Ezekiel stole the advantage, kneeing him hard in the shin. The blow caught Daniel off-guard and he faltered, nearly falling to the ground. He grabbed for the wall to steady himself. Out of the corner of his eye, he saw Ezekiel slink away, clutching his throat and coughing. Half-heartedly, Daniel grabbed for him. His fingers brushed against soiled skin.

Ezekiel took off running and Daniel didn't move to follow. He couldn't.

He'd almost killed a man.

Alone in the alley, he leaned his head back against the cold stone wall. His breath came in pants. He should have ended the bastard, denied that little voice in his head that said to stop when he felt Ezekiel's life slipping out of his body. Now, Ezekiel would return to Jasper Finn with several new bruises. Finn had seemed like a cocksure scoundrel. He would retaliate for the damage done to his property.

A life for a life. Dalton's life to protect Jasper Finn's operations. Kate's life to clear his name.

Daniel scrubbed a hand through his hair, clutching at the roots until his scalp protested. He ought to feel pain, ought to bear the injuries done to Kate. No matter how she justified it, he couldn't help but feel responsible. She never would have been at Friggard's Pawn if it wasn't for him.

Pushing back against the wall with his foot, he shoved his hands into his pockets. Kate needed new clothes to replace those damaged in the explosion, and he had little food left in the flat. One step at a time. He proceeded down the street, finally coming to the secondhand clothes shop Atlas had recommended. With the help of an overly friendly shopgirl, he purchased a dress, stays, and a shift for Kate.

By the time he left the market, it was mid-morning. He had crossed through seven other streets instead of taking a straight route back to the boarding house. By the time he turned the corner to take him back toward Madame Tousat's, he was certain that no one was following him—no one person stood out.

He passed by the open doors of a public house. People spilled in and out, the cheery sounds of music pouring forth into the street. Daniel lingered in the doorway, readjusted the bag of groceries in his arms.

He breathed in deeply. A year ago, he was in a tavern like this one, gin in hand. Convinced he'd never return to London, that the only thing he had to keep him sane was the spirits. He wanted the blue ruin—no, he needed it, if he was to keep Kate safe. Without it, he'd cave under the stress.

His head pounded. His body ached. Every injury was magnified in this door frame.

A man emerged from inside the public house, leaving through the door where Daniel stood motionless. "You goin' in?"

Daniel started, gripping the groceries closer to his chest. "No." He shook his head, cheeks burning.

"Best move on." The man nodded at him, getting lost in the traffic of the street a minute later.

Torn from his daze, Daniel's eyes finally focused on the guests inside the public house. He saw their imperfections: the reddened nose of a boy chimney sweep, perched high on the stool with as much world-weariness as a man twice his age; the harsh growl of a man as the bar wench came to take his glass without letting him finish the dregs. The bar wench's crimson bed jacket was rumpled, the apron tied at her waist heavily stained. He watched as she snatched an abandoned drink from an empty table, knocking back the contents.

She smiled at him but no feeling echoed in her bleak eyes. Once, he'd been just like her, but not anymore.

He turned away, out into the street.

THE DOOR OPENED. Daniel's head poked in, his flaming red hair glinting in the sunlight. Relief clutched at Kate's throat, tightening until she could barely gasp out a breath.

"Good morning," he said with a sweet smile that loosened up her chest, making it possible to breathe.

He'd come back.

"I hoped to sneak back in before you noticed." In his arms was a bag of groceries, a loaf of bread sticking out of the top. He set the groceries down on the table and drew out a folded bundle, tossing it to her.

She was starving, had been for hours. Catching the bundle in one hand, she looked toward the food with longing.

He chuckled. "Your present first, then the food."

She looked up at him, eyes widening as she took in his harried appearance. A bruise colored his cheek. His pants were ripped at the knee and his greatcoat was stained with grime.

"What happened to you? Who hurt you?"

He shrugged off his greatcoat, tossing it to the side. "I don't want you to worry. I've taken care of it."

"That's not an explanation."

"You are recovering, Katiebelle. Let me take care of you." He motioned to the package in her lap. "Open it."

She sat up straighter on the bed. Her grip upon the sheet increased, knuckles whitened. She could bloody well handle life on her own terms—and if he was hurt, she wanted to be able to help him.

"I won't be coddled by you," she avowed. "Either tell me who hurt you, or I shall rise from this bed, get the gun, and bash it over your overprotective head."

He rolled his eyes, the image of insolence. Like her threats meant nothing to him anymore.

"I am not going to embark upon a battle of wills with you, Daniel. *Tell* me."

"You are a wretched patient." He removed his coat and rolled his shirtsleeves up. From the bag, he lifted out bread, meat, and cheese.

"And you are a wretched liar."

Daniel picked a knife up off the table. "Do you remember the beggar we saw outside the Red Fist?"

"No. London is full of beggars," she replied.

With quick, precise movements he sliced the bread. "I saw him before we met Mason, and then after. There was something strange about him but I didn't place it until he bumped in to me today. I knew it somehow, that he was connected to Finn. When he said his name was Ezekiel—the same Ezekiel from Atlas's list—I cornered him and I told him to take a message to Finn."

"Shit." She swung her legs over the side of the bed. One foot on the ground, then the other, and she could be closer to him. Run her hands over his chest and make sure that the wounds didn't need more attention.

He turned around, arching a brow when he saw her trying to stand. "Careful now. I need you in better shape, if this is an indication of what's to come."

She stayed put on the edge of the bed. Her head swam with explosions and fights and everything in between. If she went to him now, she'd never come back.

"How are you feeling?" She pulled on the edge of the white shirtsleeves she wore. His clothing.

"I've had worse. He was spry, I'll give him that." Daniel set down the knife to rub at his ribcage, wincing. "And he had rotten placement to hit me where the shrapnel cut. But at least now we know another player in the game. I don't know if I made things worse for us."

"At this point I don't think it makes a bit of difference." Kate sighed. She couldn't get rid of the sinking feeling that there was something they were missing, beyond Finn, beyond Bartleby, beyond Dalton's murder. Originally, she'd gotten involved in this to save her father's memory from further tarnishing.

It should have been simple. Now that she knew Emporia wasn't involved, she should leave.

But she wouldn't.

He passed her a plate full of bread and meat. "I know you said you didn't want to move, but I really must insist upon it now. That letter was slipped under your door—so someone obviously knows where you live."

She took a bite of the bread and sausage and then another to buy time. He was right. But where else could she go?

"But my flat has my goods for fencing," she said, as if that could negate his logic.

"I'm not saying you have to leave forever. You can move back when we catch Finn."

"It is not as if I can afford another flat." She barely had enough money to afford this place. The landlord here was lenient because he knew Jane; she couldn't count on that connection somewhere else.

"You could move in with me," he suggested, ever-hopeful. "We don't have to stay here. We can go wherever you like."

Move in with you when your trunk remains packed.

She glanced down at the food again. He had sliced the sausage in two and placed on top of the bread. The meal was simple, neat in arrangement. Everything that getting back together with Daniel was not.

"I'm not ready for that step," she said.

His face fell, but in a second his expression had returned to normal. "I'll have Atlas find you a temporary flat. Something Finn can't find."

Her fingers tightened around the plate. This little flat was her entire world. A chair by the door, the bed with the lumpy mattress, her armoire and the portrait of Papa on top of her desk. When she couldn't deal with the rest of the world, she'd come home to the flat.

"It won't be so bad, Katiebelle." Daniel smiled encouragingly. "We'll leave in a bit. But for now, open your present."

The bundle was on the bed next to her. Lifting it up, she untied the ribbon holding it together. A simple cotton chemise was on the top, which she lifted out and placed on the bed. Underneath the shift was a hunter green gown printed with tiny flowers and dots. The long sleeves held a slight puff at the shoulders and the empire waist was pleated, dropping down to a full skirt.

"For me?" She ran her fingers across cool, crisp cotton.

"No, I thought I'd start a collection of women's millinery," Daniel teased. "Of course it's for you. As much as I'd like to keep you forever in my shirt, you'll need something to wear if you want to leave this flat."

She spread out the dress on her lap. Daniel's gaze swept down her frame, hooded eyes taking in all her curves. Her nipples tightened at the heat of his stare, arching without her permission. Ready for his touch.

If they fell back into bed, for a few moments she'd think of something other than the threat surrounding them. That would be easy, but it'd only add further complications.

She brought the dress up to her shoulders. "It's beautiful. Where did you get it?"

"They're not stolen, if that's what you're asking. I went to a bow-wow shop. I remembered one Atlas had spoken of last week, and told the owner I was a friend of the Gentleman Thief. He gave me a good discount." He pulled the last item from the bag, ivory small boots.

The leather was worn along the heel, and there was discoloration at the tip of both boots, but otherwise the boots appeared to be in good condition. Far better than her own dilapidated boots, with the soles separating and the leather cracking.

She shrugged. "I wouldn't care if they were filched."

He looked at her skeptically, one brow arched as he sliced into the hunk of cheese.

"I forgot to thank you for not calling the doctor," she said, for it was the first thing she could think of that wouldn't add to the heat between them.

Neither of them had the money to afford a house call from her old Bloomsbury physician.

In Ratcliffe, any man could open a shop and claim he was a surgeon. Hell, she'd even seen a man wheeling about the street with a monkey on his shoulder, "free medicine" painted on the back of his donkey cart. There was nothing to stop those unscrupulous doctors from taking advantage of their patients.

Daniel grinned. "Given our current problems with exhumators, I wasn't about to chance someone might decide you'd make a lovely fit for their anatomizing."

"How sweet of you, to not want to share the room with a dissected corpse." She smiled in spite of herself.

He chuckled. "My healthy fear of maggots has served me well this far. I see no reason to repent."

They ate in silence for a moment, a companionable, too-familiar quiet. She opened her mouth to speak, as Daniel set down his hunk of bread onto the plate.

"I didn't kill him."

She blinked, surprised by his admission. "I've said before that I knew you didn't."

"No. Not Dalton. Ezekiel."

"I see." She took another bite, chewing slowly.

He clasped his hands together over his knee, the plate balanced precariously in his lap. "I'm not that man anymore, an uncoiled bruiser who will brawl over anything." He didn't look at her, a flush spreading across his cheeks.

She refused to give in to the urge to take his hand in hers.

"So you fought before, and you drank before. In the past."

"I didn't want you to think I'd gone back," he said.

"I don't think that," she countered. He was not the man she'd loved before.

This version of him was even more dangerous to her, for he was sincere, passionate, and doggedly determined to win her heart back.

CHAPTER 16

THE FOLLOWING AFTERNOON, Daniel knocked on the door of Kate's transitory flat in Bethnal Green. His heart beat fast, pulse rapid.

His skin was cold and clammy to touch. The late morning breakfast together had only gone passably well, and she had been reluctant to stay in the quarters Atlas found for her. How reticent she was to separate from this new identity, when she'd so gladly shove him away for what he'd done.

She opened the door mid-way, the point of her pistol stuck in the gap. "Whatever business you have, turn around."

"Christ, Kate. It's just me," he said, stepping back from the door so that she could see him in the tiny crack.

"Oh." She lowered the gun and pulled the door open all the way for him to enter. "You could have told me last night that you were coming."

"I didn't expect you to be armed." He shut the door behind him. A frown crossed his lips. They'd slept together again. He ought to be able to show up without a reason.

"I am always armed." She looked perturbed that he didn't already know that, as if he'd offended her sense of self. Placing the flintlock down on a chair, she moved toward the tea kettle.

Shrugging off his coat and hanging it on the doorknob, he looked around her room. Sun penetrated through the midday fog. This flat was bigger than her last place, or perhaps it merely looked that way when it wasn't crammed with her furniture. She'd taken a few dresses with her, the portrait of her father, that gigantic greatcoat, and her gun. Atlas had provided a few essentials, but the flat felt sparse when compared to her own.

It was temporary, something to make do.

God, he hoped she didn't think that about him.

She opened a paste box, nose wrinkling at the contents. "I have no tea. I'm afraid I am a rotten hostess."

"I had tea before I left."

"Oh," she said again, setting the box down.

Her hair was done up nicely. Despite the dull gold fabric of her dress, her skin no longer had a languid pallor to it. Good. Even the cut to her forehead appeared less vivid. He breathed a sigh of relief.

"I wanted to see how you were feeling," he said.

"Better. The thrumming in my head has ceased." She nodded, forcing a half-smile.

"And the aches?"

"Better as well. I am still sore though."

He sounded like a bloody doctor, emotionally detached. Asinine. He took a step forward, wanting to reach for her hand but stopping himself in time. She didn't meet his gaze.

"Have you had any more thoughts on my proposal?"

She spoke at the same time. "I was thinking we should visit Bartleby."

"I wanted to tell you—" He paused, as her words sunk in. "You want to pay a call on the man who might have tried to kill us?"

She tilted her head to one side. "How else do you think we should get information?"

"You almost died. Pardon me if I'm reluctant to drop my card and have a spot of tea with a potential madman."

"We will prepare more this time." She picked up the flintlock, rifling through the top drawer built into the table and drawing out a cloth and lead balls. Methodically, she began to load the pistol. She slid the rod into the barrel, pushing the cloth and lead ball inside. His mouth grew dry at the motion.

Up and down she pumped, like her hands on him before. He wanted to return to that place of passion, where he'd been so damn convinced of her feelings for him.

"I don't think it's wise, Kate." His voice sounded strangled.

She didn't seem to notice. "We have no evidence yet, only a set of accusations from a bruiser looking to blame anyone he can and a prostitute. When they arrested you, the constable at least had an eyewitness who claimed to have seen you. False, I know, but more than we've got." She latched the rod back onto the gun with practiced precision. "I don't see that we have any choice. Besides, I'd sincerely like to shove the barrel of my Forsyth in his face."

He rolled his eyes. "We need a plan outside of you barging in with a pistol. One can't succeed on bravado alone."

"I disagree. It's gotten me this far."

"Be smart about this."

She set the gun down on the table by the window and turned to face him, jaw set stubbornly. "The bastard conspired to end us, and I want an explanation. You said Atlas found his address, so I think we should go there. Better to question him than to go after Jasper Finn directly. Finn has a gang of men to protect him, while Bartleby is a messenger."

"Shoot the messenger, win the war, or something like it?"

"Or in your case, beat the messenger to a bloody pulp."

He met her gaze with a smirk. She looked quickly away but he'd seen it: a wink, so quick that if he blinked he would have missed it.

Cheeky chit.

"You like it when I defend your honor." He crossed the room, closing the distance between them. "Yes, I know,

Katiebelle. You're brave and strong. I love that about you, but you need me."

"No, I don't," she objected, her lower lip quivering.

"You know you do, and that's not a sign of weakness. I need you too. I'll keep you safe if you keep me sane." He grabbed her waist, tugging her closer to him. Her hands went up, as if to fight him off, and then fell on his shoulders to brace herself.

His lips crashed down upon hers. Press to press he devoured her, tasting her until he had his fill. He pulled back to gauge her reaction. Breathing ragged. Hands shaking.

She grabbed for him, pulling him closer to her and kissing him fiercely. Angling his chin, she took the kiss deeper, tongue thrusting in his mouth.

Didn't love him, his blooming arse.

He turned her, forcing her up against the wall. Her palm stretched out on the glass pane to hold her steady, chest pressed up against the window. She was his and his alone.

His hands roamed her body, squeezing her waist, massaging her taut breasts, falling in at the pockets on her dress and pinching the tender flesh of her upper thighs. He pushed her hair away from her neck, bringing his lips down hard. Her head lolled back against his chest and with better access to her neck, he bit at the point where her swan neck joined her shoulders. Like a cannon, her breathing came quick-quick-fire. Her hand went back to tug his head closer upon her skin.

Then he was off of her, stepping back without remorse, ignoring his own hardened erection in favor of teaching her a lesson. She played loose and fast with his heart. A step forward with her meant two back.

"I'll see you tomorrow to go to Bartleby's then. May we find our bomber."

She inhaled deeply, desire-clouded eyes popping open. For a second she looked surprised.

He'd left her wanting.

LAURENCE BARTLEBY RENTED a small townhouse in Westminster, far enough from the edges of St. Giles to be deemed reputable yet too far from the fashionable district to be desirable. His section of the four-story narrow building consisted of the left half of the stucco-fronted exterior.

"For a man who lost his job, he certainly is doing well," Daniel said, as he extended a hand to help Kate down from the hack.

Her hand came to rest on his arm as a proper woman did with her escort. He turned to her, brow arched and about to comment, when he saw her face. Her lips were set in a line so thin as to be barely visible. Her eyes were dark.

Of course she'd be upset, he realized with a start. The snake Bartleby, culpable in the bankruptcy of Emporia, resided in relative wealth. She instead had been forced from her family's home through no fault of her own.

"Shall we?" He asked, cocking his head toward the looming townhouse.

Sunlight splashed across her high cheekbones as they stood on the street. She ran a hand across the folds of her skirt to straighten out the wrinkles from the carriage. She wore the same blue plaid dress as when they'd gone to Jacob's Island, but this time she'd paired it with a gray pelisse instead of her father's greatcoat. Regally, she held her head high and her shoulders back. The dress suited her willowy frame perfectly, from the full skirt to the circular bodice. For a second he simply watched her move, struck by her.

She was magnificent, and soon, he'd make her realize this.

Her nose wrinkled as they stepped onto the stoop, as though she'd smelled something rancid. Daniel knocked.

No one came.

"You'd think he'd have servants, the pompous arse," Kate sniffed.

He could easily imagine Bartleby deriving great joy from

being able to order around servants. He had lost count of the number of times the accountant had barked a racial slur at him, even though he had been Bartleby's superior.

Daniel knocked again. Still no answer.

On his third try, Kate stopped him mid-raise of his hand. She pulled out her flintlock, ramming the door with the butt of the gun. "Bartleby, you pathetic mongrel! You worthless coward! Come out here, before I break this door down and drag you out by your balls!"

Daniel would have paid good money to see that. "Are you quite done?"

"No." She banged the door once more with the pistol butt before turning to face him. "Now I am."

The lock turned. The door was partially opened. "Listen here, I don't know who you think you are but—" A lean, cavernous face peered out the door and stopped mid-sentence as he recognized them. "Miss Katherine," the man sputtered.

"Bartleby." She greeted him flatly, disdain chalked on her face. "Pardon me if I don't bother with an honorific. You did try to kill me, after all."

"What?" Bartleby blinked rapidly.

"Let us in." She pushed at the door with her flintlock, opening it wide enough that Daniel was visible as well.

Bartleby's thin face turned ashen. His nostrils flared. "O'Reilly. I heard you were dead."

Daniel shrugged. "I'm sorry to report that rumors of my demise have been greatly exaggerated."

Bartleby could not close the door with Kate's pistol wedged so firmly. Morgan had kept Bartleby because he was a "damn good accountant." Kept him despite his surly manner, kept him despite his lack of regard for anyone but himself.

Kate pushed the door open all the way, barging into the townhouse.

"You can't—"

"Best not fight her." He closed the door behind Bartleby.

Daniel took a good look at Bartleby. His shoulders were

hunched, his gaunt frame so insubstantial that a steady push might send him reeling to the ground. Bartleby had never been this reedy before. The accountant wore a silver waistcoat of good quality cloth that didn't taper to his chest, yet his fitted shirt was of cheap linen. His breeches were large and baggy.

"I really don't have the foggiest notion of what you're gadding on about, or why you're here. Please leave, and take O'Reilly with you." Bartleby looked furtively toward the door, as if assessing his escape routes.

"What? No 'Paddy'? No 'Bog-Trotter'?" A slow smirk slid across Daniel's lips as his leaned back against the door. Unless there was another entrance onto this side of the street, the accountant would have to use the window if he wanted to leave.

It wasn't exactly equal revenge for Bartleby's attempts at humiliating him over the years, but it'd do.

Bartleby followed his movements uneasily. "I don't want any trouble. Whatever money I've got you can take."

Daniel shook his head. "I don't need to steal from those who are ill."

"He tried to blow us into tiny-sized Kate and Daniel bits. I should think his mental sickness is obvious," Kate scoffed.

"No." Daniel gestured to Bartleby. "Your waistcoat and breeches are of good quality but your shirt is cheap, as though you had to replace it recently with ready-made. Probably due to your weight loss from the illness, I'd think. Medical bills can be quite harsh on the extravagant dandy's budget. Pity for your wardrobe you haven't the blunt to pay your tailor."

"No one pays tradesmen," Bartleby huffed.

"You do realize you were an accountant, correct?" Kate walked further into the house, ignoring Bartleby's attempts to herd her back toward the door. She entered the small parlor off to the side, plopping down in a gold embroidered armchair. "Cushy." She stretched out in the chair, head back as a cat in a sunbeam. The flintlock lay across her lap.

She was enjoying herself far too much, but he couldn't

blame her.

Bartleby perched on the couch. Like a bird's talons, his spindly fingers gripped the arm with nails dug into the fabric. "Why are you here, Katherine?"

She crossed her ankles, a debonair queen on a gold throne. From her pocket she fished out the offensive foolscap. "Here is what is going to happen. You are going to tell us exactly why you sent this note." She leaned over, passing the foolscap to Bartleby.

Bartleby put his glasses back on, reading the note. "I never sent this." He passed the paper back to Kate with a shrug.

"It is your signature," Daniel said.

"That it is a decent representation of my name I don't doubt. Regardless, I never sent it."

"Then who did?"

"King William?" Bartleby's sarcasm was broken off by a coughing fit. His entire body shook, head falling to his knees from the violence.

"How long do you have?" Daniel asked.

Bartleby rose shakily, hobbling to the wine cabinet by the window. He poured from the glass bottle of claret, drops of the red liquid splashing onto the wood.

Red, red drops like the blood in Ezekiel's nose. Wine that once had danced on his tongue seductively in spirit's kiss.

"Two months, to approximate." Bartleby took a sip of claret, gasping as the alcohol burned his throat. The accountant made his way back to the chair, absorbed in his own thoughts. "I hate approximates. There's no beauty to be found in a number one can't define."

He should feel some level of pity for the accountant, but he felt nothing. Did that make him deadened inside? He didn't know, and at that moment, he didn't care.

Bartleby sucked down another sip of wine. Daniel watched as he swallowed, the muscles of his throat straining. Claret had never been his favorite, but it'd do the job as well as any other. It would help him to make sense of the insanity that was his relationship with Kate.

He shook his head to rid it of the images. This was not the time to submit to old habits.

"But I guess death is the final number of them all." Bartleby sighed.

"I'd think you would like obscure mathematics. After all, isn't that what you used to hide your stealing from Papa's company?" Kate's voice held an edge he could not place. Anger, bitterness, fury...or a combination of all three that seethed and bubbled under her icy exterior.

Bartleby's glance flickered to Daniel, ignoring Kate. "You wonder why Morgan would keep an odious bastard like me on staff. He always liked charity cases—you should know that best of all."

Daniel bristled, his hand clenched around the arm of the chair. "I believe Morgan had his reasons."

Reasons which he had begun to suspect were not so noble after all. Could Morgan really not have known about Bartleby's misappropriation? The two had met weekly to go over the books.

"Daniel worked for his salary. He didn't steal, unlike you," Kate sneered.

Her defense of him made up for Bartleby's rudeness. In fact, he half-wished the accountant would insult him again so he could see the outraged flush of color on her cheeks.

No matter how she might protest, she cared for him. He needed no further proof.

"Grin all you want, O'Reilly, but I know you suspect the truth. Good for you." Bartleby's voice was laced with condescension. "That's the wisest you'll ever be."

Kate huffed. "Daniel knows my father had nothing to do with this. *You* tried to have us killed, Bartleby, and I demand to know why."

"Miss Katherine, I will tell you what really happened with your father's company. I've got two months left, what are they going to me now?" Bartleby tilted his head toward Daniel. "But not with him here. I may be dying, but I still have my pride."

Kate sent him a disbelieving look, so hard that the accountant cowered under the weight of her stare. "He stays."

She wanted him to remain, wanted his help to fight her battles. Daniel was buoyed, even though he knew she'd deny it all.

"And you will tell me what I want to know," she continued. "Because of the people in this room you should be afraid of, it's me, not Daniel." She lifted the flintlock from her lap, distractedly fingering the trigger on the half-cocked gun.

"You honestly expect me to believe Morgan's spoiled pet would know how to shoot that?" Forgetting himself, Bartleby crowed with laughter.

In the blink of an eye, Kate had the gun fully cocked, and aimed. She squeezed the trigger. The bullet sailed, smashing into an expensive-looking vase on the mantel. The vase shattered, mint green tulip shards flung across the oriental carpet.

Bartleby dissolved in another fit of coughs.

Daniel grinned, shamelessly proud of her. Damn, he liked that gun when it wasn't pointed at him.

"You were saying?" Kate snickered.

"Ah." Bartleby flinched. "I was saying that I have been many things in my life, but a smuggler is not one of them. Whatever money I hid on the books, it was because Morgan requested I do so. It was he who was embezzling, not me."

"You lie." Kate was up on her feet, furious. The pistol swung at her side.

Devil take it, she'd shoot Bartleby. He crossed over to her, reaching for the gun. When she wouldn't release it, he covered her hand with his own. "Come, Kate," he urged, voice low. "Release the gun, love."

"Adorable," Bartleby muttered. "Kate blusters and her Paddy defends. Nothing has changed."

Daniel wrenched the gun finally from Kate's grip, uncocking it. He turned on Bartleby, words uttered through clenched teeth. "What did you say?"

"Nothing." The accountant propped his jaundiced chin up on his hands, as if the act of holding up his own head was becoming too taxing.

Two months. Doubtful. Whatever information they wanted from Bartleby, they better get it fast.

Bartleby blinked. "Morgan would come to me periodically, in the last few years of Emporia."

Kate took a deep breath, chest shaking with barely contained fury. She opened her mouth for another harsh retort. Daniel grabbed for her hand, squeezing it. She inhaled again, composing herself. In a second he felt her squeeze back.

"He got involved with some very bad people, Miss Katherine. Have you heard of resurrection men?"

CHAPTER 17

EVERYTHING LAURENCE BARTLEBY said was false.

Kate's heart beat once against her chest and stopped. Her breath died without being released. There could be no other explanation but that he was a vicious liar out to smear the last shreds of her father's good name.

"I am aware of such villains." Her voice was eerily flat, when all she wanted to do was scream.

Daniel's hand clenched around hers. He rooted her to this spot. She couldn't even throw her hands up around her ears and block out the vile sounds of Bartleby's nasal words.

"I would not call them villains, when your father was in league with them." Bartleby's reddened eyes took on a gleeful sheen. "Unless you wish to class your dear Papa as a dastardly blackguard, in which case I should rightly agree."

"My father was a good man. A better man than you, you unrepentant arse." She spat out the insult, for it was dirt on her tongue.

Grave dirt.

"Oh, Miss Katherine, how I have missed your spunk." Bartleby's thin lips curled into a sneer.

"I'll show you spunk—"

Daniel maneuvered himself half in front of her, cutting her off. "Let the man talk, Katiebelle," he murmured.

"So that he can spread more lies? I think not." In a fit of rage, she wrenched her hand from Daniel's. Quick steps took her toward Bartleby.

"Hit me, if you like. It shall not change what your Papa did. How do you think I got the funds for this townhouse?" Bartleby shrugged bony shoulders.

She clenched her fist, nails biting into her palm. The quick sting of pain centered her. "You stole from Emporia."

"Only what your father failed to provide for me. We had a deal, him and me. I'd hide his illicit activities so the Board wouldn't realize he was taking from the company, and he'd make sure I was set for life." Bartleby's eyes narrowed, slits seen through his wire-rimmed glasses. "Then the bastard died. What I was supposed to do? No one wanted to hire the accountant from a business that had gone bankrupt. As if it was my fault!"

"How exactly was Morgan involved?" Daniel faced Bartleby with a blank expression.

His lack of emotion shot through her. Did he not care at all? This was her *father* they discussed as if he were a common criminal!

Bartleby tapped his fingers against the arm of his chair. "I learned of the smuggling a year into my employment at Emporia. Morgan started small at first, just a few crates of wine every other month to avoid the duty."

Six years. Six years Papa had been working with Bartleby. She had known he smuggled wine crates occasionally—every shipping company did—but this sounded far worse. It couldn't be true.

"He was overly cautious, afraid the authorities would find him."

Yet that sounded like Papa. He'd always had an exit strategy.

Daniel didn't hide his skepticism. "That's a hell of a leap

to make, from smuggling wine to selling bodies for ready money."

"When I confronted him I convinced him to seek other lucrative means." Bartleby had no shame, proud of what he'd done.

"You! You're to blame." Her voice shook.

"For the resurrection men? Hardly. That was all Morgan and Finn. I merely convinced him we could up the cases without anyone noticing, as long as I hid it. I needed to make it worth my while, Miss Katherine. Surely an enterprising woman such as you can understand that." He arched a brow, his viper gaze sliding down her form.

A chill settled in her spine.

Daniel was by her side in an instant. His eyes glinted, dangerous and wild. "If you insinuate one more thing, Bartleby, I will make sure the Runners know exactly what you've done."

"How do you plan to do that, O'Reilly, when they want you far more than they'd care about a dying man?"

"I have contacts," Daniel asserted.

"Through who, the Gentleman Thief?"

Daniel's hand faltered halfway to her arm. "How did you—"

"Did you think I didn't know about Atlas Greer? Morgan knew too—in fact, he thought it'd make you more willing to help him. Why do you think he encouraged Miss Katherine to set her cap at you?" Smugly, Bartleby smiled, paper-thin skin stretching ghoulishly.

Daniel's face hardened. He took a step back from her, a step so small it was barely noticeable, but she felt it like it was a chasm.

"Daniel, you know Papa never thought that," she cried, bridging the gap between them. She reached for his hand, his palm hanging limply in the grasp of her slighter fingers. "He hired you because he knew you could do the best damn job of anyone. Because you're smart, and you work hard, unlike *some* people."

Bartleby snorted. "When you turned out to be honorable, Morgan backed off of you. He realized he was never going to push you into our world."

Daniel's jaw clenched. His shoulders were set back, his free hand balled into a fist like he would gladly punch the nearest person. He believed every lie Bartleby spouted, ignoring what he'd known before of Papa's character.

"Let's go." She tugged on his hand, pulling him toward the door.

He didn't move. His hand clenched tight around her own. "I want to hear the rest."

"You can't believe this." Her pleas fell on deaf ears, yet she had to keep talking. No one would defend Papa but her. "He's telling you whatever he can to incriminate Papa because it makes his sick mind feel vindicated."

Bartleby stifled a yawn. "Miss Katherine, I don't have to invent stories. Richard Morgan was a pathetic waste of space. He lacked the vision to turn the enterprise into something truly lucrative. In fact, if Jasper Finn hadn't uncovered his smuggling in the first place, I doubt there would have been enough money left for me to survive on."

Papa had always been there for her. After her mother had left when she was eight, instead of hiring a governess and forgetting about her entirely, he'd taken an active role in her education and life. Almost every night he made a point to share supper with her and ask about her day. He'd provided her for every step of the way, until he left her alone with no funds.

Papa couldn't have anticipated that Daniel would leave her, or that he'd become ill so quickly. He'd intended for her to be set for life.

She glanced toward Daniel, yet he looked at Bartleby. He had no eyes for her, no condolences for the ruination of the man who had raised her. That was fine; she didn't need sympathy when she knew Bartleby's claims to be false.

"How did Morgan get involved with Finn?" Daniel asked.

"I'm not sure how he managed to uncover what we were doing. I learned early on to never question how Finn got information, only to trust in its veracity. But what did I care, when it meant thrice my normal income?" Bartleby took a long sip of wine. "Finn needed a better place to store his cadavers before transport, and what better place than Emporia's warehouses? If they were found, his hands would be clean."

She'd finally caught him in a lie. "I knew those warehouses better than my own house. If there were dead bodies stored in them, I would have known about it."

"Do you remember the long boxes that Morgan claimed were full of fresh fish for the butcher?"

Her mouth fell open, but she couldn't think enough to shut it. "You can't possibly mean—"

"What better storage for a Subject? Filled to the brim with ice to slow the decomposition, the body could sit while Finn found a wanting surgeon. Sped things up dramatically, for he could take more corpses without having a prior buyer. I could be living in Mayfair now, if Finn hadn't cut me out." Bartleby's drawn, unhealthy face darkened. "But I'll have my revenge, if the look on your lover's face is any indication."

Kate glanced over at Daniel. He was stoic, lips pursed and shoulders back. No reaction anywhere but his cold eyes. It was if something had been turned off in him, leaving him void.

"Why me?" He asked the simplest question.

When she had so many questions that she couldn't sort through them all to find the truth.

Bartleby blinked at him. "Why you, what?"

Like a dam breaking, emotion spilled into Daniel. His pale Irish skin flushed, his voice broke with rage. He stood directly in front of Bartleby's chair, his knees smashed against the elderly man's. Grabbing for Bartleby's cravat, he pulled the accountant up until Bartleby met his gaze.

"If Morgan wasn't going to involve me, why was I drugged and left in a goddamn alley? Why was I framed for Tommy Dalton's murder? What did you gain from ruining my life, you self-serving prick?"

His hand wrapped in the cravat, twisting. Bartleby let out a strangled gasp. Kate held her breath. Everything was happening too fast for her to stop it.

But then Daniel released Bartleby and backed away. He exhaled, shoulders trembling. Bartleby descended into another coughing fit. Kate crossed to the wine cabinet and poured him another glass of water. That was as much charity as she could muster; she wanted to let him suffer, to die before them a shriveled wreck ravaged by illness. Exactly like her father.

The accountant found his voice, his eyes never leaving Daniel's face "Because you are a monster. You are a bog-trotting brute, not fit to wipe the dust from my boots. And Finn knew it. He saw you for what you are: a disease, contaminating good solid English flesh when you tupped Miss Katherine here. You think I didn't know about your little nightly activities? Everyone could see it in your eyes."

"You are vile." Kate's hand darted forward. The glass of water tipped as her fingers connected, upending the contents in Bartleby's lap. He sputtered, brushing at the water frantically. The glass remained intact.

Devil take it.

"Morgan didn't think that. He defended me," Daniel murmured.

"No, it was Morgan's damn belief in you that made Finn peg you. He needed to get rid of Dalton and you'd harm our operations," Bartleby said. "You'd be the first to rat us out, when the time came."

"I'll kill Finn," Daniel vowed.

"You and your copious contacts?" Bartleby scoffed. "Best of luck to you then. Send him my regards."

She tugged on Daniel's hand in an attempt at leading him toward the door. He remained, Hessians pressed deep into the luxurious carpet, jaw clenched.

"We are done here," she hissed, with another pull to his hand.

He started, as if registering her voice for the first time. His grip on her hand tightened. Allowing her to lead him toward the door, he stopped when Bartleby called to them again.

"Oh, Miss Katherine?"

She didn't turn around. Let him call, for she was done with his lies.

But Daniel cocked his head, urging Bartleby on. The chair creaked as Bartleby pushed himself up, hobbling over toward them. He went to slide something between her right arm and side.

She caught his wrist, digging her nails into his tender flesh until he yelped in pain. "Don't you touch me, you bloody blackleg."

"I thought you would want your father's ledger." He held out a leather bound volume. Embossed on the front cover was the seal for Emporia. For three years she'd looked for it in every secondhand shop she passed.

She snatched the journal from his hands, the weight of it somehow reassuring. "I ought to shoot you for keeping this."

Bartleby held tight to the door frame. "Would you prefer I have handed it over to the Thames River Police? I did you a favor."

"Don't do us anymore favors," Daniel said.

As they left, Kate's mind spun with frantic possibilities. Finn had taken Daniel from her and tried to kill her. Had her father really had been involved with resurrection men?

She feared even her memories were no longer whole.

CHAPTER 18

THE HACK THAT pulled up to the waystation in Westminster was intolerably small. Every rut in the road jostled them on top of each other. Kate's skirt was flung up over his leg, while his shoulder rubbed against hers. His scent filled her nose, penetrating every last crevice in her mind until she breathed in only Daniel.

Kate needed silence. She needed to be alone. In the temporary flat, she could sprawl out on the bed and comb over her father's ledger in peace. There she'd find the answers she sought: Bartleby was a liar and Papa hadn't been involved at all.

She smoothed a hand over invisible wrinkles in her skirt. Had her father truly helped to set up Daniel? She thought of the O'Reilly ring, tucked away until she could bear to fence it.

Daniel broke the quiet. "Christ, that meeting."

"Hmm?" She blinked at him.

"He told us everything." Resting his elbow on his knee, two fingers spread across the bridge of his brow, he was a man bereft.

"He told us nothing. Surely you don't believe Bartleby's falsehoods." She undid the knot underneath her chin and removed her bonnet. There was no clarity to be found in this carriage, but at least, she could dispense with the obscurity of the wide-brimmed fabric.

"What reason would he have to lie? The man is dying, Kate. The doctor was being charitable in his estimation. I doubt he has more than a month left." Daniel sighed.

She turned to face him. "Hatred for my father is as good of a reason as any."

Daniel grimaced. "So he lies to your face, and takes the real murderer with him to his grave? That defies logic. Bartleby is not a valiant man. If he could earn a small bit of fame by lording his knowledge over you, he'd do it. By his own omission, he wants revenge on Finn for ending his windfall."

This was not the time to discuss this. Later, when she'd had a moment with the journal, they could broach the subject. "Remember who you are speaking about, Daniel. You expect me to believe the words of a fraudulent accountant over what I knew of my own father?"

"When it could save my neck, yes, I certainly do," he snapped.

He asked too much of her. He started to reach for her, but stopped when she spoke.

She didn't flinch from his gaze. "I can't do that. Can't you see I need time?"

He pulled back completely from her, pressed himself up against the window. "Do you love me so little that you wish to see me hang?"

"My love for you—whatever I may feel—has little to do with my feelings for the man who raised me. Don't try to draw comparisons when none can be made." She spoke through gritted teeth, each word a warning to him that he should drop the issue.

"I've done everything you asked, Katiebelle," he pleaded, desperation lacing his voice. "I've stayed by your side every time you'd have me these past two weeks. I've let you use me as a veritable punching bag. I've apologized more times than I can count, only to have you hurl my sins back into my face. And I'd do it all again, if it meant I could win your heart, but I won't put my life on hold so you can play pretend with your memories."

He thought everything she did—everything she was now—was naught but a joke.

She spun on him, shifting her weight so quickly that she elbowed him in the chest so hard it knocked his breath away.

"You left," she hissed, low and lethal. "Then you returned out of nowhere. You were kind to me, and so I should fall at your feet, forsaking all else for the greatness of Daniel O'Reilly. Forget what I knew before, forget the family I mourn every day, forget the woman I've become because you decree it to be so. Because some wretch claims what is obviously a lie!"

"Your father worked with resurrection men. How much more evidence must be put before your eyes before you open them?" He snatched the ledger off her lap, waving it in her face. "How about this? Will you even looked at the contents, or are you too damned scared of what you'll find?" He flipped through the foolscap. A page ripped under his harsh thumb.

She cried out, snatching the journal from him.

"You care more about this bleeding journal than you do for me," he spat.

"That's not true." She cradled the journal in her hands, as far from his reach as she could get in the jammed hack.

"Admit it, Katiebelle. Admit that you'd rather have me take the fall for your father's crimes than him." He reached forward, grabbing her chin between his forefingers in a vice grip.

"Let me go!"

He didn't release her.

"Daniel, please," she pleaded. "Please, can't we rest? I need time to process all of this. I bedded you again, for God's sake. Do you really believe that means nothing to me?"

He dropped his hand to his side. Her shoulders shook as

she sucked in air. Her cheeks burned, but she didn't retreat, her face so close to his she could snatch a kiss from his quivering lips.

His hand fell upon hers, skin that sizzled through her resistances. She wanted to give in to his touch, to believe that eventually, with time, he'd understand. He would move on from the rage that built up within him and realize that this was lunacy—surely Papa could not be involved. She laid her forehead down on his, breathed in his spicy scent. This could all be fixed, if she simply waited.

She tilted her head back, kissing him. Lips to lips in a desperate lock that left them both breathless, yet unwilling to pull away, for then the moment would be over and they'd have to face the coming end. He ran his tongue against the seam of her lips, as if memorizing the taste of her for the last time. She opened her mouth to grant him access and his tongue darted in.

They kissed like adrift sailors, their lips the only raft to keep them afloat in stormy waters. Greedily, she drank in everything about him.

She blinked, and then it was over. Leaning against the cushion, she patted at her upset hair and straightened her dress. Order where there had been passion. She schooled her features into a careful mask and suddenly she knew that he'd kissed her for the last time.

The hack's wheels churned in time to the brutal pounding of her head. Sapped of strength, she laid her head against the blue benchseat and breathed in deep. Everything smelled like him; he was inescapable. Her thigh pressed up against his.

Yet that closeness lied and twisted her until she had nothing left.

"TELL ME YOU love me." Daniel didn't know why he said it. He couldn't be patient any longer, couldn't give his heart up for her to stomp upon it in her half-boots.

Kate drew back to the furthest reaches of the carriage. Her shoulders hunched.

"You promised you wouldn't push the issue. You said you'd give me time." She spoke in a half-plea, half-reproach.

"As you vowed you'd help me to find Tommy Dalton's murderer." He kept his gaze fastened on the hack's window, for if he looked toward her, he'd fall right back into her arms. "If what we have means something to you, come with me to the constable. Tell him we've found new evidence in the Dalton murder and they need to talk to Laurence Bartleby before he dies."

"You know I can't do that." She looked away.

"No, you *won't* do it."

"If what Bartleby says about my father is true, then Papa must have had a good reason for partnering with Finn's resurrection men. Perhaps he was trying to protect us—"

"God damn it, Kate, how can you be so worldly and so immature at once?"

Pain flashed across her face. He'd hurt her. In her mind, the worse thing she could ever be was innocent. She sputtered for a second. He could almost see the wheels that turned in her head.

"How can *you* be?" She flung back. "So I go the constable. The first thing he will ask me for is evidence, and then what should I tell him, Daniel? That he should arrest a man based on the words of a Jacob's Island prostitute, a pugilist, and an accountant cited in the bankrupting of a shipping company? He would laugh in my face."

He cursed in Gaelic. She was right. No one would listen to them. While Jasper Finn would face trial by jury if arrested, they'd need some impregnable evidence to get him to that point. Something to make Finn, with half a dozen law officials on his payroll, more appealing to the jury than the Irish son of a farmer.

He scoffed. "Why bother, is that what you are saying?

Accept my fate, and let them hang me for the pathetic drunkard I am. Is that it?"

"You're not being fair," she protested. "I never said any of that. You put words into my mouth and persecute me for them. Ask me for my opinion, Daniel. Don't condemn me without it."

"You don't have to voice it. I know what passes beneath the surface." He was utterly aware he'd never be worth anything. Not to her.

"So now I don't get to speak, either? Is there nothing left that is truly mine? I should be nothing more than a sycophant, perhaps?" She was as far away from him as she could get in the cramped hack.

"I didn't mean that," he protested. "I've said I support the life you lead. I support you, damn it."

"As I support you, but you don't seem to understand what's going on here. Tommy Dalton was murdered." Her voice, with its quietly rhythmic lilt that once sounded like an angel's harp to him, tore at his insides.

"I am well aware. I see his bloody body every night as I sleep." He couldn't make her understand that pain.

Patiently, she ignored his outburst. "Murder requires evidence and we have none. It has nothing to do with your religion, your heritage, or your blooming class. There's a justice system in place for a reason, Daniel. I know you don't believe in it, but I do."

"Do you really?" he retorted. "If it was your Papa set to face the hangman's noose, would you blame him for escaping? If you could save him, wouldn't you risk everything you could?"

Her eyes fell to her clasped hands in her lap. "You know I would."

He cupped his ear mockingly. "What? My apologies, I've grown a bit deaf from the blast."

She met his gaze, steely like a razor's edge. "You know I would."

"Yet you can't forgive me for doing the same."

For a second, he thought he had her. She'd admit she was wrong. These past three years she'd been harboring resentment against him that she should have released. She loved him, needed him, wanted to start a new life with him.

But the seconds turned into long minutes and still she said nothing.

She finally spoke. "It is different."

One pithy statement to end it all for him.

"Yes, it is." He sighed, the weight of her betrayal crushing him. "It is different because I love you and I've never once lied to you."

"He raised me. When my mother left, it was just us!" Clear and loud, her history rang out in the carriage, over the din of the wheels.

"He was my mentor, Kate." Daniel let out a shaking breath. "Don't think for a second that I don't understand his impact on your life, because he changed mine too. Plucked me from the obscurity of the warehouse and made me his assistant."

It had all been spurious.

Morgan and Finn had needed an easy target.

"He *cared* about you. Why can't you see that?" She turned back to him, her eyes burgeoning with tears that didn't fall because she could not let that one sign of weakness be shown. God forbid she be anything but impregnably strong around him.

Her finger ran across the journal's cover, a delicate, intimate touch. She undid the leather ties and flipped the journal open. Her brows furrowed as she peered at the contents. Then, she passed it over to him.

He looked down at the scrawls in handwriting he recognized as undeniably Morgan's. Yet none of it made sense: combinations of letters and numbers in a seemingly endless and indiscernible tangle. "It's encoded."

"So it would be no help to the constable even if I were to

hand it over." She couldn't hide the joy in her voice any more than she could erase the relief on her face.

"You knew him better than anyone. You could decode it," he suggested. "You studied ciphers."

"That was years ago."

"You could at least try."

"He's dead, Daniel. Let his memory stay unblemished."

The matched team's hooves struck the ground in a constant beat. Shouts echoed from the outdoor market. But nothing echoed more in his ears than Kate slamming the journal shut.

"At the expense of my freedom," he said, as the truth of it hit him hard. Knocked out his breath, clutched at his chest. There could be no place for him in London as a persecuted man. He might be able to avoid discovery, but the accused crime would linger over him until he succumbed back to the drink to make the nightmares abate. The world thought him a murderer and he had let them think that. He had run when he should have stayed; now he stayed when he should run.

"Why must it be a trade?" She reached for him. Her hand upon his in a tender caress, smaller fingers between his larger ones.

Always filling his gaps, giving him back sanity when he had none.

He didn't pull away. He remained transfixed by the feel of her skin against his, soft and unchangeable. Countless nights he'd spent in Sussex brothels, losing himself in the most depraved ways, yet nothing could ever compare to the subtle grace of her touch. He was undone by it, the seams of his consciousness frayed and transmuted into something entirely different. A new form of him, who wanted only to be loved by her, to finally be chosen above all else.

When she'd been his before, he'd been second in her heart and he'd understood that because she owed her father fealty. This woman that loved fiercely and felt deeply would be his upon marriage. The depth of her loyalty had astounded him.

Now, he wondered if she would have ever been his.

"I can't choose between the two of you, Daniel. My memories are the past and they are as much a part of me as whatever this is between us. We are but the sum of our experiences, don't you see? To ask me to deny what I know to be true—that my father was a good man whose vices were not so dark as Bartleby claims—is to ask me to deny a part of myself." She stroked her thumb against his in small, interlocked circles. Past and present, together in one.

"You can love the man and recognize what he did is wrong," he said. Surely she could understand that. The two were not mutually exclusive.

"Not when I know in my heart that he has been as falsely accused as you." Her fingers slowed, the circles she drew no longer connected. "I believed in your innocence, Daniel, when the constable had a witness. I believed in you because I loved you, damn it, and I loved Papa. I owe him the same allegiance."

Because I loved you. Always he would live in the past tense with her.

"A man in the ground, however dear he may be, is not alive. I am, and I am here." He wanted to scream at her that she should choose him over a dead man's memory. Over and over again, he chose her. Needed her.

Her thumb movements along his knuckle ceased, her face taking on a more contemplative bent. "I can't help but think London is poisoned. We could leave this hellhole, go back to Dorking and see Poppy's daughter grow up. Raise our own children."

On the docks as they waited for the ferry, he'd imagined their children with wistfulness. A daughter with Kate's high cheekbones and his red hair appeared before him and faded away into the mists of his mind. Left in the carriage without the wisps of a dream, he was alone. Her touch failed to chase away the darkness of his mind.

"Or we could start an entirely new life somewhere. I remember how you said you'd like to see where your ancestors grew up. I might make a wretched farmer's wife, but I suppose I could learn to cook. I made my own lock picks, after all. It can't be much more difficult."

He could see her surrounded by the lush greenness of pastoral Ireland, her curls a shining halo around her flushed face. She'd pat her flour-drenched hands against her apron as she called to him in the fields of their farm. Her pistol would rest against the door frame of their thatched cottage because she could never be separated from it for long.

An aura of violence would shroud them always.

"We'd raise our children to be sons and daughters of an accused murderer." He didn't want Poppy's daughter Moira to know that shame, let alone his own children.

"We needn't tell them that. We'd be free of London and its lies. I know you didn't do it and you know it. Is that not all that matters? Why must we concern ourselves with the opinions of others?" She shrugged, unconcerned about the dent to his reputation and honor. Her grip tightened on his hand and she tilted her head toward him. Her lips parted, ready for a kiss from him. Wanting. Willing to be with him in a physical sense but never allowing him access to her heart.

He would live with the sins of his past, apologetic for a crime he hadn't committed. Forever haunted by Dalton's corpse, begging for justice.

Without the drink, he had nothing to take away his pain. Nothing but her.

"Don't be like this, Daniel." Her gaze fell on him, implored him to choose another path. She scooted closer to him, so that their legs overlapped. Another edge forward and she'd be in his lap, his for the taking.

She used his words against him. "Let me love you."

Her dress had slipped down. Two pert orbs crested above the v-shaped pointed bodice, tempting him with their perfection. He wanted to fling her skirts up, tug down her drawers and rut himself in her tight cavern until she cried out her release.

That was the only damn thing that made sense between them anymore.

He could see it now. They'd never be anything more than this. The rhythm between them didn't extend farther than the beast with two backs.

"Because we only get along when we're fucking," he muttered.

"What?" Her head snapped up, eyes narrowed.

"You and I. You shag me, I shag you, and we achieve *nothing*." Daniel threw up his hands. "I told you I loved you, Kate, and you can't even say it back. All you can say is how you felt about me before I left. We almost died and still you won't let me in long enough to be anything more to you than the bloke who shares your bed. You're caught in grief for a man who died two and a half years ago, and you'll never move forward with me until you can deal with that. It's not enough."

She fell back against the bench. "It's all I can give you now."

He tore from her, though that took every ounce of willpower he had left. "I want more."

His throat burned, needing relief but coming up empty. There had to be something to cut the pain. His mind was surprisingly silent, offering no other alternative but to pursue the course he'd started.

She didn't look at him, staring out in the carriage darkness. "Then I can't help you anymore. I'll get my things out of Atlas's flat and be gone."

He'd never heard such sadness in her voice. Not when she'd spoken of the attack upon her person, not when she'd mourned her father, not when they'd almost died. It was almost fitting that as she crushed his dreams, she was worn down from the effort.

"I will no longer waste my breath trying to prove to you we are worth fighting for." He turned from her, toward the door of the carriage.

She took his declaration with stony silence.

The hack stopped at the station closest to Ratcliffe. He would go back to his flat, while she'd return to the temporary housing Atlas had set up. He grabbed the door handle, not waiting for the driver to disembark.

"Goodbye, Kate."

CHAPTER 19

KATE STOOD ON the gravel road long after the tenement houses began to settle into evening routines. Fathers returned home from work, rejoined their wives and children at the table for dinner. A woman scooped up her washing from her second- story landing. The smell of soda bread drifted from Mrs. O'Malley's open first-floor window. Familiar sounds, familiar faces that bled into a kaleidoscopic haze.

Her stomach rumbled in a dull register she would not regard. She had gone back to the lodgings in Bethnal Green to get her greatcoat, the portrait of Papa, and her dresses. That small room smacked of Daniel, of the Gentleman Thief, of everything that had been her complicated existence these past weeks.

She ached for what had been before he came back. When her life had made sense and could be easily categorized. Danger be damned. She'd protected herself before and she could do it again. Did her endurance really matter, when her beliefs in Papa were challenged, and Daniel had left yet again?

This tenement house was where she belonged.

She leaned back against the building, hands clasped behind her back. The sack with her dresses hung from her fingers. The rough, cracked wood scraped at the exposed skin between her gloves and the long green sleeves of her dress. She stayed, fixed to the point, eyes half-closed. The pain pierced, but it was immaterial when everything she knew was painful.

Cold air stung her cheeks, chapped them red and raw. Pressed up against the building underneath the awning, the black night shrouded her.

The journal in the pocket of her destroyed greatcoat weighted her down, like the lead balls in her pistol. She knew what she'd find, yet her stomach tightened inexplicably. Papa was blameless, wrongfully accused like Daniel. Those hastily scrawled words were nothing more than notations on shipments.

Daniel wouldn't believe that. He clung to the idea that the world was against him. Never mind that Papa had hired Daniel to Emporia in the first place and promoted him to shipping assistant. Someone must pay for Tommy Dalton's murder and he'd gladly believe it was her father.

Daniel didn't want her. For if he did, he wouldn't trust Bartleby's lies over her knowledge of her father. She'd believed in his innocence when all evidence was to the contrary, but he couldn't do the same for her family.

She didn't want to go to Sussex, to live on a blasted green farm in commune with bloody sheep. But she would've done it for him. She'd agreed to set herself up in Bethnal Green until his guiltlessness could be proved.

She'd put everything on the line for him.

Inside the building she headed up the stairs, into her rooms, each step taken automatically. Vaguely, she heard voices. She might have uttered a greeting; she was not sure.

She should have told Daniel she loved him. She should have told him that Finn had given her the ring, and she hadn't pawned it because it was too dear to her. But there was no use in saying what could never be, no use in being weak.

She'd show him he was wrong. Lighting the candle, Kate surveyed her room. Her body ached still from the explosion and she sunk down into the chair gingerly. From the pocket of her greatcoat she pulled out the journal. A few attacks to the nib of her quill sharpened the tool.

She traced the seal of Emporia with the tip of her index finger wistfully, breathing in the rich scent of leather and ink. As a child running through the warehouses at the London Docks, she'd thought the company indestructible. Her children would grow up under the tutelage of Emporia, and their children after them, on and on throughout the Morgan lineage.

But nothing was constant. She grasped the edge of the journal as though it were Papa's hand once more. Consumption had rendered him useless, unable to recognize her as his daughter. He had still clung to her hand, intrinsically able to understand she offered him support. In death, his grip loosened and his sallow skin was cold.

She opened the book and surveyed the contents. Daniel had been right—she could decode this easily. Almost too easily…had Papa intended this for her to find?

The pages were coded with a simple Caesar shift, her favorite as a child. Papa used to leave coded messages for her with "K" as the key, with each letter of the alphabet substituting accordingly. "B" when replaced turned into "L" and so on. She scratched quill to paper and within no time, the first line became "40, Man, English, no visible scars. 7p."

Her grip tightened around the quill.

Underneath the top line, another set of coded words were indented. Transcribed from the code they became an address in Bethnal Green. That part of St. Mary's Street opened up onto Whitechapel Road and the burial ground of those who died in the workhouses. She had been there before and received a sapphire ring from a thief who believed the Met would not track them to a graveyard. Like the funeral processions of the wretchedly poor were sacred cover.

Nothing was sacred. It was the only truth that remained in her twenty-three years.

She blinked. The page was still there. Her translation was unmistakable. Every bloody word Bartleby had said was the truth. Papa had done this.

Sobs wrenched from her throat, shaking her whole body. The ink blurred before her watery eyes. *This is all a lie,* she repeated over and over again, yet she knew in her gut that the only inaccuracy was her own avowal of virtue.

Clumsily, she rubbed at her eyes with the back of her hand. Her fingers hit against the scratch on her forehead, a jolt of pain driving through her body in protest before her vision cleared.

From the pocket of her greatcoat, she pulled out the last portrait of Papa painted before he'd gotten sick. Laying it up against a chipped blue flower vase, she stared at his dark eyes. He smiled slightly, for the artist had caught him after she'd said something that made him laugh. There was a crease down the center from where Kate had folded it to fit in her valise before the bank evicted her from the Bloomsbury townhouse.

That man was gone, gone like her old life, gone like Daniel.

The list went on another two pages, cramped script stuck in the margins, words written across each other in inter-lapping fashion until her eyes crossed from the effort it took to decipher. When she was finished, she had a total of forty-three entries and five cemeteries in London: St. Mary's Street in Bethnal Green, the workhouse cemetery of St. Sepulchre's-without near Smithfield, Tower Hamlets Cemetery in Southern Grove, and Manor Park on Serbert Road.

Forty-three graves disturbed. Families without peace, knowing their loved one's eternal rest was shattered. Forty-three cadavers kept on ice in Emporia's warehouses.

God only knew how many more murdered for what they'd raise on the black market. The Metropolitan Police estimated that one of the Italian Boy's murderers had stolen over a thousand bodies. Jasper Finn had bodysnatched for at least three years, and if Atlas's surmise about his connections with May and Bishop were right, his reach could be much more fatal.

And her father had been right in the middle of it.

Kate's mouth hung open, yet no sound escaped. No words came to her as cries wracked her trembling frame. Her stomach churned. When she was calmer, she looked back at the ledger. One last line to read.

Bile rose in her mouth as she worked out the last entry. "Woman, 25, mangled, no profit." The doctors didn't want corpses they could not rip apart themselves in the name of science. The dead were only useful when they were whole.

Kate would never be whole again.

Her stomach seized. She lurched to the window, barely managing to raise it in time before she upended the contents of her stomach. Doubled over, acridness coated her tongue and the frigid air stung her cheeks. Kate gasped for breath before heaving again.

She sunk to the ground. The window remained open. In the alley below, a beggar railed against her harsh treatment of his living quarters. Another window sprung up and a slurred reprimand to the beggar for his loudness echoed. From there, a few more windows opened and an out-and-out shouting match ensued in the alleyway. The bandied insults became one long string in Kate's mind. The coarsest language could not encompass what her father had done.

She rested her chin on her knees, pulled up against her chest. Papa must have known she'd find the journal eventually. He was an expert with codes, collecting ciphers with each business trip to another country. If he'd wanted to keep this from her, he had plenty of alternatives to choose from.

A bottle of gin rested within arm's reach on the bedside table. Kate knocked it down, catching it as it fell. The smell of junipers and coriander wafted to her nostrils as she lifted the bottle to her lips. She knocked a sixth back in one fell sip, as Daniel had taught her, remembering the long, lean line of his throat as he swallowed enough shots to stun a horse.

The gin burned. It cleansed her palate, leaving nothing in its wake but the astringent boldness of a cheap distillery.

Gripping the glass bottle in one hand, she turned it around.

It wasn't Daniel's brand, yet gin would be forever his in her mind. She hugged the bottle to her chest. Pressed in between her breasts, arms wrapped around it securely, the bottle stayed when he could not.

Kate drifted off that night, head lolled against her bedroom wall.

DANIEL'S HEAD BEAT in a staccato pulse that bit at his temples and continued on to his forehead. He had not slept well. Without the aid of gin, he doubted he ever would again.

In his dream, he knelt by Dalton's body as he always did, but this time he didn't dream of the false witness and the patrolman. He mouthed the Irish funeral prayer helplessly, unable to bring back Dalton. From the back of the alley, a shadow emerged, passing through the light of the oil lamp attached to the warehouse's fixture. He knew her instantly, her willowy frame encased in the destroyed greatcoat. The wraithlike Kate moved with an aquiline grace, scuffed boots barely touching the ground as she advanced upon him. She drew up her arm and a glint of silver caught the lamplight, dully registering in his mind. Her fingers closed around the hilt of a serrated knife, blood dripping from the blade onto Daniel's hands.

"I can no longer help you. You'll always be alone." With one sudden thrust toward him, she plunged her dagger into his heart.

In the clouds of the morning, he knew little hope. Four days had passed since his fight with Kate, four long days where he had only left the flat to fetch food and water from the pump two streets over. She had not made any attempt to contact him. No one came by his door, and Madame Tousat had no new messages for him.

If Kate wanted to be with him, she would have chosen

him.

He sat at the desk, sharpened quill in his hand. A half-finished letter to Poppy lay across the desktop. What would be the point? He had no good news for her, nothing that would justify her blind faith in him. She had been so certain that Kate would take him back. He didn't want to tell Poppy he'd ruined that too.

Since returning to London, he had been stalked, almost blown up, and he'd choked a man within a millimeter of his life. He believed he had found Dalton's killer, but he had no evidence to convict Finn outside of the unreliable testimony of a pugilist and a prostitute.

He needed Morgan's journal if he wanted a solid case. Atlas could decode it with little difficulty. He could get Atlas to steal the ledger. Kate had made her choice—she protected her father's memory over him. Shouldn't he choose his own sanity as well?

But he couldn't.

For no matter how she had hurt him, she was still his Kate. So he stared at a dingy wall in a rundown flat in Ratcliffe. He drummed his fingers against the desk in time to the drubbing of his head because he didn't know how to continue on without her or his freedom.

On the foolscap before him, he had scrawled "I will return home soon." There was nothing left for him in London, nothing but his pathetic visions of justice for a man he had only met twice before finding him dying in that damn alley. This was a crusade for another dead man, where he was as trapped in the past as Kate.

But if he didn't clear his name, he returned a failure, the exact same man he'd been before he left. Only now he could not console himself with an illusion. Kate had not married into a perfect life. She haunted the rookeries like she haunted his dreams.

Crumbling the parchment in his hands, he threw the balled up paper against the wall. He'd been a stalwart shipping assistant with a taste for drink, an alcohol-abusing blackguard, and a sober man with no reason to continue. Out of the three, he'd choose the one that allowed him to function. He would be careful this time. Watch his intake; only use it to cease the dreams. Then when he'd cleared his name, he'd come off of it again and he'd be better.

"PRETTY RING," JANE said, as Kate passed her a steaming mug of coffee. "The boys brought it to you, I presume."

Kate took a seat on the edge of her bed. Her pinky finger curled delicately around the edge of her mug; some habits died hard no matter how long she lived in Ratcliffe. She brought the mug up, swishing the hot liquid around in her mouth. The coffee was bitter and in desperate need of sugar, yet that would have exceeded her monthly budget. She swallowed it down, grateful for the heat that swum in her stomach and the excuse it gave her to not speak.

"Kate." Jane tapped the gold ring on her friend's finger twice, her tiny index finger the width of the heart. "Did you think I wouldn't recall?"

"I hoped you wouldn't." Kate nibbled at her lower lip, setting the mug down on the table.

Jane smiled ruefully. "I can tell you the favored drink of every single member of Chapman Street, and I don't even like the majority of them. I should hope I could remember the ring that your betrothed gave you. It meant something to you."

"Once it did." Wincing, Kate flipped the ring around so that only the gold band showed. Out of sight, out of mind—or so she'd thought. But the bloody ring had called to her from inside the secret compartment in her flat. *Wear me*, it said, *wear me and remember all you gave up because you made the wrong choice.*

"He'll come back. He loves you. I could see it in his eyes." From any other woman, such a proclamation would have sounded maudlin, but with Jane it became certain fact.

Kate exhaled a shaky breath. "He'd be a fool to want me now."

"Those in love generally are." Jane shrugged.

"My father—my father did those horrible things, Jane, and I stood like a bloody addle-pate rambling on about how virtuous he was." Kate's thumb pressed against the engraving on the ring, tracing the contours of the heart. *My heart will always be yours,* Daniel had said when he gave it to her.

She didn't deserve his heart. She didn't deserve any damn part of him. All this time she had been the unseeing daughter of a man who sold corpses to be chopped up like slabs of cattle. How could she have never noticed this? Papa had been away at night often, but she had considered that part of his job. He had functions to attend, investors to speak with about new opportunities. She had never cared, especially in the last year when his absence had made it easier to sneak Daniel in and out of the townhouse.

"You're loyal. Why do you think I like you so?" Jane tilted her head thoughtfully. "Loyalty is a rare quality here. People come and go. Alliances are forged with no more reasoning than 'he's got the bigger knife, so I shall support him.' But not with you, Kate. You choose because your heart tells you to believe in someone."

"Every single time I've been wrong." Kate sighed. "Papa, Owen…I should have believed in Daniel more. Should have written letters to him in Dorking."

"And I should have prevented Penn from going on the job that got him collared." Jane squeezed her hand. "Life is full of regrets, dear. You decide what to keep and what to toss into the rubbish."

"How can I possibly accept the idea of my father as a…resurrection man?" She hissed the last words out, the term as dirty to her as the cemeteries they dug into. She couldn't picture Papa with a spade in his hand, bent over a grave and plundering the soil.

"Sin is sin," Jane said. "Pithy, perhaps, but I don't know a single soul who has not committed some despicable wrongdoing. Penn is not an honorable man, yet I love him because he's family and I don't know how to do anything else."

"I won't forgive Papa." Stubbornly, she clung to that, as if she could punish him for what he'd done.

"That's the choice you make then," Jane frowned, concern creasing her brows. "But I hope for your sake you learn to come to peace with it."

CHAPTER 20

DANIEL LINGERED OUTSIDE the dram shop. "Dram hole in the wall" was a better term, for it took up no more width than that of the door. One unmarked, heavy door in the middle of Wapping, known only to those who sought the strongest of spirits sold within. Every gin distillery of London was represented inside, from the bootlegger's poison that would leave one blacked out for days, to the well-known manufacturers. Bottles were sold, or single shots for those with less blunt but who needed a hit to get by.

Today, he would rejoin those ranks. Kate would never want him back, but he could pretend that it didn't matter.

His first stop had been to the Prospect of Whitby. He'd had a mind to reunite with his old drinking friends, if they were still there. Yet that was a place too visible and frequented by the Bobbies. The threat of discovery loomed as long as he was in London. He'd lingered at the door and then left.

It was better this way. His return to vice would be less public. The little bit of pride he possessed wanted to hide his failure, to be alone when he got so rousing drunk that the world became nothing but mottled images.

He doubted the proprietor would recognize him, but he remembered this place well. On the route from Emporia's old warehouses to his prior tenement, he'd visited weekly; sometimes two or three times a week if the shipments had not come in on time and Morgan was in a rage.

The gin staunched the pain, every time. Until it was gone and reality crashed down upon him with the weight of all his inferiorities.

He'd been lied to by Morgan, by Kate. Yet the worst lie of them all was the one he told himself: he didn't need the crank. He could get by without it, even as his head swam anytime he smelled it. Even as he was surrounded by it in the public houses he'd visited with Kate.

He did want it, and he needed it.

He needed it like he needed Kate to keep him sane.

His hand wrapped around the tarnished doorknob. No gloves today. No more pretending to be a gentleman. The metal was cool under his fingers, a reminder that he was unfortunately alive.

He turned the knob and pulled the door open. The cylindrical shop was lit by three oil lanterns, strategically positioned around a counter that stretched the full length. The counter had a glass front, displaying at least one hundred different bottles of gin. There were no shelves; thus the bottles were crammed behind one another and set on top of each other hectically. The ceiling hung so low that Daniel had to stoop once he entered.

Behind the counter, a skeletal man stood, shoulders hunched and elbows perched on the glass. Stringy gray hair streamed from underneath his floppy, crushed top hat. He peered down his hook nose at Daniel through wire-rimmed glasses.

"O'Reilly," he said, his thick Irish tones containing no surprise at Daniel's return. No one escaped the lure of gin.

"Mathias." Daniel nodded crisply. He dropped a brass watch-fob on the countertop. It had arrived on his doorstep the other day, brought by one of the grubby children Atlas kept in his employ to run errands. He'd meant to pawn it to buy Kate something special.

"Been long time, lad." Mathias palmed the fob, deposited it swiftly into the scrap of cheesecloth he used as an apron.

"Took off to Sussex. Now I've returned."

"What say ye? My Lady's Eye Water?" Mathias ran his index finger over the bottles, snickering as he stopped on a dark amber tub. "Or Cuckold's Comfort? That suits, cub."

Daniel stiffened. The dram owner most likely used that insult on everyone. It stung nonetheless, a pinprick to the exposed sore of Kate's betrayal.

"Lady's Delight. Can you use the fob or shall I take it elsewhere?" He stuffed his hands into his pockets, pulling his greatcoat tighter around him.

"Aye, still a classic man." Mathias's beady eyes flicked from Daniel to the door and back. "Ye've got a ladybird fence. Don't ye know what'll 'appen to me if I go a-stealin' 'er payday?"

Damnation. Was there a soul in Christendom that didn't know he'd been back with Kate? He needn't worry about smashing his brains out on gin, if the Peelers would soon be at Madame Tousat's.

Daniel blinked. One wretched problem at a time. First the gin, then a plan to leave town. Dubious statement of criminal loyalty aside, he sincerely doubted Mathias would refuse to serve him. "You ought to demand a refund from whatever snitch you paid, as he's fed you nothing but deceptions. I've barely been back in town long enough to see the Gentleman Thief. How'd I get a fence too?"

"As if I be a-needin' a snitch to be doin' my business. Insultin' me 'onor." The receiver's sharp nostrils flared.

"And you apparently don't need blunt either, since you won't take the fob. It's worth three times a bottle of Lady's Delight. Hand it back and I'll take it to someone with the balls to move it."

Mathias's lips curled back, bearing his teeth. Daniel half-expected him to lunge forward and sink those yellowed, decayed canines into the flesh of his neck.

Perhaps today was the day he finally died from poking a bear with a flaming baton.

"'Ere's a-warnin', O'Reilly. I'll take yer paltry an' a-give ye some ruin, but if ye come back again—"

"Come now. Do you think the Gentleman Thief would like it if you threatened me?" Daniel leaned back on one foot, hands shoved into his pockets, a picture of nonchalance. "Lest you forget, the constable thinks I murdered a man. Care to see if I'm innocent?"

The dram shop owner's teeth gnashed. "Ye's a spoiled sop, bloody Irish. I liked ye better when yer 'ands were a-shakin.'"

"Just give me the crank."

Mathias knelt. His crushed hat bobbed in the window glass as he poked at the various bottles with long, bony fingers.

Daniel waited with bated breath. He didn't have more than the fob on him to pay. If Mathias demanded more he'd be royally tupped. The dram shop owner had already put it in his apron. He'd be hard pressed to get it back from him—the counter Mathias stood behind stretched the width of the room, with singular access to the inside through a padlocked section in the gate.

Mathias stood back up, a sick little smile twisting his thin lips. "This what yer lookin' for?" He held the dingy bottle up in two fingers, precariously balanced. In a second, the gin might tip to the counter and splash out.

Daniel's throat tightened. He managed to nod. His gaze never wavered from the bottle.

Readjusting the bottle so that his right hand clenched it, Mathias tapped a finger against the wart on his cleft chin. Daniel's hands gripped the counter, as hard as he wanted to wrest the bottle from Mathias's spidery fingers.

"Fob'll do." Mathias set the gin on the counter.

Releasing his held breath, Daniel snatched the bottle up.

Mathias's leathery voice reached him as he left the shop.

"Welcome back, O'Reilly."

"MISS, I DIDN'T think I'd see ye 'ere again." Sally Fletcher perched on a straw mat, her back to the wall.

I hadn't thought to come back. Hadn't wanted to, for being in the bordello reminded her of the girl Mei that she'd left in that hellhole. Reminded her of telling Daniel her secret and falling asleep in his arms.

Rigidly, Kate leaned against the door-frame. "Here," she said, thrusting a sack toward Sally. "I brought you these things."

Sally smiled impishly, her pale cheeks flushed with joy. "My thanks, miss." She tipped the sack over next to her. A loaf of bread and a hunk of cheese spilled out.

"Please, call me Kate." She didn't deserve a title of respect, not after what she'd done.

Sally spread out across her lap an amber dress with a full skirt and lace across the bodice. "This—this 'ere's quality. Ye certain ye want me to 'ave it?"

Kate nodded.

Tilting her head to the side, Sally fixed Kate with a quizzical look. "Why ye bein' so nice to me?"

"Because I believe you should have niceness." Kate dropped down on the mattress next to her, sighing. While Sally's feet tucked nicely underneath her, Kate felt like an Amazon in the cramped room.

Sally blinked, unconvinced. She fell upon the bread, devouring hunks at a time and barely pausing to chew. In a minute, the bread was gone and she'd latched onto the wheel of cheese.

Kate's voice softened. "I do think that you warrant better treatment, Sally. No one should be treated as an object."

"'Tis not so bad. Got me a bed and the rain don't come through the ceilin'. If I were a flower girl, I'd not be sayin' that, now would I?" Sally shrugged. The horsehair pad stuffed into the puffy caps of her dress showed through a rip on her right sleeve. The hair was rough and matted, speckled with dirt.

"That is certainly one way to look at it," Kate mused.

"Pardon, for ye've been awfully kind, but why are ye 'ere, miss? We don't get charity. Not 'ere on Jacob's."

Kate opened her mouth, and then promptly shut it. She swallowed. No other convenient reason came to mind. For the first time since her father had passed, she'd choose the truth, ripping apart her old wounds and bleeding red. "I had a plan once. A plan inside a plan, and then another inside of that, to cover for all contingencies. Work with the putter-uppers and thieves, fence their goods, stay alive. It was a sound plan."

"Then ye met Mr. O'Reilly," Sally said, with the all-knowing air of one far older.

"Met him again, if one can say that when we've both changed." Kate's sad smile didn't reach her eyes. "We are nothing now, and all I've got is this blasted journal of my father's." Kate pulled out the notebook from her petticoat pocket, handing it to Sally. The decoded foolscap stuck out of the bindings.

Sally flipped through the ledger, her brows furrowed. She lingered on one page too long, turning another over so quickly there was no way she could have seen the contents. She didn't bother with the foolscap pages. A few minutes later, she pushed the journal back to Kate without comment.

"You can't read," Kate observed.

Spine stiffened, Sally drew herself up to her full petite height. "'Tis not a skill needed 'ere."

"No, I suppose it's not. It's not a failure on your part, Sally. One can't be expected to know things unless you are taught them." Kate's fondest memories of her childhood involved curling up in the over-sized leather armchair in her father's office, reading a book from Ackermann's Repository while he worked. He'd scribble away in a journal like the one on her lap now.

How could father, who had taught her to read when the governess insisted she was far too young to comprehend, be the same person who assisted in the robbing of graves? How could Papa allow the only man she'd ever loved to be accused of murder?

Kate pocketed the leather book. She felt suddenly lighter once it was away, as if by keeping her father's words hidden away she could somehow make them not exist.

I'm going to do the right thing. She heard Daniel's voice, the catch in his throat.

In one breath, Kate explained to Sally the death of her father, Emporia's closing, and the contents of the journal. Sally kept silent, her expression blank. Her gaze remained fastened on Kate, yet her ocean blue eyes showed no indication of recognition. She seemed to have retreated somewhere inside herself. Her toes curled around the side of the mattress.

Maybe she had erred in telling this to Sally. But the girl had loved Dalton. She deserved to know why he had died.

Finally, Sally spoke. "Ye say yer father was in league with Finn?"

"So it appears." Kate scrubbed at her face, pinching the bridge of her nose.

Sally followed her hands, worry lines writ into her forehead. She drew back from Kate, tentatively tracing her own brow to mirror. "Yer head—who struck ye?"

"An errant block of wood. There was an explosion and I was in the middle of it." Kate touched two fingers to the scratch gingerly, wincing when soreness flowed through her. The cut had not healed yet.

Sally grabbed for the dress, clutching it to her chest. Her fingers dug into the fine muslin, creasing it. Eyes wide, mouth half-open, she seemed small and helpless. She could not have been more than nineteen, a victim of circumstances who knew no better life.

"Miss, a bomb's more than I care to be riskin'." She pushed herself up from the mattress.

"I am here under an assumed name, and I paid the fee as anyone else would. I held to the schedule of Wilkes's appearances and came when he wasn't present. You're not in any danger.." Kate forced false certainty into her voice.

A decoded journal was not enough against a confirmed witness statement. Cyrus had claimed Dalton worked with the resurrectionists, and Sally had verified his connection to Finn. It was all speculation, lines drawn to connect one incident to another. Nothing incontestable to hold up against a corrupt magistrate's decisions.

Sally stroked the dress in her lap, looking at it with rapt attention. "What are ye wantin' to know? I already told ye what I recall. If Finn's been 'ere, I 'aven't seen 'im."

Kate's stomach clenched. "As much as I want to find Finn, I'm more interested in if you recall anything about my father."

"I don't know." Sally's expression was guarded. Always in expectation of a blow, for her luck to turn against her.

Kate brought the shreds of her father's greatcoat out, cradling the burnt fabric. Her tone was gentle, firm in its intent and aimed at setting the girl at ease. "I'm trying to put the pieces together, Sally, and I can't do that without you. The constable does not care who actually killed Dalton, as long as he can send a soul to Newgate."

Sally looked up, her eyes locking on Kate with blistering outrage. "I want to stop Finn."

Kate's breath hitched. Sally had loved Dalton, understood his quirks and lived with his wrongdoings. That was what love was, an acceptance of one's partner for all that they were and all they could be someday.

She and Daniel could never come to that raised comprehension, no matter how much she longed for him, or how soothed she was by his presence, because she'd failed him. Chosen the wrong side in his war because her damned memories had been more important.

She brought out the portrait of her father, reluctantly

handing it over. One more memory gone, sold off in the name of veracity.

Sally held the paper gingerly, seemingly aware of its emotional importance. Her lips pressed together so tight her bottom lip disappeared almost entirely. She exhaled, her breath shaking the edge of the paper.

Sally recognized Papa.

Sally handed the paper back to Kate. "'E came by once or twice. They never let Tommy at the meets, but I saw Wilkes talkin' to 'im. 'E gave that man some paper before Finn came 'round. Didn't know 'e mattered before, 'cause Tommy never talked to 'im."

"Did you hear what they said?" Kate folded the portrait back into her pocket.

"I didn't get close. Wilkes don't like it if ye come up on 'im discussin' business. They 'ad a fight, I think, for that man—yer father—left lookin' like 'e'd punch Wilkes." Shyly, Sally looked up at her. "I 'oped 'e would. Wilkes deserves it."

"If I ever run into him, I shall punch him for you myself," Kate vowed, which made Sally smile. "Did he come by again?"

"Not that I saw. But we don't get much time outside. 'E might 'ave come by and I missed it."

Kate fished out her pocket watch. Time was nearly up, lest she want to alert the brothel-keeper to her presence by overstaying. "You've been very helpful, Sally, and I thank you."

"'Tis nothing, miss," Sally blushed prettily.

"Kate," she corrected.

Sally smiled, gathering up the sack's contents. When the girl relaxed, she appeared innocent. Kate swallowed, forcing herself to turn toward the door. The girl had a home here in this foul place, possibly the only home she'd ever known. If she tried to tear Sally from that, she couldn't guarantee she'd live a better life somewhere else.

She couldn't keep Sally from being hurt.

Sally stood, the sack held against her chest. She wore no coat, only a plaid cotton dress with short sleeves that hung awkwardly from her thin frame. The sack covered her jutting clavicle, and she rested her chin on the top. If Wilkes found out Sally had new things, he'd filch them from her to sell to the dolly shops, if he didn't beat her bloody first for acquiring without his permission.

Kate's hands fisted around the fabric of her greatcoat. With one long scratch running up the back seam and a dozen other rips, it was still more than Sally probably owned to keep warm. Mechanically, Kate unloaded the contents of her pockets. Load pouch, pocketknife, a roll of twine, and the portrait all went into the pockets of her skirt.

"You should take this. I don't need it anymore." She shoved the greatcoat toward Sally.

The girl readjusted the sack to fall on her hip, her brows furrowing, but she didn't speak. Instead, she accepted the coat and nodded.

"Good luck to you, Sally." Kate stepped to the door, hand on the knob.

"Kate? Don't be givin' up on Mr. O'Reilly. Love is worth fightin' for."

CHAPTER 21

WRAPPED IN A cloth sack, the thin-necked bottle of gin fit as though it was made for his grip. The voluptuous middle and plump bottom hung in motion as he walked, tempting him like the well-rounded curves of a woman.

His hands didn't shake. He caught his reflection in the butcher shop glass as he passed: ginger brows arched, lips flat in grim determination. His neckcloth wrinkled from where he'd tugged upon it on the walk to the boarding house. His red locks were mussed from his fingers. With his black greatcoat swathed around him, he was man on his way to a funeral, the bereavement of his blighted self-ambitions.

No one was in the hall when he returned to Madame Tousat's. As he passed by the doors, the muted discussions of families flitted to him. Thousands of poor men lived in the rookeries across London. If one of those men went missing, their wives, their whores, their children would mark their absence.

He wondered if anyone would remember him when he was gone.

He heard a violin as he rounded the corner to his flat. This place had begun to feel like home, but it was home for a few weeks and no more. Now that Kate had left him he'd be gone soon.

The music grew louder as he came closer. He put his hand up to his door. It vibrated with the violin's melody. He knew the song, a pithy country tune about John the Fiddler and his bonnie lass. It was Atlas's favorite.

Opening the flap of his greatcoat, Daniel slid the bottle inside and buttoned up the coat again. The music stopped as he opened the door.

"You might have sent word, Danny." Atlas's crisp accent was as good as any peer. Violin in his hands, he reclined back on Daniel's bed as though he hadn't a care in the world.

The very bed Daniel had shared with Kate, arms curled around her bare body, legs intertwined with hers. In feigned nonchalance Daniel slouched against the door, head and shoulders back, using the heavy wood to hold himself up. He folded his hands at the waist to keep the bottle from falling to the ground.

He couldn't face the concern in his friend's eyes. He looked instead at the violin next to him on the bed, to the bow propped up against his headboard.

My failure is mine and mine alone.

"The last note I received from you said you were going to Bethnal Green." Atlas cocked his head to the side, his usually merry features concerned. "Then I hear a bomb was set off at Friggard's and the place was completely demolished. I thought you were dead, Danny, until your landlady said you stayed in last night."

"Finn tried to kill me, but he didn't succeed."

Atlas reached behind him, plumping the pillow. He lay with his legs outstretched, his shoes polished to a shine on the top of Daniel's elderdown. "Sound a bit happy about it then. Not many men can say they've avoided death's hand so many times."

"Get your feet off the bed, would you?"

Atlas sighed melodramatically. He pulled off his shoes

slowly and dropped them to the floor.

Daniel rolled his eyes. "Now that you've seen I'm alive, you can leave me to sleep in peace."

"I fear it may be more complicated than that." Atlas moved the violin over, snatching up a piece of paper. He didn't need to look at the contents; he had likely memorized it upon first reading. "Laurence Bartleby is dead."

Daniel stiffened, posture no longer loose. His mouth fell open dumbly; only after a moment did he think to close it. He should feel something, anything other than the overwhelming emptiness.

"According to whom? I went to his townhouse two days ago. You were right, he was living in Westminster."

"According to several very good sources who expect anonymity."

"This is no time for your thieving code, Atlas, if there even is such a thing." Daniel clenched his hands together, right thumbnail digging into his flesh. Balanced on his folded hands, the bottle underneath his greatcoat moved slightly.

Atlas's eyes narrowed in on his hands. Daniel gulped. If he didn't distract Atlas soon, he'd discover the gin.

He'll take the bottle away, and I need it to survive.

"Did they say how he died?"

"What do you have underneath your greatcoat, Danny?"

"Nothing."

"Dishonesty I can abide by and even praise, when it is executed flawlessly. You, on the other hand, are a bloody bad dissembler and an even worse thief. The Runners would mark you upon first glance." Atlas shook his head in barely suppressed disgust. "Doff the coat, or I'll embarrass you with a lift."

He had no doubt the thief could filch and pocket the bottle, all without him being the wiser. He reached up underneath his greatcoat and pulled out the cloth sack to protect the gin: not because he wanted, in some unrecognized part of him, to be caught with it.

"Again, I see." Atlas's gaze flipped from the sack in Daniel's hands to his face and back to the bottle.

"Just this once." Daniel yanked the sack off the Lady's Delight, placing the bottle on the table by the door.

"And when it leads to another?" Atlas swung his legs over the side of the bed, both feet landing on the floor. He pushed himself up and off the bed.

Protectively, Daniel stood in front of the bottle to hide it from the thief's vision. "I haven't been sleeping. Kate's gone. I've got nothing else."

"So you tupped her." Atlas's voice held no note of inflection.

The thief had predicted all along that the state of affairs between Daniel and Kate would lead to this. All-seeing Atlas had made his own rules as an orphan in St. Giles and succeeded because of it. He did not need gin to succeed— Atlas had no limitations.

Anger flooded Daniel. He welcomed it because it made him feel alive, something more than a burned-out soul responsible for the ruination of everything he'd ever wanted. Conceivably, it'd be easier to believe that the bond between him and Kate had been nothing more than two bodies rutting.

But it had been real and true in those moments with her. He could no more deny that than deny his nationality. "I won't let you make this into something vulgar."

The edge to his words provoked a raised brow from his friend. No apology, for Atlas didn't believe in apologies. "I warned you about getting involved with her for precisely this reason."

"What would you have had me do? I love her, Atlas, I love her and I bloody need her." He scraped his hands through his hair, gripping the base of his skull and holding on as if the motion could bring clarity to his overwrought mind.

He'd never have clarity, not now.

"This is why I only bed whores. Far easier when it's a business transaction and both parties are well-informed." Atlas shook his head. "When you dally with the civilized sort, it ends badly."

"I've tried that. It's not the same. It's not Kate."

Atlas came to stand next to him, laying a hand on his arm. Daniel stiffened at the touch, an intrusion on his space when all he wanted was to be left alone with the gin to his degradation.

"You can't go back to the ruin." Atlas didn't step back, ignoring Daniel's reproachful grimace. The thief made a move toward the Lady's Delight and Daniel shifted, blocking him. Daniel had at least a head and a half on the thief and twice the bulk.

Grabbing the bottle up, he held it up above Atlas's head. "One drink. I'll have one drink."

"And if anyone else said that, I'd believe that. Gin is good for the soul, I'd say, because it's the rookeries and it passes the time. The sixth is a way of life, but it can't be yours." Atlas's eyes narrowed as he stared up at the bottle, examining all the angles to identify the best way to steal it. "You don't function properly, mate. When I met you down by the docks years ago, you were dependable. Then you took that job at Emporia and you met that dimber mort Kate and everything changed."

Daniel sighed, bringing the bottle down to level again. His hands still clenched around it, but he was too tired to keep up the fight, too tired to defend himself. "It doesn't matter. She chose her father's good name over our future. Morgan was involved all along."

"As I told you before," Atlas shrugged. "You need to take the freedom you've got and run again, Danny, because it will be common knowledge soon that Laurence Bartleby had his throat slit."

"I shouldn't have to run—Christ." Daniel stopped, rubbed at his eye with his free hand. "His throat was slit? Nobody deserves that, not even that horse's arse."

Atlas nodded. "The Met will think you did it, if they hear you are back in town. Look, it's not that I want you to leave. I like having you around again, but not if it means your life. Go now, go back to Dorking."

Daniel held the gin in his hand, taunting him with its presence. He couldn't think when it was near; couldn't think without it. Depositing the bottle back on the table, he ran a hand over his scruffy chin, index finger curled underneath and thumb pressed into the middle.

It would be so simple to run. Gathering up what little he had brought with him would take a matter of minutes. He sank into the chair by the door, closing his eyes. Dalton's blood-drenched corpse lay in that alley again, killed by Finn's men. Bartleby had faced the same fate and Kate had almost died in the explosion. If he fled, he was a coward.

Better a coward than dead.

"I don't know. I'll take a drink and I'll sort this all out with a clear mind."

"What about Poppy?" Atlas's question surprised him.

Poppy, set up as a seamstress back home, raising an illegitimate child. Poppy, who had stuck by his side despite his abandoning her. He'd find a way to make it up to his sister, when he could think through the pain.

"It's not necessary for her to know. By the time I go back to Dorking, I'll be off the drink again. Now, I *need* it." His fingers snaked around the lips of the bottle.

"Do you truly believe that?" Atlas asked. "Because those sound like the words of a man laboring hard to convince himself of something he knows is wrong."

"It doesn't matter what's wrong," Daniel shrugged. "I shouldn't have to remind the Gentleman Thief that—how many laws have you broken, Atlas? How many losses have you profited from over the years?"

Atlas frowned. "It's not the same matter, and you know it. But I can't change your mind, old boy. If you do decide to go back to the drink, then I'll support you, because you are my friend and that is what one does."

"I'll manage it." He sounded more confident than he felt,

intent on convincing himself.

"No, you won't," Atlas said quietly. "But when you give it up, it'll have to be for you and you alone."

ALMOST OUT THE door without incident, Kate breathed a sigh of relief. If she could get through this last stretch of the bordello, she could slip out into the night unnoticed. The flintlock pistol remained in her pocket, loaded and half-cocked. She no longer felt solace in the ability to defend herself. Violence bred violence until nothing was left but the decaying flesh and filthy scalpels.

Sally had seen Papa. Kate repeated that, beating it into her mind in hopes it'd sink in and she'd find some sort of peace with it. All this time, Daniel had been right.

"He's a good man, Katiebelle," Papa had said, when she told him Daniel had asked for her hand. It shouldn't matter if his defense of Daniel was genuine, not after all he'd apparently done, but deep down she knew it did. He'd become sick shortly after Daniel's escape, and once the consumption had hit him he wasn't coherent.

"Certain I saw 'er, Finn." A man's voice sounded at the end of the hall.

Her throat clenched. *Finn was here!* She turned the knob to the closest door and ended up in a narrow hall. Underneath the one lantern, mold spun up the walls, filled in the cracks in the sealant. The lantern's reach extended only to this corner of the tunnel, leaving the rest in darkness.

With Finn and the other man present, she couldn't go back to the hall. The exit she had taken with Daniel before was now blocked. She had no idea how long the tunnel was or if it ended up in the street. If she could see further, she might be able to ascertain if it was worth it to proceed or wait for people to leave the room she'd come from.

Kate reached up to the lantern, attempting to pry it loose.

The fixture had rusted over and could not be broken from the wall. The top of the lantern was cracked, so that the flame was accessible. Quickly, she tried to think of what she had left that would provide light when burnt.

She'd given up the greatcoat, and she couldn't afford to ruin another dress by ripping off the hem. The lead bullets would do no good, unless she wanted to draw attention to herself with another explosion, and she couldn't hold the twine easily when it was lit. That left only the portrait.

"No," Kate mouthed.

"Aye, she left from there. Been with Sally." Again the man's voice penetrated the door.

"I've already dealt with the whore. She doesn't know where the bitch is going." The malice in the second man's tone sent a shiver down Kate's spine.

She knew that voice, once so bright and flirtatious. Owen, or Finn as she knew him now. How had he "dealt" with Sally? Was the girl still alive? Fear gripped Kate's throat, dropped down to her stomach and seized her internal organs. She was suddenly cold, stricken.

"Been askin' questions. We can't be 'avin' that." The other man's voice was closer now, like he'd taken another step toward her hiding place.

She pressed herself up against the wall.

"You think I don't know that?" Finn snapped. "You set the explosion wrong, you bloody arse, otherwise we'd be rid of them both by now. O'Reilly lives and that's on your head."

Kate gulped. The portrait flitted from her hold, down to the ground.

"Blaster said charges were good, what ye want from me?"

"For you to do your bleeding job, Wilkes," Finn hissed. "I shouldn't have to send Ezekiel out to get rid of one drunk, miserable Paddy."

"S'not my fault Ezekiel failed too," Wilkes protested. "Why don't ye be yellin' at 'im? I got the girls to tend to."

Daniel.

Her hand shook. She remembered Daniel saying he had fought Ezekiel before, and he'd been injured. Daniel would have no idea Ezekiel was coming after him this time. He'd be exposed. She needed to get the hell out of here, back to Madame Tousat's and warn him.

The doorknob turned.

Her heart in her throat, Kate fell back up against the wall, until a female voice broke the silence. "I heard the girl went out the west entrance."

"That's my girl, Amelia. Knew you were worth every penny this old bastard here charges." Something that sounded vaguely like a smack upon a bottom echoed, followed by a woman's coo. High-pitched and over-exaggerated, clearly done for Finn's benefit.

"Coming, Wilkes?"

"Aye." Two sets of footsteps retreated.

"You'd better go." The woman's voice was so soft Kate was not entirely certain she'd spoken at all, or if the prostitute's words were the manifestations of her own thoughts.

There was no time to question Amelia's help. Kate looked down at the portrait. In the golden light of the candle, her father's face appeared ethereal. Kneeling down, she picked up the paper and rolled it into a tube. "I'm sorry," she whispered.

Daniel waited, likely alone and unaware of the danger about to befall him, convinced that she cared nothing for him. She held the paper to the lantern, orange flames licking at the edge of the paper and eating away the charcoal lines. Lifting the paper from the flame, Kate held the bottom of the roll.

She'd have to move quickly to reach the end of the tunnel before the paper burnt completely. The flames had already devoured the top of Papa's head. Arm outstretched with the paper as a torch, she walked quickly, afraid to run for her footsteps would resonate and give away her location.

Light bounced off the tunnel walls, flicked onto the cracks in the wall. The air smelled dank and dismal. It had begun to rain outside, droplets hitting the brothel roof. She plowed through the rushes and rubbish lining the tunnel, ignoring the damage to her boots and the sluice of noxious liquid sliding up her ankle. Her pale pink skirts dragged in the mess. The paper burnt down three-fourths, precariously close to singing her fingers.

She kept moving. The tunnel was straight at least, with little room for deviation in the path. In the distance, she could discern a light underneath the door. Heat started to spill onto her fingers from the burnt ember of the papers. She let go quickly, stomping out the flames before they could catch onto what little dry tinder beneath her feet remained.

She stopped, putting her ear to the door to listen for voices. Over the sound of rain, traffic echoed, horse's hooves clopped and the drunken slurs of conversation sounded further down the street. Kate exhaled. She'd finally found the exit.

Opening the door, she stepped out into the last rays of daylight. Twilight streaked the sky, casting everything in a hue of gray. She breathed in the cold night air and instantly regretted it. The tunnel had been moldy, but it could not compare with the stench of the side streets and back alleys of Jacob's Island.

Rain pelted the alley. In a moment's time, she was drenched, her dress clinging to her soaked skin. She turned to leave the alley and smacked right into the solid confines of a man's chest.

"Going somewhere, Kate?" His hand grabbed her waist and held her to him.

She tilted her head back to look up, her stomach plummeting.

Jasper Finn leered down at her.

CHAPTER 22

"IT WOULD HAVE been so easy, Kate, if you'd accepted me before." Finn's hands tightened around her waist, digging through her broad skirt into the tender flesh of her hip. Layers of clothing dissolved as if nothing were underneath his hold. "If you'd spread your legs for me like the whore you are, we wouldn't be in this position."

"I'd rather die," she spat, mind reeling.

"All in due time," Finn sneered. "Unfortunate, really. I would have enjoyed the poetic justice of having Morgan's daughter as queen of my operations. But I'll settle for a bit of flesh before I slice your throat open."

Finn leaned forward, his breath hot on her neck. He smelled of cheap perfume from the whore he'd laid with, his breath soaked in even cheaper port. How had she ever found him attractive as Owen? Her body revolted at the very idea now. His hands seared her flesh.

"I cheated you when I fenced your goods," she hissed. She hadn't. She'd been bloody honest with him.

"No, you didn't love, but it's charming you want me to think so. You haven't even fenced your dear Paddy's ring." Finn let go of her right hip to brush his hand along her neck.

Her body went rigid at his touch. "Why did you give it to me? You must have had an end game."

"I wanted to see if you still cared for the bastard. You picked the wrong side." He plucked up a curl of her hair. Rubbing the strand of hair between his thumb and forefinger, he brought it up to his nose, breathing in the scent of her hair. "Mmm. Jasmine, and what else is that? How perfectly bourgeoisie of you."

She snapped her head quickly to the left, wrenching her hair from his fingers. "Touch me again, and I'll kill you."

"With what weapon?" He ran a finger up across the curvature of her ear, so light she shivered.

Her pistol was out of reach in her pocket, half-cocked. If she could manage to retrieve it, she wasn't certain she could get a good shot. This close, she'd be better off using her fist to plow into his nose, like she'd done with McNair in the Three Boars.

"I don't need a weapon," she said.

"Barbaric, are we? But I much prefer civilized combat. A knife to the gullet, for instance." He tweaked the bottom of her lobe with a sick chuckle.

A chill slid across her bones. Water streamed from the heavens in a steady downpour. If she didn't get free—but she wouldn't think of that. She'd be calm. Logical. In control. Keep him talking long enough to develop an exit plan, and then rescue Daniel.

She'd doomed them all with her refusal to face her father's past. She had to get to him, had to take him away from this, and then apologize for refusing to dignify what she'd known deep down all along. Papa was a criminal and Daniel had almost paid with his life.

Daniel had to still be alive. She would have felt it if he was dead. She had to believe that.

"There's nothing civilized about what you did to Tommy Dalton." Kate shuddered.

"Ah, Dalton. That was a hatch job, wasn't it? I let Wilkes

do the first blows before I finished him. Wilkes has a bit too much fun with the knife, as your friend Sally Fletcher has discovered." Finn tilted his head toward her downed knife. "Shall I demonstrate what he did to her?"

"Don't hurt her. She did nothing to deserve that." Kate pleaded, disgusted with the weakness in her voice but unable to bite down the rising panic.

"*Au contraire.* She told you about me. How else would you have found me? That idiot pugilist? He's been bashed in the head so many times he can't tell his head from his arse. Or your Paddy's friend, Atlas Greer? The Gentleman Thief does not scare me." Finn worked his forefinger down her neck, slowly dancing across her bared skin until he got her to where her shoulder bone and clavicle joined.

A storm brewed above. The dark clouds threatened to upend, and she was going to die in this godforsaken alley.

"I've no love for Bow Street and I won't be caught like Bishop and Williams. They were careless and paid the price. I taught them better than that. Kill if you can to get a fresh Thing, but don't leave a mark. Dig up what Subjects you can't overpower." Finn sighed, seemingly put out by the ignorance of his old colleagues.

"You taught them?" She didn't need to feign surprise.

"What, did you think the Spitalfields gang had all the fun? I've been running bodies since Bishop was still a pathetic carter doing errands for other snatchers. I took him in, him and his damned neighbor Williams, and they've repaid my generosity by bringing that arse Thomas down on everyone's head."

Kate thrust her chin up to look him in his steel blue eyes. "The Superintendent will find out what you've done."

Finn smirked. "But then everyone will know what your dear Papa did too."

"The Met should know what he did. I was wrong to try and hide it. What Papa did was despicable."

"You say that now, but when it comes out, will you feel the same?" Finn chuckled. "That was a boon, finding out

Richard Morgan was shiver-tapped. The cut of my Subject money kept you in that fancy townhouse you loved so much, so you could continue to screw your lover under your Papa's nose. You should have heard O'Reilly the night I found him, cup-shot and bleary-eyed. A man will tell secrets when he's foxed." He pinched her clavicle bone, pressing deep into a bruise from the explosion.

Kate winced, barely managing to stifle a cry of pain. "You bastard."

"You'd like it if I was, wouldn't you?" He dug his nail into her skin, chipping away at the scabbed portion of the bruise. Blood oozed from the wound, stinging in the air. "It'd make me more attractive to you. You like the lost causes, Kate. How else can you explain why you'd be so willing to lie on your back for a popery drunk?"

"Daniel is ten times the man that you'll ever be." If she could back up more, possibly maneuver her foot hard into his shin—

"Only ten?" His lips twisted into a smirk, hand starting to trail from her neck down her arm to cross underneath. Her breast fit in the palm of his hand. He cupped it, squeezing. She gasped.

One, two, three—*now*. As he released her waist to readjust his hold, she slammed back into him, driving her foot into his shin. He stumbled and she whirled around.

She only got a few steps across the alley before he caught her again. Drops of water fell from her hair, into her eyes and down her nose. Seizing hold of her, he slammed her up against the stone wall of the brothel. She grunted with the impact, head hitting hard against the stone. Her vision darkened. She blinked, focusing on the details of the stone squares. The wall was solid; it provided no exit.

He'd pinned her hands behind her back. His weight pressed into her, his height a perfect match to her. With his knee, he parted her legs, fitting himself in the space now left. His front to her back, his hardened arousal pressed at her.

"Do you feel that?" Finn asked. "That's a real man. A man who'd knock you and slice your throat in the same breath. That's what you deserve. I wouldn't send you to the labs, for I knew you were special the first time I saw you with your father. I was going to make you mine, if that old codger hadn't kept you away from me."

She swallowed down bile, determined not to let him see her cower. Her father must have warned Finn off of her, threatened to retract his warehouses if he approached, for she couldn't remember meeting him before she'd moved to Ratcliffe.

In her ingenuousness, she'd let Finn into her life because he could utter a few pretty words and he seemed genuine.

"Why get rid of Dalton?" She struggled to keep her mind sorted. Anything to keep him talking and distracted.

His body tensed, bringing her into closer contact with his erection. She squirmed against his hold, desperate to get away from him. Rain slicked their bodies, yet his grip remained firm. He pinched her wrist hard, twisting until she cried out in pain.

"Stay put, love, or I'll be forced to do something you won't like," he murmured into her ear. "As to Tommy Botch-it, his death was inevitable. He stole from me, and you know what I do to those who pinch from me. Getting rid of O'Reilly at the same time was a bonus."

"How did you get Daniel into that alley?" She tilted her head away from him, able to gain a few centimeters of space. Far enough away to no longer feel the burn of his breath on her skin.

"I'm sure you've already surmised that I drugged him. It was not difficult, for your Paddy's a creature of habit. Every night at the Prospect of Whitby before he'd come to see you, he'd stare into the bottom of a glass. So earnest, like a dog in heat, hanging around your ankles for a chance to rut. Let's see what he was desperate for, shall we?" His hand moved again, down her hip to her thigh, stretching around toward her front.

She swallowed down a sob. He wouldn't see her cry.

"I've always wondered what it'd be like to taste you, Katiebelle." His fingers crept up toward the closure between her skirt and bodice, expertly finding the brass clasp. The light rose fabric, which she had thought so demure when finding it in Spitalfields, was polluted by his touch.

With his hands otherwise occupied, he didn't keep a good grip on her waist. Kate slammed her head into his nose with a horrible crack. He staggered backwards, stunned by the impact. Squirming out of his embrace, Kate slipped past him, apart from the wall.

Finn's hands cupped his nose in a futile attempt to staunch the blood. Crimson rained through the slits of his fingers. She'd wounded him, probably broken his nose.

"You bitch!" he shouted.

"That's for Daniel." Vindication flowed through her, though she knew she was not out of danger yet. She took off running, out of the alley and into the street.

Rain beat heavily around her, swirling puddles about her feet. Finn's voice was almost eaten up by the storm.

"You'll never get to him in time! My men will slit his throat like the dog he is."

She looked over her shoulder quickly. Finn gave up on his bleeding nose, letting it flow naturally. It coated his neckcloth, turning the blue pattern into a red mess.

He grabbed for her as she ran, blood-stained fingers curling around the pink sleeves of her dress. She pried off his hand, throwing every ounce of energy she had into the action. Fueled by panic and fear, she bent his pointer finger backward. Finn howled with pain. The bone crunched as it broke.

Finn wrenched his hand back. His finger was now set at an odd angle, tilting precariously to the left side. She jerked back from him, fumbling in her pocket for the pistol.

"When my men get done with him, he'll be unrecognizable," Finn snarled through clenched teeth.

He didn't move. He held his good hand crossed over his injured one in a sort of makeshift sling. For a second, his attention was not on her, but on his wounded hand.

Her fingers closed around the pistol. She raised it to his head, moving it into a fully cocked motion. Her left hand steadied the gun, right index finger on the trigger. Finn was there before her. In an instant, she could end his life, if she only aimed right.

She didn't hesitate. He'd hurt Daniel, convinced her father to do terrible things. Finn looked up and for the first time fear shone in his eyes. Pistol positioned between his eyes, Kate squeezed the trigger and waited for the recoil.

Nothing happened.

The shot had not fired. The powder might have been wet from the rain. Or the gun may have jammed. She didn't know, only that her trusty flintlock had failed her.

Finn's exhale of breath was audible. Recovering quickly, he took a step toward her. Bullet used, Kate didn't wait to load another. She turned and fled, past shops and houses, through crowds of gin-addled thieves loitering outside the public houses, down alleys and passageways. She ran like she'd never run before, heart echoing in her chest, useless pistol in her fist. She ran until she reached the ferry. Leaning all her weight against the same precarious rail Daniel had warned her about, she searched for Finn. He had not made it onto the ferry on time. He'd have to wait for the next one.

Rain slapped her face, pouring down from the sky in veritable outrage from a god above. She looked out at the night sky as the ferry crossed the Thames. She saw no boot in the water this time. The slow moving sludge of swamp and decay was quiet. Bodies wound up in the Thames, to be found months later when the river had finally released their bloated flesh.

Daniel would not be one of those dead men. Once she hit the shore, she'd keep running toward him. If she had to kill every bloody snatcher from here to Westminster, she'd make damn sure he survived.

DANIEL'S TRUNK WAS packed. One would never know when looking at the crisply folded clothes arranged in straight rows that his hands had shaken as he laid them inside. Madame Tousat had fetched the schedule of the mail coach routes from London to Sussex. In the morning, a carriage would leave from the station and he intended to be on it, royally in his cups and oblivious to the jostling and crowded conditions. From the station in Sussex, he'd stay a night at the coaching inn and hire a hack to Dorking.

Daniel stepped back and surveyed the fruits of three hours of labor in his rented room. His truncheon rested against the wall closest to the door. The room was otherwise bare, except for the bottle of gin placed in the center of the table and a small glass.

Two weeks in London with Kate and all that remained was the bottle of Lady's Delight, a piss-poor substitute with a taunting name.

Closing the trunk, he knelt down on the ground to latch the padlock. The click of the catch echoed in his bones far louder than the barely audible sound. The click meant soon he'd leave for good, taking the easy way out.

Rain pelted the windows. In the distance, a storm gathered up strength to besiege Ratcliffe. If the wretched weather traveled toward Sussex, his journey would be delayed.

He stood and crossed the room in three strides. His hand shot out, wrapping around the bottle. The bottle had three rows of clay stacked on top of each other to form the lip. His mouth would enclose the top two rows in a blighted kiss, knocking back the first sip. Harder at first, the burn bright and fierce until he got used to the taste once more. Then he could afford to nurse the drink, give it proper attention.

The burnt orange clay should have seemed right. Familiar. Comforting. An escape when he'd lost control of everything else.

Clasped around the bottle, his hands were still bruised and battered from the explosion. He looked down at his right thumb pressed over the "Lady's Delight" etching, a furious red slash from the bottom joint to the middle of his thumb. The cut festered, exposed to dirt and grime.

Carefully, he tilted the bottle over his thumb, splashing the alcohol onto the infected flesh. He gritted his teeth against the sting of sizzling inflamed skin, swallowing down a yell. The pulsation of the rain against the patched roof of the lodging house continued on, filling up the silence.

Rubbing his thumb against his pants, he dried the alcohol. The cut ached, a pain that ebbed and flowed with each passing second. It reminded him he was alive, senses alert.

How much could one man be reasonably expected to handle? He didn't know the answer.

In the past, he would have believed the bottle contained a deep-seated secret and if he simply imbibed enough she would finally share the truth with him. Lady's Delight was always a woman, like Emporia's old ships that sailed from the harbors at the London Docks. She had been the only relationship he'd trusted when he fled back to Dorking.

Daniel leaned his head back against the chair, grip tight around the clay. He could remember Kate straddled across his lap, but he didn't have the power to pretend she was here with him. Memories, that was all he had, memories that transmuted and faded over time until all that was left was the subtle scent of her soap and the whisper of her voice.

He lifted the gin to his nose and inhaled. Crisp juniper and pine needles, an astringent bouquet designed to knock him down. "I can smell it on your breath," Poppy had said. "You never hid it well."

Poppy wouldn't need to know. When he got to Dorking, he'd buy another bottle to get him through the visit, but he'd chew mint. That would mask the scent. He'd be more careful this time, control the urge around Moira so that she wouldn't grow up to know her uncle was perpetually in his cups.

Yet that was a lie like every other lie in his life. He breathed in one last breath and set the bottle back on the table next to him. He settled back into the chair, eying the gin, unable to staunch the feeling that it might disappear from him if he didn't watch it.

It would not be his first relapse. He'd stopped when Poppy had given birth. But the cries of her daughter had been too much for his worn down nerves. Seeing Moira had reminded him too much of what he could have had with Kate. He'd fallen from grace and submitted to the ruin's hold.

Seven months without a drink. Moira had been three months old. The air was clear, the sun shone, and it had all seemed so unbearably perfect that he couldn't stand to view it hazily. He'd handed the bottle to Poppy and told her he was done, for good this time. He couldn't stop that bastard from seducing her, but he'd be strong and have a positive effect on her daughter's life.

But he was a failure and failures drank.

Pragmatically, he knew Jasper Finn would kill him if he stayed, for Daniel had gotten too close to Finn's resurrection men. Finn knew where Kate lived. He had prior ties to her. Would Finn go back and find her? Daniel's stomach wrenched at the thought. If he left, Finn would have no reason to hurt Kate. He had to hold on to that hope.

Women who helped him paid the price. He was powerless to defend them.

Outside his window, the storm continued to brew. A clap of thunder penetrated the walls. Shaken from his thoughts, he stood and picked up the bottle again. One hand wrapped around the base, he poured out a sixth into the glass and swirled the gin.

But he didn't drink.

Instead, he thought of Kate. How she'd rested her head against his shoulder and fallen asleep in his arms. How content he'd felt, without the gin to hamper his faculties, fully alert to everything that had happened between them. The pain stung and ripped away his reserves but it was real, so achingly real. It sang of truths he'd never comprehend, but knew existed in the grand scheme of life.

I want more. It's not enough.

Kate had chosen another path, clinging to her memories and not the life they could have had together. The gin that sat so complacently in the glass across from him was a passageway to his old life and the man he'd been then. If he went back there, the last seven months were undone. The man he'd tried so hard to become—a better version of himself, free of the taints of vice—would no longer exist.

He wanted to *be* more. To exist on a plain outside of his basest needs, to live a life he could be proud of and to help those he loved. He wanted to know that he'd done everything he could to eradicate the sins of his past.

He wanted justice.

Picking up the glass, he walked to the window. Rain flowed in through the cracks in the panels, dribbled down onto the floorboards where already a puddle formed. Daniel raised the glass to his lips, breathed in the aroma of gin, and then poured the contents through the split panel.

Sober, he'd mourn the loss of Kate in his life like he should have three years ago. He'd feel every bit of the hurt and become something new from it. "You are stronger than you think," Poppy had said, and for the first time in his life he believed her words.

He was done hiding.

THUNDER ROARED IN time to the frantic pounding of Kate's heart. Panting, she skidded to a stop in front of Daniel's door. Water streamed from her dress, her hair, even from her hands as she tried the doorknob. The pink fabric was now brown in places, thickly coated with mud.

Locked. She pounded on the door, shook the knob,

screamed as loud as she could. "Daniel!"

No answer came, nor was there any light emanating from beneath the door. She could barely see in the hall—what few sconce candles there were had burnt out before this late hour. If Ezekiel had found Daniel before she'd gotten here, then Daniel would be on that floor, gasping for his last breath. Provided he was even in the room, for he could be anywhere in London at this moment, and she'd not be able to get to him.

She couldn't think like that. She'd save Daniel. She had to, if she could get inside the damn room. Fishing in her pocket for her set of lock picks, Kate forced herself to take a deep breath.

Calm, clear mind.

She jumped as another clap of thunder shook the house's foundations. Lightning crackled in the sky, casting an ethereal golden glow from the window at the end of the hall. Seizing the sudden light, Kate inserted her pick into the upper part of the keyhole in the door. The rest she could do by touch, feeling for the pins and coaxing them into compromise.

"Come on, come on," she muttered under her breath, leveraging the torque wrench and the pick in the lock.

One pin wouldn't move.

"Daniel!" she yelled again, her voice breaking as she pushed at the stubborn pin. Not too hard, enough to get it to move, when all she wanted to do was rip the lock off its hinges. "Daniel, please. Oh bloody, bloody hell."

She felt the pin go down.

Without hesitating, she used the tension wrench to rotate the cylinder and unlock the lock. She turned the knob, yet nothing happened. Something blocked the door. Was it Daniel's body? Had Ezekiel beaten him and then left him there to die?

She shoved the door. Kept shoving, kept yelling out his name.

CHAPTER 23

IN THE ROOM, something cracked and fell to the ground. Kate pushed harder.

"Christ, Katiebelle, you'll break the door down." Daniel's voice cut through her panic.

She stopped immediately, hand on the knob. The door opened.

He was alive, unharmed, and without a shirt. On the floor behind him were the remains of a wooden chair, shoved up underneath the doorknob as a failsafe lock. He pulled from his left ear a cotton plug, grimacing at it. "Neighbors were bloody loud this evening. I'm sorry I didn't hear you the first time."

He continued to speak, but she no longer heard him. His voice melded into the most harmonious of songs, Sussex accent with that hint of Irish brogue on the edges. Without hesitation, she flung herself into his arms, landing hard on his chest.

"Oof!" he grunted, but his arms wrapped around her waist to pull her closer to him. Instinctively, like he'd been expecting her all along.

She forgot about her damp dress, the storm outside, even the danger. Clasping her hands together behind his neck, she leaned back in his hold to look him in the eye. Strong chin with the hint of stubble, his fiercely red hair and wide forehead, everything she held dear in that face.

"I didn't expect to see you again," he said.

Brazenly, she told the truth. "I didn't expect to be back again."

A small crowd of interested parties had assembled in the hall from the noise. Quickly, she shut the door behind her. She knew Finn hadn't followed her. She'd been vigilant about checking behind her, and with the storm the roads were close to impassable.

But if she'd been able to pick her way into Daniel's flat, so could Ezekiel—born and bred in the rookeries as he appeared to be, it was a safe assumption he'd been picking locks since childhood. The armchair to the right of the door was solid and would serve as a better stop-gauge for the lock.

"Help me move that chair." She went to the side, beginning to shove it to the left.

He complied, lifting up one end of the chair. Chair moved against the door, Kate stood back, somewhat satisfied.

Daniel tilted his head. "Katiebelle, you want to tell me what's happening?"

"Finn's sending Ezekiel after you." She stepped closer to him, grabbing his hand in hers, needing to be close to him. "I went to the brothel to see Sally Fletcher. Finn caught me outside."

She didn't want to think about Finn. Squeezing Daniel's hand tighter, his touch made it all seem surreal. The heat from his body warmed her frigid fingers.

Daniel's gaze locked on hers. "Did he hurt you?"

"No." She shook her head. "Not much, at least. He...he tried to touch me, but I got away."

"Bastard," Daniel cursed. "I'm going to tear him apart by his bloody limbs. This happened tonight?"

"Before I came here." A shiver went through her frame, either from the chill in the room, the wet of her dress or the memory of Finn's attack on her. "You've got to get out of here, Daniel. Ezekiel will come after you."

He dropped her hand to envelop her in his strong hold. Running his hands up and down her arms to warm her, he held her close. "With the storm raging, we won't get far, love. Madame Tousat said the hack routes are a mess."

She looked back toward the door and the chair. It would stick, at least until the rain lessened. She'd barely made it here in the first place.

"We'll leave as soon as the storm abates," Daniel assured her. "I'm concerned, of course, but any attempt at venturing outdoors is going to get us wet and lost. At least here, we've got a roof over our heads. I've kept watch for anyone following me, and I take a variety of ways to get to the flat. I'm registered under an assumed name."

She leaned her head against his chest, the smell of bergamot and cloves surrounding her in something that was utterly male and utterly Daniel. They were strong once, and they could be strong again.

"I've got my gun, and you have your truncheon, yes?" She pulled from him to look about the room, finding the gun on top of his trunk. Standing back from him, she surveyed the room. "Though I think my powder's wet, as the gun didn't fire off properly at Finn."

Daniel scowled. "Hate that you had to use it at all. He'll pay for this, I promise."

She barely heard his words. On the table by the door was an empty bottle of Lady's Delight.

Kate's stomach wrenched.

"Oh, Daniel. I'm so sorry. I didn't mean for you to go back to the bottle." She picked up the bottle. It was feather-light in her palm, deceptively so when it was the root of his past problems. He'd been so determined not to return to that.

She couldn't help but feel it was all her fault.

Daniel's larger fingers covered hers around the clay bottle. "I didn't drink it."

She exhaled. He squeezed her hand before prying her fingers off the gin. The bottle returned to the table.

"I bought it with every intention of drinking it. I thought it'd be easier, if I could find some peace, if the dreams would stop. But then I thought of you, out there with Finn on the loose." He cupped her chin in his hands, truth reflected in his jade eyes.

He had worried for her safety, while she'd rushed back to protect *him*.

"And I thought of Poppy, back home with Moira. I want to bring them to London and give her a fresh start where no one knows the story of Moira's birth. Poppy could pass as a widow. I can't bring them here if I'm still wanted."

"We will find a way to make that happen."

He gave her a grateful smile. "But mostly, I don't want to be a shell anymore. Forever apologizing for what I've done in the past. I want to make it right and then move on, live life as I should have all along." He let his thumb trace the curve of her jaw.

She shivered at his soft touch, leaning into his hold. "I have every confidence you will."

Daniel's fingers ceased moving. He tilted her chin up so that she looked him in the eye. "Where do we go from here, Katiebelle? Obviously, we need to avoid Finn's men, but you and me...where do we stand?"

"My father was guilty," she said simply, closing the little bit of distance between them. She laid her head down on his chest, heard his heart beating. Only now did she feel back at rights, able to deal with the atrocity of her father's past.

She followed Daniel's movements, noting with relish the sculpted lines of his bare chest. How could she ever have thought she could live without him? Every part of her had ached for him, died a little bit more without him.

"Yes." Daniel didn't inquire further, and for that, she was glad.

She could tell him all about her father's deeds in the

morning, when the threat had passed and they could fathom some way to go forward. She shivered and he put an arm around her, running his hands up and down her arms to warm her.

"Finn said Papa had been broke even then. Oh, Daniel, what have I done? If I'd only known, I could have provided the ledger and you might have gone free..." She sniffled, unable to stop the sob that escaped. She'd ruined everything by believing in the wrong man and trusting her memories over facts.

No one was perfect, yet she'd held her father up on a pedestal.

Tears streamed down her cheeks, melding with the rainwater until she was a torrential downpour. As if the unrest in her mind had been amplified to unnatural volumes, thunder boomed as her shoulders shook.

"Quiet," Daniel murmured. "That's all in the past. Neither of us is faultless."

He pulled her closer, the warmth of his bare chest and arms surrounding her. There was no fireplace in the room. Out of the corner of her eye, she saw the windows were patched ineffectively with a bit of red cloth. The scarf he'd lent her because again, in a moment like this one, she'd been cold and worn out from exposure to the elements.

It had been so long since anyone had done anything to bring her comfort. She'd been on her own for two and a half years, lost to the emptiness inside of her and certain she needed no one else to survive.

But she did. She needed him. It was not weakness to want to share her life with someone else. That knowledge burned within her, burned like the flames of Friggard's Pawn, licking at her insides until she could not stand on her own two feet without effort.

She sagged against him. At her falter, he lifted her from the ground, his arms wrapped around her legs, her feet hanging idly off to the side. He brought her to the bed and set her down gently.

Going to the closed County Cork steamer trunk, he pulled out a blanket. She blinked at the ordered rows of his clothing. He was never that orderly, unless he was trying to bide his anxiety with menial tasks or he was to go on a trip.

He had been about to leave.

"Daniel?"

"Yes?" He wrapped the blanket around her shoulders.

She tugged the blanket tighter around her, her gaze on the neat stacks. "Are you going somewhere?"

The bed creaked as he sat down next to her. His arm draped over her shoulders and he scooted her closer so that she could rest her head against his shoulder once more. She snuggled deeper against him. His clothes smelled faintly of lye from the washing soap, something good and clean in this hovel of waste and rotten food. She fisted the end of his shirt, clinging to it as if she could stop him from leaving simply by hanging on to it.

"I had thought to return to Dorking," he said. "But I'm not going anywhere now. I don't want to turn tail and run anymore, Kate. I want to stay and do what's right."

Her heart was suddenly lighter, the pent-up stress of the past few weeks released. They could look toward the future together, if only they could deal with the sins of their pasts. She wanted that, wanted it with every fiber of her being.

Before, she had feared admitting love for him again. It would leave her vulnerable, a prisoner to her emotions. But as she leaned against him, his heartbeat echoing in her ears, she felt stronger than she had in ages. She was no longer alone, but part of something bigger than herself, this union between them that enriched her life and brought out a better side to her.

The blanket fell from her shoulders as she reached for him. Her hands came to rest on his shoulders, for she could not imagine not touching him, not being near him. He was everything that made sense. Everything she'd ever loved.

He grasped her left hand in his, running his thumb across

the gold on her ring finger. "I thought you pawned this."

"I did. Jasper Finn found it and gave it back to me."

"That's...odd." He stretched her hand out in the light, surveying the ring.

"Finn wanted to test my reaction to it. I was going to pawn it again—even went to a fellow fence in St. Giles that day we met with Atlas." She leaned in to him, right hand still on his shoulder. "This ring was part of your family and knowing what you've struggled against, I just...I couldn't bear to part with it."

His eyes glistened with hope, but his expression remained cautious. "What exactly are you saying, Kate? Do you want to be with me?"

She smiled, a wider, happier smile than she could remember in a long time. Sitting here so close to him, his hand on hers and their shoulders touching, she couldn't imagine wanting to be anywhere else.

"If you'll still have me, I want to fight by your side. And when the day comes that Finn rots in Newgate like he should have all along, I want to start a new life with you. I bloody love you, Daniel, and I always have."

HE OPENED AND shut his eyes. Surely, he must be asleep, for he could not be this lucky. Not him, who a few hours ago had been so certain he'd never see her again.

But he felt her hands on his shoulders, the pressure of her fingers as she dug into the knots of tension. Her bottom lip quivered. He saw her dark eyes brimming with hope—hope and a little fear—and he knew this was real.

He leaned into her touch, angled his forehead against hers. Her cold skin met the fire burning in his limbs. His pulse pounded in his ears. Desire raced through him like a runaway phaeton. He held her gaze as the most wonderful of emotions stirred with him, that of acceptance and appreciation and all the rest that came with being held in her esteem.

Concern flickered across her face. So lost was he in what it was to be near her, he'd forgotten to speak.

"Do you still love me?" Kate's voice was soft, devoid of her usual bluster. "Will you forgive me for not believing you?"

"Katiebelle, I've never stopped loving you. Every day that has passed, I've wanted you in my life." He pulled back from her enough to tuck her hair behind her ear, his fingers brushing against her creamy cheek.

So smooth, so delicate was her skin, yet she was the toughest woman he'd ever known. She loved with a dogmatic determination and a need to protect those she held dear. He hadn't earned her trust before but he'd earn it now, if doing so took his last breath.

Previously, he'd thought her his salvation. Now he knew he needed to save himself.

"You get a broken man," he murmured. "A man who has done wretched things, but a man who wants desperately to be something worthy of your love. Can you handle that?"

"You get a stubborn woman. A woman who told herself she didn't need anyone else to survive, but now realizes she's better off with a broken man to heal her hurt. Can *you* handle that?" She took his hand in hers and pressed it against her lips, the calluses on his fingers against her tender lips.

"Absolutely," he murmured.

From the moment she'd set foot in the room he'd been hard. She'd be his undoing, with her devious pink tongue darting along the tip of his forefinger. He groaned, unable to hold back any longer.

His lips came down upon hers. Mouth to mouth in furious rhythm, the taste of her lips better than any bottle of Lady's Delight.

"I love you, I love you, I love you," he gasped in between kisses, reluctant to part from her for more than a moment. Yet it was necessary to let her know, to repeat the words in litany because they'd been caged within him for what felt like an eternity. He was free with her. His heart soared so high he believed it to have fled from his body entirely.

"I'm so sorry. I should have listened to you. If I'd been less stubborn—" She tore from him to look him in the eye.

Silencing her with another kiss, he relished the feel of her lips hot upon his, the tangle as their tongues met and played within their joined mouths. "I like you stubborn," he said, undoing the first few closures of her gown. "It keeps me on my toes."

Her head fell back in a full-bodied, throaty laugh. "God forbid we let you slip. Shall I pick a fight with you whenever you feel too complacent?"

"Yes." He was mesmerized by the rise and fall of her chest with each erratic breath, the imperial line of her neck.

"What shall we fight about? I don't like the new Forsyth." She leaned back against his hold, granting him easier access to her neck.

"I quite like them." He found the pressure point at her neck, nibbling on it.

"But the mechanism—" She gave up mid-way, her speech descending into a breathy moan.

"Dreadful mechanism." He grinned against her skin. His tongue darted out against the hollow where her neck met her shoulders. Her smell filled his nose, blessed jasmine and black pepper. She was supple in his hands, so achingly perfect that for a second he could not believe she was real.

He pulled back to look at her, at her kiss-swollen red lips, flushed cheeks, and disordered chignon. Undeniably his Kate. His hands tangled in her dewy hair, plucking pin after pin. He barely heard the clink as the metal hit the floor. She shook her head, her silken curls tumbling down her shoulders wantonly. A groan tore from his throat. He was so awed by the wild goddess in front of him, this woman who had beaten the odds and survived the rookeries only to find him again.

Huddled against him, her dress fell around her shoulders, half-opened to him. Her breasts strained against the fabric, her pert nipples pebbled. The blanket had slipped completely from her shoulders and lay in a lump on the bed.

Four buttons on the back of her dress kept her from him, four devious buttons that when undone would give him the greatest joy imaginable. He undid the closures in record time, hands shaking but determined. The pink dress pooled in her lap. He helped her wiggle free from the mountains of fabric and settled her across his lap. Her bare legs peeked out from beneath her chemise and drawers, the sight of that milky skin enough to make his mouth water.

"Touch me," she whispered, her smoldering gaze holding his.

He didn't need further encouragement. His fingers slid against the smooth skin of her legs, up to the hem of her drawers. Grasping the fabric between his thumb and forefinger, he scooted it down her legs. He placed a kiss to each bit of skin revealed, drunk off the taste of her.

By his bedside table, the candle began to flicker. He undid the first lace of her stays before she stopped his hand, her gaze burning with such heat that the room felt ten degrees hotter.

"Light the candle again. I want to see you as you come inside me," she said huskily.

As if her bawdy words weren't enough to send him reeling, her lips curled into a little smirk. Desire shot through him, his breeches uncomfortably tight.

"Christ," he cursed, close to the edge already without even getting to touch her completely naked skin.

With her still in his lap, he fumbled in the drawer for a match. He shifted through several scraps of parchment and three lead bullets before he finally found one.

Once the candle was lit, he sat back for a second to look at her in the new light. "So beautiful." He planted a kiss on her neck, under her ear. She squirmed in his lap as his tongue shot out to lick the delicate bottom of her lobe. He nibbled on the base, each shift of her body against his erection sharpening his bliss.

Her hands spread flat across the expanse of his stomach. Daringly, she kept going to the fall of his breeches, working open the clasp and freeing his shaft. He breathed a sigh of relief, but his breath was quickly stolen by her attentions.

One hand placed over the other, she worked him up and down. She knew the exact rhythm that would crest him quickly. He was both overjoyed she remembered the rhythm of their bodies and shamed that he might fade too fast.

This felt right, the slide of his solid shaft in her hands, the way his eyes rolled back in ecstasy and his breathing became ragged with every stroke. Kate surveyed him from her perch in his lap. His sinewy chest muscles strained, raw power held within him. Her body thrummed, alive from the feel of him, awake to his every gasp.

"Love, if you continue, there's not much chance we can turn back," he moaned.

"I don't want to turn back." She pumped him again, grinning wickedly. She never wanted to leave him.

He stilled her hands. He made quick work of her chemise and stays, flinging them off the side of the bed. She helped him from his breeches. Pushing her down on the bed, he climbed on top of her, settling in between her thighs.

"My wild Kate." He kissed her again, playing in her mouth, stirring the basest longings within her core.

"Let me show you how wild I am." She grasped his wrists, rolling them over so that she was on top. She moved to straddle him, leaning forward so that her breasts fell close to him and then pulling back when he went to grasp a pebbled nipple in his mouth. Repeating the process, she stretched out, basking in the feel of being in control above him.

He grabbed hold of her waist and yanked her forward. Suckling on her nipple, he massaged her other breast with firm, circular movements. He knew every curve of her body better even than she, as though she had been created for him and him alone. In that instant, with his lips wrapped around her breast, tongue teasing the firm tip of her nipple, she didn't doubt that she had been.

He was everywhere at once. His hand dipped into the juncture between her thighs, tangled into her coarse curls. He came close to her center, never touching her where she needed it most, taunting her with his nearness. She let out a frustrated moan.

He chastised her with a nip to her breast. "All in due time, Katiebelle," he grinned.

She was on top; she was in control. Bracing herself against his shoulders, she held herself aloft from him, beyond his mouth. Two could play at this game, and she was quite certain she could win.

Until he reached up and tugged her down, his arms wrapping around her back in a strong grip. Suddenly, she didn't want to be freed from him, but instead to fall against his muscular body, to feel the warmth of his skin against hers.

She remembered that this was close to how it had been before. Before she had known only a part of him, what he chose to show to her. In this present moment she knew it all, every damn broken piece of him that added up into a wonderful whole, and that made each touch more potent.

She placed a kiss on his shoulder, licking his hard muscle. He shuddered, her hot breath against even hotter skin as he released his hold on her. He pulled up his knees, so that she lay cradled in his lap. Sitting in this position, angled with her rear against his erection, she was utterly on display for him. She felt no shame, for she was long past the world that would have condemned her for sex outside of the strictures of marriage. She had become something different entirely.

He let out a strangled moan as she leaned back, his eyes widening as he scanned her naked frame. "You're enough to kill a man."

"But it'd be a valiant death, don't you think?" She

grabbed for his hand, guiding him where she wanted him most.

He was quick to comply, thumb finding her bud and rubbing against her. From her position, she could see everything he did, see her own folds spread out for his ministrations. She gulped down a breath of air, for his fingers rubbed so softly against her clitoris she thought she might die from the torture of it, stroke by stroke toward a distant pinnacle that could not be reached.

"Faster," she pleaded, no longer concerned with who held the control as long as he continued touching her. He complied, thumb rubbing against her center in time with the flick of his forefinger. The pressure built within her steadily, and she was primed and ready, like a lead bullet wrapped in a cloth.

"Is this what you want?" He inserted a finger inside of her, the rod to her gun, his thumb still at work on her as any good trigger finger would do.

She whimpered in reply, the loudness of her own pleasure-soaked voice surprising her.

"That's good, moan for me," he urged, continuing with his wicked strokes. "I like to know that I've pleased you."

Her body lifted up as he set a blazing rhythm, taking her so close to the edge. "So good," she gasped, as the sensations grew.

"I need you," she said, for if she didn't have him in that instant she'd come without him and she wanted him deep inside her. She felt no mortification at the admission, only love for him. Together they'd become something greater. Their affection would strengthen them.

"Then have me." He released her so she could scoot back.

Lingering with the tip of him brushing against her entrance would drive her mad. With one hand, she guided him all the way into her. He slid in slowly, stretching her in the most exquisite torment.

"Oh, Daniel," she breathed as he withdrew and plunged deep into her. He filled her to the brim.

In all the times they'd been together, she'd never felt so at peace and aroused all in one. His hands fell to her waist and he helped her to push back and forth, finding a rhythm that would send them both reeling. Each thrust stirred the fire within her.

"I'll be everything you need, Katiebelle." He stilled within her, fingertips digging into her shoulders.

"You already are." She met his lips in a fiery kiss, echoing the surge and fall of his thrusts with her tongue. Quicker he thrust, erratic as he pumped everything he had into taking her higher.

For the second time she felt that building pressure within her, as he took her up and then held off to lengthen the climax. This rhythm went on until she knew he'd squeezed the trigger in her gun. The bullet shot forward and she was exploding in pieces around him. A second later he joined her, pulling out at the last moment.

"That was amazing," he said a moment later better, head back against his pillow.

They lay languidly together under the covers, her head on his chest once more and his fingers stroking idly up her arm. The only sound became the quiet of their breathing, gently lulling her to sleep.

In his arms, she knew exactly where she was supposed to be. The rest—the peril and the conflict—they'd figure out together.

THE MORNING WAS as gray and cloudy as the night prior. Rain splattered down from the crack in the window, a steady throb that would make traveling difficult. The roads would be slick, the horses's hooves stuck with mud. None of that mattered to Daniel when he awoke the next morning with Kate next to him. She fit into the curve of his side as a matching piece to his puzzle, her brown hair splashed across his outstretched arm.

His hand cupped her breast, finding that soft spot instinctively as he slept. He could move his hand, but in a fit of wickedness, he lingered and enjoyed the suppleness of her flesh. She stirred, glancing down at his hand.

She arched a brow. "Already lustful, I see. Was I not enough for you last night?"

He chuckled at her teasing and readjusted so that she was against him. Lowering his head, he stole a kiss from her that silenced any doubts she might have had about his satisfaction. She bore his mark where her collarbone joined with her neck, if he needed a further reminder that last night had truly happened.

I love you, Daniel, and I always have.

He rested his weight on his elbows, leaning over to properly survey her. He wanted to commit this new version of her, well-sated and hopeful, to his memory. When they had been together before, their mornings had been scarce, for he'd had to flee from her chambers before her father awoke.

Her cheeks flushed under the weight of his gaze, a pleasant pink that he'd missed so much. She sighed, yet for the first time since he'd been back she sounded content.

"Good morning," he said, remembering the very words he'd said to her a few days prior.

This time, she met his greeting with a private smile, brushing a fallen lock of hair out of his eye. "Good morning."

"I wish I could offer you a proper repast, but I didn't think to restock before." He didn't say that he'd thought only of bashing out his brains on the gin. It hung in the air, recognized but no longer needed.

Kate stretched, wiggling her toes underneath the blanket. "I'll go out and fetch some food." She intertwined her fingers in his. "Later."

He brought their joined hands to his lips, caressing her knuckle. He'd lie here forever, basking in the joy of being with her, but that was optimism they could not yet grasp. If they were to have the endless nights he dreamed of, he had to protect her now.

Releasing her hand, Daniel sat up. She reached to stop him from rising from the bed, but he slipped from her grip.

"Must we return to reality?" Her voice was muffled by the pillow, for she had turned on her side.

"I fear so." He stepped into his breeches.

Her dress lay in a heap on the floor, while her stays were flung haphazardly onto the tea cabinet. The chemise was harder to find, thrust between the headboard of the bed and the wall. He collected each and deposited them in front of her.

He pulled his white cotton shirt over his head, sneaking a glance at her as she did up her stays. She crossed the laces over the eyelets and then brought them together in a bow in the front, then did up the back hitch in a similar manner. He took a seat on the bed next to her, pushing her hair off her back so he could see the closures. He doubted she needed his help, yet it made him feel useful.

"Perhaps someday we'll be rich enough that you can have a lady's maid again."

"I quite like the independence." She batted his hand away from the back of her dress, doing up the last fastener on her own. "Besides, if I wish to lie around in my chemise all day, I can without feeling as though I am on display. For anyone other than you, that is."

Her saucy wink had him hard, ready to push up her skirts and take her on the bed again. He gulped.

"I wouldn't feel right giving orders to a servant now." She shrugged. "Not when I've been lesser in class than they are."

"So you're content with your station? Your life?" He eyed her skeptically.

She laughed, wrapping her hand around his. "Do I enjoy being bloody poor? Of course not. But this—fencing, going out on my own, being something more than a prim society maiden—I wouldn't exchange for anything. You'll have to pry the flintlock from my cold, dead hands."

He winced.

"I quiz you, Daniel." Kate squeezed his hand. "Although I will say my loyalty to my flintlock might be fading. When Finn cornered me, I tried to shoot the bastard but the Forsyth backfired."

"Bloody bastard."

"More like bloody Forsyth. The powder may have been bad. I didn't think to check it this morning. But the nerve of that gun!" Her nose wrinkled in annoyance, lips pulled down in a grimace.

"I love that it's not the fact that you needed to shoot Finn, but that the gun failed that is troubling you." He hid behind sarcasm, for the reality of their predicament was far more troublesome.

Daniel ran his thumb along the juncture between her index finger and thumb, mindlessly stroking her skin. They should get up and seek shelter somewhere else. The more he moved, the less likely it was that Finn's men could track him. Kate leaned on him, shoulder against his.

Where would he go from here? Another tenement house, most likely, in a deeper and more obscure part of the rookeries that wouldn't be as easy to find. No one had time to care about their neighbors. It took fourteen hour days for a menial laborer to earn enough to pay the rent on a tiny one-room flat with broken windows and walls that let in the cold.

"We should go. The rain may provide some cover from Finn's men." He didn't pull away from Kate, loathe to separate from her. Lift up the trunk, hail the hackney, and locate a safer place.

"I know." She covered her mouth with her hand, yawning.

He tilted his head toward her, winking. They'd gotten little sleep last night, too caught up in their reunion to stop. She'd had him begging for release at least three times; after a while he started to lose track of anything other than her hands and lips on him.

She laughed, winking back at him in shared secret. He

pulled her close to him.

"I love you." He kissed the top of her head.

"As I love you." Backing out of his hold, she kissed him.

Several minutes later, when they emerged breathless, she sat up straighter. Her lips pressed together in resignation. "What are we going to do about Papa?"

Daniel sighed. "The ledger had the proof in it, then?"

"Lists and lists of bodies and the amounts received for them. Daniel—" She bit at her bottom lip. "I'm not sure how to equate the man who would strike a business deal with Finn with the man I knew as my father."

Her fingers fiddled with the lace trim on her dress. "I believed in him. I defended him when the rest of society blamed him for Emporia's collapse. If the company was already in the red before his illness, it really was his mismanagement. I've been a fool all along."

"Don't think that way," he cautioned. "You were doing what you thought was right, and holding true to the memory of your father. Your loyalty is to be admired, not thought of as a weakness. I should have given you more time to process this before."

She shook her head, her unbound hair flying about her face. "How can you say that? He didn't care about me enough to set aside funds, and I've made excuses for that this entire time."

Gently, he tucked a lock of hair behind her ear. "Because I know he loved you. We all have sins we've paid for, Kate. Emporia was a huge company. Whatever mistakes Morgan made, I can hope that he made them thinking he was saving you and his workers. He can't explain what he did now and I choose to believe he was not a monster."

"But his dealings with Finn cost you your old life."

The empty bottle of gin stood on the table. So many nights wasted when he could have been with Kate. From now on, he vowed, he would live life fully. "I didn't deserve that life before. If we'd gotten married, you would have been getting half a man."

She followed his gaze. "So you're truly done with it?"

He would not lie to her. "I'll always be struggling with the need to drink. It is a disease that if left untreated will fester until the need becomes too much. So I'll remain vigilant, aware that it might strike me in the quietest moments. But I can manage it now, I think."

"And I'll be here to help." She leaned forward and laid a kiss against his scruffy cheek.

"Aye, I shall be unstoppable." He tweaked her nose.

Quizzically she tilted her head toward the window. He didn't see anything of interest outside, other than the droplets of water that pebbled on the glass.

"What is it?" he asked.

She held up her hand so he would not speak again. He sat in absolute silence, not daring to breathe.

"I thought I heard something," she said finally. "But I suppose it was just the rain."

Exhaling, he turned back around so that he was opposite the door. The armchair held fast; it had not budged since they had positioned it. No one had tried to seek entrance to the room.

For now at least, they were safe, forgotten about by Finn's men in the relentless weather.

CHAPTER 24

LULLED BY THE sense of relative normalcy, Daniel clung to Kate and what it was like to exist in this state of bliss.

The night before, they had sent Madame Tousat's errand boy for fresh gunpowder for Kate's flintlock. The boy delivered it mid-morning, awaking them from slumber. Daniel set the gunpowder down on the desk and pulled Kate into his arms for a quick embrace. One last kiss, one last touch, and then they'd leave for a new tenement house. The rain had slowed enough that they could finally travel.

He broke away from her, patting his hands against his breeches to smooth out the wrinkles. They had tarried long enough. Departure could no longer be avoided. He picked up the bottle to chuck it into the rubbish receptacle.

Then in a blur it all changed. A scratch to the window cut through the noiseless room. The movement happened too quickly for him to react—the glass was already removed. An instant later, a man's head occupied the space where the window had been.

The flintlock lay on the table by the bed.

"The gun!" he shouted at Kate, thoughts stirred to action. She vaulted off the bed, toward the gun.

He took a step forward to the door, where his truncheon had been leaning up against the closest wall. It was too far away from his current position for him to grab quickly.

The man shimmied further into the room. Daniel recognized Ezekiel as he rolled once, executing a quick flip that popped him up into a standing position. Chest tightened, heart pounding, Daniel scanned the room for something he could use as a weapon, a sharp implement or a bludgeoning tool. Only the bottle of gin struck him.

Daniel smashed the bottom of the bottle against the table. The clay broke into jagged pieces. He grasped the base of the bottle, crouched in a fighter's stance.

Ezekiel faced him with a malicious leer. The notched blade in his hand was rusted. Panic welled in Daniel's throat, threatened to seize hold of him and transfix him to this spot.

He would die in the very room that had begun to feel like home.

He searched for Kate. She knelt on the ground by the bedside table, unable to see the top of the table without sitting up and alerting attention. She'd made it to the gun. But she was too close to Ezekiel for his comfort.

As she reached up, her hand smacked the candlestick holder. The metal and wax clunked to the ground. Furiously, she kept patting at the table as Ezekiel twitched. He turned around, no longer focused on Daniel. The flintlock fell, landing outside of Kate's reach.

"You came for me. She's nothing to you." Daniel took a step forward and another, but Ezekiel was too near to her. He thrust out with the knife and Kate threw herself downward, the knife barely missing her ear.

Ezekiel's boot connected with her chest in a sickening thud. She coughed, gasping for air. Another kick like that and he'd fracture her ribs.

God, Kate had been hurt for him again. He hadn't protected her.

Daniel bolted forward, so focused on Ezekiel that he didn't register the second head in the window until the man was already in the room. The other exhumator launched himself at Daniel, blocking his way to Kate.

He heard Kate groan in agony as Ezekiel's foot rammed into her rib cage once more, but the second resurrectionist jabbed at his side. Daniel staggered back. Pain throbbed through him, for the man had hit his earlier injuries from the explosion.

Finn's man took advantage of his distraction, moving toward Kate and Ezekiel. Forcing the pain down, Daniel ran towards the man.

He had to get to Kate before the other man did.

Skidding on the floor, Daniel collided with the brute. The force of the impact threw both men back against the wall. Daniel elbowed the resurrectionist, and he groaned in protest. For a second Daniel thought he'd gotten the upper hand.

He reeled back to punch him but before he could draw his cork, the Burker's hand wrapped around the back of his skull. A cloth slammed against his mouth, and suddenly he was sliding downward.

The last sound he heard was Kate screaming as he slipped out of consciousness.

KATE DOUBLED OVER, her breath wrenched from her body. Sprawled out on the floor behind the bed, Ezekiel leered over the top of her, his short, stocky frame suddenly gigantic. His foot connected again with her midsection, sending searing pain through her body.

Her rib must have been broken. That pain laced over the ache of her other injuries, a bright, bitter layer.

She couldn't stop screaming.

He leaned down, snatching up the fallen flintlock. "Quiet, bitch." He hit her with the butt of the gun.

She didn't cry again, even as the gun smashed into her cheek. Sputtering, she tasted blood in her mouth from where she'd bitten her own tongue. She saw spots where the wall had been before, flashes dimmed by the blackness that crept over her eyes.

No, fight it, get Daniel. The resurrection men would kill him; she had to save him. If she could only move…

"Got what we came for," Ezekiel said to the other man.

"Get 'is 'ands, would ye?" The other man called. His voice sounded further away, like he was closer to the door.

"I finish the whore off first, ye know the rules, Templeton. No witnesses." Ezekiel stepped near to her. "Besides, I been wantin' to slit a bitch. Wilkes got to do the last one."

She didn't risk looking up to confirm what she knew she heard: a blade being sharpened. They meant to slit her throat like they'd done to Bartleby, and likely blame Daniel for it too. She huddled on the ground, not even daring to breathe.

"Finn'll be 'oppin' if you make 'im wait." The man named Templeton tapped his foot impatiently. "'Tis already mad ye botched the last attempt."

There was a loud thump, as if Templeton had dropped something heavy.

Did they have Daniel?

Footsteps sounded. Templeton was coming to survey Ezekiel's conquest. "Bitch is almost dead, Zeke. Ye gotta take the bogger to Sepulchre's. Ye really wanna make 'im wait?"

"Bloody 'ell." Ezekiel scoffed. He came toward her but then backed off, instead approaching his cohort. "All right. We can come back for 'er. Where's she gonna go? She's so beat up, won't last long."

"Can't think of why Finn wants 'im alive," Templeton grumbled. "'Tis a damn waste. 'E learned nothin' from Bishop's arrest."

"I say, ye sell the corpse and pay the cutter to slice it. Ye don't bury it."

"Bollocks, all of it," Templeton grunted. "Lift, ye bleeder!"

From her place on the floor, she couldn't see their exit, but she heard a sliding motion as though someone was being dragged. They'd done something to Daniel to subdue him. She wanted to scream, to bolt after them. If she screamed, she'd lose all chance of helping Daniel. They'd come back and kill her.

Kate struggled to get up. Against her chest, her left wrist bent at a nearly impossible angle, the outline of a tall boot imprinted onto her palm.

Her breaths were shallow, each exhale sending an echo of pain through her. Leaning heavily on her right wrist, she leveraged herself up from the ground, using the bedframe as support.

When my men get done with him, he'll be unrecognizable.

There was no doubt in her mind that Finn would keep his promise. But the men hadn't killed Daniel outright, which gave her a smidgen of hope. Already, he'd escaped the immediate fate of Dalton and Bartleby. If all they had wanted was Daniel's death, they wouldn't have taken him with them.

Finn feared being tied to May, Bishop, and Williams—feasibly, he intended to set up Daniel for his resurrection crimes as well as Dalton's murder. Without the attention on him, Finn could return to the resurrection game in peace.

Kate twisted the blanket in her hands, gingerly scooting across the bed. She had to stand on her own two feet, breathe through the pain.

Any chance Daniel had of survival depended on her.

A sob escaped, followed soon by another. Her father had brought them into this mess, and Daniel's life would be paid as penalty. A torrent of tears streamed down her cheeks, but she was standing and that, at least, was something.

She crept toward the door. Finn's gang had left it wide open, the armchair pushed out of the way as though it weighed as much as a pence. The pouch of gun powder had fallen from the desk and she collected it, reloading her flintlock.

Skidding into the hall, Kate took off, ignoring the

throbbing pain in her side that begged her to slow down.

She continued on, down cramped alleys and past street signs with colloquial names like Cat's Paw and Dead Man's Door. Noise poured out from the Three Boars public house, but she didn't stop. Where would Finn have taken Daniel?

She gasped for breath as she rounded the corner. Her chest heaved.

Stopping—she'd stop for a minute and go again—she leaned against the side of a building. The most logical conclusion was that Finn had a base of operations somewhere near Ratcliffe, for he'd wanted to use Papa's warehouses and most of the entries had come from around East London. The less distance the carters needed to carry the resurrection baskets the better. Chance of exposure would be higher if they carted over a longer distance.

Take the bogger to Sepulchre. Kate couldn't be certain she'd heard Templeton right over the noise in her ears, but she knew that name. Her father's journal mentioned the workhouse cemetery of St. Sepulchre's-within, located on Chick Lane in the heart of the Saffron Hill rookery. The parish had built two workhouses, which they sectioned as Sepulchre's-within and Sepulchre's-without. Chick Lane was also close to Smithfield and the Fortune of War public house, which Finn had been known to frequent.

She had to assume then that they would take Daniel to the burial grounds. What was Finn's plan? Ezekiel had spoken of selling the corpse, but if they intended to trade him to a hospital like St. Thomas, it would have been easier to kill him in the flat. She had to believe that Daniel would be safe, at least for the present. One didn't transport a body simply to kill it upon arrival without fanfare, and fanfare took time.

There was only one man she knew of that could quickly ascertain Finn's motives.

Kate started forward again, fighting the fatigue threatening to take hold of her body. She was so tired, tired of running and fighting only to have her happiness ripped from her.

A child skipped by, bare-footed and in rags. She snagged the edge of his coat, the sudden motion stabbing her ribs with pain. The child skidded to a stop, dirt flying up onto her skirt.

She searched her pocket for a coin, sandwiched between the twine and her load pouch. Her breathing was jagged. "If I give you a tuppence, would you take a message to the Gentleman Thief for me? I don't think I have to tell you twice what will happen to you and yours if he does not receive the message."

"'E'll make it 'ard for me kin." The boy rubbed at his running nose.

Kate nodded crisply. "Precisely."

"I'll take yer message." He snatched the coinage from her fingers.

"Tell him that Finn has taken Daniel to St. Sepulchre's-within at Chick Lane." She repeated it two more times before she was satisfied the boy had it down. "Remember, if anyone can find a small boy in the middle of Ratcliffe, it's the Gentleman Thief."

The boy's face whitened. As soon as she released his sleeve, he took off down the road. The message was a last resort, for in the current traffic the boy would not reach Atlas's for some time. She would have been better off with a carriage messenger, yet she didn't trust that the driver would deliver the message. A boy was easier to intimidate, though not easier to find when there were thousands of child thieves in London alone.

She palmed the remaining coins in her pocket. Enough to get her to Saffron Hill, but not back. She'd worry about the return journey later.

Lord hope she was not too late.

DANIEL CAME TO slowly. He knew without opening his eyes

that he was no longer at his flat in Madame Tousat's, for nothing felt right. This place didn't smell of rotting wood and burnt boxty. A soft surface was behind his back, and that too was wrong, as his mattress at the lodging house had been regrettably stiff and uncomfortable.

More concerning was the taste in his mouth, not of gin or tea; in its place was something sickeningly sweet he could not identify. His tongue lolled at the roof of his mouth, uselessly thick.

In such a state, he could not call out for help, if he'd dared to chance it. Instinctively, he sensed that he should not draw attention to himself. He drew in another breath and sniffed the air. Dank, musty, thick with pungent dirt. He was all too aware of the numbness in his limbs, gradually receding with each waking moment, but not completely gone.

He was outside.

But where? His head thumped so loud, he found it hard to believe the sound had not alerted his captors. Too groggy to compute the exact locale, he recognized the basest of sensations: cold bit at his joints with restored feeling. For a second, he wished he'd remained inert, for it would be far less painful to die of frost if one slept through it.

At least, he *thought* he was awake. That too was uncertain, and in a few seconds he might find himself at the London Docks once more with Kate plunging a dagger straight into his heart.

Kate. Her name startled his mind from his doldrums. Where was she? Had she been taken too? It could only be by foul play that he'd arrived here.

He hazarded to open his eyes, the blackness of nightfall offering little change. At first, he could not discern anything outside of gray outlines, indeterminate large shapes. He wiggled his hand. One finger responded, tap-tap-tapping against a wet leaf. Was he in a garden? Such spaces in the sprawling city were limited mostly to the *bon ton*. No, he reasoned, the smell was off for a garden in the wintertime, and no self-respecting gardener for the Upper Ten Thousand strewed leaves about a manicured path.

His vision began to focus. One man stood to his right, a lantern held high in his hand. The oil flame had burned halfway down, its meager light flickering over the tiny party. Three pairs of feet, he counted, recognizing the man with the lantern as the same who had attacked him in his flat.

Metal clanked against rock, dirt flung upward and fell back onto the ground. His eyesight continued to clear. Blood flow had returned to his neck and he moved his head to the side, biting his heavy tongue against the tight tingles. The man with the lantern swung forward, shining the light on his companions. He said something under his breath that Daniel could not make out, but in the glow Daniel saw all he needed to.

Finn and Ezekiel huddled together.

Damnation.

He was going to die tonight. Die without knowing if Kate had escaped their capture. Die without Poppy knowing what happened to him. Die without getting to make good on his promises.

At least he'd told Kate he loved her. That thought anchored him in the darkness. Kate knew his true feelings—she'd at least have that to comfort her when she mourned his death.

He should get up and fight. If only he could feel his legs. He could crawl away like a dog, to be hit on the back with the precariously long stick in Ezekiel's hand. The ruffian leaned down, one hand clasped at the top of the stick, the other hand halfway down. The metal attached to the stick caught the light. It was a shovel. Ezekiel struck the ground once, twice, depositing the dirt onto the growing pile beside him. The hole was already quite deep.

Deep enough for a human body.

A scream waited on his chapped lips. But who would hear him, or more importantly, who would even care? No one would stop to investigate. No one would find him.

Hell, he didn't even know where he was.

Finn turned away to say something to his lackey. Seizing the opportunity, Daniel propped himself up on his elbows to survey the area. Rocky terrain, overhanging trees with dew on the limbs, a few paths drawn between the different sections. They'd set him in seemingly the only spot that didn't suffer from cragginess.

He made out faint outlines of grayed granite. Headstones. A graveyard. It all clicked at once: where they were, his gruesome fate, their eventual plans for him. Finn was too careful now to risk a murder that couldn't be pinned on a scapegoat, and the surgeons were being watched. A body with obvious signs of struggle would alert them to foul play. A surgeon's assistant might report the body to the Peelers, as had happened with the Italian Boy. It was too much of a risk to kill him the way they'd done Bartleby and Dalton—that had come back to haunt Finn.

Better to smother him, bury him, and resurrect him in a few days. Let the surgeons do their work disfiguring him, and then Finn could spread the rumor that he'd come back to town and disappeared again as the police started to investigate Bartleby's murder. Bartleby would have appreciated the justice in that—his death would clinch it in the minds of the English that Daniel was just another Irish rogue with a fascination for blood and guts.

Daniel made another attempt to push himself up, hating how powerless he was over his own body. Finn would eat him alive in this weakened state. Down with the pain, he had to get away.

He pulled himself into a sitting position, back straight, knees hunched beneath him.

Finn's spine stiffened and he grabbed the shovel from Ezekiel, whacking Ezekiel's leg with it.

"Ay! What're ye doin'?" Ezekiel yelped, jumping back. He rubbed at his leg.

"Dig, you fool. Do you think I stand here for my health?"

Finn thrust the shovel back at him. "O'Reilly needs to be in the ground before anyone notices us here. Templeton," Finn gestured toward the man with the lantern. "Remind me again why it was a good idea to leave the trollop alive?"

Kate was alive. Bless it all, she'd managed to fight them off. Relief flooded him, frantic, eager relief.

Templeton hung his head. "S'not a good idea. But ye wanted us back and she's half-dead anyhow—"

Daniel needed something, anything he could lean on to stand.

Finn leaned forward. "Fuck it up again, and I'll deposit you on the steps of Newgate with all your crimes tied 'round your neck. You think the Chapman Street Gang would like that?"

"Ye wouldn't—" Templeton stepped back, eyes widened.

"Spare me your protests." Finn rolled his eyes at Templeton.

Turning toward Daniel, a sneer spread over Finn's lips at Daniel's propped-up state. "So the potion is wearing off."

Daniel wouldn't be intimidated. That was his last vow: he'd go out like a man. A man who didn't have control over all his extremities, but a man nonetheless. His voice was rough from lack of use. "Is that what you used on me before, Finn? What a coward you are, to have to resort to drugging me. You'd never be able to fight me while I was sober."

"Sobriety is a rare state for you, is it not? You were so easy to get to, pathetically draped over your gin. I could have assassinated the old King and placed you at the scene, and you wouldn't have known the difference." Finn advanced on him, towering over him.

He tapped a long, double-barreled pistol at his side. If Daniel could snatch it from him, then lever himself up using it, he could maybe stand, maybe run away. It was an idiotic plan, he was sure, but he had to try.

In the meantime, he would keep Finn talking, for every moment that they were engaged in conversation was a moment where he was not in the ground.

"I highly doubt that," Daniel scoffed. "If you'd crafted such a well-laid crime, you wouldn't be here with me now. You'd have covered my escape, made sure I swung from the noose."

Finn gritted his teeth. "An oversight that won't happen again."

Good. He was beginning to understand his captor's weaknesses. "Are you so certain of that?"

"I have leverage this time. Do you think I don't know where your whore is? That I can't get to her at a moment's notice?" Finn grinned. "I'm a reasonable man. If you can't behave, I'll take it out on her. Give me a reason to tup her, any reason, and I'll be so deep within her they'll never be able to pry me loose."

Rage filled him, purged the looseness from his muscles until he could feel the blood pumping. He was alive, he was aware, and he'd kill Finn with his bare fingers for threatening Kate. "She has nothing to do with this."

"She has everything to do with it." Finn turned his head. "But I think planting you in the ground will be my real reward. You've been a pain in my arse since the day you joined Emporia, O'Reilly."

"Terribly sorry my presence caused your criminal operations such trouble."

"Templeton here—" Finn gestured to the second man. "He said we ought to kill you and drop your body in the Thames. But I said, why not have a little bit of fun with it? All these years digging up bodies, we've never once unearthed a Thing we put there ourselves. You have to admire the poetry of it: you wanted to know more about our activities, and here you are, becoming a part of the resurrection game. Ezekiel, shall we show O'Reilly how we welcome guests?"

Daniel lunged forward, wresting the flintlock from Finn's hand. He shoved it hard against the ground, leaning his weight against it. He was up on his two feet and he was about to go for Finn when his body lurched forward...

He smashed to the ground. Ezekiel had brought the shovel to his back. A rock split against his skull. Blood trickled down his brow, and then there was nothing.

CHAPTER 25

THE HACKNEY STOPPED close to Cow Cross Street. The door
swung open to the carriage and the driver extended his hand to
help her out. She pushed the curtain back on the window and
peered out. The brick walls of St. Sepulchre's workhouse were
nowhere to be seen.

Every moment she dallied, Daniel's chance of survival
dimmed.

"Please, you've got to let me off closer to Sharp's Alley,"
Kate pleaded.

The driver shook his head. "Can't, miss." He extended his
arm out, pointing down the street. "See that lot of traffic there?
Backed up from here to West Smithfield. You'd be better off
walking."

She hopped out of the carriage, her boots landing in filth.
The muck clung to the hem of her gown, making it difficult to
move.

The coachman shrugged. "Cow Cross Cattle Market. It's
either them or the damned horses. No way to get a hack
through that mess. Bloody nuisance, I say." With a grimace,
the coachman climbed back into the carriage and drove away.

Kate swallowed down her panic. With the activity of the
cattle market, no one would notice as Jasper Finn crept into

the workhouse cemetery. Even if they did, Finn probably had someone at St. Sepulchre's on his payroll.

If Atlas hadn't gotten her message, she'd be entering this cemetery blind with no one to help her. She sent up a silent prayer that she'd find a Peeler near the market.

She set off running, weaving in between the crowds. Sheep and pigs were packed into the marketplace in temporary pens, while cattle and oxen were tied up to posts. The animals awaited the butcher with feverish anxiety. Endlessly, the squeal of pigs met with the shouts of hawkers. Her head pounded.

The further she got into the market, the less hope she had that she'd reach Daniel in time.

"Yer head, lady," a young boy called to her.

Kate reached up to her forehead, her gloves coming back bloody and wet. *Shit*. The injury didn't matter; it couldn't, not now. She kept on running, past public houses that teemed with people coming from the market.

Soon, she had reached Sharp's Alley. The sickening smell of butchered meat and manure assailed her nostrils. Insects buzzed in the air around the shop doors of the carcass-butcher, next to the bladder vendor and the catgut vendor. Her hand on her stomach, she fought the urge to vomit.

Her ribs screamed in agony. Dark spots swam before her eyes. Daniel needed her, needed her to get to him…

The spire for St. Sepulchre's-without rose high above the rest of Sharp's Alley. In the distance, a tall flash of blue and black appeared. Her heart sped frantically, drum-pounding in her ears. Had she imagined one of the Metropolitan Police? She couldn't be certain.

She cupped her hands around her mouth to project her yells for his attention. "Help! Help me, please!"

The Peeler turned around, his hands clasped around his truncheon. That wasn't comforting—she'd forgotten the police didn't carry guns. Finn's men wouldn't hesitate to shoot.

Taking off at a jog, the Peeler was soon at her side. Without the constant rush from running to drive her onwards, the effort of standing still became monumental. Her knees shook. She slid downwards. Her vision blackened.

Suddenly, she stood upright in the street, something sturdy supporting her weight. A glance upwards confirmed she was in the arms of a Peeler, the very place she'd spent two and a half years trying to avoid as a fence.

It was worth the risk of discovery if it meant Daniel's safety.

"Miss, you're going to be all right. I'm Sergeant Thaddeus Knight and I'm going to get help for you." The Peeler's deep baritone was filled with concern. "Can you tell me who attacked you?"

She sucked in a breath, tilting her head to look up at him. Her knees had steadied with his support. "Jasper Finn."

"His name isn't familiar to me. You can tell me what happened on the way to the doctor, miss." Knight spoke in slow, calming tones designed to soothe her. Likely, he assumed she was another victim of robbery who needed to be coddled.

But she didn't need reassuring. Daniel was hurt. She wrenched herself from Knight's grip, forced herself to stand on her own feet. "Finn broke into our flat. Please, you have to help me find him. He's got my betrothed and he's going to kill him!"

A change shifted over the officer's body. He stood up straighter, his gray eyes suddenly more alert. He ran a hand across his uniform, straightening it. The brass buttons gleamed.

"Where might they have gone?"

"St. Sepulchre's-without. The workhouse's cemetery."

"I know the place." The truncheon smacked against Knight's leg once, twice. "Very odd indeed."

"Please, please help me," she begged. "Jasper Finn is a resurrectionist. He's got ties to May and Bishop. He kidnapped Daniel. He plans to kill him!"

"Damnation, another exhumator. Didn't expect one so soon." Knight's gaze darted up the road quickly and back to her, as if assessing the chance of success of their mission. "Superintendent Thomas will have my head if we lose a resurrectionist."

Hope buoyed Kate. The ache of her head lessened, if only for a moment. "So you'll help?"

The officer grabbed hold of her arm. "Let's go!"

They took off running down the street, his hand on her arm to tow her along with him. He was lanky with lean, hard muscles and the ground-eating strides of an athlete. Without his help, she wouldn't have made it to the church steps.

ABSOLUTE DARKNESS CLUNG to Daniel like a velvet noose, softly sucking out everything he knew and leaving black in its wake. Torn between the notion of cleaving at his throat and sliding back happily into oblivion, he stuck his hand out to test the boundaries of where he was. His fingers pressed against the wood, jagged and roughly made. A splinter pierced his skin, drawing forth a curse.

That quick jab of pain brought him to reality. Where the hell was he?

He spread out his arms, finding he could barely reach beyond his own chest. The space was rectangular. If he wiggled, his feet struck against the walls. Extending his arm upwards, he prayed he would not strike what he thought he would.

Christ.

His hand beat against wooden top, too. He was in a box, all sides closed up with no easy escape that he could ascertain. Stretched out on his back, he could not move more than six centimeters in either direction.

Giving in to the panic that welled in the pit of his stomach, he screamed. His voice came back to him hopelessly. Frenzied, he thrashed within the box, striking the sides with all his might. He slammed his fist on the ceiling, over and over again until he finally gave up.

Nothing had changed. Finn's men had placed him in the

box and had no intention of freeing him.

His wrist was bruised, his fingers bloody from scratching into the wood. He fell silent, holding his breath as he concentrated entirely on picking up any ambient noise. In the distance, well above him, he thought he could discern a shovel smacking against the ground.

The realization plowed into him like the back of Ezekiel's shovel before. So this is how it would end for him, buried alive in a graveyard in the crux of the rookeries. Lost to Kate. Convicted in death for the murders of Tommy Dalton and Laurence Bartleby in the eyes of all.

All except for Kate, who at least would know the truth.

It would go easier if he stopped fighting. If he gave in to the unconsciousness that seethed at the edge of his vision, calling to him like the siren gin. He wished for the pine needle bite one last time, because in his death he knew it would not matter what wrongs he'd committed. If he'd stayed away, if he'd remained in Dorking, none of this would have happened.

But he wouldn't—couldn't—trade his time with Kate. This could be the fate he deserved, avoided three years ago by Atlas's quick engineering of an escape.

No. He was better than this, a stronger man who had paid for his sins. He was supposed to live a long life, to marry Kate and provide for her and their family.

Years ago, when he'd first come to London, Atlas had regaled him with the story of one of his greatest heists. He'd stowed away in the Duke of Cumberland's townhouse closet for two hours, until the Duke had finally left. The closet was little bigger than the box Daniel was in now, and the air almost as tight. But Atlas had regulated his breathing, saved his strength and kept himself from panicking. In the end, he had made off with a great sum of jewels.

Daniel took in one last deep breath before he crossed his arms over his chest and relaxed his muscles. This might be a futile exercise, a prolonging of his death, but he owed it to Kate to attempt. To trust that she would find him and bring help.

His memories would keep him company until that time came.

ST. SEPULCHRE'S-WITHOUT was shaped like a rectangle and built in stone—if one did not think of the workhouse, it almost looked peaceful. Knight pushed open the wrought iron gate to the porch. Atlas leaned on a nearby tree, waiting for them.

"You brought help," Atlas noted derisively.

Kate ignored his tone. "Finn's got Daniel."

"Bollocks." Atlas pushed himself off the tree, striding forward into the graveyard.

Knight's gray eyes flitted over Atlas's frame, cataloguing the thief's spotless black clothing and top hat. He lingered for a second watching Atlas, his arms crossed over his chest. As Kate followed Atlas, Knight jogged after her. "That's the Gentleman Thief. He's the most brilliant thief in all of London. What exactly are you involved in here?"

Kate glanced over at him. His lips were slightly parted, his posture alert. He held the truncheon perfectly poised for attack as he ran. This, she decided, was a man who excelled under conflict. It was in her best interests to keep silent.

They ran around the back of the church toward the workhouse cemetery. Kate cut a tight corner, half-boots skimming over the rocks in the St. Sepulchre-without's cemetery. Another storm was coming, worse than the former, as if the weather realized the injustice of Daniel's disappearance and wished to protest.

The cemetery was not particularly large. On the whole, it took fifteen minutes to search.

He had to be here, he had to be here, he had to be here. Such was the constant refrain that beat down upon her brain. For if he was not here, he'd been taken somewhere else entirely. Somewhere she could not find him and all would be lost.

She couldn't give up hope, even as she heard nothing from Officer Knight to indicate he'd found activity in his quarter.

Then she saw it, in a glen with two large overhanging trees. Three men huddled in a small circle with their backs to her. One man held a lantern, while the other shoveled dirt onto a rising pile. Graves rose up around them, solitary stone meant to commemorate the lost but instead marking the place where the resurrectionists would dig next.

The man closest to her resembled Finn from the rear. He had the proper height and build, and the other two men with him vaguely resembled his associates that had broken into Daniel's room.

I've found them!

She gestured to Knight and Atlas, not daring to cry out and alert the men to her presence. Knight crested the hill from the other direction, Atlas shortly behind him.

Where was Daniel? He had to be here, if Templeton, Ezekiel and Finn had all assembled in this one place. Templeton clutched a shovel. What cause did they have to bury something?

Kate looked from one end of the cemetery to the other. Nausea washed over her. They had taken Daniel to a place where his murder could be easily disguised, lost in a sea of corpses. They had intended for him to be forgotten about until they dug him up.

"They buried him." She barely forced the words out.

Atlas whistled. "Damnation."

Hearing them, Finn turned around. He said something to his men, and Templeton and Ezekiel turned as well. Templeton hoisted up the shovel, while Ezekiel pulled out a knife.

For a second, it was as if time stopped. The two groups stood there in silence, facing each other, weapons ready. No one dared breathe nor move.

That was insane. Finn was right bloody there, not even a

yard away, and he stood over a pile of rocks and dirt. She planted her feet firmly in the ground, and cocked her pistol. Her left hand balanced her flintlock and her right thumb went to the trigger, squeezing it.

In a cloud of gray smoke, the flint sparked the frisson. The powder in the pan ignited. Bursting forth from the gun, the shot sailed through the air, but did not meet its mark. Finn still stood.

Shit!

Scattering quickly, each man dived in another direction. Ezekiel ran closest to Knight, who took off after him. Ezekiel kept attempting to strike out, but Knight was firm, blocking his punches. He struck out with his truncheon, connecting with Ezekiel's shin.

Looking over his shoulder, Finn took off toward the edge of the graveyard.

A patch of dirt was exposed in the middle of where they had been standing. Kate started to race toward that space, the gun grasped firmly in her hand. If the men came at her, she'd beat them away until she could get to Daniel.

Atlas grabbed her arm. Gesturing to her flintlock, he motioned her onward. "Go help Knight. I promise I'll get him free."

The thief ran toward Templeton. Out of the corner of her eye, she could see him wrestle Templeton to the ground, wrenching the shovel from his hand. Templeton took off running. Atlas ignored him and began to dig.

Finn had made it halfway through the cemetery. Quickly, she reloaded her pistol. Finn would be hers now, to rip him limb from limb and make him pay. For bringing her father into this horrible trade, for falsifying evidence so Daniel would be arrested for murder, for taking him from her when they'd finally admitted their feelings. A simple shot to the head would not be justice.

She needed to make him suffer.

Finn took another step toward the gate. From this

distance, she wouldn't be able to make the shot.

She ran toward him, seeing Finn and only Finn. His smug smirk, manicured good looks and the easy way he used to quiz her over the day's activities, like they were two colleagues. The goods she'd fenced to him appeared before her eyes, her father's journal entries imprinted on top. Every ounce of suffering that she'd experienced went back to Finn.

"Come to end me, have you?" Finn called, when she stood but a few paces from him.

She was enough to shoot him with almost assured accuracy. The pistol was loaded and ready, cocked fully. She braced it properly, finger upon the trigger.

Finn did not move, his eyes fixed upon her flintlock.

"I suppose you are not your father's daughter after all. Do you know that Morgan begged for me to take his life? In the last few months, when the disease had set deep into his bones and he knew he'd die. But I wouldn't because his death wouldn't do anything for me. He could go in a month or two, in pain or not, and it'd change nothing."

She gritted her teeth. He tried to bate her.

"Where's Daniel?" She hoped to God that she wasn't right—that Daniel was somewhere safe, dropped off to the police perhaps so they'd arrest him again.

Anywhere but in a fucking hole in the ground.

"I think you have already discovered what I did with him." Finn looked toward the mound of dirt scornfully. "You'd best hope the Gentleman can dig quickly, as it is highly doubtful the human body can sustain more than a half hour without air."

"I caught you." Yet she felt no form of relief, no vindication.

"So you did." Finn shrugged. "Will it matter? They'll take me in and I shall face the same trial the others did. But they acquitted May, and they'll do the same for me. With my connections, I'm worth more to the Met alive than dead."

He reached for her, so quick she could not stop him. His

hand came down on her shoulder, hard, hitting her existing bruises. She grappled with the gun, trying to position it so she could get off a shot, but Finn was too fast.

His hands closed around her arms in a lethal lock. He spun her around, dragged her back against him. "You're just like us," he murmured in her ear. "You're no better than your basest impulses."

She couldn't let him go, never paying for the crimes he'd perpetuated. If she shot him here now—if she hit him in the chest, like she'd meant to in that back alley—then no one would be hurt again.

His blood would be on her hands forever. He'd never feel the pain and suffering he had intended for Daniel. To have to face trial for his sins and rot in Newgate waiting for his execution—that was the bloody fate he deserved.

She would not bear the mark of another's sins any longer.

She thrust her shoulders back with all her might, slamming into his chest. The movement threw him back enough that she could squirm out of his hold. Turning around, she faced him.

Swiftly, Kate grasped the butt of the flintlock. She swung out, bringing the side of the gun down on Finn's temple. It met his face with a stomach-turning thud. He slipped to the ground, unconscious.

"I am nothing like you," Kate said, and in that instant she believed it.

She had a full life ahead of her with Daniel by her side. She was more than the daughter of an old shipping magnate, more than a fence.

With a bit of twine from her pocket, she tied Finn's hands behind his back. The bastard would live until he was hanged for his crimes.

CHAPTER 26

IN THE CHAOS, Knight had subdued Ezekiel. Finally, he held the man in a vice grip, while Atlas ran behind him, tying the man's hands.

"First time I've ever been on the opposing side of this," Atlas remarked.

Out of the corner of her eye, she saw Knight pass off Ezekiel to Atlas. The thief held on to him, even as Ezekiel dove backwards, smashing his head into Atlas's chin.

"Enough of this," Atlas cursed, releasing him long enough to land a bruiser across the man's jaw. Ezekiel fell to the ground and Atlas dropped him.

Templeton had made it to the edge of the cemetery. Knight went after him, as Atlas and Kate knelt on the ground next to the hole Atlas had dug.

The wooden coffin had emerged from a pile of fresh dirt and rock. In tandem with Atlas, Kate lifted up the top of the box, grunting from the sheer heft of it. Barely registering the weight of it, she moved without thought, up and over as they hurled the lid away from them.

Daniel laid peacefully, arms crossed over his chest and feet pointed upward. No breath came from his lips. They were too late. She'd failed trying to save him, failed because she'd been too damn stubborn to admit she was wrong, failed because she couldn't face the hurt of giving her heart away.

But no amount of pain had prepared her for this.

"Please, Daniel, please be alive, I love you." Tears streamed down her cheeks, unbidden. She had not the strength to stop them.

Atlas knelt on the ground across from her, silent and stone-faced. Sadness appeared wrong on his cherubic features, and made her cry harder.

"I'm so sorry, I'm so sorry," she gasped out between sobs. She beat her hands against his chest, twisting the fabric of his coat in her hands violently. "You can't be gone, not yet."

Pulling her back from the coffin, Atlas laid a hand on her shoulder. She shrugged him off, grabbing Daniel's hand and pressing it to her chest.

His skin was still warm.

She flung his hand down as though his flesh had singed her skin. Kate leaned down, ear upon his chest. Only silence greeted her.

They'd found each other again to be ripped apart.

Another Peeler had come by as Knight was restraining Finn, likely lured by her gunshot. She tilted Daniel's head back slightly, opening his mouth. Pinching his nostrils closed with one finger, she slid her mouth over his and breathed.

No response. Struggling not to panic, she breathed into him again and pulled back. Nothing.

Once more she breathed.

His chest rose.

Kate lifted her fingers from his nose and pulled back from him. He blinked once before his eyes opened, focusing in on her. She fell back on her haunches, relief flooding through her bones.

He was alive.

"Kate?" He tried to sit up, but could not complete the attempt.

"Stay still," Atlas ordered.

Confusion flickered in Daniel's cloudy green eyes. "How did I—" He stopped, apparently deciding better of the inquiry.

Kate rested her elbows on the edge of the coffin, unable to keep from him for long. "I thought you'd died."

He reached out for her, taking her hand in his. "This is getting to be a habit with us. We really must put a stop to it."

"They've got Finn, Danny." Atlas grinned, tapping a cheery beat on the edge of the coffin. "We got ourselves a bloody resurrectionist."

"Let's get you out of there," Kate said, extending a hand to help Daniel from the coffin.

With Atlas's assistance, soon Daniel was sitting on the grass beside Kate, his head resting on her shoulder. She ran her hand through his hair slowly.

"There's Knight," she said, as Knight emerged from the other side of the cemetery, Templeton in hand.

Atlas squinted. "Old chum, if you don't mind, I think I'll take my leave before the Peelers get a hint of who I am…"

Kate nodded. "Thank you for coming."

Daniel's gaze flitted from her to Atlas and back to her. The smile on her lips never faded; stretched so far across her cheeks she thought her face might split in two. She'd smile forever. He was back in her life and she'd never let him go again.

"I don't know what miracle happened to get you two to behave around each other, but I do wish it hadn't started with me in a coffin." Daniel chuckled, a throaty laugh that shook his entire frame and sent him coughing.

"Careful," she cautioned.

Knight returned with Templeton subdued. He dragged the man next to Finn, unconscious and bound on the ground. Knight looked at Finn for a moment, then back to Ezekiel, stricken not far from Daniel and Kate.

His brows arched. "This is one of the most unusual cases I've ever encountered." He pointed toward Daniel. "I suspect that's your affianced?"

"Yes," Kate said, squeezing Daniel's hand.

Knight pursed his lips. She suspected he knew far more than he was letting on. If she had to face time in gaol for her fencing, she'd do it—Daniel was safe and that was all that mattered.

"Daniel O'Reilly." Daniel's voice was weak.

"The man accused of murdering the warehouse laborer." Knight did not wait for Daniel to confirm his statement. "I followed your case before I joined the police. I have a bit of a hobby in behavior studies, you could say. It fascinated me, your complete lack of motive. Because of you, I kept myself up-to-date on the downfall of the Emporia shipping company, trying to find an explanation for what you'd done."

Kate gulped.

"Miss Morgan." Knight's eyes narrowed. He angled his body toward her, his expression a strange mix between curious and appalled. "I've sent out for other officers to help me take in the criminals here."

She knew it. He was going to arrest her. "And you'll be taking me with them?"

Knight fell silent. His forehead crinkled as he thought. Daniel's hand did not waiver from her own.

"I'll keep you safe," Daniel whispered in her ear.

Knight watched them. Finally, he stood up straighter, shaking his head. "At the moment, no. You've suffered enough today, I think. If Finn truly has ties to the Italian Boy's murder, then I suspect that's all my superiors will care about."

Kate breathed a sigh of relief. "Thank you."

"But if you come across my notice again...I won't think twice about arresting you." Knight stepped back from her, going to collect Templeton again. "Don't think that I won't be watching you."

Dragging Templeton to the front of the cemetery, Knight went to await the other officers. Ezekiel and Finn lay in the grass, both incapacitated.

Kate ran her hand up Daniel's arm, marveling in the sheer aliveness of him. Bold, strong, and powerful…to think that a few minutes later, she would have lost him. "I love you, you know that? I love you more than I've ever loved any damn thing in my life."

He smiled. "That is quite satisfactory, as I love you too." He squinted, reaching up to run his finger along the cut at her temple. "Finn's men—did they hurt you?"

She shrugged. "I thrashed Finn with my gun. I think whatever hurt Ezekiel did is inconsequential by now."

"You didn't kill him." He sounded unsurprised.

Pride welled within her. He'd never believed the worst of her, never thought she had it in her to take a life. The rookeries had not changed her so much after all. Ratcliffe had made her independent, forced her to understand the worst of the world, but she'd kept the one part of her that made her human.

She would not regret these last three years now, not when her experiences had formed her into the woman she was today.

The woman Daniel loved.

HE STOOD AT the edge of Upper Shadwell, silhouetted by the street light. Bruised hands shoved deep into the pockets of his greatcoat, he leaned against a two-story tenement building. He wore no hat and his ginger hair was not darkened by soot. A long scratch ran from underneath his eye to his left lip, on the cusp of healing. If one looked close, the lump on the back of his head from the hit of a shovel was visible.

But none of that mattered to Daniel O'Reilly.

For up the shadowy alley that joined Broadwell Street to Upper Shadwell came a tall woman, her chocolate hair tucked up underneath a broad grey hat. She stepped out of the darkness to join him. No greatcoat masked her green dress with little white flowers, flared out at the waist and padded at the top of her sleeves. Against her leg tapped a half-cocked

Forsyth pistol, once errant but now fully accepted back into her good graces.

"Shall we depart?" she asked.

He held out his arm for her and she took it without hesitation. Standing back, he watched her for a second, eyes flicking over her willowy frame.

She tilted her head to the side, smiling quizzically. "Do I want to know what you are thinking?"

He tugged her closer to him, wrapping his arm around her shoulder. Pressed up against him, she fit perfectly.

"You're giving me devilish ideas." Narrowly avoiding the brim of her hat, he breathed in the jasmine of her hair while his hand squeezed the rounded curve of her hip.

"If you tell me them, I might be amendable." She let her lips glide along his in a feather-light kiss.

It wasn't enough to satisfy him. He took the kiss deeper, holding her steady against him, tasting and exploring her delectable mouth until a shout from the street tore them apart. One hand clutching her flintlock, Kate touched her lip with a gloved finger. He'd knocked her hat askew.

"If I was not still a wanted man, I'd take you here now," he whispered as he righted her hat.

"Perhaps I shall miss the criminal." She stepped away from him, smoothing out the wrinkles in her skirt.

He wrinkled his nose. "I certainly won't. Hiding is not a way to live, Katiebelle."

"Knight said it shouldn't be long until you are properly dismissed of all charges." She laced her fingers through his and they headed out of the alley, down the street that would take them to the Three Boars.

"I still don't like the idea of Knight having information on you," Daniel said. The officer had received so much credit from Superintendent Thomas he had agreed not to bring up Kate's fencing, as long as her illegal activities never came across his desk again. "I feel like there's far more to him than meets the eye. How is it that a man of his deductive abilities ended up in the rookeries?"

"He's going to be a bloody Superintendent himself before long with this arrest. I highly doubt he'll do anything." Kate shrugged.

They stopped on the edge of the street to let a carriage pass. Roguishly, he leaned over and patted Kate's bottom. "I love you," he whispered in her ear.

She leaned her head against his shoulder, the grin on her face everything to him.

Before long, they had come to the Three Boars. Music filtered out of the public house, blending with loud conversation and hoofbeats as carriages passed by in the street. They entered and made their way to the crowded bar. To the rest of London, this night was like any other, different only in that it was unseasonably warm for January.

To Daniel, it was a reminder of his freedom. The last three nights with Kate in his flat at Madame Tousat's had been idyllic. Lost in the exploration of each other's bodies, they had awoken each morning tangled in his sheets. But as the almost balmy air hit his face, he thanked God he was no longer caged in a wooden box. *Coffin*, he corrected himself, because this time he refused to shy away from the past.

He had not had a drink. Even when nightmares took him again, his mind placing him not at the London Docks but instead in that damned box, he stayed strong. Kate was right there with him, and through the clasp of her hand in his he knew he would be fine.

"Wondered if you'd show up, mate," Atlas grinned, clapping him on the shoulder.

Kate slid onto the last bar stool. "We were perhaps a bit waylaid." She had the grace to blush.

The thief grimaced. "Devil take it, I don't want to hear about your pitter-patter love. It's enough to make a self-respecting man retch."

Daniel chuckled. "You say that now." Standing behind Kate, his hands worked at the knots in her shoulders. He never tired of touching her.

Kate leaned back against him. "I think we ought to find a nice chit for Atlas here, a woman who could best him at his own game."

"Such a woman doesn't exist." Atlas snorted.

Jane approached from the other side of the bar, holding a tray of drinks. She set the tray down on the bar-top and passed a tankard of ale to Kate, a glass of gin to Atlas, and a mug of coffee to Daniel. Another patron cried for Jane's attention, but she waved him off, focusing on the small group before the bar.

"Busy night?" Kate asked, patting her friend's hand.

"When is it not?" Jane pursed her lips. "Since the capture of Finn and his network, the boys are reckless. All that unclaimed territory with no one but Wilkes to rule it—it'll spell trouble."

Atlas raised his glass in toast to the barmaid. "Let the jackanapes fight. The dumbest shall die, and the thieving world will be better for it."

Jane's eyes narrowed. "You would not say that if your brother's fate waited on them." She propped her elbows on the bar-top, resting her chin in her hands. Lowering her voice, she brought her face closer to Kate. "Penn's going to rot in there. I can't let him die."

Jane turned around as the patron called again for her, banging his empty tankard against the counter. "I'm coming, you lot!"

"Please, think about this," Kate cautioned, but then Jane hurried off to tend to the other customers. "That is going to end badly."

"Nonsense." Daniel laid a kiss on her cheek. "I escaped prison and it turned out lovely."

She looked up at him, a smile crinkling the corners of her lips. "Yes, yes, it did."

EPILOGUE

London, 1833
One year later

THE LITTLE COTTAGE in the south side of Wapping was not entirely impressive from the outside. Like many similar cottages, it had a once-white exterior, the paint chipping from years of disrepair. It didn't have its own courtyard, but rather a communal one in the back that stretched behind three matching houses. The walls were solid, though lacking in heavy insulation.

Within walking distance to the London Docks, yet far enough away that the cacophony of voices and activity didn't penetrate inside the quarters, the cottage sat on the far end of a street that had once been classified as part of the neighboring rookery but now took on a distinctly lower middle-class bent as new families settled in the row houses.

In total, the cottage contained three rooms: a parlor, a bedroom, and a kitchen. The entire length of No. 4 was less than half the size of a small townhouse in Bloomsbury. Yet to Daniel and Kate O'Reilly, it was a palace containing all the space they'd ever need. Leased from the money made in their new shipping venture, it was under their own names.

Kate had been to see Sally after the Metropolitan Police

had formally dismissed Daniel; the girl was alive, but with several new scars from Wilkes's knife to show for her attempt at helping them. The Police had no evidence to connect Wilkes to any of Finn's murders, and so Sally stayed at the brothel, fearing another attack if she left.

Nothing could persuade Sally to change course, but at least she had the comfort of knowing Dalton's murderer had been punished in one of the most highly attended executions since the first ringleader of the Chapman Street Gang.

Kate stood on the third ring of the ladder, hand poised above the new spice rack. "You don't arrange your spices alphabetically?"

Daniel looked up from across the room, where he unpacked the last of their boxes. "I've never had need for a spice rack before, love." He stood up, crossing the room to hold the ladder steady for her. "I'd tell you to be careful, but I know you won't listen."

Kate's hand drifted to her abdomen. "Any O'Reilly child will be made of stern stuff." She grinned down at him.

"It's the Irish blood," Daniel winked. He moved one hand from the ladder to rest on his wife's calf. "We must be aggressive to fight off you marauders."

"Marauders or not, I must warn you not to get your hopes up," she called, as she placed the cylindrical jar of thyme next to the turmeric. "I've not increased in cooking skills."

He grinned at her. "So you're saying I should continue to purchase those meat pies you like so much?"

"Either that, or we shall be forever at Poppy's for supper." She surveyed the spice rack, each vial symmetrically arranged on the two wooden shelves.

Shortly after the trial, Daniel and Kate had married in a small ceremony outside Emporia's old warehouses, with Jane, Atlas, and Poppy present as witnesses. Daniel's sister had come to London after his name had been cleared, accompanied by the old woman who had watched Moira in Dorking, Mrs. Daubenmire.

No gin was allowed in their house, as it had been almost two years since Daniel had touched a drop. He liked to claim he hadn't time to drink now if he wanted, for the business kept them so occupied that the little free time they had they spent together in their new cottage.

With the baby on the way, this cottage had become more like home than any other place either of them could remember. He couldn't recall anywhere he'd felt more welcome, not even at his uncle's farm in Sussex. With Kate, he had crafted a new world.

"Do you really need this much gunpowder?" Daniel held up a long tin box containing more powder than any one person would ever need, even in the darkest corners of St. Giles.

"You call it unnecessary, I prefer to think of it as preparation." She shrugged.

He grinned. Her flintlock had saved them more times than he could count. He crossed over to her to stand behind the ladder, his hand resting on her lower leg as she placed the last spice. His gaze flickered over her the lean lines of her back, encased in a blue gown tailored to her svelte figure. He'd gotten used to this life, working with his wife and coming home to her.

"I shall never quibble about your flintlock again," he promised, stepping back so that she could get down from the ladder. When her feet hit the ground, he spun her around, gathering her up into his arms.

"Always knew you were a wise man, O'Reilly." She smiled up at him.

He held her close to him. "I picked you, I must be."

AUTHOR'S NOTE

While my villain Jasper Finn is fictional, the Italian Boy case is quite real. In England in the early nineteenth century, the Murder Act of 1752 prohibited surgeons from anatomizing bodies that were not of convicted criminals. Unfortunately, the amount of crimes that one could be executed for was diminishing, for the preferred sentencing was often transportation, time on one of the giant prison ships moored in the ocean (referred to as "hulks"), or confinement in a prison like Newgate. If a surgeon wanted to succeed in his field, he needed a fresh supply of bodies for medical research. Unprincipled doctors would often enlist bands of resurrection men. The Select Committee that looked into anatomization in 1828 estimated that around 500 bodies were supplied by resurrection men every year to surgeons.

By the time the grave robbers in the Italian Boy case were found, London had already become aware of a new kind of resurrection man: one who killed his victims and sold their corpses, instead of waiting for fresh bodies to turn up in the cemeteries. In 1828 in Edinburgh, Scotland, two serial killers had been convicted in the deaths of sixteen victims, all sold to a surgeon. Their names were William Burke and William Hare.

Yet it is not the Burke and Hare case that truly changed the laws in England, but instead that of the Italian Boy. On November 6, 1831, surgeon George Beaman of the St. Paul's parish in Covent Garden began to examine an unusual corpse. The fourteen year old boy's body had come to him from the usual source—a few grave robbers—but the corpse had signs of trauma. The freshness of the corpse shocked Beaman, and there were no signs that the body had ever been buried.

Beaman and his associates Richard Partridge and Herbert Mayo tricked the resurrection men into waiting while they called the Metropolitan Police. The Met arrested John Bishop, James May, Thomas Williams, and the carter Michael Shields. After much investigation, the corpse was finally identified as that of an Italian street peddler, who roamed the streets with his little white mice asking for money. Perhaps it was the youthfulness of the victim, or perhaps it was the Londoners' fascination with the culture of the Italian street performers, but the case took hold of the town's attention fast.

John Bishop and Tom Williams lived in Nova Scotia Gardens in Bethnal Green (the same rookery where I have placed Friggard's Pawn). Williams had married Bishop's daughter, and little was known about his past. Eventually, Superintendent Joseph Sadler Thomas of the F-Division of the Metropolitan Police would realize that Williams was actually Thomas Head, a petty thief who had graduated to grave robbing. John Bishop was an accomplished resurrection man, and it is estimated he stole about 500-1,000 corpses before finally meeting his maker at a hangman's noose.

James May had known Bishop for approximately four years. On that fateful day, when going to drink with Bishop, he met Williams for the first time. After much drinking at the Fortune of War public house—a noted hang-out for resurrection men that in the early part of its tenure is rumored to have allowed men to stash their wares in the pub's benches—the men began to discuss the resurrection trade. Money hadn't been as good as they wanted it to be, and the drunken men decided to take matters into their own hands. Fresh corpses paid better, and so they'd murder to get one.

The London Burkers, as they came to be called, were an odd set. May turned state's evidence and so he avoided execution. The carter Michael Shields was released after it was determined he had no prior knowledge of the murder the Burkers had committed. In the beginning of the investigation, Bishop displayed an egotism and pride that I have used as a model for my villain Finn. When asked what he did for a living by Thomas, Bishop is reported to have said, "I'm a bloody body snatcher."

But that megalomania couldn't save Bishop. He and Williams met their fate in December of 1831, and their bodies were given to surgeons for anatomization. In the end, I suppose, they had come full circle with their chosen profession.

After the case of the London Burkers, a reexamination of the Murder Act became imperative. In July of 1832, the Anatomy Act was passed, which legitimized corpses from the workhouses and unclaimed bodies to be dissected. By the end of the decade, the profession had almost entirely disappeared. I have placed *A Dangerous Invitation* in the winter months after Bishop and Williams's execution, before the passing of the Anatomy Act.

Kate and Daniel's visits to Jacob's Island most likely could not have happened, due to the cholera outbreaks on the island at this time. But for the purposes of the Rookery Rogues, I have chosen to place those cholera spreads at a later date.

For further information about resurrection men and the Italian Boy case, I highly recommend reading Sarah Wise's book *The Italian Boy: A Tale of Murder and Body Snatching in 1830s London.*

Look for the next installments in
The Rookery Rogues!

A WAYWARD MAN
The Rookery Rogues 0.5
Prequel to *A Dangerous Invitatio.*
February 2014

SECRETS IN SCARLET
The Rookery Rogues 2
Coming in Summer 2014

SCANDAL BECOMES YOU
The Rookery Rogues 3
Coming in Winter 2014

Please turn the page for a preview

And check out other titles by Erica Monroe

BREAKING UP THE GIRL
Poems
Available Now

London, 1832

THE TWO-STORY brick Larker Textile Factory should have looked ominous. Steam roiled out from the chimneys in thick gray tendrils, obscuring the moon. But that was expected when London had exchanged reliance on cottage laborers hunched over looms for churning machinery and ready-made clothes.

The variable speed baton power loom sounded to Thaddeus Knight like the devil's own calling card. Clack-clack-clack the looms went in their steady jig of brimstone and hellfire. Once, he had thought the industrialization of England was a sign of progress. Country folk migrating to London would build a new social order, one free of the restraints of low income and hypocritical aristocracy.

Perhaps he was still an idealist. He wanted badly to believe that the work he did as a Sergeant in the H-Division of the Metropolitan Police Force was meaningful. He was making a difference in the lives of those doomed to the rookeries, or so he told his mother every time she questioned why he chose to spend his days patrolling the streets of the East End with only a truncheon for protection. *They're people too, Mother. They deserve justice.*

But what was justice in a world that failed to mourn the lives lost to poverty, famine, iniquity, or murder? He shook his head. Thaddeus had studied Plato, Descartes, Confucius. Hell, he'd even read the social treaties of a male prostitute he'd arrested for protesting nude in the middle of the Smithfield market. He spent his nights poring over crime reports from the Old Bailey, but he was no closer to the truth.

His hands clenched around the worn handle of his truncheon. He tapped the bully-stick against his leg sheathed in the dark blue uniform common to the Met. The blue had been meant to make the public believe they weren't a military unit, but rather a civilian peacekeeping organization. Most days, he did feel as though he was doing his part to help the borough of Stepney.

Today was not one of those days. Nor, he suspected, would the next two weeks be any better. From his supervisor, Superintendent Jonah White, he had received a maxim: solve the case at Larker factory or move the hell on. Thaddeus had been given release from his patrol duties only after he'd begged to investigate the crime.

The corpse of the young woman he'd found outside the Larker factory haunted his dreams.

"The duty of the Police is to prevent the crimes," White had said that morning. "We're not the bloody Runners. You're destined for greatness, lad. The work you did on catching those bloody resurrectionists was brilliant. Don't botch it by dodging your regular duties."

He had fourteen days to uncover why someone had left a young girl beaten to a pulp outside of the factory. A day for each year of the girl's too short life. As he stood outside the factory, cloaked by the lack of street lamps in this godforsaken part of Shadwell, he could not shake the sight of the girl's face. Blood dribbling down her lips as she coughed. Her slight frame was suddenly bitterly cold like this February night. She was gone.

The factory had let out an hour ago. There was an alleyway behind the butcher shop in front of the factory, which left him able to view the factory without being seen. He should be back at the H-Division station, combing through records for any mention of the factory owner Boz Larker. Instead, he stood outside of this factory as if by his presence he could prevent another murder.

A light bobbed in the distance. Thaddeus lingered in the alleyway. He pulled his coat tighter around him to shut out the chafing wind. The light came closer, closer until the body of a young woman appeared, surrounded by golden luminescence.

His breath died in his throat. He gulped down the rising panic that always accompanied the sight of a gorgeous woman; crimes were his specialty, while flirtations had him facing definite heart palpitations. She was beautiful, with a crown of flaming red hair that stood out bright from underneath her brown straw bonnet. With skin pale like ivory, he ached to touch her heart-shaped face to see if it'd be as perfect as statues in the British Museum.

Then she smiled, and he was lost. Instantly, he was struck by the vision of what it would be like to make her laugh. To take her into his arms and kiss those sweet lips.

Man is only as strong as the woman he chooses. He had no idea where the thought came from. Man was only as strong as his leaders, or something equally socially conscious.

She turned down the next alley. Damnation. Where were his police instincts? A woman like that needed to be protected from the ruffians that roamed Shadwell.

Thaddeus set off down the road. He skidded to a stop in front of her, careful to keep his truncheon at his side.

"Miss," he said, stepping closer so that he'd fall within the light of her lamp. He doffed his regulation top hat and inclined his head in greeting.

She arched a perfectly sculpted auburn brow at him. "Mrs."

Devil take it. She was a married woman. He had standards and rules, none of which contained coveting another man's wife. But damned if she wasn't stunning.

"Mrs. Please accept my apologies." He sounded stuffy even to his ears, like he'd shoved a handful of cotton in his mouth. "May I escort you home? These parts can be particularly nasty at night. I'm a Sergeant with the H-Division."

Thaddeus stretched out his hand to her, expecting her to take it so he could escort her to safety. She slipped underneath his outstretched arm and moved past him. Devilish minx, didn't she know how dangerous Shadwell could be at night? He wouldn't let her get away.

Another woman would not die on his watch.

He jogged after her. She spun around, the lantern shaking to and fro as she frowned at him. She wore a brown dress that tailored to her slender figure at her bodice, yet bore the wide skirts so in fashion. On top of the dress was tied an apron of coarse cotton, with scissors and a cylindrical case sticking out of the pocket. A case for a needle, he surmised from the shape of it. He'd bet an entire month's salary she worked at Larker's factory.

"What do you want?" Her voice held a slow draw to it, mixed with something distinctly Irish. It was the most melodious sound he'd ever heard.

He swallowed. "It isn't safe for you to be wandering about at night by yourself. I only want to make sure you get home without harm."

Her eyes narrowed. "I assure you, I can take care of myself. I don't need help from the likes of you, Peeler." She spat the last word like it was the worst curse she could imagine.

She pierced him with her vivid green eyes and in that stare he was quite certain she saw everything about him and didn't care to know more. His palms grew sweaty, despite the blistering cold.

Somehow, standing within arm's length of her with fury radiating from her tiny frame, he was quite certain he'd met a woman who could pierce his soul with a single glare.

POPPY O'REILLY HAD three core beliefs: one should protect family, one should be loyal, and one should avoid officers of the law at all costs. The last dogma was born out of both experience and necessity. Her brother, Daniel, had been charged with murder by an incompetent constable. He had faced certain death until he and his now-wife investigated the case themselves, and the evidence they found exonerated him.

As for herself, Poppy would be damned if she let the Peelers poke about in her past.

Yet the man across her proved a formidable opponent. Not because she had any doubt she could slip past him—she may not have grown up in these parts, but her brother's wife, Kate, had taught her the tricks to police evasion—but because he looked so wretchedly concerned.

It had been a long time since anyone had looked concerned for her wellbeing.

Lean and athletic, the Metropolitan Police officer moved closer to her. He had a straight, long face with a hawkish nose. He was, she thought, not perhaps classically handsome. There was an earnestness to him that made his features look almost boyish. His dark wavy hair fell across his eyes in the most casual of ways, making her heart flip-flop precariously in her chest. That was irrational, and she was not an irrational woman.

She forced herself to meet his gaze. Kind, soft, intelligent. She hated that she had to look up to see him. But Mama had been short, so there was little Poppy could do about her diminutive height.

"I've got to get home, guv," she said. "Don't have time to be gadding with you."

That at least wasn't a lie, unlike her fabricated husband. Daniel and Kate were minding her one-year-old daughter, and soon they'd start to worry about Poppy if she didn't return to their flat in Ratcliffe.

The officer frowned at her. "Madam, I'm sure your husband would agree my escorting you is the proper precaution."

"He's dead," Poppy snapped.

The longer they stood on this corner conversing, the more chance she had that the officer would sense something was off with her story. Better to play the offended widow. "I doubt he'd agree with anything you say, except that the ground is particularly frozen this time of year in Dorking."

"Oh." The Sergeant blinked. "I'm devilishly sorry for your loss, madam."

He sounded so apologetic, as if he truly grieved the demise of her nonexistent husband. Poppy steeled herself. Moira deserved a second chance in London, one where she wouldn't be ostracized by society for her mother's mistake. The lies were for a good purpose, no matter how heavy they made her heart.

Poppy sighed. She looked up and down the empty alleyway, considering her options. The hour was growing late. The sun had set. The Peeler was right: soon Upper Shadwell would be brimming with ruffians. Daniel was friends with Atlas Greer, the greatest thief in all of London, and he had issued a warning that she was not to be harmed. Combined with her friend Jane Putnam's associations with the Chapman Street Gang, Poppy went about the streets without fear.

But she couldn't explain all that to the Met officer in front of her. An officer in the H-Division already knew about Kate's fencing activities and had promised to keep quiet only if Kate didn't come to his attention again. Poppy's avoidance of the Police wasn't just for herself, but for her loved ones too. The best thing to do then was to allow him to accompany her home, and drop him off about a block before her house. He'd think he had fulfilled his civic duty and forget she existed.

"Fine," Poppy said. "You can escort me."

"Very good." The officer doffed his top hat to her. "I'm Sergeant Thaddeus Knight."

Drat, drat, drat. Did God hate her? Was she being punished for all the wrongs she'd ever committed? The very officer Kate had found to help her rescue Daniel stood before her. Poppy took Knight's arm as he offered it to her, her touch so light her fingers barely brushed the blue fabric.

"Poppy Corrigan." A new name for a new life in London.

Knight smiled, a slow smile that reached from his eyes down to his lips. "Pleasure to meet you, Mrs. Corrigan."

"The pleasure is mine," she said, and that wasn't as much of a lie as it should have been.

THANK YOU FOR READING

Out of all the books you could choose, thank you for picking up *A Dangerous Invitation*. I hope you'll take a few minutes out of your day to review this book – your honest opinion is much appreciated. Reviews help introduce readers to new authors they wouldn't otherwise meet.

THE ROOKERY ROGUES

A Dangerous Invitation is the first book in The Rookery Rogues. While each book reads as a stand-alone, the series is best enjoyed in chronological order. Joined by the poorest neighborhoods in London, called rookeries, the heroes and heroines in this series defy social expectations and find love in the darkest of circumstances.

To keep up to date on The Rookery Rogues, sign up for Erica's newsletter and get exclusive excerpts, contests, and more: **ericamonroe.com**

ABOUT THE AUTHOR

Erica Monroe is a bestselling author of emotional, suspenseful romance. Though she has a Bachelor's degree in writing, she's been a secretary, a barista, and a retail assistant. Now Erica spends her days crafting lovable rogues and feisty heroines for her historical and new adult series. She is a member of the Romance Writers of America, Heart of Carolina, and the Beau Monde Regency Romance chapter. When not writing, she is a chronic TV watcher, sci-fi junkie, lover of pit bulls, and shoe fashionista. She lives in the suburbs of North Carolina with her husband, two dogs, and a cat.

Erica loves to hear from readers, so please feel free to contact her at the following places:
E-mail: ericamonroewrites@gmail.com
Web: ericamonroe.com
Twitter: @ericajmonroe
Facebook: ericamonroeauthor or ericamonroewrites
Pinterest: regencyerica